ANCIENT EVIL UNLEASHED

Tull, the ancient mage, addressed the Stone of Konnard, exhorting it as if it were a living mind to be persuaded. He was coaxing, wheedling, cajoling. Nolar wanted to cry out, "NO! Do not listen! He plans to thieve your Power and use it for ill!" Her very impulse to warn was beaten back by the unheeding pressure of Tull's spells. Nolar was mentally voiceless, stricken mind-dumb, as she had been physically paralyzed by Tull's earlier spell.

Unbidden, a vision slid into her mind of a great sphere of dull gray stone rolling inexorably forward. Despair and blackness swept over Nolar, afflicting her with repose without rest and sleep without dreams. . . .

Tor books by Andre Norton

TALES OF THE WITCH WORLD (editor)

WITCH WORLD: THE TURNING

MAGIC IN ITHKAR (editor, with Robert Adams)

FLIGHT OF VENGEANCE

WITCH WORLD: THE TURNING Book 2
Andre Norton with P.M. Griffin & Mary H. Schaub

TOR
fantasy

A TOM DOHERTY ASSOCIATES BOOK
NEW YORK

This is a work of fiction. All the characters and events portrayed in this book are fictitious, and any resemblance to real people or events is purely coincidental.

FLIGHT OF VENGEANCE

Copyright © 1992 by Andre Norton, Ltd.
Maps copyright © 1990 by John M. Ford

Cover art by Dennis A. Nolan

A Tor Book
Published by Tom Doherty Associates, Inc.
175 Fifth Avenue
New York, N.Y. 10010

Tor® is a registered trademark of Tom Doherty Associates, Inc.

ISBN: 0-812-50706-1
Library of Congress Catalog Card Number: 92-27463

First edition: December 1992
First mass market edition: June 1994

Printed in the United States of America

0 9 8 7 6 5 4 3 2 1

FLIGHT OF VENGEANCE

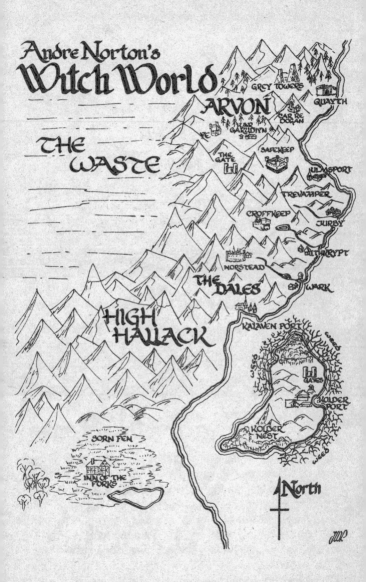

The Chronicler

ONCE I was Duratan of the Borderers—now what shall I call myself? I am in part a Chronicler of the deeds of others, I am one of such as Ouen and Wessel who help with the preserving of the framework of Lormt so that those who come to delve there for knowledge have lodging, food, that which will keep life in their bodies while they labor among the records of the past they love.

I am also a seeker. Bit by bit I gain a little here, a fraction there, striving to make clear to the questions within me answers of what I have to do in a world which was overturned by Power and in which so many of us have been set adrift.

When Estcarp stood in direct threat from Pagar of Karsten, and all who were clear-thoughted could foresee (without any recourse to the uses of Power) that we must be indeed overrun, it was the Witches who themselves interposed all that they were or could be between the coming of chaos and their land. Binding together in one embattled body and mind they brought all their famed strength to bear upon the earth itself, forced nature to bow to their united wills.

Those mountains, through which Pagar's forces moved to crush us, were shaken, put down, raised up. The land split, was gashed, wounded, scarred. Forests disappeared, rivers were rent from their age-old beds, there was a madness in the world.

For this there was a heavy price. Of the Council in Es City, there were no survivors. Others were as husks, burnt out by the force they had summoned. The Witch Rule died with the majority of those who had held it. Though still along the borders there were enemies such as Alizon where Witch Rule was considered an abomination.

The Kolders, who had come upon us through one of the gates, bursting outward as might the vile flow from the lancing of a festering wound, began the last travail of the world as we knew it.

But Champions arose. The Witches gave those their full backing. Simon Tregarth, an outlander from another gate world, came. To him joined the Witch Jaelithe, also Koris of Gorm (that ill-named place the Kolders had first befouled), and Loyse of Verlaine; others also whose deeds the songsmiths have wrought into many ballads.

It was Simon and Jaelithe who closed the Kolder gate. Yet war continued, for the evil the Kolders had sown was far from harvested.

In the Dales of High Hallack there was fierce fighting, for the Kolders had encouraged those of Alizon, aiding them in an invasion of that land with strange weapons, that a path might be cut into storied Arvon beyond where the Old Ones were rumored to have concealed treasures of power. When the Kolders fell, Alizon's failure followed and her force was hunted through the Dales to the sea and died there because there was no escape. For the Sulcars, ever friendly to Estcarp, had swept away their fleet.

Yet Alizon was not yet defeated in the minds of those sword lords who ruled there. They licked their wounds, ever looking south. For, though they hated the Power, they also cherished secrets which were of the Dark.

Karsten arose out of the Kolder chaos under Pagar, but

what happened there after the Witches put an end to the invasion? Or was it a beginning?

For, just at the turning, the Tregarths again played a part. There were three of them, the children of Simon and his Witch wife, Jaelithe, born at a single birthing which was a thing unknown before: Kyllan, the warrior; Kemoc, the warlock; and Kaththea the Witch. They broke the age old block laid upon our minds and went eastward, over mountains, into Escore, from which our race had fled a millennium before.

However, their coming into Escore had troubled the ancient balance held between the Light and the Dark. Once more war and fearsome things, born of the filth of evil, broke forth. However, there were those of the Old Race who arose, took their households, and kin-lieges, to cross the eastern mountains and use their swords there, to bring once more forces of Light to meet Dark.

I was in Lormt and not at the forefront of any battle when the turning came upon us. Kemoc was my shield comrade and he had dwelt in that storehouse of knowledge for a space before he had ridden to free his sister from Witch hold. I had visited him there. Surely no geas was laid upon me, still the desire to return to that place held me after I was sore hurt in a rock fall and my fighting days so ended.

Though Kemoc was already gone, I stayed, sometimes torn two ways—yearning for the Border life I had always known, and again for this seeking among the many old and rotting accounts of an earlier world and time. I would have sworn while I was a warrior that I had none of the Talent in me. It was always believed that that went only in the female line among us. Yet I discovered that I did have strange gifts.

Since I was young and active, and not too hindered by my limp, I had much to do with Ouen in Lormt after the Turning. Of the four towers of that age-old fortress of knowledge, one and part of another fell as a result of the great earth movement, taking with them the connecting wall.

However, though there were injuries among us, there were no deaths. But what was the most surprising was that the structural collapse revealed sealed chambers and crypts in which had been stored chests and great jars filled with all manner of scrolls and books.

Our scholars were frantic and it took those of us who were more level-headed and less wrapped up in research to make sure that none of them came to harm in their assault on places where there was treacherous rubble. Thus I was greatly busied in those first days and hardly aware of what chanced, except for what was directly under my eyes.

We sheltered a trickle of refugees. Among them was a young woman who had ridden to us in search of healing for her aunt. I did not see the older woman, but I was told that she had suffered a head injury which put her into a sleep-walking state. There was with the two of them a Borderer whose troop had been scattered during the catastrophe and he had taken service to see them safely to us.

Those who employed him spent much time with Morfew, one of the scholars always more helpful than others. Shortly the three of them made a sudden departure, as I was told by Wessel who supplied them. Morfew said that the maid Nolar had discovered among some of the newly salvaged material reference to an ancient place of healing. I was a little disturbed, for surely the many changes in the landscape might have obliterated any landmarks they would travel by. Almost I was moved to ride after them but there was so much to be done and I fully expected them to return shortly in disappointment.

When I had first visited Kemoc at Lormt he had given me a bag of colored crystals and I had discovered that these answered to some talent of my own. When I threw them they would fall into patterns. Dwelling upon those, thoughts and warnings sometimes became clear. So it became my daily custom upon arising each morning to throw a handful and try to read what might lie before me for the day.

There were no thoughts of the three who had gone on the morning days later when I made my throw. But what lay there was indeed a warning.

That red which is near black (signifying the worst of evil) was centered. Fronting it were three other sparks, one of green, which was small but clear, and two others which blazed higher. One of those was blue, the other a clear white, and from each came a beam to lick at that smear of dark. As if I stood in sight of what passed I knew I witnessed a mighty battle. My hand clenched upon the edge of the table. The hound Rawit, who always witnessed my throw growled, and from the back of my chair the female falcon Galerider screamed as she might when about to war. Three lights against the dark—in my mind those three were the ones who had gone forth from Lormt. Mightily I strove to reach them by thought-send. Instead there was a rush of the crystals and not by my will.

I feared—unnaturally. Perhaps something had been loosed again, even as the Tregarths had unwittingly loosed the Dark in Escore. Yet I thought this was no warning from Escore, but what happened was not far from Lormt itself.

That day and for four following, I rode the boundaries of our fields and watched my crystals, throwing them twice, thrice a day. I visited Morfew. He showed me a copy the maid Nolar had made from fragments of an ancient scroll which spoke of the Stone of Konnard. That this was part of a dire ensorcellment I was sure, and I was angry with them for what they might have loosed upon us.

Arming myself I gathered supplies, though what good I might do I had no idea. Yet there was danger and I was still fighting man enough to be drawn to it. For the last time I threw the crystals.

And this time I was successful. That which blazed with evil was gone. There remained only the white, and those pulsed evenly like the beating of a heart.

I heard the barking of Rawit and sudden sharp cry of

Galerider. So I looked out beyond that space where the gate to Lormt had once hung and saw riding, with weary drooping of body in saddle, the two who came again. Though at that moment I did not truly realize why there was such a surge of gladness in me, I thought it was only because some threat was past.

Urging my mount forward I went to meet Nolar and Derren. And indeed they had for me a mighty venture to add to the Chronicles.

EXILE

by
Mary H. Schaub

*S*omething was wrong with the air. It wasn't visible, like a haze of smoke or dust to stifle breathing. The late summer air was as clear and fresh as usual in Estcarp's foothills nestled beneath the higher peaks. And yet . . . there was a gnawing sense of unease.

Nolar thrust aside the herbs she had been sorting and strode yet again to her narrow window facing south. She had felt uncharacteristically restless all day, as if an undefined danger were looming just out of sight. It was, she thought, like glimpsing the shadow of a hawk, and not knowing just when it would swoop down to strike its prey.

She stepped outside for a better view of the sky. The sunrise had been clear, but during the day, an ominously dark cloud bank expanded across the southern horizon. In her efforts as a healer, Nolar had seen that same black-purple hue on severely bruised flesh. She heard no distant thunder, but she knew from experience how the worst high peak storms could break with terrifying swiftness. They were almost always preceded by a breathless calm, much like the unnatural stillness now.

Similarly, Nolar was aware of a nervous tingling in her hands and face, and her breathing was as rapid as if she had just run up the steep path near Ostbor's house. She concentrated on what else normally preceded storms—something elusive, some common element. She knew there had always been an oppressive sense of power intensifying until it found release in the actual storm.

Abruptly, Nolar stopped pacing. She had grasped the vital distinction. What had been troubling her all day was not a gathering of power; instead, it was quite the opposite. What she had been noticing unconsciously was the draining away, the diminishing of the area's ordinary vitality, that sense of living plants and animals comprising a natural order. Throughout this day, something had been interfering drastically with that energetic wholeness.

Nolar again observed how abnormally quiet the hillside was. No birds called, no small creatures scurried about. She was accustomed to the solitude of the foothills and peaks, but this profound stillness was unsettling. Inevitably, the thought of power and its manipulation brought with it the complex image of the Witches of Estcarp.

For as long as she could remember, Nolar had been simultaneously drawn to and repelled by the Witches. They were Estcarp's rulers and ultimate defense. The fate of the Old Race lay in their hands, since only by their concerted use of the Power could the ancient land of Estcarp hope to hold its borders against the repeated attacks, first from Karsten to the south and then from Alizon to the north. In recent years, the primary threat had emerged consistently from the south, where Pagar of Geen had fought his way to the dukedom, uniting Karsten in an extended effort to crush Estcarp. Despite sea raids by Estcarp's faithful Sulcar allies, Karsten had continued its armed forays along the border, slowly but surely bleeding away Estcarp's limited number of fighting guardsmen. Even in her remote mountain area far north of that embattled border, Nolar had heard fragmentary accounts of the struggle.

Suddenly, the words of the traveling cloth merchant

echoed in her mind. About once a week, Nolar customarily walked down to the nearest foothill village to barter herbs for the supplies she could not make or gather for herself. Two days ago, she had been weighing some dried frostflower seeds when the stir of new arrivals had drawn her attention to the front of the village's sole all-purpose shop. A dusty, middle-aged man with a sharp-eyed, weathered face was clearly relishing the attention he was attracting. Nolar easily heard his complaints, for he had a true merchant's voice, pitched to carry above any competition.

"I should never have left Garth," he exclaimed, "but that fool of a ship's captain assured me that the market in Es was active." He gave a snort of derision. "No doubt it was active, perhaps a hundred years ago. Oh, I grant you, there are ample numbers of people there—too many people, all rushing about in different directions, and not one of them interested in buying cloth." Pausing for effect, the merchant appealed to his listeners. "You have seen my goods. I carry fine cloth for all needs. Would they deign to examine my lace edgings? Would they feel my superior velvet? No. They were far too busy making room for Borderer troops coming down from the mountains. And that's another thing—there was no room for a man to display his goods properly, or even to lie down in comfort. Every inn was packed with people—guardsmen, Sulcar seamen, even some of those outlandish Falconers with wild birds perched on their saddles."

Nolar drew farther back into the shadowed interior as several of the hill farmers' children crowded in near the door, jostling a herdsman who was demanding a remedy for sorefoot. The shopkeeper, anxious to hear more of the merchant's news, brought out a flask of the strong local wine and poured him a measure. "Here, try some of this wine. Tell us, if you will, how stands the border to the south?"

The merchant willingly accepted the wooden beaker. "My thanks for the refreshment. As to matters along the border, that tale is tangled far beyond the ability of my wits to unravel it. Cloth is my business, not the high affairs of Witches, dukes, and armies. You may have heard some time past that Sulcar ships were rumored to be taking some from Estcarp to safer grounds over the sea. That is, of course, an old tale, scarcely heeded of late, but I can tell you one thing from the sight of my own eyes—a Sulcar fleet has massed now in the bay near the Es's mouth. There is much feverish talk of a last escape by sea should some grand plan by the Witches fail. Frankly, no one agrees just what the plan is, but I know from careful listening that the Council is plotting some elaborate trap to swallow the Duke of Karsten and all his harrying forces." The merchant shook his head, frowning. "Not at all good for trade, this fighting and plotting." Then his face brightened. "Still, I am now well away from that, set on this fair road to the north, where sensible folk recognize quality and value when they see it. I tell you, the signs in Es were plain—any merchant keen to trade should seek better markets, not to mention safer ones."

"But what trap?" "How plans the Council?" Several voices clamored for more details.

The merchant threw up his hands. "Does the Guardian gift me with a sending so that I may be aware of her intentions? All I can tell you is what I heard and saw among those trading rumors in Es. More rumors were changing hands than goods, I can assure you. Yes, yes—the details, such as I could make them out. One Borderer told me in confidence that his troop had received a sending to withdraw down from their mountain posts, but carefully, so as not to be noticed at once. When I pressed him for the reason, since it was obvious to me that many other troops must have received similar orders, he said the Witches expect to deal Duke Pagar a blow from which he and Karsten will not soon recover." The merchant twisted his wine cup on the rough board trestle. "It was whispered privately that this undescribed trap will either end the threat from the south, or else Estcarp itself may be lost. It was clear to me that either way matters go, trade will surely not benefit, so I packed my goods in all haste to leave Es behind. And now I must be on my way, for the day promises more heat to come."

The shopkeeper caught at the merchant's sleeve. "But someone in Es must know the nature of this great impending trap. Have you no idea what the Witches plan against Pagar?"

The merchant grimaced. "There was only such wild talk as would make a sensible man laugh . . . or cry. I tell you freely, I am myself a man of Verlaine, and we pride ourselves on keeping our eyes on our own business. It is wise not to meddle in high matters." He stopped at the door and peered back at his audience of hill folk. "From what I have heard of Estcarp's Witches, I would suggest that you bar your doors to the south and abide within until whatever is to be done has been done. For me, the road awaits—good fortune to this house."

Nolar stored her bartered packets of salt, meal, and a small flask of wine in her scrip, then slipped out by a back door to avoid being seen. The hill farmers's children, however, had loitered on the path to watch the merchant's pack horses slowly pace out of sight. One lad pointed at Nolar and shrieked in mock fear. She as usual ignored the ragged chorus of taunts and walked steadily away up the slope.

From her earliest awareness, Nolar had known that something was wrong with her appearance. People would look at her face and then quickly avert their eyes. As soon as she had seen herself reflected in the shining surface of a kettle, Nolar recognized that her face was different from other people's faces. She had been told that her birth had been long and hard; her mother died of it, while she herself had been thought likely to die for some time afterward. Whatever the cause, she had emerged branded across her face by a dark red swath, spangle-edged as if wine had splashed on the skin and could not be wiped away. Nolar suspected that people avoided looking at her for varied reasons—revulsion, fear that the strain might somehow be transferred to them, and even perhaps embarrassment. The prevailing view seemed to be that her disfigurement could be denied if the observers refused to look at her. As a result, Nolar had been a lonely child, shunned by the other children, and excluded from games or group activities. She was also rejected by her father, who bitterly mourned the loss of his wife and blamed the child. When Nolar was five years old, she developed a dangerous fever that prevented her from being examined for potential Witch talent as she should have been tested according to tradition. It was at about that time that her father remarried a sturdy woman of Falconer blood, to whom the presence of a deformed child was unthinkable. Although the lady herself had fled from one of the secluded villages where Falconer women were kept to bear children, she held to their harsh belief that children with defects should not be allowed to live. To avoid strife, Nolar's father decided to send Nolar away to be fostered out of his sight and that of his new wife as well. Nolar remembered the parting words of her old nurse, a kindly woman who tried to provide the only comfort Nolar ever received. "Do not cry, little one. It is better that you go away to the mountains. Every time your father sees you, it is the face of your poor mother that must torment him, for you move as she did, and bear her eyes and hair. Never mind, there will be new birds and animals to see in the mountains, and fine forests to wander in, and the hill children to play with, more than there are here . . . and kinder, too, I trust," she added under her breath, for she was well aware of the scornful way the local children called Nolar "Mistress Wash Her Face."

So Nolar made the long journey into the sparsely settled hills, being received at last by a stolid family of farmers. Unfortunately, the hill folk, if anything, seemed more offended by Nolar's birthmark than the town children had been. Perhaps it had something to do with the sour nature of Thanta, the local Wise Woman. The first time Nolar encountered her at the village shop, Thanta flourished her gnarled staff at Nolar and growled, "Mark of evil on your face— avaunt you from honest folk!"

Stung by the words, Nolar abandoned her usual polite silence and blurted, "I am no more evil than you! It is not my fault that I look this way." Thanta turned her back ostentatiously, and everyone else in the shop edged away from the child.

Nolar quickly learned to wear a loose scarf to cover as much of her facial mark as she could. No matter how hard she tried to be friendly, she was always rebuffed or actively driven away. She worked hard to accomplish the many chores she was assigned on the farm, but she was seldom thanked or praised. The weary months stretched into years. When Nolar wasn't required to be working at the farm, she often wandered alone in the hills. Her nurse was right in one respect—the animals and plants of the mountains did become Nolar's companions. She longed to learn more about all living things, and watched and listened to anyone who seemed to know about such matters.

After much thought, Nolar even dared to seek out Thanta at her hut in the hills. As she had feared, the Wise Woman was not at all pleased to see her. Nolar haltingly explained that she wanted to learn about the uses of plants for healing.

Thanta squinted suspiciously through the smoke rising from a squat brazier near the door. "Who sent you?" she demanded.

Nolar had taken a steadying breath. "No one sent me. I have heard several of the farmers say that no one hereabouts knows more about plants than you do. I hoped that you might let me help you gather them, or just watch you at work. I would not trouble you."

Thanta seemed to consider for a moment, then shook her head decisively. "No. I have suffered much to learn the secrets I have mastered. I will not gift them to an outlander—

especially not to one marked as you are. Go away—do not come here again."

Nolar trudged back to the farm, her cheeks burning as much from keen disappointment as from the icy north wind.

Although they did not welcome Nolar, some of the hill farmers would at times let her watch them tend to sick animals and accept her shy offers to fetch things or help care for the beasts. In that way, she accumulated scraps of lore and practical healing methods, but in an unsatisfactory, fragmentary way.

She was almost eight-years-old when she stumbled—literally—upon her singular experience of good fortune. She was walking slowly along a forest path, her eyes focused high in the branches seeking the plump green leaves of mistletoe, when her boot caught against an unexpected irregularity. Nolar pitched forward, hands thrust out to break her fall. When she sat up on the soft drift of leaves and shed evergreen needles, she rubbed an abraded knee and uncovered the cause of her stumble. It was not a misplaced rock, as she expected, but instead a smoothed section of tree branch, capped at both ends by age-darkened metal. Nolar's interest soared—it had to be a scholar's carrier for scrolls or parchments. She had seen only a few such at her father's house, for he was not a scholarly man by nature, preferring to keep his written records at his trading house. As Nolar turned the wooden cylinder in her hands, she saw regular scratches on the flat metal surface of one end, probably the name of the owner. Unfortunately, the marks had been meaningless to her since she had never been taught to read. She decided that the carrier was too clean and unweathered to have been lost or discarded for very long. She had not walked along this path before, so it was possible that the owner was still nearby. The early winter afternoon quickly darkened toward dusk, so Nolar immediately noticed the warm spark of candlelight farther up the path to the left. It belonged, she found, to a ramshackle hut much built onto, with oddly shaped rooms branching off in several directions. Nolar tapped at the door, and when she heard no response, she pushed it open a crack.

"Confound that draft," a peevish voice complained from some interior room. "If you're a bear, go away. If you're a visitor, shut the door . . . if it is the door that's open. How can I be expected to keep my scrolls in order with a gale blowing through the house?"

Nolar stepped inside cautiously, shutting the door behind her. A pale light preceded its bearer around a shadowy corner. Nolar's first impression was of a long, thin nose flanked by piercing eyes beneath white tufted brows. The figure then resolved into a tall old gentleman muffled in countless layers of antiquated clothing.

"And who are you, hmm?" he inquired in a voice unexpectedly deep for a man of such a gangling frame. "I haven't seen you before." Nolar shrank back when he extended his candle toward her. "No, don't run away," he added hastily. "Is that—have you found—oh, do let me see. I have been searching everywhere for my scrolls on the House of Inscof."

Nolar held out her find. "It was in the leaves on the path. I fell over it."

The old man, who was happily rummaging inside the cylinder, paused to gaze at her with obvious concern. "I do hope that you didn't hurt yourself. You must have something warm to drink. Where did I put that kettle? For that matter, where did I put the cups? But I forget the proper customs. I am Ostbor. Some call me 'Ostbor the Scholar,' which is kind of them, I'm sure. As you may be aware," he continued with an air of one sharing a great confidence, "it is true that I spent some considerable time at Lormt." He stopped, courteously awaiting her reaction.

"Forgive me, sir," Nolar said, unsure of what she was expected to say. "I have been sent here to the mountains by my family because of my face."

Ostbor blinked, looking rather like a curiously featherless

owl. "Face? Face? What about your face? You have one, I have one. What is so unusual in that?"

"The mark, sir," Nolar admitted in a low voice.

"Hmm—that." Ostbor dismissed the mark with a negligent wave. "Think nothing of that, child. It is no more than a minor stain on a new parchment. So long as the writing is clear, what matters the appearance of the material? Speaking of writing, I presume you brought my scroll carrier to me because you saw my name on the cap. I engraved it myself," he added, proudly fingering the scratches that Nolar had noticed.

Nolar cringed inwardly. "I cannot read, sir. No one ever thought to teach me."

Ostbor was momentarily speechless. "What! Can't read—of course you can read, and write. I shall show you how. It is really quite simple. Hmm—to be truthful, some folk find it easier to master than do others, but it requires no great wit, and I can see from your eyes that you have sufficient spark. Here, sit down—wait, let me move some of these records. There are those who call me 'Ostbor the Pack Rat,' which I think entirely unfair." As he made an expansive gesture to emphasize his words, Ostbor precipitated a cascade of loose parchment strips and scraps. "Hmm—perhaps not altogether unfair. I do tend to accumulate things—chiefly written things, you see. It's because of my interest in families. Who was whose great-grandfather? Did they come from here or there, and who married whom? Which reminds me, who are you?"

Nolar straightened up from retrieving parchments from the floor. "I am Nolar, sir, of the House of Meroney—that is, Meroney is my mother's House."

Ostbor had given an encouraging nod. "And a fine House it is. I am more familiar with the branch that settled near Pethel, but I have certainly read of Meroney. See here—we are still standing in this cold room with nothing to drink. Come back by the fire and tell me about yourself while I look for that kettle. I know I had it out yesterday, but where did I leave it?" He swept Nolar ahead of him down a twisting passageway into an even more cluttered room, which was comfortably warmed by a brisk fire. The area around the rough stone hearth was surprisingly clean and orderly. As if noticing her appraisal, Ostbor explained, "One can never be too careful about fires, especially when it comes to manuscripts. One must keep them well away from any flames. Some of the older scholars at Lormt, now—I can remember one who would let his candles drip on his work—most unsafe. He lost an entire scroll one day when it ignited. Dreadful."

"Was he hurt?" Nolar asked.

"No, no, silly fellow—although I do believe he did scorch his sleeve in putting out the fire. I had told him a dozen times to be more careful. And you must be equally wary. When one is handling parchments, particularly old ones, the material is nearly always dry and very fragile. A mere spark can set it off. That's why I take such care to keep my hearth clear and place my candles securely out of drafts. Which I must say," he added as he triumphantly excavated a small kettle from beneath a mound of scholarly debris, "can be a problem in this house. I cannot imagine how the wind penetrates the way it does. Let me fetch some water. You will, of course, stay the night." Before Nolar was able to protest that she had to get back to the farm, Ostbor bustled away down another narrow passage.

That was the first of many nights there for Nolar. In retrospect, those few precious years with Ostbor were the happiest that Nolar had ever known. On long winter evenings, the snow-hush was broken only by the snapping of the fire and Ostbor's muttering as he pored over his records. As a special treat, he occasionally let Nolar mull some wine. Later, there were exhilarating spring afternoons striding through the mountain meadows trying to match flowers and plants to the curious old drawings that Ostbor had collected.

He insisted that someday he would write and illustrate his own catalogue of plants. "For then, you see, the people could have an organized record and not have to depend on the scattered memories of Wise Women. Not that some of them aren't very well informed, but some of their lore is mistaken, and they do persist in teaching it unchanged to their apprentices, so errors aren't corrected."

Ostbor's true interest, however, was bound in his genealogical researches. He spent countless hours sorting through dusty records, forgetting to eat, and often sitting so long that his bones would creak when he finally did rise. He was scrupulously honest, always attempting to consider objectively all the facts in a dispute, and speaking the truth as fairly as he could. He primarily bartered for his supplies, trading decorated scrolls commemorating events in the family lives of the hill folk. Although unschooled themselves, the hill folk respected learning, and prized Ostbor's work. He was also paid in gold and silver for his researches for wealthier families from the distant towns who sent kinship queries in letters delivered by servants.

Nolar awakened her first morning at Ostbor's under a mountain-sewn down quilt far warmer than the threadbare blanket she was accustomed to at the farm. She found Ostbor by following a discordant clanging that had led her to the kitchen. Ostbor somewhat sheepishly confessed that his household affairs were not perhaps as well organized as his scholarly work, and from a rapid survey of the deplorable state of his pots and pans, Nolar heartily agreed. Having spent some time in the kitchen run with ferocious efficiency by her father's cook, Nolar knew how a kitchen was supposed to look. She hesitantly suggested that she might help clean a few pots for Ostbor, if he had any fine sand for the polishing. He appeared much relieved to encounter anyone at all familiar with such matters, and showed her as best he could where everything was stored before retreating to his researches. Nolar scraped, scoured, washed, and polished most of the morning. When Ostbor had appeared at the door just after midday, absentmindedly assembling a platter of bread and cheese, he suddenly stopped, amazed by the progress she had achieved.

"This is splendid!" Ostbor exclaimed. "You are a treasure—but I have left you laboring away here for too long. Let us divide this bread—I think I have some sausage tucked away over here—and after we've eaten, I must show you how to read. Then you can be my assistant, and not merely a cleaner of pots, which I must say you have improved significantly. I had no idea that one was copper—fancy that."

Although often distracted from the point at hand, Ostbor proved to be a fine teacher. He was delighted to find that Nolar could distinguish the tiniest letters, for he confessed that his eyesight was not so keen as it had once been. "It is an advantage to a scholar to see better those things close by," he suggested. "One is scarcely diverted by grand views when all one sees is a blur. Give me a nice crisp list of descendants—now that is worth examining. Look at this one. See that large letter? Yes, quite so, and what about that one?"

Nolar absorbed his intermittent teaching like a thirsty man long denied the very sight of water, who beyond all hope was allowed free access to a flowing brook. Every minute that she wasn't trying to bring some order to the house, Nolar immersed herself in mastering the intricacies of reading and writing. Soon she was able to puzzle out the crabbed and faded letters on stacks of scrolls that Ostbor had set aside as unreadable. He was enchanted when she found a fragment that filled a gap in a lineage that he had reluctantly abandoned as forever flawed. For the first time in her life, Nolar felt that she was contributing something useful—that she was needed. It gave her a sense of contentment unlike anything else she had ever experienced.

That first day they were together, Ostbor at once sent word to the farmer fostering Nolar so that he would not think her lost in the mountains. Ostbor then prompted Nolar to describe her life at the hill farm. Slowly at first, and then with more fluency, Nolar detailed the grinding work that had occupied most of her waking hours. Almost incidentally, she related her experiences of being actively scorned and more recently, being simply ignored and isolated. When she finished, Ostbor sat thinking in his big chair, then he began work on a new decorated scroll. As he assembled the bright colors he used to ornament prominent letters, Ostbor explained that it was only fair to offer the farmer something in exchange for Nolar's services.

"I trust that you would prefer to stay here, if that were possible? I thought so. I know that farm, by the way—they have ample helpers without you, whereas I do not. I must, however, write to your father to request that you be allowed to stay here as my apprentice. That is the proper thing to do, as well as the polite thing."

Some weeks later, a passing hunter had delivered Nolar's father's brusque reply. He had starkly assented, with the clear assertion that he did not intend to pay Ostbor; if Ostbor chose to keep the child, then he could support her as he pleased. Ostbor chuckled at this rather cold dismissal. "Hmm—the hill folk bring me far more food than I need for myself, and your assistance with my records will speed my work considerably. Ordinarily," he confided, "I do not consider myself a keen tradesman by nature, but in this matter, I am obviously getting the better end of the bargain. Let us celebrate with a little wine. Now where did I put that flask? I'm sure it was on that middle shelf yesterday . . . or was it last week?"

Among all of the many subjects that Ostbor talked about, the one that intrigued Nolar the most was Lormt. She was fascinated by his tales of his studies there. Once the world of writing was revealed to her, Nolar felt a burning desire to learn, and the notion of a place where ancient knowledge was preserved and cared for spurred her to ask Ostbor about Lormt again and again. Lormt took on fantastic dimensions in her imagination. Finally, one early spring day when buds were beginning to swell on the trees and the icy ground was softening in the first thawing of the season, she dared to ask Ostbor if he would take her to see Lormt—the vast towers, the great buildings he had described, the walls within stacked with scrolls.

Ostbor was taken aback. "Hmm . . . perhaps I have conveyed to you too grand a conception of Lormt," he had confessed. "No doubt in former years, the edifices were most impressive; but I must tell you that these latter years have not been kind ones to Lormt. There is so little appreciation for the value of preservation, you see—most people don't really care about old manuscripts, peculiar though that is to those of us who know how priceless they are. Of course, I can understand that writing is difficult to appreciate if one does not read—even you, my dear, were once in that unhappy state, and you have observed that some common folk would as soon burn scrolls for fuel as not." He shuddered at that awful thought. "And one must accept the attitude of the Council." Ostbor sighed and fell silent. Nolar begged him to continue. "Hmm . . . yes, the Witches, you see—they don't— that is, they prize their own knowledge, as well they might, but they don't much esteem knowledge from other sources, especially that compiled by men. The scholars at Lormt are nearly all men, so there is practically no communication between them and the Council. My own work, of course, has been chiefly involved in kinship records, but Lormt contains vast stores of scrolls on magic and healing and tales of the past. Lormt is a treasure house, as you have surmised. What you must know, however, is that Lormt is isolated far from most people and ordinary affairs. A few good folk have settled nearby, to farm and provide the scholars with all the necessities, but life at Lormt is extremely austere. Over the years, too, there have been occasional floods and quakes of the earth which have damaged the buildings. Indeed, no man knows when or how the massive stones were set to raise the great enclosing wall and the four corner towers. To my mind, though, the worst of it has always been the deplorable lack of order. Yes, I see you smile, and it is true that I am not the most orderly of household arrangers. You will concede, I trust, that I do keep my records in good order. I know where every single scroll is . . . hmm . . . almost every scroll. At Lormt, I regret to say, many of the scholars are less serious than they should be. Why, some of them even try to order what should be copied from the fragments before they become unreadable. There is a certain disregard for priorities and details, and from what I have heard since I was last there, I fear that conditions have become even more lax and disorderly." Ostbor shook his head. "I wish I could assure you that Lormt was the esteemed center of learning that it should be, but . . . Still, I can say that it does persist, and even the little that is accomplished there is valuable. Perhaps one day, some more energetic scholars may demand that purpose and direction be instilled—much as you have succeeded in doing here in my house!" And with this wish, Ostbor smiled, and turned back to his parchments.

Next to Lormt, the subject of Nolar's greatest curiosity was the Witches. Ostbor answered her questions as best he could, but he warned her that the Witches were jealous of any penetration of their mysteries. He cheerfully admitted that magic failed to interest him in the main, which was just as well, since men were unable to wield the Power as properly trained Witches could.

"They tend to draw apart, the Witches," Ostbor said once. "It must be a lonely life, in many ways. They put aside all bonds to family, you see, once they are selected for training."

"My great-aunt is a Witch," Nolar said. "My nurse told me long ago that my mother's aunt was a member of the Guardian's Council."

Ostbor raised his eyebrows. "Why, so she is. I hadn't thought of her for years—formidable lady. They lose their names, too, when they go away."

Nolar was intrigued. "I know they never said her name. Why not?"

"Because a name carries powerful bonds to the person who bears it. Suppose I were an enemy of Estcarp, and I discovered your great-aunt's name. Provided, of course, that I were able to work magic, I might cast a powerful spell to injure her or render her witless. Magic, you understand, is a subject which I have not carefully studied, but over the years, I have heard certain tales about the uses of magic, both for good and ill."

"But if they no longer have names," Nolar had persisted, "then how can they call to each other?"

"Each trained Witch is given a jewel which they use in exercising the Power. I would suppose that each Witch must be individually recognizable, mind to mind, for they are able to dispatch Sendings to one another over long distances. That would certainly be a helpful talent, especially when, as now, the information one needs is in Es and one is here. Hmm—I must resort to my own talent and write a letter, which is far slower, but generally brings satisfactory results."

Nolar therefore had settled happily into the quiet routine of life at Ostbor's house. The days and months flew by. Nolar became more and more useful to the old scholar, reading to him in the evenings, helping him to compile his endless kinship lists, and when his hands became too unsteady, she practiced until she could produce a creditable ornamented scroll.

Nolar was eighteen-years-old in the early spring just before Ostbor became gravely ill. There had been a late snow and days of cold, dank mist and fog. Ostbor's cough had worsened, and no amount of herbal infusions brought him any relief. He sent for the shopkeeper to stand as witness to his testamentary intentions. "I should like for you to take my riding horse," he told the shopkeeper, "for it is a gentle animal, and I know you will care for it kindly. The smaller horse is to be Nolar's, for it is accustomed to her and she may require it for traveling." Ostbor reached up from his bed to grasp Nolar's hand. "This house, too, shall be yours, dear child, for as long as you need it. I have sent a letter to Lormt concerning the disposal of my records. I expect you to choose any scrolls you care to keep for yourself. Now, there, do not cry. I have lived a long life, and in my way, I have accomplished many useful things. Do not sorrow for me." Ostbor died peacefully a week later.

About a month afterward, a gnarled old man arrived with a string of pack horses. Initially, he was almost truculent, announcing that he had come from Lormt to gather Ostbor's records, but he was mollified when he found that Nolar could read the official letter he bore authorizing the removal. She helped him shift the bundles, boxes, hampers, and loose stacks of scrolls. It took them two days, and when the old man left, the house seemed woefully empty. That encounter had provided the last mention of Lormt that Nolar was to hear until an unexpected meeting with a Witch again brought up the name and subsequently changed Nolar's life.

Nolar composed a stiff letter of her own to her father, informing him of Ostbor's death and simply stating that she intended to stay on at Ostbor's house. Her father returned a bare assent, with no other comment.

Thanta, the local Wise Woman, died early in the summer after Ostbor's death. A fire, possibly sparked from her old brazier, raged through her hut. Thanta had lately taken on an outland apprentice girl, but the hill folk felt little confidence in her. It was the frightened apprentice who brought the news of the fire to the nearest village. She lingered near the ruined hut for a few days, packed up all of Thanta's supplies that could be salvaged, and retreated to the plains.

Without announcing her availability in any way, Nolar gradually found the hill folk coming to her for plants and herbs. It was a relief to Nolar to be able to support herself that way, for as she had suspected, the hill folk assumed that Ostbor's skills had died with him. No one asked Nolar for any scrolls, but they did respect her knowledge of plants. With a sense of resignation, Nolar quickly observed that the old distance that had always intruded between her and the others again pressed her into aching isolation. The hill folk were uneasy around Nolar, so they kept their commerce with her as brief as possible. They never considered asking Nolar to be the new Wise Woman. Nolar was not considered as the new Wise Woman; she was merely a reliable source for the wild plants and simple healing potions that the people sometimes needed.

Nolar was arranging pared slices of fruit to dry in the summer sun when a stranger unexpectedly rode up to her door. The message that the young man brought startled her: her father commanded her to return with this servant to his house at once for the betrothal of one of Nolar's stepsisters. They would have to hurry to be in time, for the marriage was arranged to coincide with an important Ritual Day within the week. Nolar offered the servant some berry wine of her own making, and while he tended his tired horse, she withdrew inside to think. There had to be something more to this sudden summons than appeared in the bare words of it. It was twelve years since Nolar had seen her father; she had never met the stepsisters. Nolar allowed herself a brief smile. She could almost hear what Ostbor would have said. "Hmm—you can never know unless you venture to see for yourself. I think that sheer curiosity lies at the base of more actions than people care to admit. But what is scholarship, after all, but the cultivation of curiosity and subsequent efforts to satisfy the urge to know?" Ostbor would have gone on this trip—Nolar was certain of that.

Nolar hastily assembled the few things she would need, and she and her escort had set out for the plains late that afternoon. After so many years of isolation in the hills, it felt peculiar to Nolar to be back among such numbers of people. As they descended from the hills, Nolar carefully swathed her face in a scarf despite the growing heat. The servant's eyes widened when he had first seen her uncovered face. He had been too well trained to comment upon her simple, if uncomfortable defense against the stares of strangers.

Upon their arrival five days later, her father's courtyard seemed both larger and smaller than Nolar had remembered it. She had last viewed it through the eyes of a child, so those recollections loomed spaciously; the current reality appeared cramped, crowded with extra horses and grooms in unknown liveries busily darting about. Nolar had never before seen so many people at her father's house. She was hurried through a side entrance near the back, and a businesslike house servant had shown her to an upstairs room.

"Your father requests that you array yourself as speedily as may be, mistress." The woman paused briefly at the door. "There are special guests here to see you."

Nolar's ears pricked at that. She knew practically no one in this house any more, other than her father. Who could possibly want to see her, and why? Several bright gowns of various sizes were draped across the bed. Nolar had chosen the simplest that fitted her, a subdued blue-gray with white bindings. There was a selection of jewelry on the chest beside the bed. Nolar momentarily picked up a chain of twisted silver links, then replaced it. She had never worn such things. Necklaces were meant to draw attention to a face or neck, and her chief desire was to remain unnoticed, if not completely unseen.

The servant returned to lead Nolar to one of the larger formal rooms, then left her there alone. Dramatically, as if her arrival was trumpeted by a herald, an imposing lady swept into the room. Following a pace behind was Nolar's father. He looked much the same as Nolar remembered him—stern, self-contained, distant. Nolar had realized with a mild sense of surprise that she no longer had acute feelings for this man. He could as well have been the servant sent to fetch her. He was a stranger, and it was an especially severe pain for Nolar to admit that he had truly always been a stranger to her.

Her thoughts were interrupted by a peremptory rap to her left—her stepmother apparently did not like being ignored. Nolar studied her face with interest. She had seen the lady only a few times before her own childhood exile to the mountains. Nolar could remember her old nurse whispering confidentially to the cook about the new wife arriving from one of the Falconer's breeding villages. Much of what they had said made little sense to her, being a small child, but the word "Falconer" lingered in Nolar's mind. She now noticed that her stepmother possessed the shining reddish hair and hawk-yellow eyes associated with the Falconers. Ostbor at one time had been quite fascinated by the genealogy of the men of the south mountain's Eyrie, and had tried without success to establish a correspondence with the Lord of Wings, commander of the Eyrie's forces.

In her turn, Nolar's stepmother gazed at her with equally keen regard. Nolar reached up and deliberately removed the white veil she had drawn over her hair and across her face. Her stepmother gasped involuntarily, but Nolar's eyes were on her father's face. He flinched as if she had struck him. It was, Nolar thought, a sad effect to have on one's own family.

Her father swiftly regained his normal composure. "Nolar," he said, then with a proudly graceful gesture, "my wife."

"Lady." Nolar dipped her head, thinking wryly that no doubt there was some proper customary movement she should have made, if anyone had only instructed her about it before.

Her stepmother continued to regard her severely. For a frivolous instant, Nolar wondered if she were being assayed for sale; then an icy sense of premonition seized her. She *was* being weighed somehow, and as usual, she was found wanting. Nolar's suspicion was immediately confirmed when the double doors opened to admit a cluster of strangers—a family, to judge by their close resemblance. The ornamentally dressed matron at once took charge of the proceedings.

"So this is your daughter who has been living in the mountains. My son . . ." Her voice faltered when Nolar turned to face her. There was an appalled silence as the party of visitors stared at Nolar. Feeling very much the deformed trade animal about to be rejected, Nolar calmly returned their regard. The ornamented matron whispered rapidly in her husband's ear, then defiantly confronted Nolar's father and stepmother. "Your proposal regarding the betrothal of my son to your daughter is not at all suitable. I regret that we cannot stay for your other ceremonies. We shall be leaving at once." With a curt nod, she marched out, trailed by her party.

From the corner of her eye, Nolar caught an expression of almost smug amusement on her stepmother's face. Evidently she had not put much credence in the notion that Nolar could be so easily banished into marriage. Her father looked more resigned, as if he, too, had not really expected the venture to succeed. They might have mentioned to me that they were contracting for my marriage, Nolar thought, but it must have been a purely practical move, perhaps a corollary to the other betrothal. The one event, in fact, might have suggested the other. In any case, the negotiations on her behalf had failed, so Nolar should be free to return to the mountains after the Ritual Day observances. Unless—a daunting doubt occurred to Nolar. With all the people gathered for the stepsister's betrothal, would her father try to arrange a marriage with some other available family? She glanced anxiously at her father, but his grim expression was forbidding of any queries. He indicated another interior door. "The Council member awaits—we must present the household to her. Nolar, go through, if you will. My wife and I will follow shortly."

Nolar's thoughts whirled. The great-aunt Witch, *here*, in this house! Nolar had never before been in the presence of a Witch. Her heart raced. Could this Witch somehow discern that Nolar had never been properly tested for Witch talent? Nolar would simply have to chance it, trying to be as inconspicuous as she could. As she moved into another large reception room, Nolar replaced her veil, and sought the most distant corner beside the raised dais where great chairs were placed for important visitors.

Figures in gray gowns had already occupied two of the chairs. *Two* Witches—Nolar started toward the side of the dais, but one Witch summoned her with a peremptory wave of her wooden staff. Nolar took a steadying breath and approached the dais.

The Witch on Nolar's right spoke in a voice that was low, but firm and accustomed to obedience. "Look up, child. Which daughter are you?"

Nolar raised her eyes, and after an instant's pause, pulled back her veil. It was obvious from their initial glance that these two could not be deceived by an untrained person. Nolar turned toward her questioner. "Lady, I am Nolar of Meroney."

"Yes, I observe a clear likeness to your mother."

This, then, had to be Nolar's famed great-aunt. Nolar searched the calm face for some family resemblance, but the chief impression was one of serenity and controlled power. Both Witches had silver nets drawn over their hair, and pendants of cloudy crystal suspended from single-strand neck chains.

Although both Witches' faces appeared relatively ageless and unlined, the Witch on Nolar's left had seemed somehow the younger of the two. One of her eyes was obscured by a milky film. If she were indeed blind in that eye, Nolar thought, her intimidating staff could be merely a necessary aid for walking. Ostbor had told her that when the Witches withdrew for training, they generally renounced all personal belongings. This Witch's staff, however, was capped by a small silver bird, as if it were a House badge. To add to

Nolar's unease, the half-blind Witch peered down at Nolar with unusual intensity.

Nolar's great-aunt was also regarding her closely. "A pity about your face. Had you shown any talent at your examining, you might have found refuge among us."

So they did not know that she had not been examined! Nolar's heart thumped with relief until the horrid thought occurred that the Witch might be deceiving her on purpose, lulling her into a false sense of confidence.

The half-blind Witch stirred in the great chair, as if debating whether to speak. "Perhaps in the archives at Lormt," she ventured in a hesitant voice, "might there not be some lore concerning such stains of the skin?"

The senior Witch frowned. "You have always been overly inquisitive on matters of no moment to you. The old fools at Lormt do naught but waste their time shuffling pointless scraps of useless scribbling. They cannot even be considered laughable—they are simply irrelevant. Have done with any mention of the place."

Her companion silently accepted the rebuke, but kept looking back frequently at Nolar during the subsequent introductions when Nolar's stepmother led in the rest of the household to be formally presented. Nolar was immediately relegated to a position far to the rear of the group; after being merely named in her turn, she was allowed to slip aside out of the way. Distracted by her own worries, Nolar did not at first listen to the conversation on the dais, where her father and stepmother had been seated in the two remaining great chairs. Something in her father's tone abruptly attracted Nolar's attention. With deferential courtesy, he was inquiring about the current state of Estcarp's harried borders. The earnest concern in his voice betrayed to Nolar his intense interest. The senior Witch remarked that Facellian of Alizon appeared to be closely occupied nowadays with purely local matters. There was a dry satisfaction in her voice. Nolar suspected that the Witch knew far more than she was revealing.

Nolar's father hastened to thank the Witch for any news of Alizon. "I am certain that your recent travels near that border must have yielded valuable information for the Council. As you must know, we here in the midlands are at a grave disadvantage, having to rely on repeated tales or mere rumors. Our trade has been grievously disrupted by the raids from Karsten. Is it true that Duke Pagar has assembled a vast army? I have heard that he is actually poised to invade Estcarp at any time."

The senior Witch surveyed Nolar's father with controlled scorn. "Those who invest according to rumors may find that their gold has vanished overnight. You would do well to base your judgments on more reliable facts. The Council, I assure you, is prepared to deal with Pagar. It is convening at Es Castle shortly for that very purpose. And now we must retire, for we shall depart early on the morrow."

Nolar quietly retreated to her room. Her mountain clothes lay neatly folded on a low chest. She touched one familiar, rough-woven sleeve, wishing that she could be back in her own house, when she heard a faint scratching at her door. To her complete surprise, the impatient figure waiting in the hall was the half-blind Witch, who strode decisively into Nolar's room, shutting the door behind her.

"I must speak with you," the Witch said, so quietly that Nolar had to lean closer to distinguish the words. "There will be no opportunity tomorrow; it must be now. Pay heed to me: you must travel to Lormt!"

Nolar supposed she must have looked as stunned as she felt. At first speechless, she recovered enough to say, "Lormt—but until you spoke the name a few minutes ago, I had not heard it since the old scholar came to take Ostbor's records there."

The Witch had nodded. "Good—then you are at least aware of the place. So few recognize the value of preserving

ancient lore. You heard the opinion of the Council member;
I am sorry to say that she speaks for most Witches on the
subject of Lormt. Still, despite their low opinion, Lormt is a
storehouse of old knowledge to be found nowhere else, and
you *must* travel there. I cannot convey to you my sense of
urgency on this matter, but you must believe me. Lormt
holds that which you alone can find . . . must find."

Nolar was convinced of the Witch's sincerity, but all that
flooded her mind were more questions. "But, lady, what am
I to seek? How am I to get there? Who would listen to me?
I know no one at Lormt, nor the way to the place. Ostbor
studied there many years ago, but he was too old to attempt
the journey with me when I asked him to take me there."

The Witch remained still, except for her fingers twisting
nervously around the boss of her staff. The silver bird crafted
there was definitely a raven; it was a clear miniature of those
stately birds Nolar had often seen in the high peaks. Nolar
suddenly realized that the twisting fingers had to evidence
uncharacteristic agitation for a Witch.

This Witch's severe frown appeared to reflect her own
inner disquiet. "I cannot tell you exactly where to go," she
admitted. "The how is a simple, practical matter of hiring a
guide who will arrange for horses and such—you may dismiss that. The troubling point is the object of your quest. It
is not clear to me at all." Frustrated, the Witch had thumped
her staff on the floor, and was instantly dismayed by the
noise. Fortunately, the household had remained undisturbed. The Witch hurried on. "Our time is short—hear me
well. We are sometimes granted a Foreseeing, a vision of
what is to come. Three times I have seen you—there was no
chance for mistake, for you are the one in my vision. And
Lormt is the place; I am certain of that." She had compressed
her lips, then sighed. "Mist, fog—all else is concealed from
me, but I *know* that you must go to Lormt and seek. Never
before have I had such a powerful Foreseeing. Now I must
go. Perhaps we may meet again. I sense that we are somehow

linked together. I do not know how or why . . . but I wish you well. For the future, all good."

Deeply impressed by the Witch's evident concern, Nolar tried an awkward bow. "My thanks, lady, for your telling of this Foreseeing. I do not know where my path shall lead, but if ever I should go to Lormt, I shall recall your words."

The Witch hesitated at the door. "I can do no more. Remember—you *must* go to Lormt and search there." With a swirl of her gray robes, she hastened down the hall, not looking back.

Nolar lay awake for many hours, puzzling over the incidents of the day. She swiftly dismissed the effort by her father to arrange her marriage. So long as she bore her own face, she thought, she was likely safe from that threat. Her father was both too practical and too proud to risk further ridicule and additional rebuffs. This one failed effort would probably be his last . . . unless, a nettlesome thought nagged, some other family was afflicted with a similarly unsuitable son it could not place. She shook her head, then stopped, aggravated by the unfamiliar softness of the pillow.

She knew that she did not belong in this place—she never had. The sooner she could return to the solitude of the mountains, the better. Resolving to ask her father in the morning for his leave to depart, she then reviewed her meetings with the Witches. Ostbor had been right. There was no tie of kinship left to the woman who was her great-aunt. Having become a Witch, she had cut all ties to her family, and now she had to be thought of solely as a Witch, and an important Witch at that. Nolar did not know what to think of the half-blind Witch who had visited her room. There was a quiet warmth about her that made Nolar think of Ostbor, the only other person who had ever truly cared for her. If family members were supposed to care about each other's well-being, then this complete stranger—and Witch—seemed far more like a family member than did her blood relatives. But

Witches were not supposed to have family feelings once they took the gray robe.

It was like a knot without a loose cord to pull, yet Nolar was unable to ignore what the half-blind Witch had said and how she had said it. Why should Nolar have appeared in the Witch's vision? And how could she possibly be linked with anything in distant Lormt? A little of her old desire to see Lormt stirred in her mind, but Nolar told herself that it was all foolishness. The only place that she belonged was in the mountains, away from most scornful eyes. Curiously, her last thought before she had dropped off into troubled sleep was of the silver raven perched on the Witch's staff.

The next day began in a bustle of activity. The two Witches rode away just before dawn. More guests had arrived for the betrothal. Nolar had to wait until midmorning to see her father, but he was distracted, and seemed not to care whether she stayed or left. Nolar seized her opportunity, asking the same servant who had escorted her if he would see to her horse for the return trip to the mountains. Her packing required little time, and before midday, she rode quietly out of the busy courtyard.

Ostbor's cramped, eccentric house seemed a welcome refuge when Nolar wearily descended the last slope down to its door. She opened all of the windows that would open, and breathed the pine-scented air with relief, after all the dust from the road during her trip.

During the succeeding days, she slipped back into her former life pattern, gathering herbs, roots, leaves, and stems to be prepared in many ways for use by any hill folk who would ask for them. In the still night hours, Nolar searched through all of Ostbor's remaining scrolls for any information on the Witches and their ways. As Ostbor had told her, the Witches kept very much to themselves, so what was written about them appeared to be more conjecture and rumor than likely fact. Still, what little she found only added to Nolar's unease. The senior Witch had said that Nolar might have found a place with them in spite of her disfigurement, provided that she had shown talent.

It must, Nolar thought, be a great encouragement to feel that one truly belonged to some group, whether it was one's family or even the company of Witches. In her case, of course, the door to her family had been closed to Nolar from the very first. Nolar decided that notwithstanding the totally unexplained feeling of kindness that she had sensed from the half-blind Witch, life among the Witches must be coldly austere, submerging the individual into the group in some mysterious way that seemed to her basically threatening. She renewed her resolve to avoid all Witches in the future, if possible, although she occasionally surprised herself by wishing that she might someday again meet the Witch with the silver raven on her staff.

There had been no further word from or about Lormt. In thinking back to the senior Witch's remarks at her father's house, Nolar wondered if there could be some connection between them and the traveling merchant's speculations about a trap for Duke Pagar. Nolar had a foreboding sense that events were about to break upon Estcarp just as sea waves were said to crash against the coastal beaches. She had never seen the sea, but Ostbor had read her tales of the wreckers of Verlaine and the fabled merchants and fighters of Sulcar. If the Sulcarmen were indeed planning to help those of Estcarp to escape by ship when Pagar invaded, surely Nolar and the hill folk would be secure so far away nestled against these interior mountains. Even as she thought that, however, Nolar knew that Karsten's forces would not stop at the Es River, nor at the great walls of Es Castle. If Estcarp were to be attacked in earnest, Alizon to the north would not sit idly on its hands. But the south—Nolar's thoughts had kept turning to the south, to Lormt. She was irritated by that repeated intrusion, and vowed not to let herself be manipulated by outside pressure.

Pressure—the very word seemed to vibrate in the breathless air. There was a certain morbid irony, Nolar reflected, in her sense today of some essential wrongness. Except for Ostbor's quiet companionship, she had never felt comfortable in the company of other people. Now it seemed that the whole natural world had become somehow misaligned. How else could she account for the silent oppression that battered her from the south? It *was* from the south . . . but not, Nolar was abruptly certain, from Lormt itself. The merchant's words sounded again in her mind. "The Council is plotting some elaborate trap to swallow the Duke of Karsten and all his harrying forces." Nolar suddenly knew that whatever was wrong was related to the Witches. They had to be behind it, this draining away of all vitality. If the Council were drawing upon the energy of the very land of Estcarp, then what devastation must result when they loosed that fearful accumulation?

With the twilight darkening to dusk, Nolar shivered, as much from her daunting thoughts as from the penetrating cold. There would be no visible sunset this night; the dense southern clouds had blotted out the usual channels through which the sun's last rays ordinarily shone. Nolar stepped into the house only long enough to snatch up a woven shawl, then hurried back outside. Her feeling of urgent anticipation drove her to scramble up a nearby hill where she could gain a better view toward the south. Something, she *knew*, something dreadful was about to happen.

Alert and expectant as she was, Nolar still recoiled, startled, when a blaze of light erupted from the brooding darkness across the horizon. She caught herself unconsciously holding her breath, her hands clenched until the nails bit into her palms. She tried to relax, but another enormous flash of light, far brighter than any lightning Nolar could remember, flared against the black clouds. It had to be countless leagues away, but Nolar strained to hear the thunder that must accompany so gigantic a display. The minutes crawled by, and to her amazement, the first physical sign of the distant catastrophe resonated through the rocks against Nolar's feet. The initial movement was tentative, then more pronounced.

During her years in the mountains, Nolar had experienced a few minor quakings of the earth, which had always passed quickly with little damage, except for crockery tumbled from shelves. This deep, horrid shuddering seemed to emanate from the very roots of the mountains. Clutching her shawl, Nolar dropped to her knees. The ground shook ponderously, reluctantly, as if responding to irresistible pressures from some distance away. Sound—she could barely distinguish the sound that must be deafening to any living creature unfortunate enough to be trapped near its source. It was a low-pitched, drawn-out, grumbling, grinding sound that vibrated into the bones of the hearer.

Nolar clung desperately to her suddenly precarious position. What were the Witches doing? Was it possible that they were somehow responsible for this earthquake? The question seemed so absurd that Nolar thrust it aside, but the suggestion echoed in her mind, numbing in its awful enormity.

As she grasped the quivering rocks, Nolar tried to distract herself. Ignore the Witches, she thought, but unbidden, the image of the half-blind Witch who had urged her to go to Lormt suddenly crystallized in Nolar's mind's eye. Instantly, as if she had accidentally touched the hidden spring releasing a secret door, a spate of images and voices flooded into her mind, drowning out all other thoughts. Terrified, Nolar cried out and pressed to her forehead the only hand she could spare. Pain—pain—pressure—Power! The mind-realm crackled with Power. Nolar's eyes were squeezed shut, but she was *seeing*, seeing things and places that she had never before seen. She was allowed no time to be frightened; indeed, she scarcely had time to breathe.

The highest Nolar had ever climbed had been dangerously near the swaying tip of an evergreen tree near Ostbor's house. He had wondered whether the seed cones near the top were of the same form as those closer to the ground, so the young Nolar had immediately rushed to find out for him. She had returned much later, breathless, her skin scraped by the rough bark and sticky with evergreen gum, but triumphantly bearing several cone-laden branches. She still remembered the sweeping view from that treetop, the sense of breathtaking space beneath, stretching to the forested ridges and crags that rimmed her world.

Now, abruptly, Nolar was suspended far higher in the air than she had ever imagined in idle speculations of what a flying bird might see. She seemed to be hovering, bodiless, above a vast nocturnal panorama of mountains. Horribly, these mountains were not serenely still; they were *moving*. What should have been eminently solid, reliable earth was heaving, rolling, even rippling like the surface of a pot of thick, bubbling gruel. Oh, the poor animals, Nolar thought, then her self-awareness was crushed by a titanic thrust of outside will—a concerted, iron demand of concentrated Power reaching, probing down to the deep-buried bones of the mountains and stirring them, shaking them, pushing, pulling, tilting. The pressure seemed to build within Nolar's skull until she feared her head must burst. There was a crescendo of white-hot agony, during which she lost all sensation.

When Nolar slowly regained her awareness, she could still "see" the appalling turmoil being wreaked upon the mountains, compounded now by screaming winds, and torrential rain, and illuminated by eerie flares of lightning.

Gradually, amid the chaos, Nolar noticed disruptions, hesitations in the flow of Power, sudden brief pauses when the punishing pressure against the earth seemed to falter. The cataclysmic momentum, however, continued unabated, since all of the imbalances deliberately introduced by the Witches now had to work themselves out physically. The fabric of the hillsides buckled and slid. Immense avalanches were lubricated by the ice and water of unleashed glaciers, augmented by lakes and streams wrenched from their beds. Fires were kindled by lashing lightning, and as rapidly quenched by cascades of water and loose earth. Whole forests were being swept away as if they had never been. Nolar felt an inconsolable sense of loss as she knew she was witnessing the death of entire arrays of plants and animals—and people, should any be trapped in that unnatural cauldron of destruction.

Again, flickers of hesitancy stirred in her mind, followed by an incoherent pulse of sorrow, regret for all that was being sacrificed. Without warning, Nolar was transfixed by a pain of searing intensity. Something/someone was screaming her name against the cacophony of the storm.

"Nolar . . . *Nolar!* . . . *NOLAR!*"

Tormented, she cried out, "I am here! Here! Oh, stop, please, STOP!"

For a breath, there was a respite, then the imperative mental battering resumed. "Nolar . . . NOLAR . . . Lormt . . . LORMT! Quest . . . must go . . . Lormt . . . HEAR!"

Nolar's mind was reeling under the bombardment. Her own thoughts formed with painful slowness. Lormt . . . the half-blind Witch. This . . . this Sending had to be coming from her. Immediately, as Nolar concentrated on her memories of the Witch, the ferocious pain ebbed from the mental contact, while the linkage seemed to strengthen. Emboldened, Nolar tried to respond, to reach back to the Witch, but her every effort was overridden, crushed by the sheer force of the Sending. Nolar helplessly endured the repetition of her name and the exhortations to go to Lormt until, to her numbed surprise, she realized that something was changing. The message was fading, growing less coherent, as if the mind projecting it was near exhaustion. The once clear pattern had degenerated into a confusing jumble, but the sense of urgency and distress permeating it sharpened even as the strength behind the Sending drained away.

"Help me . . . sisters dying . . . blasted . . . too much Power. . . . NO! must not let go . . . pain . . . Es Castle. . . . Come, Nolar!

. . . you *must*. . . . HURRY!" With that final mental shout, the contact snapped, leaving Nolar cowering on the ground.

Nolar lay still for several moments, her body trembling. Then she struggled to sit up, and rose shakily to her feet. The mountain air was no longer still; it smelled of impending rain, and gusted strongly from the south. Nolar's face felt chilled. When she brushed a hand against her cheek, her fingers came away wet with tears. She stumbled blindly down the slope, frantic to find the refuge of Ostbor's house. The formerly shuddering ground had subsided into a blessed solidity, but the wind and approaching thunder heralded the fringes of that mammoth storm battering the south. Cold— so cold. Would she ever feel warm again? Empty—so much gone—so many gone. Dazed, Nolar shook her head. She had shared the thoughts of another person—the half-blind Witch—leagues away, presumably in Es Castle itself.

Nolar gasped and fell when she abruptly collided with a rough wooden wall. Her house, at last—she groped her way inside, sobbing for breath, just as the storm broke. With shaking hands, Nolar seized a fire-hardened stick and prodded the fireplace coals to life. Hugging her shawl around her, she sank down on the hearthstones. She had to try to make sense of what she had just experienced. That she had *seen* and *heard* with her mind instead of with her own eyes and ears frightened Nolar almost beyond expression. She could no longer evade the awful question: could it be that after all these unknowing years, she actually possessed Witch talent? Nolar wanted desperately to deny it, to run away from it, but she knew she had to admit what had just happened. She had received a Witch Sending. From what Ostbor had told her, few common people had ever experienced a Sending, since Witches employed that use of the Power to communicate between themselves, or, if necessary, with those few others trained to receive their warnings or instructions. Nolar could not recall any references in the scrolls to an ordinary person like herself being granted visions of faraway events. And not only the disturbing visions and sounds of the cataclysm; Nolar had also shared some of the feelings evidently belonging to the half-blind Witch.

As she sorted through her tumbled memories, Nolar knew with a leaden certainty that many Witches had died this night, burned out by the Power they had attempted to direct and control. That would explain the curious faltering she had sensed; if the Witches of the Council had fallen one by one, during this extraordinary effort to turn the very earth of Estcarp against its enemies, then the flow of their Power would have been diminished until uninjured Witches could take their places. Was her own great-aunt one of the fallen? Nolar blinked at the thought. It was the fate of the half-blind Witch that urgently concerned Nolar far more. That lady of the silver raven had called to Nolar. At the moment of her greatest trial, the Witch had dispatched a Sending . . . more than just a Sending. Nolar crept up from the hearth to sit in Ostbor's chair. She had been summoned. How had it been said? "Es Castle. . . . Come!" and "Help me." There could be no doubt of the urgency of that plea. Nolar found herself mentally calculating what supplies she would need for the journey. She drew up suddenly, trembling despite the warmth from the fire. Es Castle was the center, the seat of the Council of Witches. If Nolar should go there, how could she hope to avoid being disclosed as a potential Witch? Surely it must be known even now to the others of the Council. The force of that Sending had to have been felt by any adept near the Sender. Might not the half-blind Witch have told the others about Nolar? But had there been time? If this Sending had been simply a desperate effort by an injured or dying Witch among others similarly afflicted, could there be a chance that no one else had noticed what was being Sent? Nolar caught herself painfully gripping the chair arms and tried to relax her hands. It really didn't matter who knew what. Despite any risks to herself, Nolar had to try to reach the Silver Raven Witch. There was a double linkage between them now: first, the Witch had Foreseen

Nolar in association with Lormt, and second, she had just Sent her plea for help directly to Nolar. As the rain and wind lashed Ostbor's house, Nolar smiled ruefully. Ostbor would have understood. This was one of those decisions that truly demanded no act of choice. Nolar felt an obligation toward the Silver Raven Witch. Somehow, a bond had been forged between the two of them, and Nolar could not rest until she found the Witch and offered whatever help she could provide.

It was very late that night before Nolar wearily crawled into her bed. After a brief hesitation, she had unlocked Ostbor's treasure box and spread out on his table the entire store of precious metal. Ostbor had left her most of it, but she had earned some of the silver herself. She had no clear idea of what trials might lie before her, but it seemed prudent to carry with her all that she possessed. It took only a few moments to fold the gold and silver bits within a narrow fabric belt that she could conceal beneath her clothing. Her modest store of coppers could travel safely in her scrip. There was no need to arrange for the care of any livestock since she would be riding her only horse, and Ostbor had not customarily kept small animals as pets.

He had occasionally accepted injured creatures to be nursed until they could be safely returned to their normal home areas. Nolar wistfully recalled one bright-eyed, soft-feathered owl, whose broken wing had mended in Ostbor's attic over one quiet winter only a year or two after Nolar herself had arrived. She had been reluctant to free it, but Ostbor had been firm: the owl belonged among its own kind.

Sore at heart, Nolar had retorted, "Yet I do not belong. No one cares whether I stay or go. At least, I could talk to the owl, and perhaps stroke it sometimes." The owl had appeared to follow the conversation with great interest, turning its head gravely toward whichever of them was speaking.

Ostbor had grasped Nolar's hand. "Dear child, I care very much where you are. For this time, you belong here with me. This bird of the night needs to rejoin its kind, to hunt the mountain meadows and reduce the deplorable number of mice that insist upon chewing on my parchments. Look! See how he stretches his wings—he is ready now to fly from our care. Let us not confine him when he should be free."

Ashamed of her selfishness, Nolar had opened the shutter and Ostbor had gently set the owl on the window ledge. It had hooted once, then swooped away soundlessly, a shadow quickly lost among the night's other shadows.

So Nolar had no beasts to provide for, but she had many other tasks to be completed before she could begin her journey the following day. All of her herbs and supplies had to be carefully examined and those that could be stored for an indefinite period had to be packed away. Nolar sent word by a passing herdsboy to the storekeeper that she would be bringing him her perishable items as well as those things most likely to be needed by the hill folk while she would be traveling to Es City.

It was midafternoon when she arrived at the shop. The keeper agreed, somewhat gruffly, to supply her in return with ample journeycake and grain for her horse. After securing the grain sacks on her horse, the storekeeper surprised Nolar by pressing a handful of copper into her hand. "Here, lady. Good fortune upon your trip."

Taken aback, Nolar tried to return the metal, but he brushed aside her protests. "What you brought me, lady, fairly outweights the value of the grain and the cakes," he said. "Besides, you were friend to the old scholar, and he was a wise man, helpful to us hill folk."

Nolar nodded as she mounted her horse. "Then I thank you gladly, for Ostbor's sake as well as for my own. Good fortune upon you and your house."

During the hot, weary days that followed, Nolar drove both herself and her horse to their physical limits. League by dusty league, she pressed on, her conviction sharpening, knowing that every moment was vital, that she must hasten with all possible speed. As before, on her trip to her father's house, Nolar kept her face swathed and stayed apart from other travelers when she could.

Every night before sleeping, Nolar paused and concentrated, straining to reestablish that remarkable mental linkage with the Silver Raven Witch. Each effort left her frustrated. If only she knew *how* one was supposed to reach out—but there was never the slightest indication of any response. Nolar kept telling herself that the Witch was probably too weak or too ill to attempt another Sending. With each failure, though, Nolar's sense of urgency burned stronger.

The best times to ride, Nolar quickly discovered, were the very early and late hours. The air was cooler then, the dust less, and the company on the road generally sparser. She would have ridden exclusively at night, had there been enough light to see her way, but the destruction to the south appeared to have affected the weather. The farther south she went, the darker and cloudier the skies became.

As she drew nearer to Es City, Nolar met fewer people on the road, and those she saw were close-mouthed, their eyes fixed on the road before them. Perhaps, Nolar thought, they were reluctant to talk to a stranger, but after several days of observing, she concluded that the people must still be stunned by what the Witches had wrought. Even at this distance from the southern border, the signs of physical damage kept increasing. Trees had been uprooted or splintered by the winds, and gravel and soil had been swept across the road. In places, the road itself vanished, scoured away by the unnatural storm.

On the fifth day, Nolar slowly rode through one of the narrow gates set in the massive gray-green wall encircling Es City. As she approached across the plain, Nolar marveled at the great round towers set in the wall. This was the largest city she had ever seen, and she was profoundly impressed by the sense of immense strength and age that emanated from its stones. The midmorning sun flashed briefly through the clouds, but Nolar felt a foreboding internal chill despite the sultry air. She recalled the cloth merchant's description of how crowded Es City had been only a few weeks before. There still seemed to be a large number of people hurrying through the streets, but they were self-absorbed, their faces drawn and grim. Nolar had no need to ask directions to Es Castle, for it loomed in the middle of the city, dominating every view. She felt drawn to it, but also dreaded every step that increased her danger of being recognized as an untested potential Witch.

As soon as she ventured into the Castle's main courtyard, however, Nolar realized that for once her deepest fears might be unjustified . . . at least for this moment. If Es City and its inhabitants appeared to share the dazed obliviousness that she had observed in travelers along the road, Es Castle was evidently demoralized into nearly complete inactivity. She searched without success for a watchman or doorkeeper. The few distant figures she sighted all scurried away before she could attract their attention. At first, Nolar was relieved not to be accosted. She was not at all certain how she would fare when asked for her reasons for invading the Castle grounds. As the minutes passed, however, she became increasingly uneasy. Someone should have intercepted her. Feeling curiously like an outlaw seeking plunder, Nolar decided that she must enter the Castle itself, and simply search for the Silver Raven Witch until or unless she was physically barred.

Tethering her horse in a shaded area near a water trough, Nolar forced herself to cross the threshold into a warren of passages providing access to the lower halls and storerooms. Once inside, she stared in wonder at the clusters of pale globes set in metal baskets near the arched ceilings. They seemed to contain no candles or brazier coals, yet they shed a white, constant light. Nolar assumed that they must be part of the Witches's magic. As her footsteps echoed from the worn stone paving slabs, she felt oppressed by the silence and by what had to be the unnatural emptiness of a place that should be bustling with people. How could she possibly find the Silver Raven Witch in this enormous structure?

Her hand brushed against a heavy wooden door that swung back quietly. Hoping to find someone within, Nolar pushed the door open and entered a storeroom whose shelves and bins stretched away into the shadows. She was about to withdraw when a metallic glint caught her eye. Above one section of shelves and cupboards, a metal House badge was inset into the dark wood: a silver raven. Nolar was just reaching up to touch it when she was startled by a sudden voice behind her.

"What are you doing here?"

Nolar whirled to find herself confronted by a gray-clad man whose face seemed creased in a permanent frown. He must have shared Ostbor's shortness of sight, for he stepped quite close, peering accusingly at her. He carried a short staff or thick wand in one hand, and a great bunch of keys in the other. Nolar recalled a similarly harried-looking man who had always flourished such a staff in her father's service, and decided that this man must also be a steward.

"Please forgive my intrusion," Nolar said, "but I could find no one outside to ask where I should go."

"Speak up, speak up! I am the Chief Steward, and I have many important things to do." The man rattled his keys, but his eyes looked oddly distracted, as if he weren't really sure what he planned to do next.

"Sir, I have come many leagues to seek a . . . relative of mine. I have been sent . . . word that the lady is ill and requires my assistance. I am Nolar of Meroney, late assistant scribe to Ostbor the Scholar."

The steward fastened on her family name. "Meroney—I fear that the Council member from your House is dead. The Turning, you understand." His pale, lined face looked stricken, as if the recent disaster had brought him near his breaking point.

Nolar bowed her head in respect. "I feared that might be

the case, sir, but my message came from a living Witch." She pointed to the metal raven. "That is her House badge. I cannot, of course, say her name."

The steward gazed at the badge and sighed. "Ah, poor lady. Come." As he preceded her up stairs and through endless halls, the steward explained that the Castle was in great disarray. Few fully functioning Witches were left; many had died outright, and many others . . . his voice dropped. "Husks. They may never again come back to themselves. There has been a Sending to draw here safely from afar those Witches who remain, but they have not had time yet to arrive." He shook his head. "Likely, there will have to be a reexamination of all girls as soon as Witches can be spared to quarter the countryside. The ranks *must* be replenished."

Nolar stood as if rooted, horrified by the prospect of being so quickly found out. The steward, impatient, glanced back at her.

"Come along! I cannot spare this much time. Here, down this corridor." He stopped in front of a metal-bound door and unlocked it with one of his many keys.

Nolar entered the room. Her heart leaped when she saw the half-blind Witch sitting in a tall-backed chair. But . . . something was seriously wrong. The Witch was as motionless as a wax image. Her good eye was clear, but unfocused, gazing straight ahead. She was obviously unaware that anyone had come into the room. Anguished, Nolar turned to the steward. "Oh, sir, what has befallen my dear . . . aunt?"

The steward made a vaguely hopeless gesture with his staff. "Many are like this. They will eat if food is put in their mouths, and drink if a cup is pressed to their lips—but truly they are not here with us. It was the effort of the Turning. The Power was too great for even the Council to control."

Nolar's mind raced. She dared not stay here at the Castle to try to care for the Silver Raven Witch. It was only a matter of time before she would be noticed and questioned too closely. If only, somehow, she could take the Witch away.

"Sir, there are family estates where my aunt could be attended. May I take her thither?"

The steward appeared tempted, but indecisive. "I could not say—it is not my place. The Council would have to rule." Suddenly, his composure crumbled, and tears spilled down his cheeks. "The Council is no more! What shall become of Escarp?" He clenched his hands around his staff and his keys as he struggled to recover his official mien. "It is true that at present we are having some difficulty caring for our injured. If we knew when—or whether—they might regain their senses, we could make better plans. As it is, you see your aunt's jewel." He pointed to the crystal pendant Nolar had seen sparkling at her father's house. Now it lay dull and lifeless against the Witch's scarcely moving chest. "The Acting Guardian has ruled that until the jewels resume their usual fire, we must assume that the possessing Witches are lost to us. Should you have a safe place for this lady, perhaps it might be wise . . . for the present, you understand . . . and if there should be any change, you would inform us at once." The steward appeared perilously close to tears again but he straightened his drooping shoulders and assumed a brisker manner. "Your aunt's personal possessions were stored when she entered the Castle. She may require some of them for your journey. Come, I will unlock her cupboard for you."

Back in the shadowed storage room, Nolar chose several sturdy traveling cloaks and plain gowns. The steward extracted a locked casket from a drawer near the floor, and fussed with it until its lid hinged back. "Here, you may need some of your aunt's gems and silver. I really must be getting back. You will send word concerning your aunt if . . ." His voice trailed off. He turned abruptly and hurried away.

Nolar retraced the route to her purported "aunt's" door, which the steward fortunately had left unlocked. She tried speaking to the Witch, even daring to raise her voice, but she might as well have shouted at the stone towers of Es Castle. Nolar paused, took a steadying breath, and examined the room. In a withe hamper in a corner, she found a stout fabric bag in which she collected the Witch's few personal articles—comb, hair nets, underclothing, a small pot of ointment to soften the hands. Several of the formal gray robes hung in a niche behind a curtain, but Nolar felt that it might not be wise to proclaim the identity of her charge. If the Witches' views of Lormt and its scholars were so implacably scornful, how might Lormt welcome a supplicant seeking help in healing a Witch? Nolar gently removed the distinctive silver hair net, and exchanged the Witch's gray robe for a less noticeable pale blue one she discovered in a chest at the foot of the bed. Prompted by an afterthought, Nolar also slipped the Witch's jewel inside the fabric of her gown where it was not immediately visible. As she worked, she found herself talking to the Witch, even though she doubted that she was being heard. Still, Ostbor had told her of instances when folk with head injuries could not show that they heard, but upon later recovery, said that they had been aware of sounds. It somehow seemed more courteous to explain what she was about to do than just to proceed as if the Witch were a helpless statue to be pushed and pulled, forced about by another's will.

Nolar was greatly relieved to find that the Witch could stand erect and walk slowly, if guided and supported. Would she be able to sit on a horse? That would have to be determined. Nolar maneuvered the Witch to the courtyard, and then faced the problem of how to lift her into the saddle. Fortunately, by that time, more people were moving about the Castle grounds, and she was able to ask a passing man for his assistance. Stepping up on a mounting stone, he easily swung the Witch's small body astride the saddle. Nolar took the reins and slowly led her horse forward, glancing up and back frequently until she was certain that the Witch was securely balanced and not likely to fall. The man who had helped her also offered directions to an inn several streets away from the City wall.

After only one false turn, Nolar arrived at the inn and installed the Witch in a small but comfortable ground floor room. Since it was by then well past midday, she ordered some simple food that she hoped she could feed to the Witch. The steward had been right; the Witch could eat and drink in a slow, jerky fashion. The amount she would take was completely determined by Nolar, somewhat to Nolar's dismay. She realized that she would have to be careful to provide enough food and drink; she would receive no response or request for more or less from her silent charge. Nolar forced herself to eat some of the thick soup and a bit of bread, then stood up and looked critically at the motionless Witch. She would also have to move the Witch's limbs regularly and change her body position if she was to avoid the sores which she had seen develop on the old and sick who could not move themselves. Making sure that the Witch was safely balanced in her chair, Nolar went to seek the innkeeper.

She found him busily scrubbing a wooden table in the large common room. He was a burly, bald man with good-humored features. Like all of the faces in Es City just now, his was somber. "Could you tell me," Nolar asked, "where I might find a guide to Lormt?"

The innkeeper blinked, reminding her of the owl in Ostbor's attic. "Lormt, lady? No one goes to Lormt but old, half-witted scholars."

"I am neither old nor half-witted," Nolar pointed out patiently, "but I require a guide to Lormt. You have seen my aunt. Her head was injured during the recent upheaval at our mountain home. I came to Es City hoping that the Witches might be able to heal her, but they are themselves stricken and unavailable. I have been told that Lormt holds many writings on healing, as well as wise men who might help us."

The innkeeper paused in his scrubbing, obviously considering her problem. "Maybe that is true, lady," he replied in a dubious tone. "I wouldn't know myself, never having gone there nor knowing any who has, but I can ask about. With the damage to the south, few folk are venturing that way. I haven't heard whether the way to Lormt is passable. As you may know, there is only one track going to Lormt, and from what little I've heard of it, it never has been well kept."

Nolar tried to cling to some hope in spite of the inn-keeper's discouraging remarks. "I see. I would appreciate your arranging for a guide. It would be worth a piece of silver to me if you could find a reliable person."

Nolar waited at the inn for two days before the innkeeper reported with honest regret that he could find no one in the city planning to travel to or even toward Lormt. By that time, Nolar had decided that she would probably have to find her own way to Lormt. There remained the problem of transporting the Silver Raven Witch. Nolar had hoped that a knowledgeable guide could have advised her whether a horse litter might be preferable to the risk of letting the Witch ride a horse. Without a guide Nolar still needed a second horse, and frankly explained her need to the innkeeper.

He thought for a moment, and then said, "A merchant was here last night. While his party was on the road to Es City, one of his apprentices was killed during the Turning. He had no need of the extra horse, and was talking of selling it. The merchant said he was staying at the Sign of the Snow Cat. I can send a lad to ask his price, and if you like, I can look at the animal for you, to be sure it is suitable for your aunt's use."

Nolar gratefully accepted his offer. By early that evening, she was the owner of a second sturdy, well-mannered horse. The innkeeper agreed to arrange for her journey provisions. He seemed genuinely concerned that she and her aunt should be traveling unescorted.

"Lady," he said, "there are all manner of ill folk on the roads these days. Of course, you need have no fear of the Borderers and Guardsmen, but there are many other arms-men separated from their troops and ranging freely." Worried, the innkeeper glanced to both sides, then confided in a lowered voice, "It is said that all of Duke Pagar's invaders perished in the Turning, but word keeps passing of stray Karstenian spies and armsmen scattered free on our side of the mountains. And there are outlaws, lady, giving homage to no man and abiding by no law but their own greed. I urge you to reconsider. In a few days, I could find a trustworthy lad to ride with you if you must go to Lormt."

Nolar deliberately lowered her veil, and tried to ignore the innkeeper's involuntary recoiling from her. "You are kind to show such interest, Master Innkeeper, but as you see, my face is not one to attract either ardent attention or unwelcome fellowship. Outlaws, I gather, are chiefly drawn to plunder, but my aunt and I carry no great wealth to tempt any robber. My mind is set. I must go to Lormt, and I must leave early on the morrow."

The innkeeper shook his head in continued disapproval, but efficiently organized her departure. The next morning, he even walked part of the way down the street toward the City wall. "Have a care, lady," he called, as she rode on, leading the Witch's horse. "I will tell the Borderers's patrol leaders of your trip so that they may bear a watch for you."

The initial league of road from Es City was clear, so the riding began easily. Once the City was out of sight, however, the trail tended more directly east along the Es River bank, and Nolar had to dismount and lead both horses. The river had evidently flooded during the cataclysm, for large swaths of earth had been newly raked from both banks, leaving drifts of gravel, uprooted trees, and other storm wrack swept into obstructions around which high water still swirled. Near sunset, much reddened and dimmed by lingering dust and clouds, Nolar heard riders approaching toward Es City. She had already tethered her horses for the night, and was spreading a cloak for the Witch to lie upon when three men reined in on the rough track nearby. Two were riding erect, but the third was slumped in his saddle as if he were exhausted or hurt. Their leader raised a hand to Nolar and called, "Are you well, lady? Can we help you?"

"Are you Borderers, sir?" Nolar called back, and the leader nodded.

"Aye, lady. We have been searching for stragglers from Pagar's army, or outlaws, or any who would trouble honest folk. Can we escort you to Es City?"

Nolar walked toward him so that they wouldn't have to shout at one another. "I thank you, sir, but my road leads to Lormt. I seek healing there for my aunt, who was sorely injured in the Turning."

Concerned, the Borderer looked down at her. "You should not travel alone, lady. I cannot spare a man just now, for Goswik here took an arrow in his shoulder before dawn and we hasten to a healer's care in Es City. It was only a single outlaw who will trouble no one else. Truly, lady, this open country is not safe. Will you not ride with us to Es City?"

Nolar shook her head. "Thank you, no. I must seek the healers in Lormt, for we have already asked the Witches in Es City, and they were not able to help us."

The second rider had been examining his wounded companion. "The bleeding has begun again," he said gruffly.

The leader twitched his reins. "We must ride on. Take care, lady, you and your aunt."

Nolar decided to move her camp to an area a bit less conspicuous, behind some bushes that shielded the view from the track itself. The night passed quietly. As soon as it was light enough to see the trail, Nolar led the horses to the river to drink. She felt a prickling unease, as if she were being observed by some hidden watcher. She had heard no hooves nor telltale jingle of harness, but her sense of being watched persisted. As she brewed a morning cup for the Witch, Nolar listened for any unnatural sounds. There—the click of a displaced pebble. Without turning, she said in a normal tone of voice, "You need not crouch behind that bush. It is far more comfortable here on these large rocks, and I have an extra cup if you will share our drink."

For an instant, there was silence, then she heard someone walking openly toward her over the loose gravel. She glanced up, confronting a tall young man in the dark riding dress of the Borderers. "You have very keen eyes, lady," he said, taking a seat on one of the low boulders by her small fire.

"And ears, Master Borderer. It is difficult to move quietly on this kind of rock. I must take my aunt's cup while the drink is hot." On her way back to the fire, Nolar extracted their spare cup from her saddlebag. As she poured, she looked at the stranger. He had the black hair and gray eyes of the Old Race, and although his clothing and gear appeared worn from long use, it was clean and in good repair.

He returned her frank appraisal. "My thanks for the drink, lady," he said, accepting the cup. "You are some distance from Es City."

"As are you. No doubt your reasons for being here are as sound as mine. Shall we exchange them? I am Nolar of Meroney, and yonder is my poor aunt . . . Elgaret." The name had simply popped into Nolar's mind. She had to call the Witch something, and somehow "Elgaret" seemed appropriate. "I live in the mountains to the north." She was careful not to specify how far north. "During the recent upheaval folk now call the Turning, my aunt was sorely injured about the head. I sought aid for her from the Witches at Es Castle, but they are themselves much affected by the Turning, and so we must seek healing elsewhere. I am traveling now to Lormt to question their healers, and if necessary, search their ancient archives."

The young man dipped his head. "I have heard of the scholars of Lormt, lady. I hope your quest there may be fruitful. As for myself, I am Derren, son of a forester from the south. When the fighting began in our area, I joined the Borderers, and have been quartering the mountains since." He turned away suddenly, toward the dust-shrouded southern peaks. "The trees have been cruelly hurt. It will take many years for the forests to recover."

"Are you not attached to any troop?" Nolar asked. "Yestereve three riders stopped to bespeak me on their way back to Es City. One had been wounded by an outlaw's arrow. They said they were Borderers."

"There are many of us on patrol just now," Derren replied. "My own troop was disbanded a week since so that some could return to their fields and the wounded among us could be properly tended. I had thought to report to Es City to see if I could be of further use. There is obviously no point in trying to ride south for any scouting into the mountains."

Nolar could hear the regret in his voice, and his expression was withdrawn, almost haunted. She thought it advisable to distract him from his evident distress. "Would you by chance be at all familiar with the road to Lormt?" she inquired.

Derren roused himself from his preoccupation. "I have never traveled to Lormt myself, no, but I have heard that only one trail leads there. Amid the mountains as Lormt is, it may well have been damaged by this Turning, as you say it is being called. Would you allow me to travel with you and your aunt? It is scarcely safe for two ladies to take this road alone."

"So everyone is at pains to assure me," said Nolar dryly. "But I confess that I do agree with the assessment. I tried to hire a guide in Es City, but no one showed interest in traveling this direction. If it would not unduly delay you, my aunt and I would welcome your escort to Lormt."

Derren stood up, handing the cup back to Nolar. "I shall fetch my horse, then, and we may start, lady, if you are ready for the day's journey."

As he walked away, Derren was thinking hard. This unexpected diversion might provide the very security he needed. He had told the Estcarp woman some truth: he was the son of a forester, and he had been scouting for weeks through the border mountain lands. What he had deliberately not mentioned was that his father had been forester to a lord in Karsten. Pagar of Geen had seized that estate in his scramble for the dukedom. Derren had prudently joined Pagar's forces, and because of his dark hair and gray eyes, as much as for his able scoutcraft, he had been sent to spy along the Estcarp border. He had tracked the Falconers, with considerable difficulty, and had even slipped into Estcarp itself. In fact, he had been in Estcarp the night of the horrendous "Turning," and had found himself effectively trapped on what was for him the wrong and potentially deadly side of the border. Risking all, he had dared to approach a decimated Borderer troop, initially feigning deafness to excuse any obvious mistakes he might make through ignorance of Borderer customs.

He found the chaotic Turning, however, had so severely shaken the Borderers that he was not pressed with any awkward questions, but was accepted as a scout separated from his own troop. Derren's deepest fear was that he might be confronted by one of Estcarp's terrifying Witches, who were said to be able to draw the truth out of any man by their fiendish magic. When the Borderers he had joined recovered sufficiently from their injuries to ride back to Es City, Derren had stayed behind, saying that he must seek the remnants of his troop. He had tried to work his way south, but to his horror found that the land was no longer as he had known it—all landmarks had been wiped away as if they had never been, and the very contours of the land were suddenly strange and different. For days now, Derren had fought to suppress a despairing conviction: that even if he were to return to Karsten, the old familiar land there would be transformed into something both ruined and foreign. He shook himself to dispel the horrid thought. These two women of Estcarp—they must be his chief concern for the present. No one would question his being their escort. He could deliver them to Lormt and then slip away through the uninhabited mountains back to Karsten without fear of notice or pursuit.

As he led his horse back, Derren wondered fleetingly why the woman named Nolar kept her face half covered. The little he had seen of it appeared to be presentable. He had never heard that Estcarp's women customarily went veiled; certainly, the injured aunt's face was exposed. It would probably be wise to appear to ignore the matter for now. He could not risk rousing suspicion by asking questions whose answers he, being a Borderer, would be presumed to know.

It was a great help to Nolar to have Derren's physical assistance with the Witch. Nolar was somewhat surprised to find herself thinking of the Witch by the name "Elgaret." So far during the trip, Nolar had tried to say "Aunt" when she addressed the Witch. She trusted that the simple practice might protect her later at Lormt, preventing her from thoughtless or possibly dangerous errors before strangers. "Aunt Elgaret" the Silver Raven Witch must therefore be, and although she was a small-boned woman, it was still a considerable exertion for Nolar to lift her onto the horse several times each day. Nolar thankfully relinquished that task to Derren, who seemed commendably gentle, yet strong, despite his gauntness.

Their initial morning's ride passed mainly in silence. The farther south and east they went, the more damage they encountered from both the Turning and the storms that had accompanied it. When they dismounted to avoid the midday heat, they were grateful for the patch of shade beside some enormous boulders swept down by the flooding. Derren settled Elgaret on a folded cloak and turned deferentially to Nolar. "You seem uncommonly quiet, lady. Have I offended you in any way? I must tell you that I am not used to the company of women, having spent most of my days in the forests or with other men, so I can claim no courtly manners."

Nolar looked at him gravely. "If there be a fault, Master Borderer, it is surely also mine. I, too, have lived overmuch alone, and have small ease in talking to others." She thought

Derren appeared relieved to hear this, presumably feeling that he need not attempt artificial courtesies. For herself, Nolar had always preferred silence to idle chatter. When she was small, the mountain children had taunted her by calling her "Tightmouth."

Derren wiped his brow with his sleeve. "I came along this way some weeks ago, lady. A few leagues on is a broad area of sand bank by some trees where you might care to bathe this evening." He hesitated. "That is to say, it *was* there then. You have seen how fiercely the river still flows at times, and how much debris has washed down. We shall have to see whether bathing is possible."

Nolar nodded appreciatively. "That is a welcome thought. Both my aunt and I would value the opportunity if it arises."

Derren squinted at the haze-dimmed sun. "It would likely be wise to rest now during the heat of the day. I shall keep watch, lady, if you care to sleep."

"Pray waken me, then, in a while," said Nolar, "and I shall take my turn at watch-keeping."

That evening, as the shadows lengthened, Derren found the spot on the river bank that he had recalled. As he had feared, the storm-fed flood had drastically changed the whole area. What had been a fair sand beach suitable for bathing was now submerged under racing, soil-clouded waters. The entire clump of shade trees Derren remembered had been swept away. Stubbornly, he scouted ahead until he found a backwater, a side pool to the river, relatively untouched by the flooding. He helped Nolar guide Elgaret to the water's edge, then withdrew to rub down the horses and make ready their night camp.

The water in the small isolated pool had settled into clarity and although cold, was now clean and refreshing. Nolar carefully attended to Elgaret before hastily bathing herself. It was a quiet pleasure to put on clean clothing after several days of hard riding. Nolar had brought Elgaret back to Derren's campsite and was collecting the cookpot and utensils for the evening meal before she realized that she had forgotten to cover her face. She jerked her head up to find Derren staring at her, but there was no sign of revulsion on his face.

"You now see, sir, why I favor a veil," Nolar said briskly. Derren did not look away from her. "I have seen such marks before, lady. I hope that yours is not painful to you."

Nolar was astonished at this first indication in so long that anyone might care how she felt. "No, it gives me no pain, but it seems frequently to disturb those who must look upon it." She stopped abruptly. In midsentence, Derren had frozen, the color draining from his face. Nolar turned anxiously to see what frightful thing could so rivet his gaze. Her heart sank. Derren was staring at Elgaret. Nolar had of course changed the Witch's gown after their bath, and now by oversight, the distinctive Witch jewel hung clearly in view outside the fabric.

Derren raised a slightly trembling finger to point at Elgaret. "Witch!" he whispered.

It did not immediately occur to Nolar that this was a curious reactions for one of Estcarp's Borderers. Instead, she sensed Derren's intense disquiet and strove to reassure him. "Yes, Aunt is a Witch, but as you see, she has been blasted by the Turning, and can no longer respond to the world. You have nought to fear from her. Her jewel, being similarly affected, has no fire, and thus is also powerless."

Derren turned blindly toward Nolar, then focused his attention on her. "Forgive me, lady. I was startled. My troop had no Witch to . . . advise us."

Nolar smiled at the memory of her own initial introduction to Witches. "They *are* awesome to encounter in person. I well recall my first meeting with two Witches at once." She suddenly remembered what Ostbor had said, and hastened to add, "Her name, of course, is not truly Elgaret, but we in the family chose to use that name for her so that we might still speak of her."

Again, naggingly, Derren's expression seemed oddly blank, almost intentionally deceptive. "Of course, lady. I did not mean to offend."

"You have not. May I comb my hair before we eat? While taking advantage of your kind suggestion for bathing, I washed my hair, as you see."

"I must gather more wood for our fire," Derren said, quickly rising to his feet. His mind was whirling. A Witch! He was in company with a Witch of Estcarp. What if she suddenly recovered her wits and exposed his true identity? But Nolar had said the Witch was bespelled, and her dreadful jewel, now that he dared to glance at it, *was* dull and lifeless, like any common crystal. Perhaps—dared he to hope?—perhaps he was safe so long as the Witch was senseless, and what more brilliant protection could he ask while in Estcarp than to be guarding one of their premier defenders? Derren supposed that he should feel lucky, but he could not totally suppress his innate fear of Witches, no matter how hard he tried.

When he returned to the camp, Nolar was taking the last few strokes of her comb through her long black hair before coiling it back into her usual practical twist.

The motion spurred a memory for Derren, who observed simply, "You have fine hair, lady, like my mother's."

Surprised, Nolar had paused, and looked up at him. "I thank you, Master Borderer. I do not think anyone has ever before noticed that I have hair. Now I must prepare our meal."

As she warmed a simple porridge, Nolar mused over her observations of Derren, especially in his reactions to her. This was the first time since Ostbor, and briefly, the Silver Raven Witch, that anyone had seemed to view her as an individual. Appearances weighed so heavily with most people. They saw Nolar's facial stain, not Nolar herself. For whatever reason, Derren seemed able to see Nolar, not just her disfigurement. After Ostbor's death, Nolar had not expected to find any other so accepting. And yet . . . what about Derren's behavior upon discovering that Elgaret was a Witch? There was something strange about that, although Nolar could not quite identify the source of her misgivings. With a suppressed sigh, she finally dismissed the problem to be considered later.

Although the late summer days were still hot, the nights tended to be unusually chill. Nolar wondered whether the upheaval of the Turning might have somehow hastened the onset of colder weather. She unpacked heavier cloaks to wrap around Elgaret and herself. Derren admitted that he had not expected such unseasonable cold, and gratefully borrowed a spare cloak.

By late the next day, it was obvious that their progress was going to be severely delayed. The very river itself had been affected by the turmoil deep within the earth. Nolar ventured to ask whether the Es River could have changed its bed, and Derren agreed that it was no longer flowing where he had previously observed it. They reined in and dismounted to try to walk the horses between the tumbled rocks and storm-torn trees. Derren had to carry Elgaret, for in her withdrawn state, she could be led on foot only if the surface was fairly uniform. Nolar trailed behind, leading the horses. The land here had definitely been distorted by the Turning. Instead of gently rolling river plain, the new and unexpected contours thrust up and fell away on all sides. When they finally emerged from the chaotic tangle of limbs and flood-displaced rocks, Derren suppressed a groan of dismay. A vast expanse of mud had flowed across their trail, forming a trackless and treacherous surface.

"We shall have to turn aside to go around this, lady," Derren said. "We dare not risk riding onto such as that. I have seen both men and horses founder and be lost in mountain mudslides. What may appear to be flat and shallow can in truth conceal a ravine where the unwary may sink from sight."

Shortly afterwards it was Nolar who first saw the pale blotch against the darker mud ahead of them to the right. She picked her way gingerly forward until she could distinguish the shape. One of the rarely seen snow cats of the high peaks had been washed down by the flood, its lithe body impaled by a sun-bleached tree limb. The delicately mottled fur stirred in the chill twilight breeze. With a low growl of disgust, Derren moved beside Nolar. He gestured angrily at the snow cat's body.

"How many others have been slain so, lady? What has become of all the mountain beasts—the plants—the trees? It is far worse than this, to the south. Three days past, I tried to scout into the mountains, but had to turn back within a league. The land is no longer the land I knew. There are valleys now where there were none before, great springs of steaming water, new crags, and everywhere landslides. All the old vantage points and landmarks are gone. They are not just damaged; they are *gone."* Derren's voice sank to an impassioned whisper. "I tell you, lady, this Turning was an evil thing."

As Derren spoke, Nolar had again recalled her magic-borne vision of the Turning's awesome destruction. Her natural affinity and sympathy for all wild creatures spurred her to extend a comforting hand, but even as she moved to reach out to Derren, she stopped herself. The land of Estcarp and its hapless inhabitants had been tormented by the Turning, but the Witches' purpose had been both compelling and totally defensive.

"What of Pagar's army, Master Borderer?" Nolar asked. "The sole reason for the Turning was to protect Estcarp from an invasion that could be halted in no other way."

Derren stood very still. "I am a forester's son, lady. My life has been lived among trees and animals. The ways of armies and Witches are beyond my understanding."

"I lately heard a merchant say much the same," Nolar replied thoughtfully. "It did not seem to occur to him that there could be no trade unless there was order and peace in the land. Invading armies, so I hear, pay scant heed to preserving the lives of animals or farming folk, for that matter."

"I am fairly rebuked," Derren conceded. "War is not my trade, lady, but I have seen enough of it to know that your words are true." He glanced back at the snow cat one last time before turning toward the tethered horses. "I know that animals die in storms, and trees are blown down or broken. It is just that I have never before seen so much destroyed in one night's space."

"Nor had anyone before, to my knowledge," Nolar agreed. "My late master, Ostbor the Scholar, had studied all the writings he could find upon great happenings in the past, yet I cannot remember his ever reading of any such thing as this Turning. We may hope that no other may be required again to scourge the very earth, for surely the loss to Estcarp has been grave indeed."

By the following midday, they had climbed well into the foothills—or rather where the old foothills had been, for as Derren had feared, the mountain trees and vegetation had been grievously harmed by the drastic changes in the land. The little shade that could be found had to be sought beside boulders or heaps of debris. Hours of leading the horses through the blasted landscape weighed heavily on their spirits. Nolar, therefore, reacted more violently than she would ordinarily have when a small brown blur streaked up her leg onto her riding skirt. After an initial jerk of complete surprise, she snatched up the creature.

Derren peered at it between her fingers and said, "It is only a mouse, lady. Still, womenfolk often take fright from such. Here, give it to me and I shall kill it for you."

. Nolar gently cradled the quivering scrap of fur in her hand. "No, thank you, Master Borderer. I have frequently searched the meadows for plants, so I well know these little mice. They do not distress me, so long as they stay out of my grain bin. See how frightened it is. Just think how all that was familiar to it has been wiped away. It does not know where to run. I believe it can shelter in my pocket for the present. Perhaps we can find some piece of surviving meadow where we may release it."

Late that afternoon, Nolar's hope was fulfilled when Derren spied a small green area along a low hillside which had been relatively undamaged. He smiled when Nolar dismounted and carefully placed her tiny passenger in the long grass, where it crouched for an instant before scampering away.

As she remounted, Derren said, "You have a kind heart, lady."

Nolar returned his smile. "Perhaps. More likely I act because I know what it is to feel alone in a strange place. How much farther is it to Lormt, do you think?"

"This would seem to be the same trail that we had to abandon beneath the mudslide," Derren suggested. "I must admit, lady, that it could truly be some other mountain trail instead, but it must lead somewhere, and if we have strayed, we should find someone to direct us. I shall scout ahead now to see how this track runs for the morrow."

Derren helped Elgaret down and rode on while Nolar moistened a journeycake into soft mush that the Witch could swallow easily. Derren soon returned to report that the Es River had definitely been relocated some distance away from its old bed.

"The earth here must have moved considerably," he mused. "I have never before seen so large a stream displaced." Derren paused and looked keenly at Nolar. "I must be plain, lady. Not far from here, our trail has simply vanished. The whole hillside has slid into the valley below. We had best journey along the ridge until we can descend into the next valley . . . if there is one left. The morrow's passage will be difficult, so we must try to rest well this night."

In the morning, there was no question of riding the horses on the treacherous scree. Derren again carried Elgaret in his arms, and Nolar led the horses. After a hasty midday meal, they pressed on, anxious to find even a rough herdsman's track that might be suitable for riding. As Nolar repacked their now scanty supplies, Derren ranged ahead on foot. He was hurrying when he returned, and his voice was excited.

"Lady, I think we may have found Lormt. Come and see—it is beyond that rise, in the next valley."

Nolar scrambled eagerly after him, almost tripping among the loosened pebbles. After so many years, she thought, she could at last look upon Ostbor's beloved Lormt. She reached the rocky crest and gazed down, then drew back as if lashed by a whip.

"Oh, *no,*" she breathed, not knowing whether to laugh or cry. All of her shining childhood imaginings crumbled before her eyes, just as the walls and towers below had been reduced to rubble. Great, important Lormt, treasure house for all scholars was . . . was in ruins. Ostbor had warned her of the ravages of time, but he had spoken before the unimaginable violence of the Turning. Nolar turned away for an instant, her eyes blinded by tears. Angry at her weakness, she wiped her face with her neglected veil and forced herself to look again. Tiny figures were creeping across the mounds of shattered stone. Two of Lormt's fabled round towers stood unscathed, along with the remnant of a third. The fourth corner tower and most of that short wall, as well as one entire long outer wall had completely collapsed. The ground supporting that side of the complex seemed to have sheared away and dropped more than a tall man's height. From this distance, the two remaining walls appeared whole. Like the sharp-peaked tower roofs, the walls were sheltered by steep pitched roofs covered with slabs of dark mountain slate. Nolar could make out two buildings within the enclosing walls. One long, high structure nestled against the far wall, a high, horizontal strip of windows running its full length. A smaller, squatter building was tucked behind the gate wall abutting one undamaged corner tower. Nolar strained to see any glint from

the Es River, since Ostbor had often mentioned the ease of
fishing so close to the dormitory area. There was no flash of
reflection from water. The Es River no longer ran in sight of
Lormt, unless it was buried somewhere beneath the rubble.
As she scanned the surrounding hillsides, Nolar made out
little scattered fields and occasional huts such as herdsmen
used. Not all, then, had been lost in the Turning. Some
people and some housing had survived. She took a deep
breath and turned to Derren.

"That is truly Lormt, Master Borderer, although it has
suffered much damage since my old master's day. Can we
find a safe track down to it?"

Derren surveyed the rock-strewn slope. "If we walk, lady,
I can carry your aunt."

"We should not have been able to journey here without
you," Nolar said. "I thank you for my aunt and myself."

For a moment, Derren seemed genuinely abashed, then he
resumed his authority as experienced guide. "Have a care on
this slope, lady," he warned. "The soil appears loose all the
way down, and likely to give way."

Even forewarned, Nolar slipped twice during the descent,
but each time she was halted by the steadying weight of the
horses. At the base of the incline, they stopped for a much
needed rest before mounting to ride the remaining distance
to the gates of Lormt.

As they neared the sheltering walls, Nolar recalled her
recent impressions of Es City. Both complexes proclaimed
their age and solidity by their very presence, but the stones
of Lormt were far more massive, drawing the eye to their
individual dimensions. Nolar wondered how the builders
could possibly have moved such enormous blocks, not to
mention how they could have originally hewed and dressed
the stones. The seams between blocks were so tight that she
doubted a knife blade could be inserted in any crack. She
thought again of the chaos of the Turning, and marveled that
even stones of this size could have remained, unmortared, as

standing walls. Ostbor, she knew, would have been wildly curious to hear from the resident scholars how they had fared.

Nolar wondered how they might be received, even whether the gates of Lormt would be open to them at all. She discovered on close approach that the metal-bound gates were a trifle askew, and several old men and two youths were busily engaged in trying to repair the lower hinges. Old men hurried in and out.

Derren dismounted and called to the nearest old man. "Sir? Can you tell us where we should go? This lady's aunt seeks healing."

The old man, gaunt and bald, peered at them, reminding Nolar for a painful instant of Ostbor himself.

"Come in, come in," he invited. "You look as if you have traveled far. Come rest your beasts and water them. Yes, by all means—we do not yet understand why, but our well in the courtyard has suddenly commenced a much freer flow—colder, too. A result, we are sure, of the recent turmoil. This way, this way."

Despite his evident age, he moved nimbly and they had to hurry to keep pace as he preceded them through the gates into the great open courtyard. The well he had mentioned was housed in the interior corner to the right, with a sheltered opening down to the water, over which a sturdy windlass unreeled buckets suspended on braided cords. Troughs for the animals stood nearby, freshly filled and clean-scrubbed, even amid the general disarray. Derren lifted Elgaret down into Nolar's care and led the horses to a trough. At the well, the old man drew up a bucket from which Nolar dipped a cup for the Witch and then one for herself.

"Feels like snow-melt, eh?" commented the old man cheerfully. "We have lost the river, but I must say, this well is a wonder now compared to what it used to be. If the increased flow holds, we shall be fortunate. By the way, should you care to sup, our dining hall was lost when the outer wall fell, but we have made a place to eat in the storehouse. This way, this way." He darted toward the squat stone building to the inside left of the gates.

Derren called across that he would see to the stabling of the horses, and then join them. Nolar guided Elgaret into the storehouse, where makeshift trestle tables had been set up, and evidently one corner had only recently been converted into a kitchen. Settling Elgaret into a high-backed chair, Nolar sank gratefully onto a bench.

The old man bustled back into her view with two rough wooden bowls full of steaming porridge.

"We did save most of our grain," he prattled on, as if Nolar had demanded a full report on Lormt's supply status, "although we lost the greater part of our root vegetables in the subsidence. It may be possible to dig out some of them before they spoil. I understand that Ouen has plans to excavate for the root bins as soon as our more urgent digging is finished." He stopped abruptly. "But I have not introduced myself. I am Wessell. Provisioning is my trade, and I must say the earthquakes have quite upset all of our normal arrangements. Still, we were spared flooding. As you must know, nothing ruins grain so fast as having it exposed to the wet. Now that the river has shifted, I don't suppose that we shall have to worry as much about flooding, always excepting the spring rains. But there—I haven't let you speak. Forgive me. We have been so much upstirred of late that I scarcely know what I am doing. Do take some of this barley water. It is most refreshing in hot weather."

Nolar smiled at his earnest, if overwhelming, helpfulness. As she spooned some porridge for Elgaret, she said, "You have been very kind to see to our wants so promptly. Our journey here has been long and tiring. I am Nolar of Meroney, and this is my aunt, Elgaret." She paused, weighing how much she should disclose and to whom. It was rather like the decision she had made regarding concealing her face. Ostbor had assured her that knowledge and honesty were most highly prized at Lormt. Nolar had decided before she entered Lormt's gates that she would proceed as she was, unveiled. Of all the places in Escarp, Lormt should allow her presence as a seeker of healing. If her face offended them, she thought grimly, then the scholars could look elsewhere. Now that she was within Lormt's walls, however, she somehow sensed that surface appearances did not matter as they did in the outer world. Certainly Wessell had not drawn back from her, and his eyes appeared to be clear and keen.

Nolar faced him and declared, "My aunt is a Witch of Estcarp, injured by the Council's recent . . . exertions. My late master, Ostbor the Scholar, often told me that healing lore could be found at Lormt as in no other place, so I have brought my aunt hither."

Wessell looked shrewdly at Nolar. "We of Lormt have scant reason to welcome Witches, no more than they implore us to share our knowledge." He cocked his head to one side, rather like an inquisitive bird eyeing a doubtful morsel. "Our healers are overburdened just now, treating our own folk and others who have come to us for refuge. Master Ouen would ordinarily receive you, but he is thoroughly occupied with the recovery. So many are displaced. Healers." He squinted at Elgaret's still form. "Would your aunt require a healer, or a scholar to search out writings on healing?"

Nolar blinked. She had not before considered that distinction, but now that Wessell had made it, she quickly grasped his thought.

"My aunt bears no outward injury to the body," she replied. "If one of your scholars could direct us to the works that might bear on our predicament, that would be most helpful."

Wessell pondered, drumming his fingers on the table. "Morfew—that's who you need to see—old Morfew. Ever since Kester fell last month and damaged his hip, Morfew has cared for the scrolls on spell-countering and healing."

Derren entered the dining area, and Wessell broke off to

fetch more food and drink. Nolar swiftly summed up what Wessell had told her.

"Will you be returning to Es City, Master Borderer," she asked, "now that you have seen us safely to Lormt?"

Derren smiled wryly. "I doubt, lady, that my single presence is urgently required. There are ample Borderer forces available to deal with any scattered remnants of Pagar's men. What will be chiefly needed are scouts to try to penetrate the mountains and locate new trails . . . but I doubt that will be possible for some time yet. If you do not object, I can stay here a few days to see whether you may need an escort for your return journey."

Nolar regarded his guileless face. She thought to herself, Where indeed can I go if the Witch can be revived? Would Elgaret consider staying at Ostbor's house, or would she demand that I go to Es Castle to be examined? To give herself a moment to think, Nolar sipped her barley water. She had to face the possibility that nothing might revive Elgaret, and then what was she to do? It seemed that all she could prod from her weary mind was a series of unanswerable questions. She forced her attention back to Derren.

"It would be helpful to me," she said, "if you could continue to assist me with my aunt, at least until we see whether anything can be done to aid her." Nolar turned to Wessell. "Is there any space where we may stay? We have nearly exhausted our journey food, but what we have we will gladly share."

Wessell waved aside her offer. "No, no, thanks to Master Ouen's foresight, we have sufficient food as of yet for the whole community and those who have recently joined us. He urged us to shift our grain stores just before the earthquakes. Master Duratan thinks we can transplant some of our existing seedlings into our damaged fields to provide a late crop before the winter snows. And we have ample room for travelers. One thing we have always had at Lormt is room. In truth, with the hidden cellars opened by the subsidence, we have even more room than we thought! Let me show you where you may rest while I search for old Morfew. I know of three likely places he may be, and should he not be there, I can search in several other less likely sites."

Wessell trotted ahead of them to a door in the great remaining side wall, back across the courtyard. Nolar was surprised by the cavernous space within the wall. Narrow stairs led in several directions, and there seemed to be doors to countless storage rooms and quiet sleeping cells. Smaller light globes and occasional torches supplemented the waning daylight penetrating through thin slits in the courtyard side of the wall. At this level, low to the ground, the exterior wall was solid, much like a defensive fortress. Wessell soon located an available room for Nolar and Elgaret, and set off down the corridor to find another for Derren.

Nolar quickly scanned the sparse furnishings in her room. There were two low pallets for sleeping, insulated from the cold stone floor by heaps of sweet smelling rushes. A small table held a pitcher and washbowl, while a closed flask of drinking water stood on a stone ledge near the door. Nolar eased Elgaret onto one pallet and spread one of the plain but well-sewn quilts up to the Witch's chin. Elgaret's eyes closed. Nolar herself longed to sleep, but first she had to see whether Wessell could find the scholar Morfew. To refresh herself a little, she splashed her face with some cold water from the pitcher. Wessell and Derren appeared at the door while she was patting her skin dry.

"I have found Morfew," Wessell announced with evident pleasure, as if the old scholar were a particularly elusive quarry. "He often dozes over his work, so don't hesitate to prompt him. Come along."

He led them to the long building set against the wall. From Ostbor's tales, Nolar guessed that this must be the main scholarly repository. Her supposition was immediately confirmed when they plunged into a warren of cubicles and study nooks, divided and flanked by shelves, with countless tables and desks heaped with writings. The interior was fitfully illuminated by the high windows and various flickering light sources placed there by the scholars. Nolar recalled Ostbor's cautions about candles; perhaps because of past experience, Lormt now seemed to favor broad-based lamps with short wicks, unlikely to turn over or endanger the precious parchments. Nolar simply gazed at the scrolls. She had never seen so many in one place. She yearned to stop and delve into the stacks, bundles, and even heaps of scrolls, but she dared not lose sight of Wessell, who suddenly halted at a narrow opening between two towering partitions.

He poked his head in the gap and inquired, "Morfew?" After a pause, he raised his voice. "Morfew! MORFEW!"

That final bellow evidently roused the old scholar, for Nolar heard a quiet, reasonable voice respond, "You need not shout, Wessell. I can hear you perfectly well."

Nolar followed Wessell into a study nook crammed with writings on all available flat surfaces. Ostbor had only thought himself a pack rat, Nolar reflected, amused. Lormt was apparently the original inspiration for all pack rats of scholarly bent. Morfew himself was sitting at a scribe's desk, inkpot within easy reach. He looked older than Ostbor, perhaps because of his shining silver-white hair, which reminded Nolar of a rare spun sugar subtlety she had once seen at a long ago high feast at her father's house. Morfew's pale blue eyes, clear as a child's, were set above a thin nose and a mouth framed by lines of determination. Like Ostbor, Nolar thought, Morfew must have been born to be a scholar.

"These are the travelers I was telling you about," Wessell said. "Nolar of Meroney and Derren, a Borderer. Her aunt is the one injured, which is why I brought them to you, since Kester is still abed." He turned to Nolar. "If you can find your way back, I should return to the kitchen." Scarcely waiting for her assurance, Wessell disappeared into the deepening shadows.

Morfew shook his head. "Wessell has always been in a

hurry, and since the earthquakes, I fear that he has not stopped to rest at all. He'll be falling down the stairs at any time, mark my words, because he'll be reciting some report or other and won't be looking where he's going. But you must describe your aunt's condition so that I may know which scrolls to seek out." He waved a hand vaguely at the vast number of parchment rolls cluttering the shelves. "It is true that Kester is more familiar with many of these than am I, but if you help me search, we should be able to find what is needed."

Nolar stared up at the shelves with numb despair. It would take years merely to lift down each scroll and identify its subject. She recalled how Ostbor had complained of the lack of order at Lormt.

"Oh, surely," she burst out, "there must be some plan by which they are sorted. Ostbor used to say—"

Morfew, whose head had been drooping suspiciously, as if he might be drifting into drowsiness, abruptly sat erect, and exclaimed. "Ostbor! How is the good fellow? I have not seen him for years."

"He died in late spring," Nolar said quietly, feeling again the stab of loss. "One of your scholars came to gather his archives. I had been living at Ostbor's mountain house and assisting him in his work. He was truly like a father to me."

Morfew was genuinely affected by the news. "Dear child . . . I respect your sorrow. Ostbor had a brilliant mind for tracing kinships. I am sure that his records will be of great use to us here. I shall have to inquire where they have been stored. You will have noticed that one wall and tower were completely destroyed after the earthquakes. Fortunately, due to our prior warning, we had moved almost all of our records to other areas beforehand. Indeed, when we discovered previously unknown cellars unsealed by the turmoil, we found numbers of scrolls whose existence we had never suspected. It has quite confused us all—a profusion of riches, as it were, coming so soon after the violence. Had it not been for our protection . . ." His voice trailed off, and he began to nod.

Derren gave a discreet cough, and when that brought no response from the old scholar, asked loudly, "Protection?"

Morfew jerked awake. "Protection—yes, yes. Our quan iron spheres, of course. We should all have been lost without them. See here." He arranged four scrolls on his desk to represent Lormt's outer enclosure. "When Lormt was built—and no one now knows how long ago that was—a great sphere of quan iron was set in the base of each corner tower. It must have been originally intended for magical protection against evil forces, but we have been so isolated here that no such assault has been described. When Ouen and Duratan recently received warning to prepare for a great working of magic by the Council of Witches, they moved all of the community within our walls, and strove to preserve our priceless records." Morfew paused and Nolar suspected that he was about to doze again, but he was evidently recalling the order of events during the Turning. "That entire day was most peculiar," he confided. "No wind at all, and unnaturally quiet, although our animals were restless. Ouen and Duratan insisted that the flocks and herds be brought into the courtyard, you see, and they made the area extremely noisy. I could hear them even this far inside. Near dusk, several of our helpers cried out. The quan iron, heretofore always quiescent, had begun to glow. I saw it myself, later—a startling, blue illumination in the very air. It grew into an enormous bubble enclosing the whole of the Lormt, and none too soon. The most appalling storm broke full upon us, and the earth itself heaved, as if shaken like a rat seized by a monstrous dog. It was most upsetting. Every scroll was tossed from its place, and I feared that our taller shelves would surely collapse. Some did, of course, but most remained standing. Duratan, who as you know has been a far-traveled warrior, said afterwards that Lormt must have floated like a chip of wood in a millrace, secure in our quan iron's protective bubble. When the churning of the land ceased, a great section of earth dropped away from beneath our other wall, thus bringing down that wall, one corner tower, and part of a second tower. Due to our earlier precautions, none of the community were killed. We suffered many other injuries, chiefly minor, but on the whole, our community has emerged fairly unhurt. Our animals, I am told, were terrified. I must confess," Morfew admitted with disarming candor, "that I was quite unable to move at first. I simply clung here to my desk until I could creep out to see if I could help in any way. We have been working ever since to restore Lormt. I expect that you are the first far-travelers to reach us since the cataclysm."

"We found the way here much affected," Derren observed. "The shifting of the Es River has caused considerable change all along its former course. There are now numerous mudslides and landslides blocking or even entirely wiping out the old trail."

"Folk are calling it 'the Turning,' " said Nolar. "It was the will of the Council of Witches expressed against the land to turn back Duke Pagar's armies."

Morfew nodded gravely. "It was not the first time such an effort has been made." He seemed to relish their obvious surprise. "We had not been aware of that ourselves, of course," Morfew hastened to say, "but some months before this . . . Turning, Kemoc of the House of Tregarth came to Lormt to search our archives for lore from the ancient days. It was a most curious thing that he stumbled upon." Morfew paused. "As you can see from the color of my eyes, I am a man of Alizon, not Estcarp. When I was young, I determined to seek knowledge. To my sorrow, my family disapproved, so I was forced to abandon them, and came at last to Lormt, my refuge and true home. I mention this because Kemoc discovered that those of the Old Race are blocked against even thinking of the direction 'east'—most peculiar. I have seen him trying to discuss the east with our Estcarp scholars. They could not even look at the maps he drew, nor bring their minds to the subject at all. Not being so barred, I could assist him somewhat in his researches, although he was deeply concerned to keep his work private. It was while Kemoc was examining our oldest scrolls that he found fragmentary accounts of the previous Turning, which had evidently thrown up the vast mountains to our east. From the few comments he made to me, and from the scrolls themselves—for I studied them after he left—it appears that some hideous evil had to be walled away from Estcarp, and then the very memory of the deed, and awareness of the direction east was deliberately expunged so that none of the Old Race would ever venture that way."

Nolar was afire with curiosity. An earlier Turning! "Please, when was this? Was it done by the Witches of that day? How? . . ."

Morfew threw up his hands. "You sound like Kemoc—all questions and unseemly haste to know everything at once. He labored like a man under a geas—I could not intrude unless asked. I believe, however, that for all his efforts, Kemoc was not fully satisfied when he rode away from Lormt. It must have been ten days before the Turning that he left us. I am not always asleep, although I may seem to be so," Morfew added, with a smile. "Kemoc exclaimed at times while he was working, and as I say, I noted which scrolls he consulted. It is my business, you understand, to follow what is being researched in my domain. In this case, the scrolls on magic and ancient days were in Kester's care, but as you know, they have come to me while Kester is abed. Yes, yes, I see your impatience, but in scholarly matters, one must be clear about the where and when before one considers the what. It was a thousand or more years ago that the Power previously altered our land. Since the mountains to the east were raised by the Power, those wielding it must have been the Witches of that day . . . unless, of course, in that time, males could also share the Power. That is a point that Ouen and Duratan are most anxious to pursue once they can return to being scholars. As for the how of it, perhaps you should ask your aunt, for if I am not mistaken, she was one of those who brought about *this* Turning, was she not?"

Abashed, Nolar bowed her head. "Yes, she was. It was because of her taking part with the Council that she was stricken . . . and," she added slowly, "because of that same action, my great-aunt and many other Council members died outright. To return to my aunt—she breathes, and eats and drinks what I give her, and seems to sleep, but her mind is not truly aware of the outer world. Please, sir, is there any scroll here that might explain how she could be recalled to us?"

Morfew laced his fingers together on his desk, pondering. "The Witches of Estcarp have no kind regard for us here at Lormt. Yet in their way, they value knowledge and its preservation. Our reason for being here is to learn, and if we possess any ancient scroll that bears on this Turning magic and its effects on those who wield it, then we must seek it out. You say that many of the Council died. Are others afflicted like your aunt?"

"Yes," Nolar replied. "I was told that the surviving Witches had been unable to help those whose minds seem to have withdrawn, like my aunt's." She hesitated, and again decided that she must tell the truth. "For courtesy, I call her Elgaret. During the Turning, although she was at Es Castle and I was far north at Ostbor's house, I received a Sending from her. I am not trained in any way," Nolar added, half aware that Derren was staring at her with an odd intensity. "I was ill as a child when the proper time came for me to be examined, so I was never tested by the Witches. The Sending was a complete surprise to me. Elgaret had earlier experienced three Foreseeings that persuaded her that I must come to Lormt upon a quest; she could not say for what thing I must seek here. In the Sending, she called to me to come to her, but also repeated the linkage between me and Lormt. I am therefore here on a dual quest; first, to try to restore

Elgaret to herself, and second, to seek whatever it is that I am supposed to find here."

Both Morfew and Derren were silent when she finished, then Morfew rubbed his hands together and announced, "We face a most interesting challenge. As you see, our written resources are considerable, but upon the subject you require—that previous Turning—I can recommend only those scrolls that Kemoc studied, and perhaps a few others. Ouen might know where else we should look. I shall try to speak to him, although he is quite absorbed by the work of restoration." He broke off and glanced up, surprised by the comparative darkness. "Why, night is almost upon us, and you have had an arduous journey. Come to me on the morrow, if you will, and we shall begin our search. I shall be thinking where else we might seek. A good rest to you both." He waved a dismissive hand at them, and his head drooped forward.

Derren stood aside for Nolar to edge between the shelves into the passageway. "I suspect," he said in a low voice, "that old Morfew will be chiefly resting until the morrow."

Nolar smiled, then replied seriously, "We must recall what Morfew admitted to us. He is not always asleep, even if he appears to be so." She paused, remembering clearly how Ostbor's absurd clothing and distracted manner truly concealed a keen mind and an iron determination to know. "I think," she resumed, "that Morfew is a clever scholar, perhaps wiser than he may seem. He is certainly correct judging my weariness." She stretched her numbed arms. "Let us ask for some food, and then I know of no other bed to rival the pallet beside Elgaret."

When she finally lay down and pulled up several quilts against the night chill, Nolar found it difficult to sleep in spite of her physical exhaustion.

So many factors had arisen during just this one day. To learn that there had been another Turning—that was an astonishing thought. Even more arresting was the speculation that had to follow. What scale of evil could have existed in the east to force the Witches to raise mountain ranges to block it away from Escarp? Was that evil force still active in the east beyond the mountains? Could this new stirring of the southern border mountains affect the eastern barrier, and if so, with what consequences? Morfew seemed certain that the Council of Witches now in Estcarp did not know of the previous Turning. By their ignorance of the far past, they might have caused even more danger to Estcarp. Nolar tried to push aside these musings. What must concern her immediately was the search for a way to aid Elgaret's recovery. She tried to nourish some hope that this might be possible, but the prospect did not seem encouraging. As for the quest that Elgaret had Foreseen, Nolar was still as confused about that as before. It would simply have to wait until Elgaret herself could advise Nolar.

As her tired body gradually relaxed, Nolar sensed a calming influence permeating Lormt. The peaceful quiet was restful, as if the very stones had absorbed and were now reflecting back the patience of generations of scholars. Just before she fell asleep, Nolar wondered why Derren had looked at her so strangely earlier in Morfew's cubicle. It had been in reaction to something she had said. . . . What was it? It had been her admission that she had received a Witch Sending. Why should that trouble Derren? He had seemed similarly perturbed on the trail when he first saw Elgaret's jewel and realized that she was a Witch. Nolar drowsily resolved that, when there was time, she really must think further about Derren. Despite his odd disquietude, he had been very kind.

Early the next morning, Nolar brought a bowl of gruel to Elgaret in their room. It was simpler than having to escort her all the way to the dining area. For the day's examination of old scrolls, Nolar decided that it would be wise to take Elgaret along to Morfew's study area so that the scholar could see the Witch, and at the same time, Nolar could keep watch over her. There were countless nooks where a person could sit undisturbed among the shelves, bins, and desks stacked with rolls of parchments. Derren soon appeared at their door having checked on the horses, which he said were being well cared for. With his help, Nolar guided Elgaret, and settled her quietly in a comfortable corner. Morfew didn't seem to have moved since they had left him the night before. Derren gave Nolar a look that clearly said, "I told you so," but Morfew stood up spryly enough, bowed with courtesy to the unseeing Elgaret, and announced that he had located several promising scrolls with which they could begin their search. He distributed to Nolar and Derren a double handful of individual scrolls.

Nolar carefully unrolled the topmost of her bundle and began to read. After a short while, she noticed from the corner of her eye that Derren was fidgeting.

"Are you having difficulty with the old style script?" Nolar asked.

Derren looked down at his desk, evidently embarrassed. "I don't . . . that is . . . I cannot read, lady. I was never taught that skill."

The words jarred Nolar's memory back to her own painful confession to Ostbor so long before. "Ah," she said briskly, "then we are wasting your time keeping you here, Master Borderer. Do you think, Morfew, that Derren could help some of your folk outside?"

Morfew looked up from his scroll. "Outside? Yes, of course he can, if he will. I'm sure, young man, that Wessell can tell you where help is most needed. Pray do not tarry here with us if you feel of more use elsewhere."

Derren was obviously relieved to be dismissed. "I shall come back later, to bring food to your aunt," he promised, as he gladly transferred his bundle of scrolls to Nolar.

She and Morfew worked steadily all that morning and well into the afternoon. Most of the ancient material was cast as legend, and thus was often complicated and impenetrable since it referred to heroes and forces completely unknown to Nolar. There were frequent frustrating gaps in the narratives, and often physical damage to the scrolls would make the reading difficult or even impossible. Morfew did appear to doze occasionally, but Nolar found him to be as tenacious a scholar as Ostbor, always willing to examine a blot or tear or offer his opinion on how to interpret the crabbed, archaic script. That first day set the pattern for succeeding days. Derren cheerfully labored outside, rotating among the various repair projects. Twice a day, he would bring food and drink to the researchers and Elgaret, then withdraw again so quietly that they seldom noticed when he left.

It was late on the fourth day that Nolar made her discovery. She had stood up to stretch cramped muscles, and her knee bumped against a squat wooden chest wedged into a low space beside Morfew's desk. Nolar would have thought nothing of it except for the peculiar tingling sensation that pulsed along her leg when it touched the chest.

"Morfew," she asked, "what is in that chest?"

The old scholar turned from trimming the wick on a flickering lamp. "That? Why, that was brought up from one of the newly opened cellars. Duratan fetched it for me. My feet swell in warm weather, you see, and he thought I might find this chest a good height to rest my legs upon while I work at my desk."

"But what is inside it?" Nolar persisted. She had never before felt such peremptory curiosity.

Morfew blinked as he considered. "I have no idea. I do believe that Duratan said something about finding a key that might belong to this chest." He fumbled at his belt and freed a cluster of keys, which he sorted through. "This one, I believe—let me see—yes, it does fit this lock. Quite an old lock, I would say, and the hinges have stiffened with rust. Rather like my knees . . . there!" With an effort, Morfew wrenched open the lid of the chest.

Eagerly, Nolar knelt to explore the interior contents. Even

amid the slightly musty air of Lormt's archives, Nolar could distinguish the dry, unmistakable smell of very old documents. She lifted out the topmost scrolls with special care for their fragility. Beneath several layers of scrolls, Nolar found ornately carved boxes of mineral powders and dried herbs long since reduced to dust. Just as she was about to sneeze, her hand touched something that sent a warm tingle through her fingers. It was like the sensation she had earlier felt when her leg had first touched the chest. Nolar glanced at Morfew. He was happily absorbed in the ancient scrolls she had handed to him. Nolar debated with herself. Should she alert Morfew to whatever it was that had attracted her attention, or should she dissemble, try to hide her find and take it away to be examined in private? Her determination to be consistently truthful at Lormt once again asserted itself.

"Morfew," she said. "Morfew!"

"Yes, yes, I wasn't asleep. Have you found something?"

"When I first touched this chest," Nolar admitted, "I felt a strange sensation, and just now, I felt the same thing near the bottom of the chest, only more pronounced." She reached inside as she spoke, easing her fingers around what felt like folds of soft, very old cloth. She withdrew a small bundle and carried it to be unwrapped on Morfew's desk where the light was brighter.

The fabric, its color grayed by age, fell away to disclose a shard of stone smoothed on one side and rough on the other, where it must have been chiseled away from a larger piece. It fit naturally in the palm of Nolar's hand, and was not cold to the touch as she expected a stone would be. This shard was warm, as if Nolar were touching a piece of living flesh. The initial tingling had diminished, or had it? When she focused her attention on the stone, Nolar realized that the stimulating sensation had transferred from her skin physically touching the smooth surface to a gentle . . . presence in her mind. Abruptly, Nolar knew with absolute certainty that she could walk in utter darkness straight to this stone even if it were deliberately hidden from her in Lormt's farthest corner. She would simply feel where it was.

"Morfew," she said, her voice faltering, "there is something magical about this piece of stone."

Morfew did not appear to be at all surprised or dismayed. "Many objects with magical aspects have been stored at Lormt in the past," he remarked. "May I touch it?" When Nolar extended the stone to him, he gently pressed his right hand against it. He shut his eyes for an instant, then sighed, and withdrew his hand. "I fear that, to me, it is only a piece of stone. A rather pleasant piece to look at—cream, would you say, with that interesting veining of dark green?"

He did not mention its warmth, so Nolar assumed the stone must feel expectably cold to Morfew. Obviously, there was some special link between Nolar and the shard. An odd similarity occurred to her: somehow, she must be attuned to the shard—or perhaps it was attuned to her—in a way resembling the linkage established between Witches and their jewels. Ostbor had told Nolar, that as best he could guess, the jewel was matched to its possessor for life when she became a Witch. Nolar was simultaneously excited and frightened by this thought. She felt driven by forces beyond her control, pressed toward the acknowledgment that she essentially must *be* a Witch. Nolar did *not* want to be a Witch; the prospect made her long to flee, to hide somewhere safe from discovery.

Unconsciously, in her distress, she gripped the stone shard, and a second absolute certainty slipped into her mind. This stone was what she had been meant to find at Lormt. Elgaret had Foreseen an important quest for some unknown object, but had not been able to identify it. Nolar *knew* that she had now found it. A new problem immediately thrust itself before her. What was she supposed to *do* with the shard? Why had it sought her out? As she became aware of that notion, Nolar wondered at the intrinsic rightness of it. The shard *had* sought her out. She had been drawn to it, as a moth to an open candle flame . . . with better results, she fervently hoped.

Nolar looked up to find Morfew dozing . . . or pretending to doze. "Morfew. . . . Morfew! May I keep this shard? I feel it is somehow important that I carry it near me. I cannot say why." She felt keenly how foolish she must sound, but the old scholar accepted her request with complete gravity.

"As I told you, my dear, I am a man of Alizon. Objects of magic seldom come our way, and if they do, few of us can sense their presence. That does not mean that the objects are any less powerful. If you feel an influence from that stone, then it must have special meaning for you, and you should attempt to discover what you should do with it. We must tell Ouen of your discovery, of course, but would it not be wise to see whether there might be any writings associated with the shard?"

Nolar impulsively touched his hand. "Dear Morfew—you are so like Ostbor in many ways. Certainly, we must search the chest with care. Surely there would be some explanation stored with the shard. Can you help me pull the chest nearer your lamp?"

Both of them crouched down, and with considerable effort, hauled the chest out into a more accessible space. Morfew insisted that they first examine all of the scrolls that had been packed above the shard.

"It may be," he said, "that your shard is referred to in one or more of these, although I must say I have seen no such reference in the passages I have so far read. Still, we must be thorough. Here, you take these, and I shall read through this lot."

Almost frantic to delve farther into the chest, Nolar forced herself to concentrate on the musty parchments. She knew that Morfew was right. They must not overlook any possible references, however slight, to the stone shard. Her share of scrolls concerned an amazing jumble of subjects. Nolar had to assume that the scrolls had simply been snatched up at random and bundled into the chest. She skimmed through a tedious discussion of drainage methods to restore sodden fields, followed by a wordy recital of remedies for various ailments of horses. Only Ostbor, she thought, as she impatiently unrolled the third parchment, could have appreciated this interminable kinship list for some unknown noble from generations past. Her last scroll was enlivened by tiny, but clear drawings of the plants it described for use in cookery. At any other time, Nolar would have been enchanted by it; now, she raced through it, searching for any mention of the words "stone," or "shard." There were none. She looked up to find Morfew similarly setting aside his final scroll.

"No reference to your stone in these, my dear," Morfew said. "I see that you have had no better success. Let us then examine any other items left in the chest."

Nolar had shown Morfew the carved boxes of herbs and potions which she had initially discovered. Together they now opened each container to be sure that she had not missed any scrap of parchment that might have been tucked inside. Next, Nolar sat down beside the chest and handed up to Morfew each remaining item.

"More powders, I think, and a small bundle of parchment strips describing herbal remedies." Nolar leafed through the strips, naming aloud some of her old familiar friends from the meadows and forests. "Burdock, ground apple, comfrey, vervain, fennel, hyssop, nettle." The ancient cord that had once bound the strips together was now frayed beyond further use, so Nolar felt in her scrip for a spare length of new cord. She retied the bundle and handed it to Morfew. The next prize from the chest was a tight roll of age-darkened linen. An intricate design of ivy leaves and trefoils was embroidered down its entire length, displaying the skill of some long-dead needlewoman. Morfew placed it carefully on a protected shelf.

"Mistress Bethalie will be most pleased to see that," he commented. "Her needlework is a joy to behold. She cares for all our clothing, but often complains that our simple tastes give her little opportunity for ornamentation."

Nolar peered anxiously into the chest. "There is so little left within. I see only a small box or two and another roll of cloth. Oh, Morfew!" Her voice suddenly rose in excitement. "There is writing on this cloth, and I can just distinguish the word 'stone.' " She lifted out a cylindrical packet and carried it to Morfew's desk to be unrolled.

"This is indeed ancient," observed Morfew, as he gingerly loosened a narrow fabric strip binding the roll, being careful not to tear the delicate material. "Set the lamp a trifle closer, if you will. The ink has faded badly in places, but you were correct. The text does concern a stone of magical power. There is a name here. . . ." He gently smoothed out a crease in the cloth. "Konnard—it is, or was, the Stone of Konnard." Morfew paused, thinking. "I cannot recall ever before reading or hearing that name. Perhaps the text will explain the history of your shard. Let me see. I believe this must be a continuation of some earlier writing, for it seems to begin in the middle of a line. 'When the injured body is brought near to the Stone of Konnard,' " Morfew read aloud, then frowned. "Oh, fie! The next part is quite ruined by damp." He unrolled the cloth past the damaged portion, and resumed reading. " 'Let them know that great changes in both flesh and bone may be secured if the proper ceremonies be observed. Works of healing such as had never before been seen may . . .' " Morfew stopped, frustrated. "More damp. Ah, here is an admonition, or at least a part of one. 'Warned that much evil had resulted because of it, and therefore it should be destroyed utterly, but he was overruled . . . agreed that a shard might be taken for further study, but that the main Stone of Konnard must be interred, together with . . .' Really, this is most annoying. Still, as a scholar," Morfew added with a sigh, "I must say that damage to writings always seems to occur just at the most interesting points in the text. I sometimes think it must be intended to teach us patience and proper humility, not to mention the virtue of persistence. There is only a little more left—very difficult to make out. 'When the seals were set, a cry of great thanksgiving went up that such dire peril was removed. So long as the light of the sun cannot fall upon it, shall all be safe. . . .' " Morfew gestured helplessly at the damaged cloth. "I fear that is all we shall be able to read, my dear. Your eyes, however, are keen. Let me take my quill and copy as you read to me so that we may not have to touch the fabric any more than is necessary."

Her hands trembling, Nolar bent over the faded writing. The Stone of Konnard, from which her shard must have broken away, was apparently endowed with healing powers. If it had truly caused "great changes in both flesh and bone," and "works of healing never before seen," then, perhaps . . . Nolar tried to contain her soaring hopes as she read each word aloud slowly so that Morfew could record it on a fresh parchment. Morfew was completing the last few phrases when Derren arrived with their evening meal.

While she fed Elgaret, Nolar told Derren about her exciting discovery. She set aside the spoon and dish to show him her shard. When she offered the stone fragment to him, however, Derren hastily drew back.

Ill at ease, Derren declared, "No, thank you, lady. I know naught of magical things. Such should stay with those who understand them."

Nolar grimaced, disgusted with her own lack of knowledge. "I would I did understand this shard and its uses, Master Borderer. If only we knew how to employ it, perhaps it could aid Elgaret."

"There is also the question," Morfew quietly reminded them, "of where this Stone of Konnard now lies. It would seem to have been buried, but that must have been many generations ago. As I told you, I have never seen any reference to it or to Konnard, whoever or whatever that was, whether person or place."

"If only they had left us some directions," Nolar fretted.

Morfew rolled his quill thoughtfully between his fingers. "You must consider, my dear, that some magical objects may better be left undiscovered. Remember the warning that much evil had resulted from it, and that at least one authoritative person at that time insisted upon the destruction of the stone."

Stunned, Nolar slid back on her narrow bench. She had not properly attended to that warning. The proclamation of healing powers had seized her total attention. "But surely," she objected, "if the stone promoted healing, it must have been empowered as good, not evil."

Morfew shook his head, clearly recalling baleful precedents. "I possess only a scholar's outside knowledge of magic. From my lifelong observations, I may tell you my individual opinion that Power itself is neither good nor evil. It is a . . . a force, and how it is used, for what purpose and to what end determines whether its effect is fair or ill. It may be, and I merely suggest, that this Stone of Konnard was misused for evil purposes. It therefore had to be hidden away, banished, so that it might not be so used again. In some of our oldest scrolls, I have read that objects of Power can be corrupted by long use in the service of evil. Perhaps the Stone of Konnard was one such."

"NO!" Nolar was herself startled by the utter conviction ringing in her cry of negation. As she clutched her shard, she could feel its warmth both in her mind and physically against her fingers. Embarrassed by her outburst, Nolar turned from Morfew to Derren. It was vitally important to her that she convince them. "Forgive me—I cannot say why I know this, but I *do know*. The Stone of Konnard is *not* evil. It was meant to heal, and that is why . . ." She stopped, suddenly aware that her words were somehow not hers, that she was expressing thoughts that were not her own. It was an astonishing feeling, reminding her, in a way, of her reception of Elgaret's thoughts during the Turning. In that instant, Nolar knew what she had to do. She took a deep breath, and said firmly, "That is why I must seek the Stone of Konnard without delay. I see now that is my true quest. The shard has come to me so that I may return it to the Stone from which it was riven." She stopped again, abruptly aware that Derren was staring at her.

Morfew nodded serenely, as if such declarations were commonplace at Lormt.

"I have read that objects of this sort can influence their own destinies," he said. "I do not believe that a corrupted object could deceive an innocent—for you are an innocent, child, in the realm of Power—concerning its inherent nature. Nor can I believe that an evil object could have abided here at Lormt without being noticed, although," he added, with a scrupulous honesty that reminded Nolar painfully of Ostbor, "we must bear in mind that this chest was sealed away in the cellars until Duratan brought it to me. Still, I think it likely that Duratan's crystals would have warned of the presence of any object tainted by the Dark. Let us therefore accept your conviction that your shard is of the Light and meant to be used for healing. What, then, are we to do next?"

Derren had been cautiously peering into the nearly empty chest, while carefully refraining from touching it.

"There is one more parchment left inside," he pointed out.

With a wordless exclamation, Nolar stooped to see. A very old leaf of parchment had been flattened on the floor of the chest, and being aged to the color of the wood, was nearly impossible to distinguish from it. Nolar pried up one corner with infinite care, then extracted the dusty leaf.

"I realize anew why the Borderers valued your scouting," Nolar said to Derren. "I would not have recognized this as parchment, it is so dark."

Morfew centered the leaf on his desk. "Let us rub one corner with a soft cloth . . . delicately . . . and see whether that improves the reading. Ah, so it does. 'A league north of the twin peaks,' "he read aloud, " 'from dawn to midday by the river's southerly edge. . . .' These would seem to be directions, but to what place, and of equal import, from what place?"

Nolar had pressed close behind, to read over Morfew's shoulder. "It is directing us to the Stone of Konnard," she exclaimed. "I feel it must be."

"Ah," said Morfew, in a neutral tone. "A scholar generally waits to find what a text actually says before he proclaims his discovery," he cautioned.

"There! There!" Nolar pointed across his arm. " 'So deep now lies the Cursed Stone that no more ill shall proceed from it. Yet would I rest more secure had they heeded me and shattered it all to dust.' He *does* mean the Stone of Konnard; he must have been the one whose warning was cited on the fabric."

Morfew frowned. " 'Cursed Stone'—one scarcely likes the sound of that. Still, this man may have been sour because no one accepted his warning. As to these directions, I see no landmarks named."

Despite his admitted aversion to magical objects, Derren could not conceal his interest. "I have traveled much in the southern mountains. Perhaps I might recognize some of the features described, if you would read them to me."

Nolar smiled gratefully at him. "What a help you are to us! Please, Morfew, read out the directions."

Morfew read a lengthy catalogue including sequential notches in mountain ridges, turns by twisted trees, and river crossings where the sand showed black among the white.

When he finished, Derren looked deeply puzzled. "I have ridden and walked, I would have sworn, over all the peaks and valleys between Estcarp and Karsten," he confessed, "but I have to say that I can put no name to any of those places."

"For a very sound reason," suggested Morfew. "We have no way to know how long ago this list was made. Perhaps the country then was unnamed, and the traveler had thus to rely entirely on descriptive directions. I must also remind you that our mountains today are not the same as they were only one month ago. Do not be downcast, child," he said kindly, as Nolar turned her back on them to hide her tears. "Our fortune would be rare indeed were we to find in one day both a magical shard and a clear map to lead us to its missing parent."

Nolar turned back, wiping her cheeks with her hand. "Good Morfew—how wise you are. Since the Turning, I doubt that any person could find his way to a formerly known site in the southern mountains. What once was peak could now be valley, or beneath a flowing stream. It was foolish of me to hope that my path might be so simple. I do thank you, Master Derren, for your suggestion. Had you recognized any landmark, we should still have had a doubtful chance to locate it now. And if our way lies to the east, of course, there are no maps to be consulted."

Derren nodded, his expression grim. "You are right, lady. Perhaps I, too, was overly hopeful in my offer. This hidden stone may not lie in the southern mountains I once knew. As Master Morfew told us when we first arrived here, the Old Race is blocked from thinking of the east." He hesitated, for Morfew was regarding him keenly, and so was Nolar. "My . . . my mother came from Karsten," Derren hastened to add. "I have not traveled myself farther to the east than here to Lormt, but I can think of that direction." His eyes widened. "But you, lady, you are of the Old Race, yet you speak of the east, and—"

"Nolar is affected by a special influence," Morfew quietly interrupted. "I suspect that her shard of stone has effectively countered any inborn barrier against considering the east. For you have no difficulty thinking of the east, do you, child?"

Nolar felt a trifle dazed. "No, none . . . but the east is not the sole source whence I feel drawn." She groped for the proper words. "East, yes, but also . . . south! That is where I must go. Oh, Morfew, how can I *know* this?"

"In matters of magic," said the old scholar, "I have read that like calls to like. Perhaps your shard itself can be your guide, being drawn to its parent stone."

"If you will allow me, lady," said Derren respectfully, "I will gladly ride with you on this quest." *South,* he thought to himself. We shall be riding south! I can go home, to Karsten.

Nolar glanced at the oblivious figure of the Witch, sitting motionless on a nearby corner seat. "We must take Elgaret with us," Nolar said slowly, as if threading her way through the twists of a maze. "If we do find the Stone of Konnard, Elgaret must be there for its healing influence to affect her."

Derren was not at all cheered by this suggestion, but he made an effort to conceal his aversion to the Witch. In a level voice, he observed, "Your aunt is a light burden on the trail, lady. But if we are to go into the high mountains with the weather tending cold, we had best seek mountain ponies to bear us rather than horses."

"Our stables have several such which you may freely borrow," said Morfew cordially, then he turned to Nolar. "I see from your face that you wish to depart at once. Can you not tarry until Ouen can confer with you? He is our community's chief scholar, and his counsel is always well worth hearing."

Nolar impulsively touched Morfew's hand. "I hear Ostbor's caution in your voice," she said, "and I treasure your understanding, for happenings of this sort are new to me . . . and daunting. Yet I feel such a powerful attraction toward the south and east that I fear I shall have no rest until I heed the call. If you can spare us the ponies that Master Derren says we need, I would be most grateful if we could depart early on the morrow."

Anxious as he was to ride south, Derren felt obliged to assert the practical realities. "We must take at least this day, lady, to ready ourselves. Have you any idea how far we must ride?"

Nolar had to admit that she could not give any estimate of the distance that lay before them. "I shall know when we near the Stone," she said firmly, then sighed, her certainty clearly ending with that assertion. "But I do not know how far from here we must travel to reach the Stone."

"Then we must plan carefully," Derren responded, already calculating in his mind how much of what to take and where it could be stowed. "An extra pony or perhaps two might be needed to carry our supplies."

"Wessell can assist you in your necessary planning," Morfew assured them. "Go now to your night's rest, for you will be rising early, I expect. I shall try to send word to Ouen, but I cannot be sure that he can abandon his current tasks to address this matter."

Nolar doubted that she would be able to sleep at all that night, but once she had tucked the warm shard under her modest pillow, she fell into a dreamless sleep that held until she was roused just before dawn by Derren's rap on her door.

"I am meeting Wessell shortly in the main storeroom," Derren called, as Nolar threw back her quilts and reached for her cloak, "but I will fetch your morning meal first."

"We shall be ready, thank you," Nolar replied, moving to Elgaret's pallet to help the Witch sit up. Without consciously thinking, Nolar had clutched her stone shard in one hand as she rose, and she didn't realize it until she reached forward to steady Elgaret. The Witch's dull crystal had again slipped outside her gown, and as Nolar's shard brushed past it, Nolar was half aware of some flicker of light within the crystal. It was instantly gone; Nolar could not be sure that she had truly seen it. There was no time to experiment, for Derren could be back at any moment. Nolar replaced the shard in her skirt pocket and settled Elgaret's pendant back safely out of sight.

The rest of the morning raced by in a whirl of activity. Nolar packed their few clothes, guided Elgaret to the dining area, and then started back with their personal saddle bags. Wessell bustled by her as she approached the door to the storeroom, and immediately offered to help carry the burdens.

"Master Derren has told me of your new venture," Wessell exclaimed with even more than his usual enthusiasm. "You will likely require heavy clothing for mountain travel. Have you warm boots? Capes with fur? Extra blankets? By all means, let me introduce you to Mistress Bethalie, who cares for all our clothing needs. I may have mentioned to you before, but it appears to me that our weather has been affected by the upheaval. You will have noticed that some leaves are already dropping from the trees—far earlier than usual. I would not be surprised if the first snows come soon in the high peaks, which is why," he added, dropping her bags inside the storeroom and taking Nolar's arm to guide her, "I thought about the warm travel clothes. This way."

An hour later, Nolar was back in the storeroom, breathing hard from her exertions. Bethalie had proved to be as dynamic an expediter as Wessell. She had delved energetically in what seemed to Nolar to be a hundred wardrobes, bins, and chests to accumulate a heap of assorted clothing and cold weather travel gear for man and horse. Nolar had just finished sorting, folding, stacking, and stowing away all the items, gratefully filling several extra hampers that Bethalie had provided for the excess. Wessell had darted off to see to another of his vital tasks, and Nolar was sipping a restorative cup of barley water when she felt a slight tug at her sleeve. She was startled to find a small person standing silently at her elbow. He was closely wrapped in a hooded blue robe, but the exposed skin of his hands and face was tanned by the sun. Nolar could not guess his age, but she had the impression that he must be very old, older even than Morfew. His eyes were pale gray, like the clear shallows of a mountain pool.

"Pray excuse my intrusion," he said in a low, quiet voice that Nolar had to lean forward to hear. "I am Pruett, one of Lormt's herbalists. Master Wessell just now accosted me and said that I should seek the lady in the storeroom, so here I am."

For an instant, Nolar was unable to imagine why Wessell should send an herbalist to her, then her weary mind made the connection. "My journey," she exclaimed. "Wessell must have been thinking of my store of herbs and simples. It is amazing how he recalls so many details all at once."

Pruett inclined his head in agreement. "Wessell is a most excellent provisioner. I am certain that the castle he left when he came to Lormt still regrets his departure. If you have the time now, would you care to examine our herbarium? We may have some plants that you might require."

After making sure that Elgaret was safely settled where the cooks on duty could see her, Nolar followed Pruett out across the courtyard to a secluded corner between the archives building and the remaining long wall. The partial collapse of the far corner's tower had showered debris on that area, but the repair workers had cleared away almost all of the movable rubble. Nolar expressed her interest in the little shed sided with airy lath strips, where plants could be hung up in bunches or spread out to dry.

"The original shed was reduced to splinters," Pruett said softly, ushering her inside, "but being as much air as it was wood, it has been simple to replace it. There are to be three in your party, I believe Wessell said. This leather travel satchel should be a proper size. I trust that you already have the basic remedies—or have you need of replenishment?"

Overwhelmed, Nolar simply stood, surveying the neat bundles, bunches, and plaited strands of herbs suspended from the ceiling and walls and distributed on wooden benches.

"I have never before seen such a grand profusion," Nolar said. "This is a wondrous place, and I could spend hours just looking and learning. But," she added with regret, "I cannot linger." Nolar cudgeled her memory, trying to recall what supplies remained in her own modest herb wallet. "I could use some angelica, please, and perhaps some of that lovely trefoil."

"Would you need the salve or the dried blossoms?" asked Pruett, delicately separating out some bundles of the dried red clover.

"Some salve, if you can spare it," Nolar replied. Her eye was drawn to a spray of dense white flower heads branching above leaf pairs united around their hairy stems. "Isn't this agueweed? I prize it for coughs and fevers."

"We call it also feverwort," said Pruett. "Have you some catmint? I find it helpful for treating skin eruptions, swellings, and small wounds or burns. One must be sure," he advised, "to steep it, of course, not boil it."

Nolar eagerly accepted the packet of dried leaves and stems. She held up some newly gathered catmint to sniff its refreshing scent and touch the clusters of fringed, pale violet flowers.

"May I have some of these fresh stalks?" Nolar asked. "I have seldom seen better prepared samples. Oh, here's hyssop—so good for insect bites or stings. And fennel, and angelica—thank you."

"I gathered this fine comfrey myself," said Pruett, offering her a branching plant with large, veined leaves and clusters of creamy flowers each curled at the tip beneath a winged stem. "Now that the river has shifted, I shall have to seek it farther afield, where the ground stays moist."

"Both roots and leaves, please," said Nolar. "I have heard it called slippery root, which certainly describes its stickiness."

"It is also called knitbone," added Pruett, "for its use in the healing of broken bones. Folk will insist upon giving many names to the same herb. More names seem to emerge whenever new uses are found for a plant. Unless one hears them all, one might not learn of the additional applications. By the way, these yarrow leaves make an effective astringent."

Nolar handled the dried fern-like leaves with special care to avoid crumbling them. "That is positively *all* that will fit within this satchel," she announced. "I am most grateful, Master Pruett. As Wessell may have told you, I am seeking healing aid for Elgaret, my aunt, whose mind was injured by the Council's Turning of the mountains. While I know of no herb that might help her, some of these good plants will surely increase her comfort during our journey."

Pruett bowed gracefully. "You are most welcome. Should you encounter any plant previously unknown to you during your travels, we would value a sample, should you have time to gather it."

"I shall certainly be alert for any," Nolar agreed, "but from my experience on the trail here from Es City, I fear that the damage to most plants and trees has been extreme, especially in the mountains."

Pruett shook his head sadly. "I, too, have received a few such reports from our local farmers who have ventured onto the nearby peaks. It may well be that we shall have to try to reestablish some plants from our stores here. Perhaps we may reasonably hope that the stronger rooted varieties and those stemming from bulbs may survive the winter, as well as their recent dislocation."

Nolar secured the straps on the satchel. "I hope I may be allowed to return this to you as well-stocked as you have entrusted it to me."

"A fair road before you, then, and a swift return," said Pruett, as he walked with her to the shed's entrance.

"Good fortune to you and your endeavors," Nolar responded, with genuine warmth. "You have here a life's work that draws me to beg an apprenticeship. But Master Morfew's scrolls, too, call to me. Truly, if I could stay here, I should likely be torn between the two of you."

"When your quest is accomplished," suggested Pruett quietly, "perhaps you may choose to join us here at Lormt."

Nolar gazed around the great courtyard. "For now, I must

follow the stronger voice bidding me on. I do not know where it leads, but I must seek its source. Yet there is something here at Lormt that seems for me, rightly . . ." She paused, surprised by the word that came to her lips. "Home," she finished.

Pruett searched her face for an instant, then, with a muffled, "Wait!" he darted back inside the herbarium. He returned with a sprig of flowers that Nolar had never seen before. The slender stalks were crowned by nine-petaled flowers, pure white at their tips, but shading through azure to a center as dark blue as the night sky of summer. Nolar was aware of a faint sweet fragrance as she accepted the flowers.

"These are beautiful!" Nolar exclaimed. "What are they?"

"They are rare," Pruett replied. "To my knowledge, our one nearby site in the uplands is the only place where they may be found. The shepherd who first brought them to me called them 'Noon and Midnight,' but I call them 'Lormt Flower.' I know of no medicinal use for the plant, but it holds its scent very well. Remember Lormt by it, if you will."

"With all my heart," said Nolar. "I thank you for the beauty of both the plant and the thought. Now I must go." She longed to stay and learn more from Pruett. She was wishing that she could just listen indefinitely to his quiet, patient voice when she was struck by a fanciful thought: if a plant could speak, it would probably sound very like Pruett of Lormt. That moment of light relief was swiftly superseded by her crushing sense of urgency. The shard in her pocket weighed upon Nolar both physically and mentally. She could not linger at Lormt; she had to ride to the south and east.

Derren, meanwhile, had been favorably impressed by the sturdy mountain ponies he had been shown in Lormt's spacious stables. He had asked for the use of four ponies—three for riding and one for carrying their additional supplies. With Wessell's zealous assistance, Derren had decided what they should take with them and how to divide it up and

secure it. As he fastened the last few straps, Derren was
surprised to realize that in one sense, he was sorry to be
leaving Lormt. He had found it to be a curiously restful
place, although he had been occupied in strenuous physical
work during his entire stay. Somehow, time seemed to run
slower at Lormt, almost as if Lormt were not affected by
time. It must be all the scholars, Derren decided, poring over
their scrolls day after day, studying the records from the far
past. They could take a longer view of life, setting it in the
ordered ranks of so many years, that present squabbles between dukes and Witches seemed but a minor ripple in the
broad stream of Estcarp's past.

Derren shook himself. What was the matter with him?.He
was being lulled into a perilous tranquility by the pernicious
influence of this place. The sooner he escaped from these
numbing walls, the better. Derren forcibly wrenched his
thoughts away from Lormt and concentrated upon his prospective journey. He had to admit to himself that he was
uneasy about the magical stone that Nolar had found.

Magic was the province of Estcarp's fearsome Witches,
and although Nolar had said that she had no Witch training,
still she had received a Sending. Now she possessed this
ancient stone fragment which Morfew agreed was an object
of Power. What if Nolar's quest led them to the parent stone,
and by its Power, Elgaret the Witch regained her senses?
Derren would simply have to flee before the Witch could turn
her attention toward him.

He did not consider himself a coward, but he did not
believe that he could stand, even armed and wary, against a
Witch. He suppressed a shudder at the thought of such a
confrontation. No, he decided, he must be practical. The
likelihood that they could even find the fabled Stone of Konnard after countless years of its total obscurity had to be so
slight as to be negligible.

And, he further encouraged himself, the upheaval of the
Turning alone should have made any former mountain trail

either inaccessible or impassable. A nagging memory nudged him. Nolar had said that she would be drawn to the site of the Stone by its magic, despite any physical barriers. Disturbed, Derren pushed that thought away. They could not possibly find the wretched Stone.

It would be an entirely straightforward matter: he would guide the two Estcarp women into the southeastern mountains as far as they cared to go, and when the quest was obviously fruitless, he would turn them over to the first reliable people they encountered who could see them safely back to Estcarp. He could then travel unhindered back toward Karsten. Derren suspected with the keenest foreboding that his beloved forests would likely be destroyed, but he promised himself that he could at least devote all his energy toward restoring the land to the condition he remembered: green, growing, full of life.

Derren heard Wessell approaching long before he could see the provisioner. Wessell was chattering to someone else.

"You found Pruett, I see, or rather he found you. I did ask him to seek you out, and I recognize that satchel of his. Very clever fellow, Pruett. He's been here as long as anyone can recall. Always seems to know just what plant to brew into a tea or chop into a poultice. Ah, there you are, Master Derren. I was just telling Mistress Nolar how much we rely upon our chief herbalist."

Nolar handed Derren the stout leather satchel. "One more thing to be packed, I fear," she said apologetically. "We shall surely need some of these herbs along our way, however, and Master Pruett has given us a wondrous variety suited to treat a number of ills."

"I hope that we shall not require any of them," Derren asserted as he strapped the satchel behind Nolar's saddle. "Still, it is wise to be ready in case bad fortune strikes. Do you wish to set out now, lady?" he added, looking up at the sun to judge the remaining daylight.

"I had the cook prepare a late lunch that you could eat here or carry with you," inserted Wessell.

Nolar could not help smiling. "Dear Wessell—you manage to anticipate everything. I expect it would be advisable to give Elgaret her food before we go. I can see to that, Master Derren, if you will bring the ponies to the gate?"

Derren nodded, "I should fill an extra water skin, then I will join you in the storeroom."

By midafternoon, the party was mounted and about to leave. To Nolar's surprise, Morfew hurried out to the gate to see them go.

"There has been another landslide in the hills," Morfew fretted. "Master Ouen and Duratan were called out in the night to help the family whose house and farm buildings were destroyed. I had hoped that Ouen could see you before you left, but I shall tell him about your stone and show him my copy of the associated manuscript. When you return with news of the parent stone, he will be waiting with great interest, I am sure."

Nolar leaned down to press his hand. "Already you speak of success—that has to be a good omen."

"May your road be a fair one," Morfew returned, "and may the sun shine upon it."

"I suspect that there will be no road and worse weather," Derren observed skeptically, "but we shall go as far as we may."

"We shall await your return," Morfew called, as the ponies ambled through the gate.

They camped that night not very far from Lormt, but Nolar still felt a sense of relief at being on her way, actually moving toward the Stone of Konnard. She was constantly aware of the warm presence of her shard, radiating from her skirt pocket. She had considered suspending it in a cloth bag on a cord around her neck, but the shard was too large to be comfortably worn as a pendant.

Their first full day of travel quickly demonstrated the value of the sure-footed ponies. As Derren had gloomily predicted, even the remnants of the trail rapidly vanished, and they had to choose their way around, through, and amid the wreckage left by the Turning. Horses, however stout-hearted and strong, could not have attempted the climbs or the descents that the Lormt ponies accepted and accomplished. On only the most difficult terrain was it necessary to dismount and lead the animals. Elgaret's pony proved to be particularly cautious and clever at choosing the safest path. Typically, Derren led the way on his pony, followed by Elgaret, then Nolar, trailed by the pack pony kept on a slack rein.

The weather at first held clear, but it grew steadily colder as they climbed higher into the mountains. Nolar was constantly grateful for Wessell's insistence upon their packing warm travel gear. While living with Ostbor, she had seen a few cases of severe cold damage when high peak shepherds and herdsmen had been trapped by winter storms. Often, despite their best efforts, the victims lost fingers, toes, hands, or feet to the deadly effect of the frost. Several times during the day and night, Nolar took care to check that Elgaret's hands and feet were safely warm, and that her nose and face were protected from the numbing wind.

The snowstorm struck when they had traveled three days away from Lormt. Derren scouted ahead briefly through the blinding blizzard, then guided the party into a cave newly formed by earthquake-shifted rock slabs. There was room within for all four ponies and the three people to shelter out of the howling whiteness. Nolar again blessed Wessell for his foresight as she warmed some meal mush over a tiny fire. Wessell had insisted that she take some bags of charcoal in case, he had said, they might be caught in rain or snow where they could not gather dry wood.

The storm delayed them more than a full day, but as soon as the skies cleared, Derren discovered a passable route into a lower valley where there had been far less snow, and movement was consequently easier. Nolar said as much, suggesting that perhaps their way would now be open, but he merely bobbed his head and grunted noncommittally. She soon understood why Derren had not endorsed her unfounded optimism. "Easier" travel proved to be a matter of comparison between nearly impossible and almost unbearable. The effects of the earthquakes in the valleys had definitely compounded the difficulties of transit. After her pony's third major stumble, Nolar dismounted and led the animal. Amazingly, Elgaret's pony picked its way slowly, but without jarring loose its passive rider.

When they stopped for the night, Nolar thought she had never before felt so drained of all strength. Derren had gathered some evergreen branches, ripped from their trees by the landslides, and laced them into a windbreak against which they could rest. He was rubbing down the ponies, his back to the small fire while Nolar tried to coax Elgaret to drink some hot herb tea. This time, there was no mistake. Nolar clearly saw a spark of light flare in Elgaret's Witch jewel. Carefully making sure that Derren was fully occupied, Nolar reached in her pocket and brought her shard close to the Witch's crystal. In the dusky dimness, she could not ignore the greenish flicker that pulsed in the jewel, then died away. Nolar peered critically at Elgaret's face. Was there any sign of life in the uninjured eye or in the facial expression? Nolar had to admit that there was none that she could distinguish, but perhaps, in time. . . . *Something* was happening within the Witch's jewel, and Nolar's shard appeared to be involved. Should she mention it to Derren? Nolar slipped the comforting warmth of the stone back into her pocket. No, she decided. Derren, for some reason, seemed . . . threatened. That was exactly the right word: *threatened* by the Witch. Nolar weighed all of his previous remarks and reactions. Why should a Borderer, of all people, be frightened of a Witch? The only answer that made sense, Nolar realized with a dreadful certainty, was that Derren was *not* a Borderer, as he claimed to be. But why would he say he was if it was not true?

Because he wanted others to accept him as a Borderer; because he was truly an enemy of Estcarp trapped by the Turning on the wrong side of the southern border. The chill that gripped Nolar welled up from within, colder by far than the icy wind that raked her face. Derren had admitted that his mother came from Karsten, Nolar recalled. She now felt certain that Derren, despite his outward Old Race appearance, was also a Karstenian, and yet . . . she could not feel hatred toward him. He had protected her and the helpless Elgaret through the trying passage of so many leagues. They had been totally at his mercy. He could have abused or slain them whenever he chose, but he had not. Nolar smiled wryly to herself. If only she could discuss this with Ostbor, or Morfew, or even Pruett. Impulsively, she reached within her cloak and drew out the now limp but still fragrant spray of Lormt Flowers.

"What is that?" Derren asked, returning to squat beside the fire.

"Some rare flowers that Master Pruett gave me," Nolar replied, holding them out where he could see the blossoms.

"I have never seen any like those," Derren said, "and I pay heed to flowers."

"Do you?" asked Nolar, curious. "Why?"

"Where there are wildflowers, lady, you will find other creatures," Derren explained, poking the fire with a short stick. "In a thriving forest, there seems to be a sort of . . ." he groped for the word he wanted, "balance. If there is an ample supply of food and water and plentiful lairs for sheltering the animals, then the forest can care for all the creatures it should. Besides, some flowers and plants will grow in only certain places where there is either much water or little, so that can direct you in turn if you note which are which. I have also learned the healing properties of a few plants, but you know far more than I about herbs and such."

"It is clear," Nolar said, "that you prize the forest and all that it nurtures and protects."

Derren gazed at her across the fire. "I belong there, lady. I know the forest in all weathers and seasons."

"Have you traveled in this forest before?" Nolar asked. "When it was forest, I mean," she added, looking sadly at the shattered stumps and dead limbs littering the surface of this decimated valley.

"No," Derren replied, with bitterness in his voice. "This is farther to the east than I have previously ventured, but I sorrow to see it thus. I think of my home mountains and the slopes and crags where my father and I ranged. I tell you honestly, lady, I dread now to go back there." He gestured angrily at their surroundings. "I must judge by what we have already seen, and we have not yet penetrated into the areas of worst damage. I fear that most valleys are choked with debris, if they are valleys still." His voice fell to a low, weary murmur. "I think that is the hardest thing to face. It would be somehow bearable to know that beneath the mud and rubble, the lasting land was still there, and might eventually be cleansed by the rain and wind, emerging once more into the light of day. But I deeply fear that the land I once knew is gone forever. The very surface is changed beyond recognition. If no landmarks survive, it will be as if it is a strange, far country instead of my familiar hills. In one night—one night!—everything that was reliable has been torn from us."

"I have also tasted something of that same loss," said Nolar quietly, when Derren fell silent. "Because of my face, I have never known the closeness of family or friends. Until I chanced to meet Ostbor, I was forever shut out. When he died, I felt that all that was solid in the world had dissolved with him. I cannot tell you that all will be well, for none of us can know what lies ahead. I think you are likely right in your fears for your forested homeland. The Turning has changed all of our lives, for it has changed the world we must live in. But I believe that time will heal the forests. A man like you, who knows the ways of the forest could speed that healing. I know of no other comfort that I can offer you, but I believe that at least is honest truth."

Derren had looked up at her, startled, then blurted, obviously surprised, "You care, lady—you do *care* about the forests."

Nolar nodded her assent. "Yes, I do care, for it has been in the mountain forests that I have spent most of the few happy hours of my life, before I met Ostbor. And although you may find it difficult to believe, I can tell you that the Witches—some of them—also share your sense of pain at the destruction they were forced to bring about."

Derren hesitated, as if he wanted to tell her something, but after a momentary pause, he devoted his attention to the fire. "I value your words, lady," he said, in a controlled, neutral tone, and Nolar did not press him further.

Later that night, as he lay awake, Derren argued furiously with himself. The Estcarp women were his enemies; the only reason he endured their company was to protect himself from disastrous exposure. But, countered a part of his mind, that reason no longer holds, not in this unmapped wilderness. You are scarcely likely to be questioned in these riven mountains by any of Estcarp's minions. Why not just abandon the Witch and Witch-friend and slip back to Karsten? Because I have promised to escort them, Derren retorted to himself. Because they would perish in this ruined country without me—I might as well strike them dead with my sword as leave them to wander hereabouts, finally starving or freezing as they slept. They are your enemies, his inner voice accused, yet you deceive yourself that you care what befalls them. They have done me no harm, he rejoined hotly. For my honor's sake, I must return them safely to Estcarp. I do not have to take them there personally—surely we must encounter someone I can entrust them to, then I can go home. Derren pulled his cloak tighter around his shoulders and strove to ignore his nagging doubts. It was a long time before he fell into a shallow, troubled sleep.

Slowly, at times so slowly as to seem agonizing, they struggled farther toward the south and east. Nolar found herself listening for bird calls or the familiar sounds of animals, but a numbing silence prevailed over the blasted land. The few birds and animals they did see were carrion eaters, and even they appeared torpid, still dazed by the Turning. Derren, too, had noticed, for one morning when they surprised two shawled vultures crouched on a dead mountain goat, Derren had frowned and halted his pony.

"I had feared," he said, "that the slaughter of wild beasts would be so severe that we would encounter great numbers of carcasses, but now I must say there seem to be far fewer than I had expected."

Nolar turned in her saddle to survey both views from the summit of the narrow pass they had just attained between two valleys. "I miss the birds. In my mountains at this time, I would be hearing owls and grouse, and the dear, silly pee-wits calling to one another at all hours. So far, on this trip, I have sighted only ravens and crows and one glutted dire-bird. I must hope that the others simply fled before the catastrophe, and have not yet returned to their home ranges."

Derren nudged his pony to one side so that Nolar could ride closer for conversation. "I have heard, lady, that some animals can sense impending earthquakes. Perhaps they ran away before the Turning. I have known deer herds to desert a feeding area for days or weeks, then return when whatever danger affrighted them had passed."

"I shall certainly hope that is true," said Nolar. "To think that this whole great expanse of land must be nearly empty of life is both sad and unnatural."

Derren sniffed the early afternoon air uneasily, and glanced up at the low clouds. "It may rain soon, lady. We should try to cross the pit of that next valley and seek shelter for the night among those far rocks."

His prediction was swiftly fulfilled, as the first heavy drops spattered down before they began the climb up the farther side of the valley. The mountain ponies shook their heads as the initial shower grew into a downpour. When he saw the treacherous character of the gravel underfoot, Derren found his sense of apprehension intensifying. He had just twisted around, beginning a warning to Nolar, when without any advance indication, the entire slope ahead and above them dissolved in a roar of cascading rocks and earth. The rock-slide swept upon them like a hideous gray-brown wave, giving them no chance to bolt or flee.

One moment, Nolar was blinking away cold rain, and the next moment, she and her pony were being whirled and tumbled back down toward the valley floor. Nolar was overcome by a thoroughly disconcerting flood of sensations—deafening noise, choking dust even amid the torrential rain, pummeling rocks that bruised the body and shocked the breath from her ribs. She was dimly aware that she had parted company with her hapless pony, and was rolling and sliding farther down the slope, now half-buried in gritty rocks and soil, now suddenly free and tumbling uncontrollably down, always down. When she finally cascaded to a stop, her legs trapped to the hips by gravel, Nolar wasn't certain for a while that she had stopped rolling. Her head whirled from all the frenzied motion, and she gasped for breath. Was anything broken? She cautiously moved her arms, then dug her legs free. She felt twinges from strained muscles and deeper aches where bruises would be forming, but no stabbing pains from broken ribs, arm or leg bones. Thanks to Wessell's ample clothing, Nolar had been covered sufficiently to prevent more than a few minor abrasions on her hands and face. She was considering herself fortunate, when she suddenly thought of the Witch.

"Elgaret!" Nolar cried frantically, and as quickly stopped, since it was unlikely that the Witch could hear her or answer. She heard a jingle of harness nearby as a pony struggled to its feet, and then, less distinctly, a muffled groan.

"Derren?" Nolar listened anxiously for a reply. The next groan guided her back up the incline. The loose gravel and slippery mud frustrated any effort to hurry, but Nolar fought her way upward until she could clearly see the dark green of Derren's tunic against the churned soil. He was lying on his right side, his head and chest swept downhill. Nolar winced to see rivulets of blood staining the water trickling among the rocks. "Derren?" she called again. "Can you hear me?"

Derren tried to lever himself up on his right arm, but fell back with a choked-off cry. "Do not look upon it, lady!" he exclaimed desperately. "It is not a good sight for a maiden's eyes."

Nolar continued to slither closer to him. "Neither is my face a pleasing sight to look upon, but while I live, I am here, and perhaps I may do somewhat to stanch your bleeding. It is your leg, is it not?"

Derren could not fully suppress a sob. "It is broken—badly. I fear I see the very bone. Oh, do not look!"

"I have seen bones before, sir," snapped Nolar, her concern so keen that it burst out as irritation. "You forget that I have lived near peaks where men and beasts fell and broke themselves with appalling regularity. Ah, you are quite right about your leg. I suspect that large, jagged rock half buried just beside you may have caused the injury. Our first necessity is to stop the bleeding. My cloak has been obligingly torn—so I shall employ the loose strip. Let me bind you here, above your wound." As she eased the cloth strip around his thigh, she glanced apprehensively at Derren, who lay back, pale, his eyes shut as the rain streamed down his face. They would have to find shelter soon, or he would die simply from the chill, never mind his blood loss. She reached out to touch his hand in reassurance. Did she dare to leave him long enough to search for Elgaret?

As if Derren had sensed her thought, he opened his eyes. "You must leave me, lady," he implored. "Find your aunt and seek shelter before full darkness. I shall follow once I have recovered my breath from the fall."

Nolar tugged her makeshift cincture tight. "I do not think, Master Derren, that you will be walking far this day on that leg. Nor, for that matter, on your other ankle, which I suspect has also been injured."

Derren had lost his left boot in the landslide, and Nolar could see that his left ankle was already discolored and swelling. His right leg, however, was in the more urgent need of care. Despite her positive manner, Nolar quailed inwardly as she examined the extent of the hurt. The bones of the lower leg had torn through the skin when they snapped, but there was also a deep gouge along the leg that sluggishly welled blood in spite of her cincture. Shelter—that was an immediate requirement, and then she desperately needed Pruett's herb satchel. As gently as she could, Nolar straightened out Derren's right leg, easing the exposed bones back into the raw flesh. Derren sighed and fainted, to her relief, for Nolar felt she had to pull his torso uphill so that his head would be elevated. The rain, at least, was diminishing, but the air was getting colder. Nolar checked the cincture, which had appreciably slowed the bleeding. She recalled that one of Ostbor's scrolls advised that the pressure had to be loosened at regular intervals if the limb below the tie was to remain alive.

Nolar staggered to her feet, searching the surrounding area for evidence of their ponies or baggage. She tried to remember where Elgaret had been just before the rockslide— she had been back behind Nolar, to her right, for she could recall glimpsing Elgaret from the corner of her eye just as Derren had called to warn them. There, far to the right, at the foot of the landslide. Wasn't something moving? As she skidded and scrambled down the slope, Nolar saw that it was Elgaret's sure-footed pony, nuzzling a dark still form on the ground. Worn out by stumbling through the gravel, Nolar simply sat on what was left of her cloak and slid down the rest of the way. Elgaret's pony appeared to be sound, with all of its gear amazingly in place, although some packs were wrenched out of order. Nolar knelt by the Witch, dreading what she might find. She did not consider herself religious, but she found herself offering a fervent prayer to Neave, Goddess of Truth and Peace. As Nolar slowly eased the Witch over onto her back, she was immensely relieved to see no outward signs of major injury. Elgaret might simply have been asleep, breathing evenly, her eyes shut against the rain. Nolar supposed that the very state of relaxation in which Elgaret rode had probably served her well during the extended fall. The Witch presumably had rolled limply down the hillside without snagging on any obstructions. Nolar carefully felt along Elgaret's limbs, but detected no broken bones.

Recalling how Derren had once attracted the ponies' attention at a streamside, Nolar pressed her fingers to her lips and emitted a shrill whistle. When she heard a faint answering jingle, she whistled again. Her own pony, limping a little, plodded into view a short distance away. Pruett's herb satchel, its leather darkened by the rain, remained securely fastened behind the saddle. Nolar hurried toward it, talking soothingly to the pony as she went. The pony trembled, but stood still and let Nolar run her hands over its joints and examine its hooves. With some effort, Nolar pried a rough pebble from its lodging in one hoof, hoping that would relieve the lameness. She then led the pony across the scree toward Elgaret's patient animal.

About a third of the way up the slope, an abnormal shape caught Nolar's eye. She left the two ponies at the foot of the slide and trudged up to the strange shape. Her worst fears for the missing animal were quickly verified. What at a glance might have been an oddly bent stick was actually the shattered forelimb of their baggage pony, whose body was buried under the slide debris. Using a broad flat rock, Nolar dug down to the body. The poor creature's neck had been broken, but most of the baggage was still intact and could be salvaged. Soft whickering sounds made her look back down the slope where Derren's pony was now rejoining its companions. Nolar slid down hastily and extracted a spare cloak from Derren's battered saddlebag, together with a blanket to wrap around Elgaret on her way back with Pruett's satchel. She noticed with a pang of loss on Derren's behalf that his small huntsman's crossbow had been ripped away from its lashings in the fall.

When she reached him, Derren was still unconscious. His swordbelt had been sheared, and his sword was gone, but Nolar saw that his dagger remained snug in its regular belt sheath. The light was dimming as twilight settled early in the depth of the valley. Nolar delicately eased the cincture, for Derren's leg below the fabric band was sallow and chill. Bleeding resumed at once, but healthier color also flushed into the leg. Nolar was delving into the satchel for the herbs she would need when a totally unexpected voice echoed across the valley.

"Ho, there! Ho!"

Nolar froze for an instant, then peered into the dusky shadows where a clammy evening mist was already thickening. "Here!" she called hoarsely. "We need help! Here!"

"Hold fast—I come!" the voice responded, and abruptly its owner came into sight, emerging from an adjoining cleft that cut into the valley. He was afoot, flourishing a heavy staff in one hand and clutching a game bag in the other.

Nolar waited, hoping for more assistance, more people, perhaps mounted on horses or ponies, but her prospective rescuer appeared to be alone.

He paused to look at Nolar's huddled ponies and the blanket-wrapped Witch, dropped his game bag, then dug his staff into the gravel and started the climb toward Nolar. He was a broad-shouldered, burly man whose tousled hair was streaked with gray. His size and evident strength reminded Nolar of the helpful innkeeper in Es City. He was wearing an old-fashioned tunic, like one of Ostbor's most ancient garments.

"I heard thy trill a while since. Thou art sorely stricken, lady," he rumbled in a deep voice as he arrived at Nolar's side. "What's to do?"

"I welcome your aid, most heartily, sir," said Nolar. "As you see, our escort has been injured in the rockslide. I have the necessary herbs to treat his wounds, but I cannot move him by myself. Our chief need is shelter for the night."

"I have been hunting," the man said slowly, as if weighing the opportunities available to him. "It is not far whence I bide. We could go thither before the dark, if it please thee."

"I should brace this broken leg so that no more damage be done." Nolar glanced about, worried. "Can you find two sturdy sticks we could bind, one to either side of the leg? I must stay here to halt the bleeding."

The burly man gave a curious half-bow and strode back down the slope, producing an additional landslide of his own. He returned shortly with two lengths of trimmed tree branches which he helped Nolar bind against Derren's right leg. Squinting along his staff, as if taking a rough measurement, the man said, "He is taller than I. Best that I carry him upon my back."

Rolling Derren to a sitting position, he squatted, his back to Derren's, reached behind and pulled Derren's arms over his shoulders as he rose in a crouch. Nolar had never seen such a lifting strategy, but it did stretch Derren along the rescuer's back, with both legs off the ground. Once at the valley floor, the man carefully transferred Derren to a pony. He helped Nolar balance Elgaret on her pony, tied his own game bag to Nolar's saddle and set off, leading that animal since Nolar insisted upon walking beside Derren to watch for renewed bleeding from his leg. As they walked, Nolar explained that most of their belongings should be recoverable from the area close by the dead baggage pony.

The burly man peered up the slope where she pointed.

"Aye," he said, "I can see a foreleg right enough. I shall return for thy goods on the morrow when the light is better."

It was almost completely dark when they reached his hunting camp. He had stretched a cord between two trees and used that line as a brace against which he had constructed a lean-to shelter from evergreen boughs. He needed only a moment to kindle a fire and carry Derren and Elgaret beneath the shelter, out of the cold drifting mist.

As he straightened up, he demanded bluntly, "Who art thou, lady?"

It seemed to Nolar that she had been introducing herself to suspicious strangers for entirely too long and wearisome a time. Her anxiety for Derren's life had worn her temper as raw as his fearsome wounds.

"Sir," she retorted, "I regret that we have not been properly introduced, but at the moment, my sole concern is to try to preserve this man's life. Can you heat some water for me? I must brew some knitbone tea and make a quantity of poultice, besides mixing an oil of garlic salve for the ankle sprain. Oh, pray do not stand there gaping at me like a fish! Hurry!"

It was only after he turned away, rummaging for a blackened kettle that Nolar realized that the firelight had likely just disclosed to him her disfigured face. The man had stared at her face for a moment, but his expression had not conveyed the familiar revulsion Nolar's appearance so often elicited. Nolar could not quite evaluate his reaction. There had been a certain glint in his eyes that Nolar halfway recognized, but amid the demands clamoring for her attention, its significance eluded her. She had no time to brood. The herbs had to be seen to. She blessed Pruett for his care in packing what she needed. If only there was sufficient knitbone; she could use yarrow as a styptic and astringent if the knitbone ran out, and red clover salve could be applied to fresh wounds, but Derren's hurts were so severe as to be daunting to even the most proficient herbalist.

The burly man gruffly presented her with the steaming kettle.

"Thank you. I shall need another pot, please," Nolar requested, "and a shallow dish, if you have one, in which to form my poultice. Could you bring me a cup from my saddle bag? That red leather one, over there."

"I came out a-hunting, lady, not carrying provisions for a troop," the man complained.

"We have some vessels in our baggage, then. I will fetch them." Nolar extracted a roll of cloth from the herb satchel. "Kindly tear some of this fabric into strips, if you will, for the bandaging. Make it about three finger widths."

Nolar fretted at every delay, but took care to mince the knitbone root and leaves so that they would mix smoothly into the salve. She set some of the leaves steeping into a tea for Derren to drink once he was awake. There were those, she knew, who pressed liquids upon the unconscious, but it seemed to Nolar more sensible to wait until the victim could swallow for himself and lessen the risk of choking. On one of their small flat wooden trenchers, she laid out a broad strip of linen as the base for her poultice. She tempered the boiling water with some of the icy fresh water the man had fetched in another jug, and plunged more knitbone roots and leaves into the pot to warm them. The mucilaginous roots helped bind the mass together as she lifted it out to drain before arranging it on the linen. The burly man assisted her in applying the warm poultice to Derren's injured leg. Nolar spread her healing salve on the raw gouge furrowed down the leg, then snugly wrapped the limb with bandage strips. With some trepidation, she loosened her cincture, anxiously watching the bandage for any sign of bloody soak-through. When the cloth remained clean, Nolar let out the breath she hadn't realized she'd been holding.

The heat of the poultice roused Derren to semiconsciousness. To engage his attention, Nolar addressed him briskly.

"Derren! You must drink some of this tea. Slowly . . . that's good. A little more, please."

"Sweet," muttered Derren, licking his lips. "Sharp."

"So I have heard. Take a little more, if you will. It will help the healing of your leg. It was very fortunate that Master Pruett packed so much of this fine knitbone, or comfrey, as he called it. Perhaps he foresaw that we might suffer broken bones." She stopped babbling as soon as Derren's eyes drooped shut.

"Now then, sir," Nolar said to the burly man, who had been listening with evident interest, "we may introduce ourselves while I rub my salve upon the sprained ankle. I am Nolar of Meroney, from the land of Estcarp, as is my lady companion, Elgaret. She was sorely injured in the recent upheaval of these mountains—the Turning, as it is being called. Our guide and escort is Derren, a Borderer from the south country. We encountered him upon our road to Lormt, where we sought aid for Elgaret." She paused in her rubbing and looked at their rescuer, the first truly close look at him she had taken.

At first glance, he had a bland, unremarkable face, with deep-set eyes that glinted red-brown in the firelight. He seemed habitually to finger a single black metal earring in his left ear lobe. His thin lips parted in a sociable smile, disclosing sharp white teeth. Odd fragments of memory rushed through Nolar's mind. She had seen eyes like those once before, and for some reason, there was a link in her mind with sharp teeth. Suddenly, the scene snapped into focus: it had been that wild boar she had seen years before, cornered by Ostbor's hunting neighbors. Her lasting impressions of it were feral eyes like smoldering coals and slashing tusks. Before the huntsmen's spears finally pinned it, the boar had gutted several dogs and savaged three men. Annoyed, Nolar shook her head. Why should she ever have thought of that dangerous animal? She concentrated on what the burly man was saying.

"I wish thee and thy party well, lady. I hight Smire, a scholar's apprentice from a distant, nameless corner of these mountains. My master and I have been lately freed from long immurement due to . . . illness. I dared to leave him briefly to hunt for fresh food. But where dost thou fare in these wilds?"

Nolar could not say why, but something about Smire deeply troubled her. Looking at Smire, she thought that "scholar" was the last term she would have thought to apply to him. With some chagrin, she tried to remind herself that few would look at her and say "scholar" either, but her disquiet persisted. She had heard of instant, unthinking dislike for a stranger—in fact, she had so often elicited that herself because of her face that she had almost ceased to care when folk drew back as soon as they first saw her. But this aversion was different.

As Smire absently caressed his earring with his left forefinger, the firelight caught the surface of the flattened ring. Nolar suddenly could see tiny marks cut into the dull metal. For no clear reason, Smire's earring struck a cold dread into Nolar. Her skin crawled at the thought of touching it. She told herself that she was being foolish, indulging in groundless fears . . . but the abhorrence stubbornly remained.

To gain time, Nolar busied herself winding a bandage strip around Derren's ankle, then deftly wrapped his cold, bare foot in a soft woolen scarf. She was abruptly aware of the warm, steadying weight of the shard in her pocket. Her decision emerged with utmost certainty: it was not safe to tell Smire the whole truth.

"The scholars at Lormt were much disturbed by the Turning," Nolar remarked in as calm a tone as she could manage. "Great parts of their walls have fallen, due to the earthquakes, and their famed records are consequently in much disarray. Still, they were able to find for us one old scroll that directed us upon this journey." A plausible tale abruptly occurred to her, and she seized it. "A secluded abbey in this area," she confided to Smire with touching sincerity, "was anciently founded near a healing spring of great virtue. Although we could not know whether it might be affected by the Turning, we determined to seek the place, and Master Derren kindly accompanied us. Of course, the disarrangement of the land has rendered the directions from Lormt most difficult to follow."

Smire nodded wisely. "How true thou speakest! I scarcely recognized this very valley from when I last traveled it some long time since. I rejoice that my master is a great sage, and may well know of this abbey thou seekest and its healing spring. If thy escort can be moved, we should hasten to my master's abode as soon as may be."

"I must see how Master Derren's leg fares on the morrow," said Nolar, wondering to herself why Smire should be in such a hurry to move Derren. "As you may know, to move a person with such a leg injury too soon can cause great woe."

"I bow to thy obvious wisdom in the matter," Smire declared. "Wilt thou not rest now, lady? Surely thou are wearied."

Nolar realized with a start that she had been perilously close to dozing. She pinched her arm through her sleeve. "I must first see to Elgaret. It has been many hours since I last fed her or gave her drink."

Smire's heavy eyebrows rose. "Can she not attend to herself?" he asked.

Nolar moved to crouch beside the Witch. "No, the injury to her during the Turning concerns her head. I must see to all her needs."

Whatever happens, Nolar thought, fighting the leaden weight of exhaustion, I must *not* let Smire see the Witch jewel. She was relieved to find that it was tucked safely out of sight. Elgaret, her eyes shut, was still breathing quietly and evenly, apparently unaffected by her precipitous tumble down the valley's incline. Nolar forced herself to search out some shattered journeycake from her saddlebag and prepare a mush of it for Elgaret. When she was through attending to the Witch, Nolar checked again on Derren, rousing him to take more knitbone tea, and making sure there was no evidence of bleeding on his bandages. Only then did Nolar pull her own spare cloak from her pony's pack and roll herself in it to lie down by the fire.

Smire assured her heartily that he would keep watch. "Fear not, lady! Thou canst rest unblenched whilst I stand guard."

Nolar murmured her thanks and sank down on the hard ground. Just before sleep's darkness claimed her, she wondered why Smire should speak in such archaic language. Listening to him was like reading some of Ostbor's oldest scrolls. And his clothing was of equally antiquated design. There must be some reason . . . but her body craved sleep, and she could deny it no longer.

Nolar awoke abruptly the next morning, unsure at first where she was, or what had roused her. An echo lingered in her memory—the ponies' harness—that was it. Cautiously, she eased her eyes open. Smire was bent over Elgaret's pony, pawing through their baggage. *I did not like that man on sight,* Nolar thought with a certain grim satisfaction. *I see now at least one clear reason why.* She yawned loudly, and flung back her cloak. Instantly, Smire stepped away from the pony. By the time Nolar sat up and turned toward him, Smire was busily feeding the fire under the kettle.

"Awake, lady?" he inquired. "I hope that thou art well restored from yestereve's sad happenings."

"Thank you, Master Smire, I slept quite well," Nolar replied. "Your timely preparations are most welcome. I shall need to change Master Derren's poultice, and if possible, he should drink some warm broth."

Smire beamed, but Nolar noticed that the smile did not touch his eyes.

"I had thought, lady, that broth might be required, so I

have stewed a fine rabbit to supply both meat and juice," he said.

Nolar felt Derren's forehead. It was warmer than normal, but wounds like his were often accompanied by fever. If the need arose, she had seen hyssop packed in the satchel. One of Ostbor's old scrolls on healing had suggested that fever could be a positive sign, so long as it did not exceed a moderate heat. Nolar turned her attention to Derren's right leg. Some blood had penetrated the bandages overnight, but it had dried, and seemed not of an alarming quantity. Nolar hastened to brew more knitbone tea.

The sun was well up in the sky by the time she had changed the poultice, applied more healing salve to the deep cut, and divided the rabbit stock between Derren and Elgaret. Nolar ate a little of the rabbit meat herself, together with some journeycake, and allowed herself a bracing cup of herb tea to which she added angelica as a tonic.

Derren's mild fever persisted, but did not seem to have worsened. He had not suffered a night sweat or chills, he assured her when she asked. Nolar was glad to see him alert, his eyes and speech unclouded by the delirium that could attend high fevers.

"It is fortunate, Master Derren," Nolar said, "that you are a strong forester and guide. In our mountains I have seen bones broken in this way with grave consequences. I believe we may hope that your leg will not produce such, not with the healing powers of Master Pruett's knitbone. Should you require an easement for pain, however, I have some syrup of blue poppies, which is effective, although it does induce sleep. Allow me now to present to you our most helpful rescuer, Master Smire, who was hunting nearby when he heard me whistling for the ponies after the landslide."

Smire favored both of them with his insincere smile. " 'Twas fair fortune indeed that wended my path near to thine. My master will be pleased to see thee when we travel to him."

"Who is your master?" asked Nolar idly, wondering if she might have heard the name or seen it in Ostbor's records.

Smire hesitated, looking momentarily flustered. "I doubt thou wouldst recognize the name," he said, smoothly regaining his composure. "My master's work, while keenly pursued and of great worth, has been in so narrow an area that few have heard aught of it. Then, too, we have been so long shut away in enforced idleness due to our debilitation that what little notice he had earned has likely been quite forgotten."

Instead of satisfying Nolar's curiosity, Smire had succeeded in sharpening it. "My late master, Ostbor the Scholar, had a wide correspondence over many years," Nolar observed. "I merely thought that I might have heard or seen your master's name mentioned in Ostbor's archives."

"Tull," said Smire abruptly. "My master is Tull, a puissant scholar whose work should have been praised instead of . . ." He paused, obviously altering what he had been about to say. "Allowed to fall into obscurity," he went on, "for I see from thy face that his name is unknown to thee."

"I fear so, Master Smire," Nolar admitted, "but I cannot claim to be a scholar myself, only the assistant to one."

"As I also labor, dear lady." Smire bent in an extravagant bow. "My days are devoted to dispatching the tedious aspects of life so that my master may be freed for his far more important work."

"No doubt he is well justified in his reliance upon you," Nolar responded, striving not to reveal her unreasonable aversion to Smire. Talking with him, she thought, was rather like fencing with words instead of with swords. She felt that each word she uttered had to be guarded, and wished fervently that Smire would take his unsettling wild boar eyes elsewhere.

Eyes—Nolar's memory suddenly disgorged the missing connection. That expression on Smire's face when he had first gazed on her disfigurement—she realized now what it had been. It was a gloating satisfaction, a smug kind of glee. Smire enjoyed other people's pain and discomfiture.

Nolar remembered where she had previously seen that same expression. Long ago, when she was a child, one of the city boys had deliberately beaten a stray dog nearly to death. She could still picture the look on the boy's face, a glint just like Smire's glowing in his eyes. Nolar had to force herself to relax, to refrain from shrinking away.

A possibly useful idea occurred to Nolar, and she turned to Derren. "We must be grateful, Master Derren, for the good that may issue from unexpected adversity. Although the landslide did injure your leg, your necessary immobility provides us with an opportunity to pursue our discussion of herbs." She smiled brightly at Smire. "During our journey, Master Derren proposed a most useful exchange of knowledge with me. He has been telling me the lore of plants and wildlife of his southern forests, and I have been instructing him in all I have learned of the herbs of my mountains. You are welcome to listen, if you care to. Perhaps in your travels and from your master, you have also learned much that you might share with us."

Without waiting for Smire's comment, and ignoring the initial blank surprise on Derren's face, Nolar plunged ahead, extracting a spray of dried flowers from Pruett's satchel. "I do not believe that I have mentioned this one before, Master Derren. It comes from a shrub or small tree called 'Fringe Hazel.' I have heard the farm folk term it 'Double Seed-spit,' since in season, the two seeds from each pod fly forth with great vigor at the slightest touch, or even by themselves."

Still looking slightly puzzled, Derren nonetheless followed her lead. Easing himself into a more bearable position, he said, "I have seen such shrubs, lady, in our southern mountains. The flowers are bright yellow, are they not, and cling close to the bare twigs?"

"Just so. The bark is what we seek for healing," Nolar went on, handing Derren a neat packet of dried bark strips.

"Extract from the bark is used as an astringent to stop bleeding, and in salves for soothing sprains, such as that swelling of your ankle. I chose to try the knitbone together with oil of garlic on your ankle, however, for such a salve is recommended for more severe injuries."

She glanced surreptitiously at Smire, who was fidgeting with his earring. As Nolar had hoped, a dry discourse on herbs was apparently not Smire's idea of an absorbing pastime. Encouraged, she resumed, "If one stews the knitbone leaves and a bit of root with sugar and blue poppy seedpod sap, one has a highly regarded remedy for cough and chest disorders. I recall that Ostbor once told me of a hill farmer whose wife's old mother had the most distressing cough." The prospect of a long and tedious tale of sick hill folk with multitudinous relatives achieved her aim. Smire suddenly rose to his feet.

"Thy pardon, lady, but I must hie me away to seek more rabbits for thy invalids' broth," Smire declared. "Unless," he added hopefully, "yon forester can be moved this day?"

"No." Nolar shook her head decisively. "I have seldom seen so severe a leg wound. It would be unwise to attempt travel today. Let us see how stands the torn flesh by the morrow."

Smire looked disgruntled. "It is not far to my master's abode. I think I should hasten there upon my way and tell him of thy tribulation. He will want to prepare for thy coming, I am certain. I shall return before night, if I may borrow a pony."

"By all means," said Nolar warmly. "We shall be quite safe here. I have noted the spring yonder whence you have brought water, so I may fetch more as it is needful."

As soon as Smire was well out of view, Nolar knelt beside Derren and pretended to be examining his bandages.

"Why . . ." Derren began to ask, but Nolar cut him short.

"Is there some bleeding on the cloth? Oh, I do hope not.

Let me see it more closely." She bent nearer, and whispered urgently, "We must not be overheard by Smire!"

Derren frowned, but did lower his voice. "Why? Is he not well away by now?"

"He may be, and he may not be," Nolar muttered, then said loudly, "It seems to be only a stain from the leaves in the poultice. Let me see how your ankle has fared since last night."

Derren obligingly bent forward as if anxious to see for himself. "What is the matter, lady?" he asked quietly. "Why do you so fear this Smire?"

Nolar spared him a brief, but genuine smile. "How quick you are. Yes, I do fear Master Smire, and perhaps we should be equally apprehensive of Tull, his master. I freely admit that I have but scant evidence for my misgivings. I saw Smire searching through our baggage when he thought we were all asleep. As soon as I made a deliberate sound, he hastened to busy himself with an innocent task. Other than his evasiveness in telling us his master's name, I confess that I rely upon my inner feelings of disquiet." Nolar hesitated, twisting a strip of spare bandage. "There is something about Smire that repels me. I fear to tell him the whole truth of our situation, especially that we know aught of the Stone of Konnard or that Elgaret is a Witch. I have instead told Smire that a scroll at Lormt cited a healing spring around which an abbey was built in olden times somewhere in these mountains. I said that you were endeavoring to guide us thither to seek aid for Elgaret's head injury, but our travel had been made difficult by the Turning. Smire appeared to accept this tale, but we must guard our tongues whenever he is near."

Derren received her warning without immediate comment. He lay back, his face drawn. Nolar wondered whether she should have confided in him, but decided that she had little choice. Should she have to try to defend herself against Smire, Nolar knew that she would need any additional help she could call upon. If only Derren's legs weren't injured. . . .

Nolar clamped down on that line of thought. Until Derren could move about, they would have to adjust their plans to what he could do, limited though that might be.

Similar thoughts must also have been occurring to Derren, for he said, "So long as I cannot stand or walk, lady, I shall be an extra burden to you. But if you are right in suspecting Smire, perhaps I can still be of some use. I shall try to draw him out in talk, which should not be difficult, for he seems to like hearing himself prattle."

Nolar nodded. "That seems a reasonable plan. In the morning, I can take Elgaret to the spring to bathe, thus leaving the two of you alone. Have you noticed Smire's speech? It may mean naught, but his style of address is oddly antiquated."

Derren didn't seem impressed by that point. "Perchance he comes from an isolated place where current speech is seldom heard. I will talk to Smire . . . carefully," Derren added, before Nolar could object. "It can do no harm to listen to him. We have great need just now of his strength, however we may mislike him or his way of speaking."

Nolar turned away to see to Elgaret, fearing that she had not properly convinced Derren, but hoping that he would be at least cautious in his dealings with Smire.

It was nearly dusk when Smire returned. He saluted Nolar, and showed his teeth in a predatory grin.

"Good fortune for us that I did seek my master," he announced. "He has opened our stores to send thee wine and better viands than yon trail food. He bade me tell thee that he awaits thy arrival with much anticipation, and hopes that the forester's wounds be swiftly healed."

As he talked, Smire unpacked a bountiful store of food: several varieties of dried and sugared fruits, pots of jam, nutmeats, salted fish, dried venison, and flasks of red wine.

"You have provided us with a feast, Master Smire," Nolar said. "We thank you and your master." She hoped that she had successfully masked her sharp prick of suspicion. Where was the bread? All of the things that Smire had brought could have been long stored away; none were truly fresh foods. Nolar didn't know why, but this niggling point bothered her.

Smire did open a leather bag of ground grain to make some griddlecakes on a flat rock by the fire, but Nolar found the one she tasted to be dry and musty, as if the grain were well more than a season old. As she continued to exclaim over and praise the food, she noted that Smire appeared to be savoring a private joke.

Smire was in an expansive mood after their repast, and prompted Nolar and Derren to talk about Lormt and all they had seen there. Curiously, Smire seemed ignorant of Lormt's scholarly reputation. Nolar supposed that Tull would surely be aware of it, if his credentials at all equalled Smire's laudatory estimation of them. She was relieved that throughout the conversation, Derren weighed his words carefully, and gave out little real information. He rambled on about the Turning's damage to Lormt and the many repairs that he had helped to make, but prudently said nothing about Nolar's finding the stone shard. Nolar, in her turn, babbled about Pruett's herbarium and Morfew's fine collection of scrolls from the old times. Smire seemed keenly interested in that latter topic, so Nolar hastened to say that she had been unable to read many scrolls because their antique script was so difficult to decipher.

"My master will be cheered to hear of it, nonetheless," Smire declared, "for the lore of ancient days attracts him mightily." He startled them both with a loud guffaw. "I doubt not that he would make himself the principal scholar at this Lormt of thine, should he travel thither." The thought seemed to amuse Smire hugely, for he chuckled to himself afterwards for some time.

Nolar had thought Smire dreadful enough while he was being serious; seeing him now amused, she decided that he was even more frightening.

"By the by," Smire observed slyly as Nolar cleaned the trenchers, "Master Tull instructed me to bring thee along on the morrow." He held up a hand to forestall Nolar's objections. "I can sling a litter between two of the ponies so that the forester can sit propped with legs outstretched. I shall walk, leading the fore animal, whilst thou dost lead thy companion's pony. We have not far to go, and the way is chiefly clear."

Nolar did not like being hurried, but Smire brushed aside her protests. She was feeling harassed when Derren interrupted.

"Thanks to Master Tull's fine feast, I feel a renewal of strength. Doubtless I can manage on the morrow, if my leg can be kept fairly straight. Besides, I smell snow in the wind—not to fall right away, perhaps, but within a day or so. Would it not be wise, lady, if you proceed as you were suggesting to me, with that bath for your lady aunt early on the morrow? Master Smire can let me help as I can with rigging the litter while you conclude the packing."

Nolar looked doubtfully from Derren to Smire, whose smirk reflected his evident pleasure at the way his plans were being accepted. Still, she thought, Derren was right. The snap in the air could presage snow, and neither Derren nor Elgaret should be exposed overlong to any snowstorm.

Feeling boxed in despite her best efforts, Nolar acquiesced. "Your judgment of weather, Master Derren, has served us well before. I yield to your experience in such matters. If your master has room for us, Master Smire, we should be grateful for the shelter of his roof."

Smire favored them with another extravagant bow. "Master Tull's welcome will likely amaze thee, lady," he asserted, laughing again with private amusement.

In the morning, they breakfasted hastily on the remnants of Tull's feast, then Nolar led Elgaret to the spring to clean away the mud and grime from the landslide and change her clothing. When they returned to the fire, Nolar was surprised by a plaintive call from Derren.

"Lady," he implored, "may I have some of that poppy syrup? My leg feels hot, and the pain is throbbing worse than before."

Nolar scrambled to fetch Pruett's satchel. "It must be diluted somewhat," she said, deeply concerned. "I shall stir a bit into water, then I had best look again at your wound."

As she bent over his leg, Derren leaned close enough to whisper in her ear, "Be sparing with the syrup, lady. I wish to appear befuddled, but be not truly so."

Nolar hoped that she successfully concealed her surprise from Smire, who was fortunately a fair distance away, working on the litter.

"Pray describe your pain, Master Derren," Nolar said loudly, "so that I may determine where I should strengthen my poultice." In an undertone, she added, "Do you need any syrup, or just the pretense of some?"

"The pretense." Derren breathed, then in a louder tone detailed a list of disturbing symptoms.

Nolar did not have to feign a shocked expression. She hoped fervently that Derren was not actually experiencing the pain and sensations he described, for she despaired that she could not alleviate them.

Smire strolled across the camp to peer at Derren's exposed leg, which was truly a daunting sight to any not familiar with wounds.

"What's amiss, lady?" Smire asked. "Can we not travel as we intended?"

Nolar handed Derren a small wooden cup of mallow root syrup, doubting that Smire could distinguish the substitution. Derren drained the cup, and grimaced.

"That may be called a syrup, lady, but it tastes bitter to me," he said.

"It will ease the pain quite soon," Nolar assured him, then turned toward Smire. "Master Derren will likely sleep during our trip because of the poppy syrup he just drank. He says his leg is hot and more painful, therefore it would be wise for us to reach your shelter as soon as may be. If his fever worsens, I must have him abed and safely out of the weather."

Smire flourished his staff. "Fear not, lady! I shall soon have the litter assembled and we may depart whenever thou wilt." He strode back to fasten his makeshift harness, enabling Nolar to dare a brief whispered exchange with Derren, whose eyes were shut and body had slackened as if he were asleep.

"Is your leg worse?" Nolar asked urgently. "I see no undue inflammation or sign of mortification."

"No, no," Derren murmured. "I find your suspicion of Smire justified, that is all. He pressed me too hard for facts he need not know. You are right, lady. He seems not trustworthy."

Nolar made a show of renewing Derren's bandages. "You must appear to be stupefied, then, during our journey. I shall ask Smire to stop frequently at first in order to check your fever. That should persuade him of our deception."

The snow that Derren had predicted began during their midday halt. Nolar "roused" Derren to drink some heated broth, and he looked worried as he tested the snowflakes's texture, rubbing the crystals between finger and thumb.

"I fear this storm will not pass swiftly," he said, shaking his head. "Snow like this can often fall for hours, if not more than a day."

Smire had drawn closer to listen to their exchange. "Then we should hasten onward," he insisted. "It is not much farther. Let us press ahead before the way becomes obscured."

During what seemed an endless afternoon, Nolar trudged after the ponies that bore Derren's litter. Dusk came early, aided by the thickening snowfall. Despite the snow cover, Nolar had noticed for the last league that the earthquake's damage was more pronounced in this area than it had been

in the territory she had previously seen. Vast slabs of rock
had been thrust up from their beds deep beneath the surface.
She was reminded of the tumbled boulders in the Es River,
but on a far grander scale. Whatever trees and groundcover
that might have clothed these hills had been scraped away,
decimated, and buried by the displaced rocks and soil.

Nolar shivered in a swirling gust of wind. She glanced back
at Elgaret, whose body was swaying rhythmically in time
with her pony's steady pace. At least, Nolar thought, Elgaret
was totally unaware of the discomforts of this trip. That
seemed a slight blessing, yet Nolar was glad to identify any
positives in her increasingly numb, exhausting ordeal. Nolar
was mistaken, however, in concluding that Elgaret remained
oblivious. The total sensory isolation that had imprisoned
the Witch for so long was slowly breaking down.

Cold . . . so cold. How could it possibly be so cold in
midsummer? The thoughts crept sluggishly through the
Witch's mind. She was still deaf and essentially blind, even
when her one functioning eye was open, but on the most
basic levels of awareness—sensation of heat-lack and motion—the Witch's mind was beginning to recover incremen-
tally. Where was she? Es Castle was never so cold except
during the worst winter storms. Movement—was she on a
horse? How could that be? So tired. The only warmth in her
darkened world seeped from her Jewel. No . . . no! Somewhere . . . nearby, in the darkness, her mind perceived a
curious glow of Power.

It was tenuous, blurred-edged, as if denying its own existence. But it blazed with potential Power, no matter how
masked or obscured. She was slowly drawing nearer to it.
Soon she would be able to open her eyes and see again . . .
but not just now. So much easier to slip back into the en-
veloping blankness where she had been resting for . . . how
long? No matter—she must regain her strength. There had
been some awful calamity, some draining of every last flicker
of the Council's Power. Her mind shrank from the enormity.

Rest now. Let go. Ease back into the quietness, the soft, dark silence. . . .

Nolar wearily thrust one foot after the other, stumbling and sliding into the tracks pressed out by Smire and the advancing ponies. At first, she was only vaguely aware of the alteration in mental sensation from her shard. Then, with something like the shock of stepping through a crust of ice into the frigid water beneath, Nolar realized that a greater depth of Power was reaching her through her shard. The Stone of Konnard—she must be nearing its actual site! There was no point in seeking it visually; her inner sensitivity would lead her unerringly to the Stone. It was very near. Nolar paused to wonder whether Tull might have stumbled over some scholarly reference in another archive. Could he possibly have located the Stone? Would he know how to use it? She felt certain that if anyone else had attempted to tap the Stone's Power, she would *know*. Nolar paced on, so deeply absorbed in her thoughts that it took a moment before she registered the sound of Smire's call from up ahead, where he had halted the snow-laden litter.

"Lady!" Smire bellowed, striding back toward her. "We have arrived! Now canst thou rest and warm thyself."

Nolar had to clench her teeth to stop them from chattering. "Your news could not be more welcome, Master Smire," she admitted. "My strength is nearly spent."

Smire loomed before her, obviously relishing his position of complete authority. "I shall attend to all," he bragged. "First, I shall carry the Borderer within—the work of a mere instant. I shall then return for thee and thy companion, and lastly see to the ponies. We have a snug space below that can serve as a stable, for it is well protected from this wind." He bustled off through the snow to extract Derren from the litter.

Nolar stood staring dully after him, then shook herself. To come this far and then allow the frost to blight her hands and feet—or Elgaret's—would be inexcusable.

In her pocket, the shard suddenly throbbed with an unmistakable vibrancy. Here! The Stone of Konnard was in this very place . . . and yet Nolar sensed an urgent warning. She must show no sign of her awareness. Even if the name of the Stone were mentioned, she must pretend to be unaffected. Nolar was puzzled by the magnitude of the warning. Could there be some danger to the Stone? That notion seemed odd, yet Nolar felt a confirming pulse from the shard. She must be acutely wary, then, and guard both her words and her actions. Her distrust of Smire, it appeared, might be additionally justified, and could potentially extend to his master. Nolar resolved to be constantly alert. She could not imagine how she might aid the Stone, but she was certain that it must be protected at all costs. For the present, she must cling to every appearance of innocent normality. By the time Smire tramped back, Nolar had maneuvered Elgaret off her pony and was walking her slowly in a circle to stimulate her circulation.

"This way," urged Smire, taking Elgaret by one arm while Nolar steadied the Witch from the other side.

Nolar had a confused impression of cracked stone slabs leaning at all angles, with the wind-blown snow lapping in drifts to conceal any original design of walls or courtyard. They descended a short incline of frozen earth and squeezed between two rough stone pillars. Smire pushed aside a huge animal fur suspended across the entry space. The passage beyond was narrow—only one person at a time could move through it—but it opened abruptly into a square chamber, scantily furnished with only a few low chests, a table, and one chair. A small fire crackled in a corner nook where a natural channel between the rock walls drew out the smoke.

Bemused by the stark bareness of the room, Nolar turned to Smire to ask, "Where is Master Tull?"

"He will receive thee shortly." Smire busied himself settling Elgaret in the one chair. He had placed Derren near the fire on a makeshift pallet formed from the drier parts of his litter.

Derren's eyes were shut, and Nolar judged that he was truly asleep. He was pale, obviously in need of rest, warmth, and solid food. Nolar looked around immediately to locate the cooking arrangements. She could see none.

"If you could fetch in our baggage, Master Smire," Nolar asked, "and direct me to your kitchen, I shall prepare hot food and drink for all of us."

Smire did not respond at once, but fidgeted with his earring. "This fire will have to serve," he asserted irritably. "We may not disturb Master Tull's chamber. I will bring in your baggage and see to the ponies."

As soon as Smire left the room, Nolar hurried to Derren's side. She chafed his icy hands and strove to rouse him. "Master Derren! Wake up!"

Derren blinked, dazed, then focused his attention on the stone walls and low ceiling. In a hoarse voice, he asked, "Where are we, lady?"

"Smire has delivered us to his master's abode," Nolar replied dryly. "It appears somewhat lacking in excessive comforts, but any shelter is welcome. Let me examine your leg and ankle. I fear that you may have been ill-protected in that litter. Smire did not halt often enough to brush away the snow."

"Nay, lady," Derren objected. "I feel scarcely any pain."

"That is my point," Nolar retorted. "Numbness precedes frost damage. Oh, your flesh is very cold . . . but not, I think, truly frozen, thanks be to Neave. If only this feeble excuse for a fire were larger. . . ."

She was interrupted by a rush of cold air, followed by Smire. He dropped the saddlebags in a shower of snow, and bent near the fire to warm his hands.

"Can you bring sufficient wood to build up this fire?" Nolar implored. "Master Derren's legs are severely chilled, and I fear for his wound. The poultice that I applied this morning is quite stiff.''

"Our stocks of fuel here are limited," Smire conceded. "I had intended to cut more wood when I finished hunting, but my encounter with thee intervened.''

"We brought with us from Lormt some bags of charcoal," Nolar said. "I believe that we must search for that now, if there is no warmer space available for us here.''

Smire appeared stung by her remarks. "My master awaits thee within. I wrongly thought thou wouldst prefer to refresh thyself before thy audience, but I bow to thy impatience. I shall announce thee now.'' With a brusque nod, he snatched aside another fur hanging in the far interior corner and stalked through the narrow opening behind it.

"Be sure I shall try to secure warmer quarters for us," Nolar promised Derren.

Smire thrust back the hanging and beckoned peremptorily. "Come," he ordered.

For the first time since Smire had gloated upon seeing her face, Nolar's fingers automatically groped for her concealing scarf. She stood up, deliberately lowering her hand, and approached the passageway. Whatever his reaction to her disfigurement, Nolar decided, Master Tull would have to accept her as she was.

She immediately noticed that the inner chamber was far more impressively furnished, and also distinctly warmer. Two sturdy metal braziers were set at prudent distances from facing wall hangings of finely embroidered fabric. Nolar had scant time to admire her surroundings, however, for her attention was at once drawn to the majestic figure enthroned at the center of the room.

Smire hovered obsequiously to one side. "Mistress Nolar of Meroney, Master," he announced.

Tull's dark eyes glittered from beneath fine arched brows. His thin, austere face was framed by a hooded robe of regal purple. He wore no other adornment except for a heavy chain of dark metal whose intricately worked links reminded Nolar uneasily of Smire's earring.

Nolar met Tull's searching gaze. His features, she thought, were artistically handsome, but the effect was coldly remote, as if he were a marble statue draped in a man's clothing. As he regarded her, for some reason, Nolar felt a strong urge to prostrate herself before him. Annoyed, she nodded curtly instead.

"Master Tull," she acknowledged. "You may perhaps have heard of my late master, the scholar Ostbor."

Tull gracefully lifted a long-fingered hand from his chair's ornately carved arm. "I keenly regret, dear lady, that both thy name and thy master's are unknown to me. I have been . . . cut off from all other scholars for a great while. But let us speak of thee. Smire has informed me of thy most misfortunate accident. I rejoice that I may offer thee my modest hospitality."

Tull's voice, Nolar thought, was like a rivulet of dark mountain honey, flowing smooth and deeply sweet. A voice to beguile the ear, to . . . As her right hand slipped unthinkingly into her pocket, her fingers touched her stone shard, and her hazed wits were abruptly jolted by an acidly intrusive thought: *entrap*. Tull's voice was meant to beguile and to entrap the unwary listener.

Startled, Nolar clutched the shard in reflex, and jerked up her drooping head to meet Tull's penetrating regard. What she saw left her momentarily speechless, for there were *two* figures occupying the imposing chair, the outline of one figure overlaying and blurring the other, as if two bodies strove simultaneously to occupy the same space.

Tull seemed instantly aware of her distracted disquiet. He leaned forward, projecting the warmest sympathy. "Whatever is wrong, lady? Art thou ill?"

Nolar ignored the specious voice. "Which are you?" she demanded bluntly. "Only one image can convey your true aspect. Have done with illusion, sir, for I am not deceived."

As before in Lormt, Nolar sensed that energetic spurt of pure conviction emanating from outside herself, pulsing from her fragment of the Stone of Konnard.

Tull frowned, his face darkening with a flush of anger and suspicion. "What meanest thou, woman?" he hissed.

"I see two forms occupying your chair," Nolar said firmly. "I think, sir, that you are not merely a scholar as Smire has said. I think you must deal in illusions and magic, although I knew not that any man nowadays could do so."

"Estcarp!" Tull spat the name, as if it were bitter poison on his tongue. "I was lured into weak sympathy by thy pitiful face, but now I see thy true blood—Witch!"

Nolar reeled back as Tull surged to his feet, his eyes blazing. In Nolar's view, the double images rippled and ran together like hot wax spilling down a candle, then stabilized into one solid figure. *This* was the real Tull—Nolar was dreadfully certain of that.

Tull's elegant robe remained unchanged, but had diminished in size to fit a much smaller-boned man, no taller than Nolar herself. His pale skin had lost its noble marble-like sheen; it now looked as if Tull had been indeed hidden away from the sun's fair light for long years in some unhealthy cave. Nolar had an unreasonable suspicion that touching Tull would be like touching the cold, clammy belly of yesterday's fish. Fish. . . .

Quite unexpectedly, a memory from Nolar's early childhood commanded her attention. The dissatisfied, furtive expression on Tull's narrow face exactly mirrored that of the fishmonger who used to scratch at the back door of Nolar's father's townhouse kitchen. The cook of that time had accused him of providing less than fresh goods, and also of giving short weight. There was little actual physical resemblance between the two men, but the glint of smoldering hatred in the eyes, the air of calculated malice—in those, the two were remarkably similar. However much Tull might desire his audience to be awed by his imposing presence, Nolar knew that she could never again look at him without thinking, "dishonest fishmonger."

"You are no mere scholar," she repeated. "You are . . ." The proper word occurred to her, and she made it a ringing accusation. "You are a *mage.*"

"I—no *mere* scholar, but a mage?" Tull's honied voice had vanished along with his earlier, more aesthetic exterior. His true voice grated on the ear, especially now as it soared to a screech. "On thy knees to me, Witch! I am Tull the Adept, Tull the Great One!" He flung up his hands, roaring syllables that resonated throughout the chamber. Streams of dark red flame erupted from his fingertips.

One part of Nolar shrank back, appalled; the steadier, inner core of her clung to the solid strength of her shard. She found herself calmly noting that despite the lashes of flame so near her face, the air was no warmer. If Tull's fire provided no honest heat, Nolar reasoned, it must therefore be an illusion. She braced her knees, standing her ground.

"How unfortunate, sir," she observed, "that these bountiful flames of your conjuring cannot warm us, for my two ailing companions could benefit from more heat than you allow in your outer chamber."

Instantly, the false flames disappeared. Tull swung toward Smire, who scurried backward several paces.

"Bring them in," snarled Tull. "Let me see what other attractive guests thou hast inveigled me to shelter beneath my roof."

Smire scuttled out, then hastily backed in, carrying Elgaret still seated in her chair. In another moment, he dragged Derren into view by simply hauling his pallet across the uneven stone floor.

Tull glared first at Derren, then peered more keenly at Elgaret.

"Thou hast quite outdone thyself, Smire," he remarked in a deceptively mild tone that rapidly swelled to a bellow of raw anger. "I behold now before me a useless cripple and yet *another* pestilential Witch!"

Smire's normally swarthy face paled, and his mouth opened and shut twice before he found any voice to defend himself. "Master—I did not know—I swear to thee by my earring! I would never . . ."

Tull silenced him with an impatient gesture. "Have done! Whatever thy beliefs or intentions, thou hast beset me with this trio." He leaned on one elbow and stared at Elgaret. "Something is awry with this old Witch. What is it, eh? She reeks of former Power, but is now as empty as a rimless cask."

Pressed beyond endurance by exhaustion, fear, and now open insult to Elgaret, Nolar strode to the Witch's side, her temper flaring. "What business is it of yours?" she snapped.

Tull revealed uneven teeth in a thoroughly unpleasant smile. "So the disfigured one has spirit, and would defend her companions? I shall tell thee what my business is, Witch. I was unjustly immured here, but now I am free to resume my activities. Thou shalt aid me. Possibly I may also draw upon the blind-eyed crone."

Tull's words made Nolar's flesh crawl. Ostbor had told her that untold ages ago, certain males were believed to have wielded Power, but Nolar had never imagined that any person posing as a scholar could be as odiously repulsive as Tull . . . or as obviously dangerous.

Nolar unconsciously clenched her hands, the left still in view, the pocketed right hand concealed, grasping her shard. "I shall never aid you to accomplish *anything,*" she vowed.

Tull gave a derisive laugh, and sat back, gripping the arms of his ornate chair. "Behold defiance, Smire. I do not brook defiance, Witch—heed this, my sole warning. Any who dare to oppose me shall feel my wrath." He drew in a whistling breath, his nostrils pinched in remembered rage. "They left me this . . . this trifling chair! They said I deserved 'a certain state.' I shall show them with whom they deal! This chair shall be my new throne, and they shall cower before it, begging for my mercy."

Nolar stared at him, an awful suspicion burgeoning in her mind. His and Smire's archaic speech patterns, their antique clothing, their long-stored food—all minor details, but they suddenly suggested a plausible theory that Nolar quailed from examining. Still, she had to know.

"You say you were immured," she said hesitantly. "Can you tell me aught of this former injustice, for word of it never reached Ostbor?"

Anxious to regain his master's approval, Smire hastened to boast of Tull's accomplishments. "My master alone rediscovered the legendary Stone of Konnard," Smire crowed. "By perilous effort, he tapped its Power and wrought great wonders. All other adepts marveled, and envied his prowess."

Nolar deliberately forced herself to remain still. Her worst fears were now confirmed: the Stone of Konnard had indeed fallen into Tull's grasp. She would have to try to displace him . . . but how? Tull was evidently gratified by Smire's praise.

At the mention of other envious adepts, Tull's thin mouth twisted in contempt. "Fools!" He ran his fingers over the broad-linked chain across his chest in a motion curiously reminiscent of Smire's habit of caressing his earring.

The closer Nolar focused on those dull black links, the more her gaze recoiled. There was something unclean about Tull's chain that had nothing to do with its physical surface. Nolar sensed that it was inherently evil, that it had been deliberately fashioned for evil purposes.

"Those envious adepts," Nolar prompted, "were they the ones who banished you? It was not Estcarp's Council of Witches?"

Tull chopped one hand in a dismissive gesture. "Some of thy meddling fellow hags thrust noses into my affairs long since, to their own cost, but I know of no Council of theirs. Nay—I was cravenly seized by the other mages. Lackwits!

Cowards! They had no stomach to dare what I dared, to risk all for the utmost prize: Control!" He held out his hand, clenching the fingers as if squeezing a soft fruit down to its solid stone.

Stone—the word vibrated in Nolar's mind. Before she thought, she blurted, "But the Stone of Konnard was meant for life—for healing."

As quickly as a striking snake, Tull lunged forward in his chair. "What knowest thou of the Stone?"

Nolar's mind raced. She must divert Tull with a partial truth. "As Master Smire just said, the Stone is acclaimed in legend. I have seen it written at Lormt that great works of healing were wrought by the Power of the Stone."

"Drivel!" Tull thumped the arm of his chair in disdain. "The Stone is *mine* to direct as I will. It has depths none suspected save I. Those fools who thwarted me guessed only the merest beginnings of what could be achieved by an adept unfettered by small-minded doubts and fears." Tull thought-fully surveyed his captives. "I begin to see a way to employ thee and thy feeble companions for the achievement of my rightful revenge. Thou shalt join thy Power with mine, Witch, and together we shall extract whatever we may from those two."

Nolar imposed herself between him and her friends. "Never," she said, and although her voice was low, her deter-mination was as evident as if she had shouted the word.

Tull chuckled, while Smire rubbed his earring and smirked knowingly.

"Smire," Tull purred, "I do believe that this Witch re-quires a demonstration of my influence upon the Stone of Konnard."

Tull rose and lifted his arms, looking, Nolar thought, rather like a scrawny bat incongruously swathed in purple velvet. She had no warning of his intent, but the instant he uttered a spate of harsh sounds, all feeling deserted Nolar's limbs. She could still breathe and blink her eyes, but she could not move or speak.

Tull pointed at Derren, who was evidently similarly paralyzed. Nolar could see the torment in Derren's eyes as he strove to move, but could not. Smire threw aside the pallet's coverings, exposing Derren's legs. He plucked Derren's dagger from its belt sheath and slid it inside his own boot top.

Tull's nose wrinkled at the faint scent of Nolar's herbs. "Cast off the Witch's bindings and vegetable trash," he ordered. "I would see the extent of these supposed injuries."

Tears of outrage and sympathetic pain blurred Nolar's eyes as Smire callously ripped away her careful bandaging and discarded her poultice.

Tull bent forward, his cruel face alight with interest. "Ah, quite a severe wound on the one leg, and a swollen ankle as well—all the better. Regard this, Witch!" He gestured at Derren, reciting some resonant sounds.

To Nolar's horror, the normal skin color bleached out of Derren's legs, to be gradually replaced by a dirty gray hue. Derren stared down, stricken, as his own body appeared to be suffering some awful transformation that he could not prevent.

Tull fluttered his fingers at Nolar and spoke more commands. "Move now, Witch. Behold the effects of my arts, and know the extent of my Power."

Released, Nolar stumbled to Derren's side. Her trembling fingers lightly touched the unnatural grayness of Derren's wounded leg before Nolar snatched them back.

"This is stone, not flesh!" she exclaimed, longing to be able to reject the evidence of her fingers and eyes.

"How acutely sensitive thou art to the obvious," Tull taunted her. "Thy acquaintance with the Stone of Konnard must be slight indeed if thou didst not know its chief attribute: to transform living flesh to its own form."

Nolar surveyed him, her revulsion evident. "To turn a great Power for healing to ends such as this is evil beyond measure. You should not have been immured; you should have been destroyed."

Tull bared his teeth. "Silence! I have no interest in thy witless judgments. Heed me—this spell may be reversed. What is now stone may once again be flesh . . . provided that thou wilt submit to my bidding."

Nolar forced herself to touch the cold, rigid surface of what had been Derren's leg. She could not condemn him to live thus, as a bipartite monster.

Nolar did not realize that tears were coursing down her cheeks as she raised her eyes to meet Tull's. "What must I do," she asked bitterly, "for you to spare my companions?"

"Ah, thou art not so witless after all," said Tull, rubbing his hands together. "Thou canst recognize a Power far greater than thine own. Hearken, Witch! I have preparations to make: high matters of which thou art ignorant. Smire shall attend me; thou shalt abide here until I require thee in the Chamber of the Stone. There we shall address the Stone and commence my revenge."

"You said that the spell on Master Derren's legs could be reversed," Nolar stubbornly reminded him.

"A trifle." Tull gestured as he turned to leave, and Derren cried out in sudden agony.

Nolar knelt beside Derren, stroking his legs, concentrating with all her might to see or feel any restoration. It came slowly, but the hard gray surface gradually softened to warm flesh. Nolar laughed with relief to see some slight bleeding in the deepest cleft of the wound.

"Hold fast, Master Derren," she exhorted him. "I shall fetch my satchel and replace your bandages."

Derren's mind still reeled from the shock of watching part of his own body turn to stone before his eyes. The pain of the return to flesh had been keener than any that he had ever felt, and he had nearly fainted from it. There was something odd now about his legs, though he couldn't quite define it. He thought it best not to speak of it until he had time to consider it privately. He lay back, spent, as Nolar worked hastily to replace the poultice and secure new bandages. With a great effort, Derren opened his eyes and scanned the room. Both Smire and Tull had gone, but Derren still kept his voice low, for Nolar's ears only.

"Lady," he apologized, "I fear that we have fallen among ill company."

To his astonishment, Nolar laughed heartily. "Oh, Master Borderer," she said, as soon as she caught her breath, "I fancy that description is without doubt the mildest and most lenient that could be applied to our hosts. Pray excuse my laughing—I am somewhat giddy with weariness." She swiftly recovered her usual serious mien. "You are, of course, painfully correct. We are sorely threatened, and I must confess that I know not how we may escape. Perhaps we may seize some chance opportunity. We must surely strive to remain ever alert, and guard our tongues. Tull is a dire foe, and Smire his willing helper." She rose to her feet, brushing stone dust from her skirt. "While we may, we should likely renew our strength by eating. Let me attend to Elgaret, then, if I am allowed, I shall hasten back with food for you."

As Nolar took Elgaret's arm to help the Witch stand, she almost cried out. For the first time since their encounter at her father's house so long before, Nolar felt a responsive squeeze from Elgaret's hand.

Covering her shock with a cough, Nolar managed to say, "Come, Aunt," and led the Witch out into the deserted anteroom, pulling the chair after them with her free hand.

Once Elgaret was again seated, Nolar leaned close, as if to adjust the Witch's robes.

Elgaret spoke in the barest whisper. "Danger, Sister-in-Power! We stand in frightful peril." She paused, as if reticent to speak the words that had to be spoken. "I sense the presence of a Dark One nearby, and also that of a lesser minion. They are of the Shadow—beware of them!"

Nolar's fussing with Elgaret's gown gave her a sudden

glimpse of the Witch's Jewel, and she gasped at the sight. The formerly dead crystal was now softly pulsing with a greenish glow.

Elgaret nodded fractionally. "Yes, my Jewel once again serves me, but I dare not wield it unless there is no other choice. Any use of Power would draw *his* attention. It is wiser for me to continue to feign dysfunction." Her whisper faltered. "There is something of great Power here. I feel it . . . old, very old . . . touched by evil, yet not itself evil."

"It is the Stone of Konnard," Nolar whispered back. "It is here, as we are, at the mercy of Tull, an evil mage, and Smire, his helper. The Stone was used in ancient days for healing, but Tull has defiled it, drawing upon it to turn flesh to stone."

Elgaret shuddered at this awful news, but made no comment as Nolar hurried on. "I took you to Lormt, to seek help for your injury, and found there ancient, fragmentary word of the Stone which set us upon our quest to find it. Master Derren . . ." Nolar paused. She dared not try to explain her suspicions of Derren now; besides, she felt convinced that in this dangerous place, Derren was their only possible ally. Nolar's inner impulse was to trust Derren, and she sensed no contrary warning from her shard to challenge that judgment.

"Derren," she resumed, "is a trustworthy Borderer who helped us travel safely from near Es City to Lormt, and then agreed to escort us in search of the Stone of Konnard. Two days ago, we were beset by a rockslide that broke his leg most pitifully." Her voice shook as she briefly described Tull's hideous spell intended to coerce Nolar's assistance in his scheme for revenge against those mages who had banished him and Smire.

Afraid to linger further in covert speech, Nolar turned aside to put a kettle on the fire. She brought Elgaret an herbal drink, and stirred some warm water into a bowl of fruit paste to liquefy it.

As she held the spoon for Elgaret, the Witch said quietly,

"This Stone of Power belongs to an age far in the past. So, too, we have always believed, did the Dark Ones, dreaded scourges upon the land. How can it be that I sense one here? Such are not supposed to exist now."

Nolar felt the renewed grip of her daunting fears concerning Tull and Smire. "Lady, I have a horrid answer to that riddle. Both Tull and Smire speak in an archaic style, consistent with their clothing. The food they have shared with us has been long in storage, none of it fresh. Smire knew naught of Lormt, and Tull just told me that he knew of no Council of Witches." She stopped to draw a steadying breath. "A scholar of Lormt told us that there had been a previous Turning of mountains, a thousand years or more in the past. Some great evil, he said, had thus been walled away from Estcarp by the raising of the eastern peaks, and indeed all thought of that very direction was deliberately blocked from future generations of the Old Race. You may think me crazed, but I fear that Tull and Smire *belong* to that past time, that they were among the evil forces to be shut away by that First Turning. I suspect that your Council's Turning of these southern mountains against Karsten must have so displaced the earth that Tull and Smire were thereby freed from their immurement."

"But the Dark One and his helper do not know of the lapse in time," mused Elgaret. "You have given me much to think upon. I caution you to contain your speculations until we can be more certain. I dare not use my Jewel, as I said, but the Power from that Stone nearby beats upon me. I sense great stores of knowledge locked within it. It is very strange, but the Power of the Stone seems somehow constrained, bound up, almost muffled. Go now, and care for the Borderer. We three must aid one another if we can, for our lives and more are at stake here."

Nolar gathered up a flask and pouches of fruit and dried meat and hurried back to Derren.

"Did I hear you speaking to someone?" he asked anxiously.

Nolar hesitated. Should she tell him that Elgaret had recovered her wits? But if Derren were truly a spy from Karsten, would he not likely be dismayed rather than cheered to know that the Witch had been restored to her Power? Besides, if Tull threatened Derren again, Derren could not reveal what he did not know. For the present, it seemed wise to try to keep Elgaret's secret.

"It was only my voice," Nolar said. "As you know, I often talk to my aunt while I feed her and care for her needs. Here is some dried meat, if you can eat it. We may have little other chance to eat for a while."

Smire abruptly thrust his way into the chamber. "Where is the other Witch?" he demanded, but did not wait for a reply, striding instead to the doorway to look into the outer room.

"I took her thence to feed and care for," Nolar explained. "You would be kind to move her back, for it is warmer here."

Smire leered at her. "Kind? A fair word, seldom applied to me, Witch. Still, it is easier to watch all one's captive birds in one cage, is it not?" Laughing at his joke, he brought Elgaret back in her chair. She had shut her eyes, and looked as serenely withdrawn as before.

"Hearken to me," Smire commanded. "Master Tull finds that his spells require the sun's rays, so we must wait out the night. Thou shalt sleep here, where I may keep watch."

"And Master Tull?" asked Nolar. "Where shall he sleep?"

"That is naught of thy concern," Smire retorted, then had second thoughts. "But what matter if I do tell thee? To my master alone belongs the solitary vigil by the Stone, Witch. We lesser wights must bide apart until summoned." He sniffed the air ostentatiously. "Hast thou not prepared hot food?"

Nettled, Nolar replied, "Our supplies are scant. I have moistened some fruit for Elgaret, and Master Derren has eaten the last of our dried meat. If you have other food to be heated, pray fetch it."

Smire grinned, like a sharp-fanged weasel. "Give me that other dried fruit. What else hast thou to set before a hungry man? Of course, once the Stone is fully revived, we shall have no need for food here at all."

Nolar's heart lurched. Elgaret had said that she sensed strange constraints on the Stone. Could it be that Tull's mastery of the Stone was actually less than he claimed? Why else would he require additional Power from Nolar and her friends? She busied herself setting out the remnants of their food.

"There is a bit of meal," she said, "and some nuts, I think . . . and, yes, a pot of wild plum jam. The journeycake was broken in the rockslide, but some fragments are still edible."

As Smire wolfed down an alarming proportion of the food, Nolar tried to probe for useful information. "You said that the Stone must be revived. But I thought that Master Tull had already drawn freely upon it to . . . impress Master Derren."

"Works better in sunlight," mumbled Smire, his mouth full. Nolar handed him one of the wine flasks that Tull had sent them on the trail. Smire downed most of its contents in two gulps.

Nolar suddenly recalled Morfew's voice reading aloud from the inscribed cloth. " 'So long as the light of the sun cannot fall upon it, shall all be safe.' " Ostbor had told Nolar very little regarding things of the Shadow. As Elgaret had just said, such perils were supposed to be confined to the far past, safely forgotten. Only . . . Nolar's spirit cringed as she had to accept what was being thrust upon her. If she was right in her awful guess, then Tull and Smire *were* from the far past.

But that part about the light of the sun—it seemed perversely backwards. Light was supposed to be the opposing force to the Shadow and all its evil trappings. If the sun's light were required for the Stone of Konnard to loose its Power, then it *must not* have become wholly a thing of the Shadow. And yet, Nolar was certain that Tull intended to use the Stone for evil ends. What could she do? What could any of them do?

Elgaret had her Witch Jewel, but surely its Power was miniscule compared to that of the Stone of Konnard. Her own shard had been cut from the larger Stone, and Nolar could feel it in her pocket, gently pulsing with warmth. So long as that source of strength sustained her, perhaps all was not yet lost. If only she knew more! Nolar felt sure that a true master of the Stone could expel Tull, defeat him utterly, and restore the Stone to its true purpose: healing.

She forced herself to look casually at Smire. He seemed to be half-asleep, the wine flask lolling slackly between his fingers. Could she dare try to ease Derren's dagger out of Smire's boot top? No.

Smire yawned and dropped the empty flask on the floor. "Best that thou rest thyself, Witch," he taunted her. "Master Tull will likely require all of thy energy on the morrow."

Nolar unpacked their spare blankets and settled Elgaret at a safe distance from one of the braziers, then rolled herself in her cloak and lay down near Derren.

Smire slyly glanced around, and appropriated Tull's great chair for himself. To Nolar's dismay, Smire now looked wide awake. He drew Derren's dagger from his boot and proceeded to carve notches on a segment of wood that he had broken away from Derren's litter frame.

Nolar despised her helplessness. She believed that Derren would try to defend her and Elgaret as best he could, but his only weapons had been lost in the rockslide or seized by Smire. With his legs injured, Derren certainly couldn't leap up and hope to overcome Smire by surprise.

Troubled, Nolar squirmed within her cloak as the cold seeped up from the floor. With her eyes shut, she was more aware that her shard's pulsing had changed to a more constant presence, almost a steady glow in her mind, as if it were a source of mental light. As Nolar concentrated on that effect, she was startled to sense a second "light" in the surrounding darkness. It was a harder light, somehow more brittle, crystalline—of course!

It must be Elgaret's Jewel. But . . . there was a *third* gleam in the mind-space. It was erratic, undirected, erupting in little leafy-green spurts. Surely it could not emanate from Smire. Nolar cautiously tried to probe where Smire was, and was rewarded by a mental impression of such deadly cold lightlessness that her whole being recoiled. No, that third spark of mental light had to be coming from . . . Derren.

Before Nolar could reach out, tentatively, toward it, a sickening vibration twanged along her nerves. Tull. The mage had to be focusing his Power on the Stone of Konnard. As her mind grew more attuned to the subtleties of this insubstantial inner realm of Power, Nolar could sense, if only obliquely, the broad thrusts of Tull's technique. He was addressing the Stone of Konnard, exhorting it as if it were a living mind to be persuaded. He was coaxing, wheedling, cajoling. Nolar wanted to cry out, "NO! Do not listen! He plans to thieve your Power and use it for ill!" Her very impulse to warn was beaten back by the unheeding pressure of Tull's spells. Nolar was mentally voiceless, stricken minddumb, just as she had been physically paralyzed by Tull's earlier spell. Unbidden, a vision slid into her mind of a great sphere of dull gray stone rolling inexorably forward. Although the shining essence of her life, Elgaret's, and Derren's lay exposed before it, the stone ground onward. Despair and blackness swept over Nolar, afflicting her with repose without rest and sleep without dreams.

Nolar was awakened by Smire, who roughly shook her by the shoulder.

"Arise, Witch!" Smire ordered. "This day thou art required to serve my master in all that he demands. Nay, do not tarry to feed the hag. I am to bring all three of thee to my master without delay."

Derren was lying still, either genuinely asleep or feigning stupor. Nolar longed for a private word with Derren, but Smire scooped up the Borderer in his arms.

"Follow me," Smire commanded. "Lead the hag thyself. Hurry!"

Nolar anxiously eased Elgaret to her feet. The Witch squeezed her hand in covert reassurance, still maintaining her outward appearance of oblivious withdrawal.

Smire preceded them through a narrow passageway barely illuminated by faint early dawn light seeping in from beyond. Nolar had no chance to whisper to Elgaret, for Smire kept glancing back to be sure she was following closely.

No furred or fabric hanging shielded the opening into the Chamber of the Stone. Huge slabs of rock flanked the entrance, one tilted well out of vertical. Nolar assumed that the Turning had shifted the slabs. When she moved into the chamber itself, she saw just how the Turning had everything to do with the literal exposure of the Stone of Konnard. Ample light illuminated the Stone, because the Turning had displaced and splintered the roof slabs, opening the chamber to the cold, pale sky. The light of the sun, she realized, was indeed once more able to fall directly upon the Stone.

It loomed in the center of the chamber, a tapered mass of stone, perhaps seven feet high at its peak, widening to five or more feet at its base, where it was over three feet thick. It reminded Nolar of drawings she had seen of ancient shields made to protect the warrior's entire body. Its surface matched that of her shard, smoothed, even polished, basically cream and white in color, veined with dark green and some spangled streaks of crystalline material that instantly brought the Witch's Jewel to mind.

As soon as she stepped within the chamber, Nolar knew exactly where her shard had been chiseled away—down on the left, near the back of the base. Somehow, she had expected that the Stone would reclaim its fragment, but she felt no attraction drawing her shard to the main mass. Nolar was, however, keenly aware of the vast store of Power resident in the actual Stone of Konnard. Her shard projected only the slightest hint of its parent's puissance. She could have stood for hours, gazing at the intricate patterns lacing beneath the clear, polished surface, but Smire, having stretched Derren out on the rough stone floor, grasped Nolar's arm and drew her to one side.

Seizing Elgaret by both arms, Smire pushed her down to sit on a stone block that had fallen down from the shattered roof. There were no chairs or furniture in this chamber, except for one low table of black wood set squarely in front of the Stone.

Nolar glanced curiously at the three objects lying on the table, gasped, and wrenched her gaze away.

Smire saw her aversive reaction and laughed. "Thou dost not care for Master Tull's implements, eh, Witch?"

Nolar merely shook her head, not trusting herself to speak. The three items should have been innocuous enough: a pierced metal hand bell, a long-bladed dagger with an ornate hilt, and a small brazier containing only a handful of coals. But each of them was made of the dull black metal that so offended Nolar's every fiber. Their aspect was so totally evil that Nolar viewed them with both mental and physical loathing. A thought beat frantically in her mind: if that hideous bell should sound, she feared that she would go mad.

Smire waved a hand casually at the objects, but Nolar noticed that he made no move to touch any of them.

"Master Tull exerted considerable effort to summon these needful things," Smire boasted. "When we were dispatched hither," he said, grimacing at remembered injury, "all of his magical implements were denied to him. They allowed only the furnishings of the one chamber to accompany us."

So that explained the scarcity of furniture and supplies, Nolar thought. Her stomach twisted within her as she realized that the food that Tull had sent to them was not from last year's storage, but had truly been over a thousand years preserved by magic.

Tull himself suddenly swept into the chamber, making up for his lack of physical presence by an aggressive energy of movement. "My hour has come," he proclaimed. "It is time to commence!"

Despite his tone of supreme confidence, Nolar thought that he looked overstrained. His eyes had a feverish sheen like those of a sick man after a wasting illness.

Tull took his place before the table, running a finger lovingly down the dark blade of the dagger. "The night was long," he said, "but I have employed it to splendid account. I have made a Seeking, and I find a most heartening absence of all those meddlesome vermin against whom lately I strove. I am thus totally free to pursue my original goal, the achievement of which they so cravenly prevented before."

Nolar drew a deep breath, and said quietly, "A thousand years and more have passed since your time. All has changed. A second Turning of the mountains has broken the spell that imprisoned you. Those who bested you are indeed gone."

She had not thought that Tull could turn any more pale, but his face blanched at this news.

Smire was similarly shocked. "A thousand years?" he whispered hoarsely. "Master. What shall we do?"

Tull drew himself up, his expression hardening into a fanatical mask. "So *that* is why I cannot sense them: they have all perished!" He gave a wild shriek of laughter. "Dost thou not see, Smire? I am now the only Great One left. This world is *mine*. I have but to use the Stone to open a Gate, and my Power shall know no limits!"

Tull stabbed a finger at the brazier, which burst into murky flame. As Tull chanted, Nolar felt again the horrid paralysis deadening her limbs. With her last conscious strength, she slid her shard out of her pocket, clutching it in her right hand. Its warmth pulsed through her palm, then spread up her arm. The dead numbness retreated. Could the shard's Power block Tull's spell? Would there be time for it to restore feeling to the rest of her body?

Tull gestured at Elgaret, who rose slowly to her feet. Her left hand reached toward her throat, and suddenly her Jewel blazed openly on its chain, outside her robe. Smire looked startled, but Tull seemed untroubled, evidently assuming that he was still in full control of events.

Nolar wondered whether the Witches of Tull's time had possessed Jewels, and if not, suspected that Tull might well be underestimating Elgaret as an opponent.

Derren, too, amazingly, was moving, raising his body to a sitting position. Without the internal support of her shard, Nolar could not understand how Derren was able to move at all, yet his right hand was creeping up to his throat.

Tull's eye caught the movement, and he paused to peer at the Borderer. "What have we here? Another amulet? Have it out, then," he demanded, "where we may see it."

Derren struggled to extract a silver leaf-shaped medallion hung on a chain around his neck. His hand fell back, spent by the exertion.

Tull dismissed the amulet with a scornful snap of his fingers. "The token of some forest godling, I've no doubt. Little good it will do thee here! Disturb me no further; I approach the heart of this spell."

He was interrupted by a calm, decisive voice. "Not so."

It was Elgaret, but an Elgaret of such imposing presence that Nolar could feel the Power radiating from her. The Witch's eyes were open, one clear, the other dimmed, and her hands moved freely to enfold her Jewel.

"You are out of your proper time, Mage," Elgaret said firmly. "Both you and your wicked schemes belong to the far past."

Enraged, Tull audibly ground his teeth, then spat at Elgaret, "Who art thou to dare defy *me?*"

Elgaret raised her Jewel. In a ringing voice, she declared,

"I am Estcarp! I stand for the Light, with the Light, and these, my companions, are held within the protection of the Light." Her Jewel flared brilliantly.

Smire cringed away from the dazzling glare, and even Tull flinched, but after a moment's recovery, Tull scrabbled on the table behind him and snatched up the dagger.

"No feeble Witch can stand before the full might of the Shadow," Tull roared. "There is no protection against that everlasting Dark which shall enshroud all things. Here, Smire. Produce for me the lifeblood of that man!"

Smire obediently extended his hand, and curled his fingers around the dagger's hilt.

"Wait!" said a sudden clear voice. It was Derren, obviously fully alert. "I have aught to say upon this proposal." To the complete astonishment of the company, he rose to his feet. "I can commend your petrifying spell in this one regard," he observed. "When my flesh was restored from being stone, so too were my broken bones. The Stone of Konnard, it seems, is still a healing force, no matter what ill you may have intended it to inflict upon me."

With a snarl, Smire threw himself at Derren, but the Borderer, evidently acquainted with knife fighting, side-stepped Smire's initial thrust and danced away, looking about for some object he could use in his own defense.

With frenzied gestures, Tull resumed intoning his spell. Elgaret countered with a chant of her own, as blinding flares of light pulsed from her Jewel.

Nolar found her body able to move, yet constrained from without, as if she were trying to swim through a vat of thick syrup. She extended her right hand, openly displaying her shard, which throbbed with a creamy light of its own, partaking of the main Stone's lustrous glow.

Smire, meanwhile, had maneuvered Derren into a corner, and now raised the cruel dagger for a mortal thrust. Tull and Elgaret fell silent, each evidently absorbed in exerting the full extent of will to influence the uneven conflict.

As Smire lunged forward, Derren touched his amulet and loudly spoke a Name. His silver medallion blazed brighter than an array of a hundred full moons. Smire shielded his eyes with his free hand, then cried out in horror as the evil dagger twisted out of his grasp, turned in the air, and buried itself up to the hilt in Smire's chest. Smire's body fell, twitching, to the floor, and before their eyes, slowly crumbled inward upon itself. Cheated for over a thousand years of its due processes, time was compressing Smire into the dust that he should naturally have been. His equally ancient clothing also fell away, suffering the same fate as its owner. Appalled, Derren gazed down at the residue, unable to move.

Tull shrieked more words and reached toward the abominable bell. Nolar, desperate to prevent its sounding, searched for any means to distract Tull. Her childhood image of the fishmonger formed abruptly in her mind, and Nolar simply thrust it at Tull, together with the whole tangle of her associated memories and feelings. She poured into her untaught Sending all of her pent-up fears, frustrations, and loathing for what he had done to Derren and what he had threatened to wreak upon her defenseless world.

Tull staggered back a step as Nolar's Sending struck him. To be compared to a . . . a fishmonger! He—Tull the Dark One, Tull the Great! It was *intolerable*. He would blast the impudent Witch where she stood . . . but the rhythm of his spell had been fatally disrupted.

"Stand with me, Sister," Elgaret called out. "Wield your Stone to free its parent of this unclean tormentor."

Nolar raised her shard and focused her mind with all her might upon the gleaming Stone of Konnard.

Tull froze, indecisive. His moment to seize total advantage had passed. A glaze of fear began to show in his eyes.

Elgaret chanted, the light from her Jewel spearing Tull so that he writhed in its glare. Nolar could see that his hand, thrust out toward the accursed bell was no longer moving, and gradually, his pale skin was turning gray. She had seen that same strange hue once before, when Derren's legs had been transformed to stone. Nolar stared at Tull's face. His expression was set in a rigid mask of malevolent spite. Even as she watched, his features grayed, his eyes dulled, and Nolar knew with utter certainty that Tull's petrification spell had been turned against his own flesh. Tull had become a statue of lifeless rock. For a moment, his purple robes hung slack, then darkened and shriveled into thready rags.

Slowly, the unearthly radiance faded from the Stone of Konnard. The almost unbearable degree of Power that had oppressed the chamber's very air now quietly drained away.

With a sigh, Elgaret lowered her Jewel. "Sister," she said, "we have wrought well this day. Master Derren, I urge you to find a suitable bludgeon and demolish that unspeakable form."

Once again master of his own body, Derren had been flexing his arms. He looked at the gray mass that had been Tull, and exclaimed, "With pleasure, lady!" He cast about the chamber until he found a metal torch bracket which Tull must have used during the night hours. Wrapping his hands in a fold of his tunic, Derren pushed against Tull's statue until, overbalanced, it crashed to the floor, one outstretched arm shattering upon impact. With powerful blows, Derren pulverized the statue until only small chunks and dust were left.

Elgaret regarded the debris with distaste. "If there be such a thing in this place as a broom, let us find it and remove this refuse."

Nolar recalled a sturdy bound-twig whisk that Wessell had insisted on packing, and ran to retrieve it from their baggage. Elgaret accepted it with an approving nod. Rather like a country housewife engaging in belated spring cleaning, Elgaret vigorously swept up what remained of both Smire and Tull, brushing the material onto her cloak, which she spread on the floor. It was such a homely sight that Nolar began to laugh, but tears soon overcame her, and she sank to her knees.

Elgaret dropped the whisk and hurried to put her arms around Nolar's heaving shoulders. "Master Derren," Elgaret asked urgently, "If you could survey the outside area and find a quick-flowing stream, it would be wise to disperse this dust therein. We in Estcarp have not been assailed by the Shadow for so long that I know not the proper means for such disposal, but I believe that running water should prevent any future reassembly of . . . these two."

Derren bowed respectfully. "Lady." He folded the sides of the cloak across to make a stout bundle, and hurried away down the passage.

Elgaret stroked Nolar's hair, and said gently, "Child, there is no need now to cry. The worst is done. You have helped prevent a great evil from afflicting Escarp and all the lands we know."

Nolar raised her head, tears shining on her cheeks. "I was so afraid that Tull would sound that bell," she blurted.

Elgaret guided Nolar to sit on the nearby stone block. "Quite a sensible aversion," the Witch commented. "We must deal now with those wicked implements." The dagger that had killed Smire was lying isolated on the floor. Elgaret wrapped her hand in her robe and gingerly placed the dagger on the table. "Smire said that Tull had summoned these wicked objects—therefore they could presumably be sent back, but they might be used again for evil purposes. If the Stone of Konnard will allow it, I think a clean flame should consume them."

Nolar felt an answering throb from her shard. "Yes, the Stone concurs," she said, sensing its wordless consent.

Elgaret held out her Jewel and sang a phrase. A bolt of shimmering heat ignited the table, intensifying to a whiteness that first melted, then bubbled away all traces of the bell, brazier, and dagger. As the flames flickered out, leaving only a scorched area on the floor, Elgaret raised a shaking hand to her forehead, and sank down beside Nolar.

Concerned by the Witch's faltering, Nolar shyly touched her arm, then exclaimed, "Your Jewel! Look!"

The cloudy crystal suspended over the Witch's heart had taken on a creamy opacity streaked with veins of green.

"It would appear," mused Elgaret, "that in working with the Stone of Konnard, one's own implements may be affected by its character."

Nolar dared to reach out and lightly touch the Witch's cheek. "The Stone healed Derren's leg," she said in a whisper trembling with hope. "Can you now see from your blind eye?"

Elgaret smiled, and in response, brushed Nolar's cheek. "No, my dear, I am still half-blind, and you continue to bear upon your face that stain which has for so long set you apart. No, do not turn away. I think I sense why we two were not healed. Tull's petrification spell caused Derren's broken bones to become whole, but that was certainly an effect not intended by Tull. I suspect that Tull's misuse of the Stone has wrenched it away from its healing purpose. In order for it to be restored, it must be refocused, and that will require much study and the aid of those with more Power than I possess."

Nolar gazed at the Witch. "But it did return you to us. Those others of the Council who were injured in the Turning as you were—if they could come here, could they not also be restored?"

"Would they believe our tale?" asked Elgaret. "You must remember that the Guardian's Council has been shattered. The few empowered Witches who remain may not choose to listen to our strange claim. Look you upon my Jewel—is this the crystal that it was before? Will the other Witches consider me their Sister still?"

Nolar wrestled with her confusion and her burning sense that the news *must* be shared. "Could I . . ." She hesitated, dreading the thought of having to face the Witches left at Es

Castle. "Could I return to bear witness myself . . . alone, if need be? I would try to explain to them . . . although I must confess to you that above all, I fear they might hold me there at Es Castle to force me to become a Witch." Overcome, she hid her face in her hands.

Elgaret gently grasped Nolar's hands in her own and eased them down so that Nolar had to look at her. "You *are* a Witch, child. It was born in you to be a Witch. You cannot deny it or hope to put it aside. But you are even more, and there lies your challenge. You have found . . . or should I say, you have been found—chosen by this great Stone of Konnard for purposes which we cannot know. I think it unlikely," she added dryly, "that any Witch—of the Council or not—could force you to do anything against your will. However, for that same reason," she went on, her face grave, "I suspect that the Council would not receive you gladly, nor listen to you with willing ears. You are different, because of the Stone. It is an object of Power from the far past, beyond their imagining. I can tell you this: because of Tull's tampering with the Stone, I suspect that forces of both Light and Dark are now suddenly aware that the Stone of Konnard has emerged, renewed. It can no longer rest here in total obscurity. You were drawn here because of your shard, a gift of the Stone. Others, for reasons good and ill, will now turn their attention to this place."

Nolar sat speechless, trying to absorb the import of Elgaret's words. "Then we cannot hope," she said slowly, "to persuade the Council to send the injured Witches here?"

"No," Elgaret answered, "not immediately. Perhaps later, when we have learned more about and from the Stone."

"What shall we do?" Tears welled again in Nolar's eyes. "Oh, Elgaret, what shall we do?"

The Witch frowned. "You name me?" she said, her voice sharp-edged.

"I needed some name to address you by to others," answered Nolar, preoccupied by her heavier burdens. "I called you my Aunt Elgaret." The Witch surveyed her with apparent consternation, so Nolar hastened to say, "It was just a name that came into my mind on the trail when I was explaining your presence to Derren."

The Witch gave a fleeting, humorless smile. "Indeed it did come into your mind, but it came to you unknowingly from me, for my True Name *is* Elgaret."

Nolar's eyes widened with horror as the implications struck her. "But I have used that name often at Lormt, and Ostbor said that a Witch's True Name could be a dire weapon if known by an empowered enemy."

The Witch's severe expression softened. "Do not distress yourself." Nolar tried to speak, but no words would come. How could she make amends for her betrayal? The Witch calmly continued, "Because of your very openness in using my name, I am all the more protected." Her smile now was genuine, its warmth evident in her good eye. "Is it not well known to all those who pry into and guess about the affairs of Witches that they keep their True Names as their deepest secret? A name used openly could not possibly be a True Name."

"I did say it was what we in the family had chosen to call you," Nolar recalled, considerably relieved that she had not unintentionally endangered the Witch. "I had to claim you as my aunt in order to remove you from Es Castle."

"Think no more of it," said the Witch briskly. "You might, however, address me henceforth as 'Aunt,' just to err upon the side of caution."

"But," murmured Nolar miserably, "you are not my aunt."

"Not by the usual bonds of blood, no," the Witch agreed, "but by the bonds of the mind, we are linked as if we did share the same blood. Perhaps we are even closer than many who share kinship, but never truly touch each other's lives. As you know, we Witches call one another 'Sister,' and it is no idle claim or mere formality. In the realm of Power, we are Sisters, you and I."

"I have so little knowledge of what such ties can mean," said Nolar, despising her tears, but unable to stop them. "I am honored that you would consider me worthy of your regard."

"You have earned that regard and respect," the Witch declared. "Let us rejoice that our linkage is more than that of mere acquaintance. The Power has taken a curious hand with the two of us, granting me my Foreseeings, which led me to urge your journey to Lormt; and then your own discoveries there, which gifted you with the shard and drew you hither. I suspect that we have not yet seen the end of what is intended for us. I know that we may not turn aside from the path that lies before us." She paused. "I hear the Borderer returning."

Derren slowly entered the chamber. Once he had carefully washed the foul dust away down a nearby stream, he had stood outside Tull's lair for some time, agonizing over his situation. His broken leg was healed, as was his ankle. The way to Karsten lay open before him: take a pony and go . . . yet he lingered. Walking back within Tull's den was the most difficult action that Derren had ever had to choose. He had forced himself to move forward, and now that he stood once again before the two Witches of Estcarp, his heart pounded and it was all he could do to keep from running away.

"Lady," he managed to say to Elgaret, "I have done as you asked. The remains of the mage and his minion have been washed away in a clear stream. I let the cloak go with them."

Elgaret nodded. "Well done. Join us now, as we decide what we must do next."

Derren gripped his hands together to stop them from shaking. "I . . . I must tell you something," he blurted, then stopped.

Nolar guessed his intention. Perhaps she might ease his

anguish. "You are not truly a Borderer, are you?" she asked quietly. "I suspected before we reached Lormt, and became certain of it during our journey here. I think you must be a spy from Karsten."

Derren gaped at her. "You *knew?* But you did not betray me." He swung to confront Elgaret. "But you did not blast me."

Elgaret looked annoyed. "Young man, I was in no condition to take any action until I was restored by the Stone of Konnard. According to Nolar, you have been completely reliable as both guide and escort. Why should we offer harm to you as recompense for fair service?"

"But . . . but it is true. I am of Karsten," Derren confessed. "I was an advance scout. The Turning trapped me in Estcarp. I thought if I escorted you to Lormt, no one would question me, and later, when we journeyed here, I hoped to send you safely back to Estcarp and go my own way."

"Then fortune has indeed smiled upon you. You are now free to return home to Karsten," suggested Elgaret, as if soothing an unreasonable child.

"But I cannot leave you here!" Derren exclaimed. "You cannot find your way back to Estcarp."

"Think carefully," Elgaret admonished him. "You must understand our situation. Nolar and I have just agreed that we would not likely be welcome at Es Castle because of our association with this unexpected Stone of Konnard. It is an object of great Power, as you have seen . . . and felt for yourself. It will draw attention now from the forces of both the Light and the Dark. For that reason, I feel that I must stay here, to listen, in my fashion, for any signs of activity threatening the Stone."

Nolar had silently risen and moved to the face of the Stone. Tentatively, then with assurance, she reached out and placed her open hand on the glistening surface. She felt the same deep warmth that she had sensed from her shard, and also an upwelling of hope. Suddenly, Nolar knew what she had to do.

"Lormt," she said, with complete conviction. "I must tell them at Lormt about the Stone, about all that has happened here. Morfew and the others will listen to me, and they will believe. Those who need to hear the message of the Stone's Power for healing will seek help at Lormt, so they may also be reached."

Elgaret nodded her approval. "Your shard was preserved at Lormt. It is fitting that you bear the news to Lormt. The scholars there should also be urged to seek any further knowledge of the Stone and how it was originally used. Above all, they must be alerted to the stirrings of both the Light and the Dark which may now be aroused."

"Any travel to Lormt must begin soon," Derren put in quickly. "The storms of winter have already begun." He paused as both ladies looked at him. "I mean . . . that is, I should hunt for some days first. We must leave ample supplies for your lady aunt." He stopped abruptly, as surprised by his own words as were his listeners.

Elgaret stood up. "I would be obliged, young man, if you could cut for me a proper staff to replace the one I seem unaccountably to have lost. A pity, for it was a staff long prized in my family."

"It is still at Es Castle, Aunt," said Nolar. "I had to leave it there with your other belongings when we set out for Lormt."

"I shall take care to reclaim it in the future," Elgaret asserted. "For the present, I require a staff. Come, Nolar, let us take an inventory of what food and accommodations we may find in this peculiar place. I shall be here for some time, I expect, and should like to know what can be done to improve the living arrangements." She pulled her robes tighter. "Quite chill here, with the roof open. Come along. I did see a brazier or two within, did I not?"

"I believe that I preserved some journeycake and other

food from Smire's notice," said Nolar, taking Elgaret's arm.

Derren hurried after them. "If there is another fur or hanging, I can block away some of this draft." He swiftly converted word to deed, pulling down one of the ornate wall hangings from Tull's former throne room and stretching it across the passageway leading back to the Stone.

That done, Derren nervously faced his companions. "Do you truly accept my service?" he asked. "I must tell you honestly that the Witches of Estcarp have always been figures of dread to us in Karsten."

"It was clear on the trail," said Nolar, "that you were not comfortable in Aunt's presence once you learned that she was a Witch."

"But she has defended me!" Derren burst out. His hand strayed to touch his amulet. "When I was forced to call upon ... My Lord of the Forest, the evil dagger turned away from me, but I could no longer move. I was benumbed. Had not you, lady, wielded your Jewel, we should all have been lost. I am obligated to repay you, if I can, by any service I may do for you."

"You have a commendable sense of honor," observed Elgaret, "but you owe me no obligation. Each of us stood forth against Tull, armed with our own beliefs. By the grace of Those who watch over Their own, we triumphed. We three are now free to pursue our separate destinies. I believe that I am meant to reside here, as a Guardian of the Stone of Konnard. I feel its Power constantly, and I long to understand its ways. Nolar feels similarly drawn back to Lormt, to bear the news of the Stone."

Derren stood before Nolar. "Lady," he said earnestly, "I fear that there will be naught for me in Karsten. We once spoke of my returning, and you gave me a great gift of hope for restoring the forests. But I have thought upon it, and what I know of the ways of men. Karsten will be in turmoil. Duke Pagar's armies had to be crushed in the Turning. Folk will spare no time for the planting of trees and the restoring of the wildlife. They will be clawing for advantage over one another, if not absorbed by the bare needs of living. Best that I leave the land be to revive as it must. I, too, would go back to Lormt, lady. I think I could be of use to the scholars there, as before. I felt as if I . . . belonged there." He paused, his face flushing pink. "I would also learn to read, if that be possible."

Nolar grasped his hand, remembering her own desire and Ostbor's welcome aid. "I shall gladly teach you, if you care to study with me. You speak truly—I, too, felt that I might belong at Lormt. It was a rare feeling for me, one that I feared to trust. If you could guide us back to Lormt, I am certain that Morfew and Wessell would receive you with joy, and likely put you to work that very day. Come with me, then, to Lormt, once we have made Aunt secure here."

Derren seized Nolar's other hand. "Lady, with all my heart," he vowed.

"Now that is settled," the Witch inserted, "will you kindly find me a staff, and a spare cloak, if one remains in the baggage? The mages of old who immured Tull here gave no thought at all to how cold these rooms would be to the unspelled."

Nolar felt a surge of happiness. Spring would follow this early winter, and in the meadows above Lormt, the Noon and Midnight plants would bloom again. Perhaps she could gather some for Master Pruett. She turned to Elgaret. "While I search for another cloak, Aunt, do take my scarf. I do not think I shall need it again to hide my face. When I get to Lormt, I shall be among friends, and for the present, I am surely among true friends."

We had news of the Witch Elgaret from time to time. Derren visited her with supplies, in spite of the heavy storms of a winter more severe than any we had known before. Once I rode with him. That was when great good came to me, for, when I looked upon the Stone of Konnard, two things happened. One, the constant ache in my leg was gone, though my injury was not entirely cured, for the once shattered limb was now some shorter than the other. But, which for me was more important, there came inside my mind the sensation (which with it first carried fear, for there is always uneasiness in the unknown) of a door opening. Straightway I found my talent was enlarged so I could communicate wordlessly with my own kind as well as with animals. Knowing this was unchancy and, in ways, an invasion of another's self, I did not practice it much, only when there was great need.

Only once did I use it and then only because I was greatly angered, though I knew also that anger is a weakening of that control which those of the talent must learn.

That anger came through a young girl who rode into Lormt and announced herself as Arona Bethishsdaughter. She had been record keeper for one of the Falconers' women villages which had been cast adrift when the Falconers left the Eyrie, a village in which there was hatred for my sex. She demanded that she be taken to a "she scholar," showing the greatest aversion to any communication with the rest of us. Nolar escorted her to the Lady Nareth, another who was without kindness for us, though she was a scholar.

When Nolar returned she was very quiet and I was concerned. She sat across from me at the table where I had been at work. Then, as if speaking of something she disliked, she said: "Duratan, with that one comes bitterness—perhaps justly in her eyes because of her past. We must not let such cut us down. Try her!"

I let my thought range out as she bade. Then I recoiled, for it was true. There was deep anger there such as might well breed danger.

"But how may this harm us?" I asked aloud, both of myself and of Nolar. "Bitterness eats at the core of the one who holds it."

"True, yet . . ." she paused and fingered that pocket within her skirt, where she carried the shard of Konnard which was to her as a jewel is to a Witch. "Yet I feel."

No more did she say then nor, for a long time afterward, but Arona Bethishsdaughter kept to quarters near the Lady Nareth and we saw little of her, nothing after the coming of the Falconer who searched for his race history. Arona did not even company with Pyra. Sometimes I hardly remembered her presence, for Lormt has so many rooms and corridors one could live a year within and not meet another who did not wish it.

With Nolar's discovery of that which had been brought to Lormt after Ostbor's death—and we had a weary search for that since it had been mislaid among the newly discovered treasures—we searched for something which might aid the bird warrior for whom I had a liking and deep respect.

Arona might have well aided us at that but she would not, though Nolar tried to get from her some ideas of what history she had brought. She told me frankly that when she urged this, Arona had looked upon her with some of the same contempt that her stepmother had once shown: that she was a marred thing. And to me, of course, the girl would not have listened at all.

However, I continued to hope. Until one morning, when, with the Falconer in mind, I threw the crystals, only to start up from the table in haste.

There was an arrow there, pointing toward me—or perhaps to Lormt—but it was red, the red of blood still flowing.

I loosed a thought search. Pain of body—pain of mind—a terrible driving need for haste as death rode close behind. I hurried to call Pyra, for help was needed, all that which we might offer, as for the second time the Falconer came to us.

FALCON HOPE

by
P. M. Griffin

1

Tarlach bent low in the saddle to cut the drag of the wind as much as possible, and cradled the still form of the probably dying woman more tightly against him.

He had been riding like this for two days, nearly three now, not stopping for food or drink or rest save only for the few seconds necessary to change mounts when the horse under him could bear its human burden no longer.

His mind was so cloaked in a numbing fog of weariness and fear that he should not rightly have been able to say how long he had been galloping thus, whether for hours or weeks, had the need for accurate reporting later not kept burning every detail into his memory with all the searing force of a brand, that and stark terror. The sight of that boulder ripping suddenly down the seemingly stable mountainside to strike the Holdruler of Seakeepdale would not leave him soon.

It had not pinned the Lady Una beneath it—nothing could have survived that even momentarily—but it had hit her and hit her hard. When he and his comrades had reached her, it was obvious that she had been broken inside. She still lived, but she would not recover, not with the cursory care they were able to provide.

His heart twisted again even as it had in that moment. Those Witches! Those thrice-accursed Witches! They had saved Estcarp, right enough, with their turning of the mountains, but they had riven and twisted the life of those highlands themselves, they had destroyed the Falconers' Eyrie, which had been their pride and whose loss might prove their end as a people, and now they had reached into the future and slain the lady he secretly loved in defiance of all his kind's custom, the lady with whom he was allied in most urgent cause, no less than an effort, maybe the last possible, to save his race from extinction.

He gripped himself once more, as he had been forced to do throughout this nightmare race. They had come here to Estcarp for that purpose, and they had been crossing these still treacherous mountains in pursuit of knowledge, of any sort of information, that might help convince the commanding Falconer officers—and the shunned, ever-feared women—of the stark necessity of the disturbing course he proposed. Lormt, the repository of ancient lore which was their goal, was relatively close to the place where the accident had occurred. He had followed his kind's usual custom and had held himself so much aloof from most of its residents during his time there that he could not even say if it could supply the help she needed, but reason declared that a community of that size was bound to have a healer associated with it, and so he had begun this ride in challenge to the Grim Commandant. While Una of Seakeep lived, while there was any chance at all that healing could benefit her, he would not give over or waver in his war to win her life.

With that determination, he had flung himself into his saddle, taking the woman up before him and fastening her stallion's rein to his wrist, knowing a second mount would be needed to spell Lady Gay when she began to tire.

He expected the rest of their small escort to follow after at a saner pace and had been surprised to see Brennan, his chief Lieutenant, leap into the saddle as well, also seizing another horse to serve him as Eagle's Brother would Tarlach. His commander did not attempt to gainsay him. Dangerous beasts and even more deadly men were reputed to roam these Witch-blighted lands, and with his arms thus encumbered, he would be able to offer no ready defense should they be challenged.

Three others shared the race with them—the falcons Storm Challenger and Sunbeam and the cat Bravery, who was to Una of Seakeep all that the fighting birds were to the men, although none knew that save only the woman herself and he. As the birds sat the perches designed for their use on their comrades' saddles, so did Bravery ride the seat made for her, a high-sided pad set behind Una's saddle.

There had been no refusing any of these, either. The bond joining them to their chosen humans was such that they would not be parted from them for so little cause as the discomfort and difficulty inherent in such a journey. Bravery particularly would not have remained behind, realizing as she did all too well that she might never feel that beloved hand stroke her thick tortoiseshell fur again.

The two men scarcely spoke during the long hours of riding as they threw all their concentration into the effort of winning more and ever more speed from their jaded horses, despite the rugged mountainland through which they traveled.

Suddenly, Brennan called out to him. His gelding had stumbled in his weariness and could carry him no farther.

Tarlach drew rein. Lady Gay was nigh unto blown herself again. They needs must change mounts yet another time.

The Lieutenant dismounted first and hurried to take the Daleswoman from his commander so that she should suffer as little jarring as possible during the exchange.

Tarlach hastened to Eagle, but before he could mount, all

the world seemed to spin around him, and he staggered against the stallion.

He kept his feet but was forced to lean heavily upon the animal for support. His eyes closed as he fought to regain control of his senses.

Strong hands gripped him.

"Come, Tarlach. We can rest now."

"No . . ."

"We need it, and the Lady must have it."

He yielded to that and allowed himself to be lowered to the ground.

It was several minutes before the reeling slowed and then stopped. After waiting a few seconds longer to be certain the world would remain steady, he sat up. His comrade was kneeling beside Una. He saw him use the edge of his cloak to wipe the pink foam from her lips.

"How does she?"

Brennan turned. "She is not greatly worse."

"But worse all the same?"

The Falconer leader's head lowered at his answering nod. He had not been able to do even this much for her. . . .

His comrade left Una and took the water flask from his saddle. This he brought to the Captain.

"She does not suffer.—Drink this. Lack of water is partly what is affecting us."

Tarlach drained nearly half the container before he took it from his lips. The liquid was both a pleasure and a torment as it worked upon his dry mouth and throat, and he wondered how it had been possible for him to have been all but unaware of such thirst until now.

He returned the flask and then smiled wanly at his comrade. "I am affected. You seem almost untroubled."

That was not quite the truth. The Lieutenant's face was strained and white, and his eyes burned red from windlash and lack of rest, but his shoulders were still unbent, his

movements still sure and strong. So much could not be said
for himself.

"I am weary enough, my friend. It is just that I have borne
no weight as yet."

He eyed his companion shrewdly. "Let me take the Lady
from you. Your arms must be nigh unto numb by now."

"I can hold," the other answered stiffly.

He softened almost in the same breath. "I do not snarl at
you, Brennan," he apologized, "but the guarding of us must
remain with you. No Falconer officer should have to confess
this, but I am not capable of it."

His comrade sighed in his heart. That last was all too
obvious. "So let it be, then."

Tarlach would delay no longer. He mounted and took Una
of Seakeep into his arms once more.

He looked into her face. She was so still, as if every part
of her will and what remained of her strength were concentrated in the awful battle she waged to draw yet another
lungfull of air into her torn body.

"Hold a little longer, my own Lady," he whispered to her,
although he knew she was beyond hearing. "Hold only a
little longer. We are very near now if we have not strayed
from our trail in our haste. Soon, this torment, at least, will
be ended for you."

2

The two mercenaries rode steadily for another hour before
entering upon a down-sloping trail that ended at the foot of
a gentle hill. This they crested and found themselves in a
narrow valley looking up at a strange keep, or what once
might have been a keep. It, like the mountains around it, had
suffered greatly in the Turning and its aftermath.

Of the four towers which had once guarded it, only two

and part of a third remained. The fourth was gone, as were two of the walls that had stretched between them. One had merely crumbled. The other and the missing tower had literally been sheared away when the ground had dropped from under them. The rubble—or some of it since a great part of the remains had probably been taken for rebuilding here and elsewhere in the area—now lay at the bottom of what was a respectable cliff bank.

One of the surviving walls held the formal gate. A path, not much worn but relatively clear, led up to it, and Tarlach turned his weary mount upon it.

Their approach had apparently been observed by someone astute enough to note the fact that the leading horseman was riding encumbered. At least, he could see two with a hand litter standing among those who had poured from the readily opened gate to receive them.

Only when he reached them did Tarlach draw rein.

"There is a healer here?" he demanded harshly. "One of our party has need. . . ."

"I am a healer," the woman standing nearest those holding the litter answered quickly. He recognized her with some surprise as the one who had charge of the materials he was studying. "Let my aides take him, Bird Warrior."

The two young bearers, both wearing the dress of either field hands or tradesmen, came to him, and he lowered the unconscious Holdlady into their waiting arms.

They were gentle despite their rough appearance when they placed her on the litter. . . .

Lormt's healer, who was of Estcarp's ancient race, knelt beside her patient. She was quick to cover herself, but he had anticipated and so did not miss her start of amazement when she discovered that she was attending, not a man, but a female. She had the grace not to remark on that fact or make any greater display of her surprise. Perhaps that fact was truly of very small significance to her in the face of the more immediate matters claiming her attention.

Speaking quickly, tersely, in response to her question, the Falconer described the accident that had struck Una down and detailed as best he could the extent of her injuries, then gave an account of his race to bring her here so that the Wise Woman or Witch or whatever she was might be able to judge the effect wrought by the strenuous journey.

The Captain was not aware of the look those listening bent upon him. He watched the bearers lift the litter and carry it inside, knowing in the depth of his heart and mind that he was not likely to see Una of Seakeep again, not as a living woman. His head lowered, and all the weight of weariness and hopelessness settled on him.

It was over. He had done all that had been in his power to do. Now Una's fate lay in other hands, in those of these strange, scholarly folk and in those of the Great Ones who commanded life and death.

He gripped himself. He could not give way, not yet. Tarlach's head raised again, and he dismounted, moving slowly, almost as if he struggled against water. His body seemed to be in rebellion against him, fighting every command to further action.

The mercenary leader faced those gathered around him, giving them his attention for the first time.

One whom he knew well immediately caught his notice, a tall man whose silver hair proclaimed a long expanse of years behind him. There was nothing weary or decayed in his gray eyes, however, and his stance was that of a young man, straight, with the pride of purpose and accomplishment. As for the rest, his appearance was that of an aged individual, frail but still sound in mind and health. His skin was unwrinkled but was pale, transparent almost, and looked as if a breath would cause it to tear or bruise. He was thin in face and body, and the hand he raised in greeting was corded with blue veins. His features were pleasant now and might once have been handsome; his expression was alert, incisive, and kind. His clothing was gray and was little different in character from that worn by a laborer in field or craft, although Ouen was head of the Lormt community. Little else was readily available here, and none of the others around him sported anything very different or richer.

Another well familiar to the Falconer stood beside him, a much younger man, also of the Old Race and also tall and thin. Duratan's dress was like that of the older scholar save for its brown color, but his bearing was that of a soldier, one who had known war. Known it and suffered because of it. He supported himself on a crutch which he held with the familiarity of long custom, and though both legs were booted, the left was stiff in a manner that told no living foot was encased within.

The others were an odd-looking assembly if judged by the populations of most towns or holds. They were in the chief male and for the greater part quite old, but with a relatively few younger people to tell that the place was not entirely dead or dying.

The silver-haired man saw the direction of his glance and stepped forward a pace.

"Lormt gives you welcome again, Bird Warrior, and welcomes your companions," he said in a marvelously soft voice.

Tarlach felt no surprise that he was recognized. The tall helmets screening the upper portion of their faces made it difficult for those of other peoples to tell one man of his race from another, but no one with eyes in his head could forget the Seakeep horse that he rode. Lady Gay had identified him as the guest who had sought information from Lormt's store of knowledge and abruptly left again saying only that he and one other would return shortly.

The Falconer's heart twisted. He had gone to the coast to meet Una's ship as they had arranged before he had left High Hallack. As Holdruler, she had been unwilling to leave her Dale in that busy season, and so they had decided that he should come on ahead and learn what he could and that she would join him in the fall when the press of her duties had eased. She had wanted to help him conclude his studies and discuss what he, what they, uncovered in depth before approaching his people. Instead, she had found her doom. He had led her to her doom, he who was sworn to defend her. . . .

"For that welcome, thanks given, Lord Ouen," the Falconer responded, forcing himself to speak steadily. "We come, as you have seen, in need of aid and as well because I would continue to delve your records. My comrade with me and eight others who follow after would remain a while to rest themselves and their mounts, if you so will, before riding to the camp of our people on the Es. We shall, of course, give payment."

"I am no lord, but only Ouen, Bird Warrior," he replied sternly, "as you well know, and as for payment, this is no inn, although need requires that we accept gratefully any just donation freely given." He smiled then, and the stiffness vanished from him as if by a Witch's sorcery. "It is our pleasure to receive you and all your party." His head moved slightly in the direction of the open gate. "Come inside now. Your animals are in need of attention, and you yourselves would benefit from rest. Your chamber is still free, and another has already been prepared for your companion's use."

Tarlach bowed his head formally. "Again, thanks given.— To the house greeting," he added in the formal guesting ritual, "to those of the house good fortune. To the day a good dawn and sunset, to the endeavor good fortune without a break."

Ouen and Duratan led their guests through the gate and across the open court within to a large barrack-like building standing lengthwise against the second remaining wall. This they entered and ascended to the level above with no delay made because of one host's age or the other's disability.

"Most of the older inhabitants are housed below since the stairs would be a trial for many of Lormt," Ouen informed them, "but our guests and those of us who do live up here find the greater solitude restful. For that reason, too, the infirmary is located on this floor."

"For us, that is well," the Captain answered for his Lieutenant, as was their custom when among those of other races. "My people prefer to remain apart as much as possible."

The old scholar led them down a seemingly endless, poorly lighted corridor but finally stopped before a heavy oaken door, which he drew back to reveal a small sleeping chamber outfitted with a square table and a couple of roughly made chairs as well as with the more usual furnishings of such a room so that it could also function as a study. A newly laid fire burned cheerfully upon the hearth and was already beginning to warm the air nearest it.

"Is this still satisfactory, Bird Warrior?" Ouen questioned.

"More than satisfactory."

His attention returned to his host after his quick, almost instinctive examination of the room. "I hope your people will pardon our lack of courtesy if we fail to give them greeting this evening. We have been long in the saddle. . . ."

"We should rather be angered if you felt compelled to come to us before you were rested." He paused. "Your saddlebags and your comrade's will be brought to you, naturally, but the Lady's . . ."

"I will assume responsibility for them."

A small dark form had silently followed the human's into the building and now rubbed against Tarlach's legs. He reached down and scooped Bravery up. "I shall keep her cat with me as well."

"Your animals, too, are welcome, furred and feathered alike."

The mercenary Captain wanted only to end this interview and be left in peace, but they had been well and unquestioningly received, and the time was come to give some account of themselves, if no more than identifying the house to which they were bound. Custom excused him from disclosing more, as it had at the time of his initial arrival. Falconers did not name themselves before those of other races or discuss their own concerns with them, nor did they let their tongues run with the business of those to whom they bound their swords.

"The woman you tend is the Lady Una, Holdruler of Seakeepdale. Of High Hallack," he added, since few of the Dales were known by name in Estcarp, save among the Sulcar and others like them, chiefly merchants—and blank shields—who had direct dealings with that continent.

"She to whom your swords are bound?" Duratan inquired.

"Aye," he answered curtly, "but as I told you earlier, I have my own work here, which I should like to resume as soon as I have rested and my other duties have been discharged, assuming that you have more for me to see."

"There are more records, some dealing directly with your race. They are very old—"

"The older the material, the more valuable to me."

"There is not much that you have not already seen," Duratan warned, "and that is very fragmented. Your kind have never been generous in sharing information about yourselves—"

"What we do possess is yours to examine," Ouen interjected hastily. "We have been pressing ourselves to seek out still more for you. The Turning opened vast stores for us, and we had not even probed all which had been free for our study before that. We have not yet been able to catalogue the half of what we have in charge here."

"I shall need everything you can produce."

"We will do our best for you. Indeed, your request is a favor to us. Many of the community thoroughly enjoy a specific search like this and relish the challenge of it."

The Captain nodded his thanks. He hesitated then, and his eyes involuntarily flickered toward the door and the dim hall beyond. "You will inform me of your healer's conclusions?"

"Of course, as soon as we have anything to report," Ouen answered.

His hosts took their leave of him after that. They led the second Falconer to the chamber to the right of his, which proved alike to it in every basic respect.

Brennan thanked them but returned at once to the corridor. "I will be a while with my Captain. Can you have food brought to us? And wine?"

"It is being prepared now."

Tarlach set Bravery down on the foot of his bed. She looked lost, he thought. She was an extraordinarily small animal, scarcely larger than a kitten of five or six months although she had attained her full growth, and the most of what one saw of her was in actuality fur. Her body itself did not weigh two pounds.

She looked even tinier now, huddled as she was with the misery she no longer bothered to conceal. Bravery knew that he was aware of her true relationship with her human and that she need not screen the extent of her understanding and suffering from him.

He sat beside her, stroking her gently, but she seemed to derive no consolation from his touch, and he withdrew his hand again. What comfort could he hope to offer, he who was utterly bereft of it?

Storm Challenger made a crooning sound deep in his throat and flew down beside the little cat. He began preening her in the manner of his kind when one of their own was lashed by loss or pain.

The Falconer's throat closed. He stripped off his helmet and carefully set it aside, then buried his face in his hands. It was as if his winged comrade was already giving condolence for the Holdlady's death. . . .

He straightened at the sound of a knock and reached for the helm again. He had no wish to deal with any of these Lormt folk with his face unscreened, particularly now. He relaxed again in the next moment as Storm Challenger announced it was Brennan who sought admittance.

To the surprise of both men, the falcon Sunbeam streaked inside and settled on the bed beside Bravery, giving every sign of a distress as deep as the cat's own, so that the mammal's pink tongue darted out to rasp along the feathers of her neck and breast.

"She realizes, too, what the Holdruler's death will mean for all of us if it should end thus," the Lieutenant said, although the depth of his war bird's obvious misery still amazed him. He had never seen one of the females grieve this intently even for the man she had chosen to follow.

He had more than that to concern him at the moment. He removed his helmet as Tarlach had done and placed it beside his commander's with a sigh of relief. It was good to be free of its weight for a while.

"We should have a few hours of peace now," he observed.

"Yes." Tarlach forced the shadow of a smile. "I, for one, can use it—you are well quartered?"

"Comfortably enough. My place is a twin to this one." Brennan glanced at the bed. "Why not lie down for a while? I have requested that food be brought to us, but I think sleep would benefit you more."

"It will not come. I am overtired, I suppose."

His eyes turned to the fire. "If the Holdlady dies, she will probably take our hope with her." His mouth hardened. "She was right as usual. We can expect to make little headway in the villages without her presence and word to support our cause."

"Maybe the women will listen to us anyway," the other reasoned. "They will fade along with us if they do not."

"Listen but hardly trust," he answered bitterly. "Why should they? What do they know of any of us, or we of them, save that bands of us go among them each season, or in some cases but once in the year, to sire young on them, as would beasts under a stockman's control."

The other frowned. "Tarlach—"

"No, let me go on. I am but trying to reason this through as they are likely to do. While we had the Eyrie and the mountains around it, we could hold them close, and even then, I think, one or two periodically slipped away into Estcarp seeking richer or different lives. When the Turning forced us into the lowlands, change became inevitable. We should have seen that. Our females' villages are now but a short space from holdings of the Witches' race. Already, we are losing women in great number. In another generation, or two at the most, too few of breeding age will remain to continue our kind as a viable people.

"They cannot but be even more strongly aware of that fact than we are, but still, were I in their place, I should be most unwilling to let myself be lured into another highland fastness where I might be even more tightly chained, and my offspring after me. The Holdruler's presence, the fact that we are working together, her testimony regarding what we are striving to build could go far in convincing them, and even that might not be enough. Without it, we have almost no weapon."

Brennan scowled. "A column still controls each village and can compel—"

"Our treaty with Seakeep precludes that."

"Ravenfield is yours."

"It is a large Dale but not big enough in itself. We need full, free access to Seakeep's lands as well, which we will be denied if we violate our agreement with its Lady." His eyes narrowed. "Even if our oaths meant nothing, we could not ride against her or any other Dale in order to seize it. High Hallack remembers Alizon's invasion all too well, and her lords would very quickly unite again to quell any such attempt on our part. Even at the height of our strength, we would not have been able to sword-carve a kingdom for ourselves there, where the Hounds with their Kolder weapons failed. If we did try, we would doom ourselves for a fact.

Who would be able to trust us enough to hire our swords after that?"

"I never suggested any betrayal. . . ."

"No." He sighed. "No. It is my weariness, I suppose. I seem able to see only gloom."

Brennan hesitated. "You are right. We have to win the females' consent if we are to succeed, but do not forget that we need the favor of the Commandants as well. If we bear ourselves too strangely in our approach, we could find ourselves outcast with nothing accomplished save our own ruin."

Tarlach shot a quick look at him. Was this a veiled as well as an open warning? Had he betrayed himself, revealed what Una of Seakeep had come to mean to him? His comrade's expression gave no sign of any such meaning, but . . .

There was no dishonor in what lay between him and the ruler of Seakeepdale, and were he a man of any other race, were the circumstances binding him different, they would be wedded lord and lady, but he was a Falconer, the Captain of a full company, one of the few such remaining to them, with five hundred men following and dependent upon him. That, he might have chosen to surrender, naming Brennan Captain in his stead pending the Warlord's approval, but chance and the generosity of the Lady Una had placed within his hands the means of preserving his race from nearly certain extinction if he could convince his kind to avail themselves of it. He dared not violate custom now, whatever the wish of his heart. Or of hers.

Falconers were a race apart from every other, walled off by the cold, strange lives they led, or appeared to others to lead. When Sulcar ships had brought them to this northern realm from their ancient hold in the south in the distant past, they had been accompanied by women and young, accompanied as herders were by their beasts. They owned no kinship with them and had settled them in several widely scattered villages, each under the control of a column, while the males, mercenaries even then, had raised and settled in their Eyrie, visiting the females of their race only to beget the next generation upon them.

Pride and shame and fear had kept them silent about the reasons driving them, and so over the long years, they had grown ever more tightly in upon themselves, ever further apart from other men even as they drew away from their own mates and offspring until only the friendship of their comrades and their falcons remained.

They had not always lived thus, but one black day, a being of the Old Ones, the Old Dark, had come upon them, and she had battened on them, enslaving them in bonds so heavy and cruel that the terror the memory of her rule invoked was still a flaming brand within their hearts.

Jonkara had been able to work her will only through females, but every Falconer woman was potentially her tool. Most whom she tried to command refused, dying in the making good of their refusal, but some she did break, and a very few gave service of their own will in exchange for the measure of her power which she bestowed upon them. Every woman so commanded was altered in spirit, becoming herself something vile and cruel, delighting in the pain and degradation of those around her. Through these corrupted shadows, Jonkara gained complete mastery over every man who had been joined by any bond of affection with the women who had been.

In the end, her power had been partly broken at great cost, and those who survived had left, fled, their old seat, for Jonkara was only chained, not slain, and they knew she waited, ever waited, for a woman to come and shed for her the blood that would set her free once more—to wreak awesome vengeance on those or the descendants of those who had so bound her.

Because of that threat of renewed bondage, the Falconer males had taken the only step that they believed would ultimately defend them should Jonkara regain her liberty. They severed themselves from all attachment, all caring and affection, for the women of their kind, cutting them completely from their lives and company save only during their brief times of mating.

This he had always known, but it was only since taking service with Seakeepdale that the other side of the tale had come to him—why the women of his race, who had been by repute as proud and valiant as any of the males, had consented to such banishment and had endured in it for so long. The men in Jonkara's thrall had been slaves and cruelly used, but they had been men and themselves still. Those women who she broke lost infinitely more and in so losing became instruments of great evil. Their fear of her return had to be vastly stronger, powerful enough to have held them—or most of them—passive through all the ages since their flight north, and even now, with the pressure to seek for better, brighter lives at last overcoming the weight of history, it was not to heal the breach with their men that they sought, but to depart from them entirely, perhaps as much in a final effort by some inner spirit to protect them as to escape from them.

A timid rap called him out of his reverie. A man's voice announced that their food was ready.

Brennan slipped on his helm again and went to the door. He took the well-laden tray with a nod of thanks and closed it again.

"They have sent a portion for the falcons and Bravery as well," he remarked approvingly as he set the big platter on the table. "Our part is plain but looks edible, and there is more than enough of it."

Tarlach glanced at it without interest. "Take whatever you will. I have no mind for food."

The Lieutenant would hear none of that. He made his comrade eat and forced wine on him, the small amount necessary to combine with his exhaustion to bring him oblivion at last.

After seeing Tarlach settled, he retired to his own chamber to take the rest he himself so badly needed.

Ouen's chamber was little larger and scarcely more richly appointed than those to which the two Falconers had been shown, but it was both home and private office to the aged scholar, and Aden, Lormt's healer and an avid seeker of knowledge herself, knew she would find both him and Duratan waiting there for her report when she finally left her patient.

The gray eyes fixed anxiously on her. "That poor young woman, how does she fare?"

"She rests and is beyond discomfort. It is too early to say more as yet, but her injuries are severe. Pyra is with her now, as someone must be until the crisis is over, for good or ill." She shook her head in mixed admiration and amazement. "That ride was hard on her, but those Bird Warriors did well in getting her here as quickly as they did.—I can hardly credit their like with rendering such service."

"Do not be surprised," Duratan told her. "I fought beside Falconers when I was with the Borderers. They do not often bind their swords to a woman, right enough, but once their oath is given, they will fulfill it in every respect, spirit and letter, however unpleasant they might find their duties. During the flight from Karsten, matron and maid and maid child were numbered amongst the refugees, and never did I witness a breach in courtesy or in the burden laid upon the able when they assume responsibility for those less strong and less skilled.

"Even beyond sworn duty, most of them seem bound by compassion as well. Had they discovered that lady injured upon the trail, they would almost certainly have done what they could for her, though they probably would not have ridden such a race for her sake."

"They have given her at least the chance for life," the

woman said, "but we now have to deal with them, or with their leader at any rate. How do we handle him?"

"Why, as we have done, by showing him such hospitality as we can and he is able to accept," Ouen answered in surprise. "That and by continuing to permit him to study our records as soon as he is rested and free to do so, of course."

"Ouen! Teacher, you know full well what I mean! It is my trove that he will be using next. Pyra is of their race, and she is also studying those same materials."

"She will have to share them. Both are not likely to want the same record at the same time."

"That is not what I am saying," she snapped in exasperation. "This is not like you, Ouen."

"Nor is it like you," he responded pointedly.

"The fear I saw in Pyra when she learned of the company we have here is unlike her, too!" She caught her temper before it escaped her. "She does not want to be dragged back to her village again before she has both the heal-knowledge and the knowledge of her people which she came to get, or to be taken to some other settlement entirely. She of a certainty does not want to be slain because she took the initiative to seek out that learning, as is not beyond the realm of possibility according to what some of our earlier guests have told us."

Her eyes went from one to the other. "It was bad enough when we were hosting but a single blank shield. Now there will be ten of those men here for several days. What could we do to prevent it if they discovered she was one of them and chose either to take or slaughter her? How could we stop even one of them, a warrior and with his war bird to help him?

"There is the matter of our own safety and that of our collection as well. No other Falconer males may have come to Lormt, but a few of their women have. One of those was so little pleased by what she discovered that she attempted to tear the manuscript she had been reading. Only the fact that

Jerro chanced to be present and intervened saved it, but all he could do against one of these mercenaries, should he respond in a similar fashion, would be to get himself killed."

Duratan let her finish speaking before raising his hand for silence. "We have nothing to fear, and neither does your friend Pyra. As I told you, I know something of these men. They are hard and cold by our lights, but they are honorable. They will not do violence to anyone under our protection after our having received them as we did, and you may be assured that none of them will be so maddened by anything he learns that he will attempt to destroy the volume in which he read it. Such lack of control is not permitted to any of their kind."

Aden sighed. "I hope you are right, my friend. I would not have much heart for turning that mercenary commander away after what he has done, but I dread to think of war blighting Lormt, and that is his work and the work of all his people, all their males at least."

"True, but it is work they often turn to life's service, as they did when they helped bring my people across the mountains in their flight from Karsten and in the fighting they have done for both Estcarp and High Hallack. They do not serve the Dark or the Shadow, nor do they knowingly bind themselves to an evil cause or remain with such a cause once its nature is discovered.—We have received many far worse here, my friends, and have suffered no harm as a result. These Bird Warriors will do us or ours no injury, and already this leader of theirs has added to our store of knowledge. It may well be that they will increase it still further."

3

*B*oth Falconers slept through most of the following twenty-four hours, and for the three days following that, Tarlach was busy with his escort, settling them in for their brief stay and replenishing their supplies for the last stage of their journey to the column to which they owed ultimate allegiance, that of Commandant Varnel, Warlord of the Falconer race. Although there were only nine men, ten including himself, the demands on his time and energy were great, for they held strictly to custom, and he alone, as their chief officer, had dealings with the people of Lormt.

It was well for him that this was so. There had been no perceptible change in the Lady Una's condition. That she still lived was taken as an encouraging sign by those attending her, but beyond that, they could give no answers and offered no definite hope, however guarded.

He contrived to see her each day on the claim that it was his responsibility to affirm that his employer was yet alive and well tended, but he derived no comfort from the wrenchingly short visits. The Daleswoman grew ever thinner, ever more frail to the eye. She retained her beauty, but it showed an increasingly ethereal cast, as if her body as well as her spirit were preparing to begin the journey on the final road that would take her to the Halls of the Valiant.

It rent his heart to see her thus, and he ached to press his lips to hers, to merely touch the small, scarred hand, but he was never left alone with her and so had to hold back, keeping to the pose circumstance decreed that he must assume. When he left the chamber where she lay each day, it was with the certainty that it was for the final time.

Despair and the anguish of irreparable loss ate into him like a canker, but the Captain did not allow himself to sink utterly into depression. He had no heart for the search which had set him on the road to Lormt, but he made himself begin it as soon as Brennan and his other comrades departed late on the fourth morning after his coming there. He had taken the fate of his race on himself and must now carry on with the work of securing it. For his own sake, he dared not do otherwise. His grief and impotence would drive him mad if he had nothing else upon which to fix his mind, even if it required the full force of his will to make himself do so.

Una slipped into natural sleep during her fourth day at Lormt, and shortly before dawn on the following morning, her eyes finally opened.

She looked about her, puzzled, then memory returned in full force, and she stiffened.

Pyra, the Falconer woman who was Aden's friend and a healer in her own right, had been sitting beside her and quickly lay a soothing hand on her arm. "Easy, my Lady. You are safe. This is Lormt, and I am Pyra, a guest here as well and a healer."

The Daleswoman nodded her understanding but did not relax. Her eyes swept the small room seeking one they did not find.

A spear twisted inside her. "The Captain?" she asked, trying to hold her voice steady, although it was an effort to speak at all. "The commander of my escort? Is he all right? I saw him spring toward me when the rock fell. . . ."

"He is well," the other woman assured her. "It was he who brought you to us. He rode with you in his arms for nearly three days, pausing only to change mounts during the whole of that time," she added with a sudden pride that would have surprised her had she really been aware of it.

Once again, Una of Seakeep nodded. She said nothing more, but her fear remained with her. She did not doubt that the man would indeed have so battled the Grim Commandant for her sake, but this stranger might also lie to her and hold to that lie until she judged her patient sufficiently strong to bear the truth.

The other woman stood up. It was easy enough to read the Holdlady's thoughts, and determination firmed within her. Una's recovery would be slow indeed with this tearing her.

She went to the door. As she expected, not one but two young people sat in the hall outside. Many of the local folk sent their children to Lormt to serve as hands and feet and laborers for the community in exchange for the knowledge they could thereby gain. Most left soon, when it was time to be apprenticed to their life's work, but a few like these two and like Aden before them either showed a bent for some trade requiring further training or a love of learning itself and formally bound themselves for service here. Youth was youth, however, no matter the strength of devotion to a course of study, and friendship flourished in these quiet, twisting halls as readily as it did in the hold of a lord, and these two boys were rarely apart when one or the other of them enjoyed any free time.

"Good," she said suddenly, enjoying startling both in the midst of what she was certain was an escape plan. There was a stream not too great a ride from Lormt whose deeper pools sheltered some very large and wily trout. "I can use the pair of you. Meron, you are studying heal-craft. Stay with the Lady Una. You, Luukey, get Aden out of bed. Tell her her patient is awake."

"With pleasure! But what about you?"

"I have something to do. I shall return as soon as I have finished. Be off now, and be quick!"

Tarlach sat by the table, not really seeing the two scrolls unrolled on its surface. He was thinking rather of Seakeep, of how his comrades and the Dalesfolk would weather the winter to come.

It would be well into the spring now before they would be

able to return there. Before he could return. It was all too likely that he would be traveling alone.

Always he came back to that!

He arose and began pacing. The most of the strange community of scholars in whose company he found himself were long since abed and, indeed, were not many hours from rising again, but he was still up and fully dressed. He had slept but little since he had thrown off the effects of his race to reach this place. There was nothing to try or tire his body here, and he was not able to chain the turmoil boiling in his mind and heart for more than a few hours at a time.

Perhaps once he resumed his own search in earnest, sleep would come to him more readily. He hoped that would prove the case, for he had little love of awareness right now and even less for these long hours alone with his thoughts.

A knock came at the door. The Captain was surprised but quickly drew on his winged helmet and gave permission for his visitor to enter.

The woman Pyra. One of those attending Una. Here it was, then.

He steeled himself, looked into her face.

Tarlach turned away from her for fear of betraying himself. Hers was not the expression of one who carried tidings of death.

She stepped toward him, although she took care not to approach him too closely. "I ask pardon for intruding, Captain, but you did ask to be informed immediately of any radical change in the Lady Una's condition."

The Falconer leader faced her once more. "There has been a turn?" His voice was deadly calm, as if he were inquiring about the morrow's probable weather.

The woman nodded. "Her crisis is over. She is awake, and she will live."

He bowed his head. Praise the Horned Lord. . . .

"Thanks given for bearing the news," he said, seeming to dismiss her with that.

Unfeeling savage! she snarled in her mind, but she had not come here for his sake.

Una of Seakeep had not betrayed herself directly, not even when the jumbled speech and restlessness of fever had gripped her most strongly, and her fear just now had been controlled. It might only be the response of a brave and caring woman to the possibility of another's dying for her, even one she paid to stand her defense. As for the Talisman, Pyra knew she could be entirely mistaken about the significance of the piece.

That it was meaningful in some sense was evident. When she and Aden had undressed their patient, they had discovered two pendants, each suspended from its own chain, which the woman was wearing close beneath her clothing. One was a tiny golden amulet of Gunnora, and this they had not thought to remove, for they welcomed the aid of the Great One who was the protector of women in their fight for Una's life. The other was silver, small as well but exquisitely fashioned, the image of a falcon diving with a blood red stone in its talons.

It proved to be a thing of Power. When she first, and then Aden, had tried to remove it, the silver bird had gently but very definitely slipped from their hands. Seeing that it was somehow bound to the Holdruler and that it rested easily beside Gunnora's symbol, they had left it be.

That there might be any connection between this woman of High Hallack's Dales and one of her blank shields seemed utterly impossible, ridiculous, at first thought, but the idea of coincidence was more incredible still, particularly since Pyra had discovered in her own reading that Falconer men had once been wont to make such things and that they, too, could not be taken from those who created them or to whom they had been freely given.

She had not spoken of her suspicion, and it seemed well that she had not, for it appeared now that she had indeed been wrong or that any feeling which did exist was only on the Holdlady's part, perhaps the very reason why she wore the piece concealed.

Maybe. Pyra could not claim to know these men, or men at all really, and knew she might well have misread what she thought she had seen in the Falconer's half-screened face when he had looked down upon the unconscious woman.

Instinct said she had not. Anguish was anguish and was in some part the lot of all humanity. No race or sex escaped its lash entirely.

She studied him carefully and without seeming to do so. Had he really received her news so coldly, or was this a man who had known such terror that all his will would not have been sufficient to master what he felt, had he given any rein whatsoever to his relief?

"I am sorry, Captain, but we must ask a service of you. The Lady Una remembers that you attempted to save her from the boulder and fears that you might have been struck yourself. Her concern is strong enough to affect the course of her recovery."

He straightened visibly. "My presence would help?"

"Yes. The sooner this worry is lifted from her, the better. You would not have to remain long. Indeed, with the gravity of her injuries, that could not be permitted."

"Let us go," he ordered tightly. "We are wasting time."

The mercenary knew his way to the infirmary room by this time, although he had been glad of a guide on his first visit there. The interior of the deceptively uncomplicated-looking building was, in keeping with the others comprising Lormt, a veritable maze of corridors and small chambers. It would take long familiarity with this ancient place before one could be completely free of the danger of losing himself, at least temporarily, in its winding ways.

Aden answered her friend's soft knock. She looked from Pyra to the warrior and nodded her approval. "Excellent. I would have sent for you myself in the morning, Bird Warrior, but this is probably better. Come in."

"The Holdlady will most likely want to confer with him alone," the other woman suggested quickly. "Seakeepdale's concerns are not ours."

Lormt's healer hesitated, then yielded. "You are right.— Very well, Bird Warrior, but warn her that she can have only a few minutes. She is not yet in a condition to conduct real business."

The Captain's heart pounded rapidly as he entered the restfully lighted room where the Daleswoman lay.

He stopped just inside the door. Una was sitting up, supported by pillows. She was pale and so thin that her jade eyes seemed huge in their now tiny setting, but her smile flashed with wonderful brilliance when she caught sight of him.

"Tarlach," she whispered.

He reached the bed in a few strides and took the chair beside it, being careful not to draw so close that he might accidentally jar her. His fingers brushed the beautiful, wan cheek, then fell away again. "I wanted to say so much throughout all this," he told her in a voice thick beyond its wont, "but now I have no words."

"They are hardly needed. Pyra told me what you did." Her eyes ranged his face, what she could see of it beneath the helm he dared not remove lest the healers return before he could set it in place again. Even with that to mask him, she saw how worn he looked and cringed in her heart because she was responsible for doing this to him.

That was past, but now that she had assured herself that Tarlach was truly all right, another fear troubled her. They were not the only ones who had been present when the ill-sent rock had fallen.

"Was anyone else hurt?" she asked.

"No. Except for you, we were fortunate."

"How is Bravery?"

"She misses you. She would scarcely settle at all until I took a shirt of yours from your saddlebag and spread it out for her to lie upon. Your scent eased her."

"Poor little thing!"

"She has succeeded in establishing herself very well. Storm Challenger is intimidating, strange and a warrior besides, but she is familiar and has made herself a favorite with the people here."

The woman nodded. That would be so. Bravery was a quiet little cat and always ready to show affection. She would naturally be pleasing company for the serious-minded, elderly residents of Lormt, and the younger scholars and those performing the labor of the place would enjoy her playfulness.

Tarlach's smile reached his gray eyes. "Most of them want to protect her, I think, to keep her as much as possible out of my unsavory company." He laughed softly as her expression clouded. "I doubt anyone actually regards me as bad, just a bit too fierce for their liking.—Now that you have returned to us, she will probably be permitted to spend at least some time with you each day."

"I should love that!" Una settled herself more comfortably against her pillows. "How does your search go?"

"I have not resumed it yet." He saw her frown and hastened to go on. "I slept away the first day and have been busy with our comrades since. They are not gone long."

"Your Falconers' clannish ways are a might hard on your senior officers," she remarked dryly.

"At times," the man admitted, "though I was happy enough to have my mind thus occupied on this occasion."

"It is just as well that you delayed. Now I shall be able to work with you as we had intended."

He stared at her. "Woman, are you mad? Do you imagine I am going to allow—"

"I can read in bed as readily as at a table, and I shall be

far better off for having something concrete to do. It will not benefit me to lie here fretting."

"We shall see what those two healers have to say about it."

Una of Seakeep laughed. "That, Bird Warrior, is a coward's escape!"

A knock silenced the retort he would have made, and he turned to see the woman who had led the battle for Una's life enter the room.

"I am sorry, my Lady," Aden said even as she scanned her patient's face to see if she had already overtaxed herself, "but you must rest now. You could too easily tire yourself as yet."

Tarlach came to his feet and, after giving the Holdruler proper salute, quit the chamber with a light heart.

4

*T*he Falconer came to the familiar reading hall Aden had specified shortly after dawn and found Aden waiting for him there despite the broken night both had known.

It was a chamber like to the very many others of its nature dividing the interiors not only of Lormt's buildings and towers but worming through the walls themselves. A number of rectangular tables filled its center, their surfaces large enough to support big tomes and scrolls and the materials necessary to copy from or repair them. The chairs drawn up around them showed more care and ingenuity of construction than he had seen elsewhere in the complex's furniture, being designed to provide support and comfort for one sitting long hours in them. Light came from the long, narrow windows lining the right-hand wall but was supplemented by candles carefully placed in broad-based holders to minimize the chance of their being accidentally knocked over or of wax damage to the documents under study.

All along the walls from floor to high ceiling were shelves, row upon row of them, filled with books and scrolls, some brightly bound in relatively new leather, others showing the ravages of the years.

The man shook his head in dismay. This was only one room, and it was intended more for human use than for storage. How much material, how much knowledge, was actually in Lormt's keeping? Seeing this, he could well understand Ouen's statement that his people had not even catalogued all they possessed, especially of the records uncovered in the aftermath of the Turning. The work of preservation alone must occupy a huge percentage of all the scholars' time, those who were able to make a significant contribution to the community's efforts. Not everyone here could do that. Age had incapacitated the minds and energies of a number of the very old to a greater or lesser extent. Though they were shown kindness and respect and most were given light tasks to help maintain their own feeling of worth, they would in actuality be of very little service to their fellows.

Because this was a public hall and one that saw reasonably frequent use, it was free of dust and of the other tokens of time and neglect so frequently encountered in other parts of the complex.

The healer had already placed a number of volumes on the table beside which she was standing when he arrived. Paper and writing materials had also been supplied for his use should he have need of them.

Her hands swept over the table. "Apart from those scrolls I gave you yesterday, which are recently made copies, the works you will be studying from now on must remain here. Some of these books are so old and fragile that we dare not remove them, not even ourselves."

"That is understood."

"This is all actual Falconer material. We have little else like it, and when you have exhausted it, you will have to go back to seeking through other works for the occasional pieces of information they might contain." She studied him closely. "You are not alone in requiring access to some of this. Once the Lady Una is enough recovered that she no longer requires constant care, Pyra will need to use it as well. We want no trouble because of that."

"There will be none," the mercenary answered stiffly.

He started to turn away from her, but curiosity pricked him, and he continued to face her. "What is her interest," he asked, "and how is it that you have charge of Falconer records? I should have thought that the history of a warlike race would come more naturally into Duratan's province or that of some other like him."

Aden smiled. "The scribe of your people who wrote and left us the bulk of what you have here was a healer. I found the trove years ago and have studied it extensively. I have also sought for more like it, unfortunately without success, because it contains much heal-lore that we had not known before."

Her eyes were grave as they raised to his. "What I learned from that long-vanished man enabled me to restart my brother's lungs when I saved him out of a trap of the Dark this last spring, and I knew how to refire his heart as well had that been necessary."

Seeing his quick interest, she described for him the rescue and the means by which she had given Jerro back his life.

Tarlach was silent for several seconds. "It is to our shame," he said at the end of that time, "but we have forgotten this ourselves. Before I begin on my own work, would you instruct me in how to do it? Every year, perhaps nigh unto every month, lives would be snatched from the Grim Commandant's grasp if we again possessed this skill."

She looked at him, amazed by his ready deference to her knowledge. Even here among her own people where her skills were well known and appreciated, she did not always receive it to this degree and could not expect to do so until many more years had added the weight of time's authority to that part of her calling. Her role as a scholar, of course, would never receive much real respect beyond Lormt's walls.

"I will teach you, and gladly, Bird Warrior, but let us wait until I summon Jerro to serve as our supposed patient. The process is hard on the ribs, and I cherish my old associates too much to inflict that abuse on their fragile bones."

Time passed slowly but not unpleasantly in Lormt. Once Una's recovery began, it progressed steadily and even rapidly considering the severity of her injuries, but it was a weary long while before she was able to rise from her bed and longer still before she could venture at last beyond the thick walls of the repository.

Winter was well established by then, but its touch was as yet light, and even the older, frailer inhabitants were rarely confined to their sleeping and work rooms by reason of the weather.

As soon as he received confirmation from the healers that the Daleswoman could ride, Tarlach suggested to her that they explore the countryside around. They would have little opportunity for that once the winter closed in for a fact, and in truth, they both needed a break from dim halls and dusty books.

They needed a break from disappointment as well. Their hosts had been all too accurate in stating that Lormt contained little on his race, and the greater part of that as yet discovered concerned the healing arts. Their time had been well spent in the study of that, for there were other techniques and potion formulations his kind had forgotten over the years and Una's had never known besides that for the restarting of lungs and heart, although none were as potentially significant, and these both made sure they recorded in mind and on paper.

The Daleswoman had worked closely with him from the first, from her bed and later in the hall beside him, and had proven very apt at ferreting out odd pieces of information from seemingly unlikely nests, but still they had uncovered very little and only a small part of that of any use to his purpose. Apparently, he thought time and time again with ever-growing despondency, the tale that a great deal of old material recorded before and during their bondage to Jonkara had been deposited in the then-young storehouse of knowledge was no more than that.

He had believed it, for his race had held to the truth of their past very closely, not yielding to the impulse to make legend of it to any extent. They had always been historians, had always recorded the events and beliefs important to them, even those they had been forced to reject and now rejected by choice. However, some of what they had carried north with them had been judged too dangerous to the life their forebears had deemed it necessary to adopt, too likely to awaken the hunger for the older, warmer way, and so the decision was made to abandon it here, in the place dedicated to the preservation of knowledge, particularly of the war between the Light and the Dark just then ebbing, rather than merely to destroy it, a deed repugnant to a people who had both loved truth and were more than passing proud of what they had been despite the disaster which had stricken them.

Una had readily agreed to the proposed excursion, and so they had ridden forth early the following morning. There was a sharp bite to the air, but it was bracing rather than unpleasant for those who were well dressed and active, and their hearts soared in response to its freshness, as did those of bird and cat, who were delighted anyway in this change in what was to them a very dull and confined routine.

The Captain watched his companion, his expression tender and full of happiness. She looked herself at last, he thought, with her own true color back in her face and her eyes alive with their old, bright light, and he knew that she was truly well again even as Aden and Pyra had told him.

He smiled to himself. It was not only their words but even more so those they did not say which proclaimed that. There had been no command not to overtry themselves, no list of symptoms for which they should watch. No instructions whatsoever had been issued save the stipulation, an unnecessary one when dealing with a mountaineer like himself, that they not ride so far that they could not return quickly should the weather suddenly turn, and a sharper warning that they must under no circumstances enter any of the caves, deep or shallow, pocking the rugged country around.

The man's gray eyes narrowed and darkened. Aden had been very definite about that and had backed her order with a chilling explanation.

Danger haunted the underground ways around Lormt at this time of year, an old, old peril that had blighted these highlands almost since they had first been settled in the dim far past, so long ago that no one now knew the story of its beginning.

A being ranged those lightless places, apparently only in winter, a woman-child, tiny by all report and exquisitely pretty, but death itself to any unfortunate chancing upon her. The Ghost Child, as the apparition had been known for as long as her grim history had been recounted, would fix her blank, seemingly sightless eyes upon any visitor she encountered in her caves and seek to throw her small arms around him. When she succeeded, she would cling tightly to him for a moment before vanishing as the sound of a child's sobbing filled the air around them. Within the hour after her touch had been received, the flesh would begin to drop from her victim, rotting off his bones as would that of a corpse long dead.

This was no legend told to raise a safe shiver in those gathered around a cheery hearth. Aden had tended such a case three years previously, a stranger who had tried to weather a suddenly arising storm in a cave and who had found living death in place of shelter.

He had been far gone when discovered but had still retained the power of speech and sufficient reason to recount

his story. All she had been able to do for him was to give him
a draught which had sent him to sleep until he had passed out
of the life that had become nightmare only, and the memory
of him was still a darkness and a lash upon many of her own
nights.

Tarlach shuddered in his heart but then put thought of the
deadly child from him. This was a danger they need not meet,
and he would not permit it to cloud the day either for himself
or for his companions.

There were other perils of which they had to be mindful,
and both humans were armed, although they had not ridden
forth seeking or expecting trouble. Wild beasts and wild men
ranged these mountains and, it was reputed, other things as
well, things wakened or set on the move by the war reviving
all over this ancient, many-scarred world between the forces
of the Light and those of the Shadow and the true Dark.

The sword at the woman's side did not rest there for display. Her father had initially had her instructed in its use, and
in the time they had been together, Tarlach himself had
taught her further, taught her that and other methods of
combat. She had proven an apt pupil, and he had ever been
known as an excellent if demanding teacher, and Una of
Seakeep was now a comrade whose backing no sane man
would scorn—a fighter whose enmity no one knowing her
would willingly court.

Content though he was in the day and in the Holdlady's
company, a heaviness settled on the Falconer's spirit as they
drew farther from Lormt.

The world about them was far from dead. It was better
than eight years now since the mountains had been Turned,
and life was resilient.

Even in that first year, that first season, a few tiny green
things must have pushed their way out of isolated patches of
soil to begin the recolonization of the riven country, a process hastened in places like this where small farms existed and

the farmers had been able to save not only themselves but the seed, or to acquire the seed necessary to set their fields anew. By this time, even trees had returned. They were little trees, young trees, not the towering climax forests that had stood there before the Witch-born disaster, but they provided shelter to the creatures who were naturally native to such country. Even with winter upon the land, it was a scene, if not of completion, at least of hope and renewal.

He recognized that in his heart and mind but was not comforted. Grief filled him, as it had not for a long time now, and he recalled vividly all that had once been, the wild magnificence of the Eyrie. . . .

Storm Challenger's call snapped Tarlach's attention back to their present situation. There was anger in it and the warning that danger might be near. The falcon took wing but soon returned and called again, this time in summons.

The man urged Lady Gay forward, drawing sword as he did so. Una, who also had the ability to share thought with the war bird, pressed after him with equal caution.

They crested a low rise and saw there what the falcon's sharper senses had already detected, three dead animals and a dead man.

Tarlach dismounted beside the nearest of the slain beasts. She was a little red cow typical of the stock kept by the local farmers, and she had been dead for perhaps twenty-four hours. Her throat had been ripped out.

They moved downslope. The other two cows had been served in the same manner. It was impossible to determine the precise way in which the herdsman had met his end. One of the animals had been well devoured, but the attackers had fed first upon the human. The throat and organs of the abdominal cavity were gone, and most of the flesh had been stripped from the chest and thighs.

"By the Amber Lady!"

He turned swiftly to find Una staring down at the ravaged

corpse. His free arm circled her shoulders, and he gently moved her away from it.

"You should have stayed back, Lady," he told her softly. "This is hard viewing even for the like of me."

"I . . . am a healer," she responded tightly through set lips. "I had to confirm that there was no life."

The woman gripped herself. "What could have done this, Tarlach? Wolves?"

"I do not know." He stooped down. "This is poor ground for spoor."

He examined the site in several places before joining her again.

"It might have been wolves," he told his companion doubtfully, "but I have never seen tracks that size. There was a horse here, too, but he appears to have escaped."

Storm Challenger's battle scream tore the air even as a sudden shift in the wind carried to them a stench so vile as to set both humans gagging, the stink that betrayed the presence of the Dark or its allies.

The pair ran for their mounts, but as they did, they heard a low, soul-freezing howl on the slope above them. It was echoed immediately by others, many others, sounding on every side between them and the horses.

This was not the familiar cry of hunting wolves, not even renegades of their kind. It was something less, more resembling the bay of a hound, yet not that either. It was, rather, a wail, insidiously terrifying in its absolute cruelty and in the eerie inconsistency of its formation.

The woman tried to fight her panic. She knew that this was a call seldom heard by one of her species, a call that few if any unfortunate enough to hear it survived to describe.

Flight was impossible! The howls had not lied in placing the things far nearer than the horses. They were clearly visible now, about two dozen of them, big creatures, taller and heavier both than any lord's mastiff, and powerfully built. They were four-footed with large, long-muzzled heads sporting three short horns on their foreheads. The eyes were red, not from reflected light but in and of themselves. Very short hair, a mixture of browns and black, covered them.

One of the creatures sprang at Tarlach, confident of an early victory, and for an instant the mercenary feared his blade would have no effect upon it, but its dying wail dispelled that doubt.

Its loss would make little difference in the end. They were surrounded, cut off from their mounts, which the attackers ignored in favor of this obviously preferred prey.

"My back!" he shouted as the next beast reached him, needlessly, for Una of Seakeep was already there. None of the creatures would take him by that route while she still held her feet.

His opponent died, and he heard a suddenly stifled whine behind him to announce the Holdruler's first kill.

Another jumped at him, a big bitch that seemed to dare his stroke as she bared fangs that were like small daggers to tear out his throat. Tarlach caught her in the stomach, ripping her open.

He leaped aside as he struck but could not move quickly enough to entirely avoid the heavy body still driving forward under the force of its spring.

One more of the things threw itself at him, triumph in its snarl. He recovered himself and brought up his defenses to meet its attack.

The spring which had saved Tarlach from being thrown down had carried him a little, too far, from Una. Terror gripped her as one of the beasts shot past her to go for his back, but her sword moved almost of its own accord to slice it across the neck.

In that instant, she herself was jumped. The big animal did not bring its powerful jaws to bear but rather lowered its head, turning the spear-sharp horns on her.

The woman dropped down, under the thing. She stabbed upward, driving her blade into the lean belly.

She could not rise! They would not give her time. Una rolled aside, narrowly avoiding the slavering jaws seeking to savage her shoulder, but she knew the dog-thing would have her on its next drive.

So it would, but the humans did not wage this battle alone. Seakeep's horses were the finest on either continent, and these two had known months of Falconer training. Iron-shod hooves crashed down upon the beast's back as it came in for the kill, snapping its spine as if it had been a twig. In the moment that Eagle's Brother struck, a small creature leaped from the stallion's back to the head of the beast nearest Una and clung there with claws that raked again and again across the exposed scarlet eyes until nothing remained of them or of the flesh around them but bloody shreds of nearly unidentifiable tissue.

Lady Gay fought, too, with teeth and with hooves, literally striking a bitch off the Falconer while her teeth ripped into the neck of another.

Storm Challenger quickly took out two of the attackers, but his second victim caught him with its central horn as its blinded head flailed back in its agony. His flesh was not pierced, but he was thrown far, well beyond the place where the battle raged, and struck the ground hard. When he tried to rise again, one of his wings would no longer bear him up.

Even with their allies' help, Tarlach knew they were fighting their last engagement. Too many of the things remained, and their losses seemed only to fire their determination to make this kill. Only minutes remained before one of them was taken down. Once that happened, the other would quickly follow. . . .

One of the beasts facing him yelped and fell, an arrow through its neck.

More shafts rained upon the attackers. He looked up to see Pyra and Jerro each loose another bolt. Others were with them, some of whom he had seen at Lormt, the rest very probably countrymen from the region around.

He had the leisure to study them. This unexpected assault proved too much for the already decimated creatures, and they broke at last, fleeing for their lives.

The mercenary felt Una sway behind him and turned to support her, but he still held his sword at ready. He would not sheathe that, not yet.

Neither did the Daleswoman. She clung to him a moment, then came erect. "I am unhurt, praise the Amber Lady. Did they tear you?"

"No. I escaped injury as well."

That was not true of their comrades. Una scooped Bravery up from the head of the arrow-slain hunter to which she still clung. Her right forepaw was dripping blood.

Storm Challenger . . . he was not dead—that Tarlach would have known—but he had been felled, and he had not yet recovered sufficiently to answer his human's call.

Lady Gay whinnied. She was standing well back from the scene of the battle, her feet firmly planted in an attitude of guard.

The Holdruler looked up. "Go," she told her companion. "She has him there. Bravery is in no peril, and the others will be back soon. I can hold the guard for us in the meantime."

As if to confirm her words, Pyra returned at that moment from the hunt. She came upslope at a lope that quickened into a run as she neared the pair.

"Come, my Lady. Sit over here where the brush has not been torn. I want to make sure. . . ."

Una of Seakeep's head raised. "I am a healer as well, and I have wounded comrades. Would you have water brought to me so that I can see how much damage Bravery has taken?"

The other woman studied her sharply, then nodded and went to fetch several waterskins which had been left with her party's horses while Tarlach hastened to his winged brother's aid.

* * *

The cleaning and examination hurt the little cat, but she bore it patiently, trusting in her human's mental assurance that this treatment was needful and for her benefit. She meowed, however, as Una started to wind the bandage about the paw, and the woman glanced up to see Tarlach walking toward them. Her stomach knotted. He was cradling his falcon against him, and his mouth was a grim, tight line.

"How bad?" she asked as he drew up beside them.

"The wing may be broken, though he himself believes that it is not." The words were calmly spoken, but she who knew the man heard the fear in them.

She carefully finished covering Bravery's wound, then gave the cat to Pyra and took the war bird from Tarlach. As she did, her fingers closed for a moment over his hand in a reassurance she did not entirely feel. Avian bones were fragile, and it did not take much of a blow to shatter one.

Una spent a long time bent over Storm Challenger while her gentle, knowing fingers probed his battered wing and side.

In the end, she looked up and smiled. "Fortune is with us, Bird Warrior. He is badly bruised, but I can detect no break. If no abscess forms within, your comrade should recover soon, though he will not be able to take to the air for a few days to come."

"Praise the Horned Lord," he whispered.

He glanced swiftly at Pyra and hastily bent to rub Bravery's head.

The cat raised it to meet his hand and purred happily at his caress. He smiled despite himself. "You seem well enough at any rate, little friend."

"She, too, was lucky. My worst worry will be keeping her from tearing at the bandage until I am ready to remove it.—You checked the horses?"

He nodded. "I did. Both are as sound as ourselves."

Tarlach turned to Pyra, who was still the only one of the

Lormt people to return to them. The distant sounds of battle, the shouts of men and howls of the dire killer hounds, explained the others' continued absence right well. None of the strange creatures, apparently, would be allowed to make its escape.

"To say thanks given is scarcely adequate, but how did you know of our need in time to meet it?"

"We did not know of your danger, but we were indeed out seeking those monsters." Her rather sharp face hardened. "That poor man there had ridden out after his cattle with his young son before him in the saddle. When the hunters surprised them, he cast himself to the ground to delay them and swatted the pony on the rump, knowing the child could ride and that terror and habit would carry the animal home.

"The little boy was naturally hysterical, but he was able to relate his story coherently enough to make his mother understand what had happened, and she raised the alarm. Dark things have invaded these highlands before and are appearing in ever-increasing number, and the local people hold themselves ready to meet their challenge lest the whole area might be rendered unfit for human existence.

"A healer might have been needed, and since I am good with a bow, which Aden is not, I came in her stead."

The warrior nodded. "A brave man," he said, glancing at the corpse and shuddering in his heart at the memory of the creatures to which the herdsman had sacrificed himself for the sake of his son. "It is a hard memory for the child to have to bear even if he was spared seeing the full of it."

"It is that," the Falconer woman agreed. She liked this man almost despite herself for what she had seen of his behavior toward his companions and for his instinctive compassion, he who knew nothing of family feeling or kin care.

"The sounds of the hunt are dying," she observed. "We should be able to return to Lormt soon and try to put the events of this day behind us."

"It will be good to have it over," he agreed, but there was a heaviness in his response. It would take more than a good meal and a night's sleep to lift the weight pressing him down from his heart.

5

The Falconer Captain had drawn his chair close to the roaring fire. The heat of it was reaching him at last, although he still would not part with the heavy cloak in which he was wrapped.

This intolerance of cold was the legacy of the fever that had followed a poorly dressed wound taken early in his career when the Hounds still had the forces of High Hallack on the run. It was a mere annoyance, not a debility, and he normally did not dignify it even by acknowledging it, much less give in to it like this, but his spirits were so low that he had yielded thus far to his body's longing for a little greater comfort.

It had worked, at least. He felt drowsy now, physically at ease, and it was chiefly languor that was preventing him from seeking his bed, not the chill which had wracked him when he had first come into the room, and which had drawn him here to the fire that one of the Lormt folk had thoughtfully laid and set alight to greet him upon his return.

His expression tightened suddenly. In truth, he was not eager to court sleep, not yet. He knew himself too well to imagine that his night would be a pleasant one once his body had recovered somewhat from the exertions of the day, not with the sense of failure and the even more violent goad of guilt so lashing him.

His eyes were bleak, leaden as a sky heavy with snow. Once again Una of Seakeep had entrusted herself to him, and once again he had failed to keep danger from her. How many more times would they be able to avert disaster? How much longer? . . .

There was a knock, and he turned away from the fire, reluctantly reaching for his helm and giving permission for his visitor to enter. The door was not barred, but he had no heart for company this night, nor had he anticipated anyone coming to him. Was something amiss with Lormt or the lands around or with the Holdruler herself?

The intruder was Duratan. He opened the door as soon as he received leave to do so but paused there. "I hope I am not disturbing you, Bird Warrior, but I did see the light of your candles beneath your door and knew you were at least not abed."

"No. Enter and be welcome. How may I serve you?"

"I merely wanted to check upon each of you before retiring myself. That was no light threat you fought today."

The scholar's eyes narrowed. Despite the relative mildness of the winter, the nights were still cold, and the fire had been laid early. It warmed the small room well, and there should be no need for that cloak, not for a sound man.

"Are you wounded, Captain?" he asked with real concern. "We have men here with knowledge of heal-craft, though none are nearly as skilled—"

"I am whole," the Falconer replied curtly as he loosed the garment from his shoulders. He felt shamed to have been discovered so studying himself. "If I trusted the Lady Una with my comrade, I would also have allowed her to attend to me. Healers are so frequently female that we are often compelled to submit to their care, though Wise Women we do try to avoid, there being more of witchery in their work."

Duratan nodded. That had been true even before the fall of the Eyrie when the mercenaries hired their swords afar and could not readily return to their own stronghold for aid.

"And the winged one, how does he?" asked Duratan.

"Well, even as the Holdruler said. He will be flying again in a couple of days.—Bravery?"

"Resting comfortably and enjoying the attention she is receiving." He shook his head in an amazement he did not try to conceal. "She is well named. I would expect no less from your falcon, but I have never before heard of the like from a cat."

"Most creatures will fight if they see one they love threatened." He steadied himself to hold his voice even although he realized the other would have spoken of it by now if he bore ill news. "The Lady herself?" It would not be taken as too strange that he should ask that in view of her role in his effort to preserve his people, which he had described for Duratan before riding for the coast to meet her.

"No ill effects, and you may believe her two guardians sought for them."

Tarlach smiled. "I am surprised they allowed you access to her."

"She is no longer ill, and I do not imagine that Una of Seakeepdale allows others to will for her very often."

"Not at all that I have observed."

"She has some rare skills to accompany her determination. Jerro reported that she was fighting like a pard when our people arrived and put that pack to flight."

"It is well for her that she can do so, is it not?" the Falconer said bitterly. "Her prospects for a long life would be poor if she were depending entirely upon the guarding she has been receiving from me."

The scholar stared at him. "I do not see how any warrior could have done more for her sake."

"My kind give and regard our oaths seriously, in spirit and word. It is mine to shield Seakeepdale and its ruler from peril, not merely to fight well once we have walked into it, yet since my taking service with her, we have moved from one near disaster to another."

Duratan frowned. He thought he had detected concern on the Holdlady earlier and saw that it was well founded. Her comrade's spirit was badly darkened, blacker by far than it had been on the night he had revealed his reason for coming to Lormt, even if this was only a reaction to the unexpected assault on top of the tension of the past weeks and the near total failure of their search.

"The Lady Una is not a fool," he said quietly, "nor is she timid. If she were dissatisfied with the quality of your service, she would have dismissed you by now."

The falcon came erect in the nest Tarlach had made for him and spread his wings with an angry hiss. The Captain's hand quickly reached out to soothe him.

Duratan studied him somberly, recalling vividly the story he had told of how his company had come to bind themselves to Una of Seakeep's cause and all that had befallen them since.

A fever had ravaged the Dales of High Hallack several seasons back, hitting men, young active men, the hardest, although none could predict the severity with which it would strike any given place.

It had been at its worst when it swept through most of the Dales in Seakeep's area, stripping them of many of the men time had restored after the war with Alizon. Only one, Ravenfielddale, had escaped with light damage, and its lord had proved the deadly foe of all the rest.

Una of Seakeep had found herself bereft of both lord and sire and threatened by a man many times stronger than her or any of her other neighbors, one determined to secure control of her Dale and its harbor, the only one of any size along all the vast stretch of coast north of Linna. Believing she had no other choice short of capitulation, she had set out in search of blank shields, a goodly number of them.

It was the Captain's company that she found. Falconers who had fought Alizon in High Hallack owed a debt of honor to Lord Harvard, her father. They had no other way of repaying it, and so they swallowed their dislike of females and accepted service with his daughter. Besides, the Lord Ogin, her enemy, was suspected of being a black wrecker.

Those renegades who lured ships to their doom in order to then claim their cargoes were foes to all and were particularly abhorred by his race, which frequently took on marine commissions.

The mercenary had passed over the weeks spent in quiet guarding but had described in detail the great gale they had weathered and the wreck of the merchantman he had witnessed at its height. He told how he had dived from the cliff into the furious sea with the rope to be the survivors' road to safety bound to him and how the line had severed as the exhausted sailors were climbing up along it. Una of Seakeep had seen it snap and had caught it, twisting it about her hands while she braced herself against the stone to which it had been tied.

Tarlach's thoughts, too, returned to that night and to the events he had so vividly described, and a chill filled him at the memory of Una's courage. She had held on there, supporting the weight of each mariner, until his comrades discovered and relieved her. Those scars circling her hands were tokens of that night's service, and the Horned Lord alone knew how she had escaped, becoming permanently crippled because of it.

He had gone on to relate how the survivors had confirmed the existence of the black wrecker and described the disastrous voyage which had left their vessel and three men dead but which had given them the proof they needed against Ogin, proof that had been delivered only after Una and he and two others had been forced to weather a second, smaller gale and the most of the day following it in an open dory. Lastly, he told of the attack that had defeated Ravenfield's Holdlord and his hirelings.

He had hesitated then, but had continued in the end. The work being done here had demanded that he do so despite the fact that there might be danger in speaking out, for himself as well as for his hope, should Duratan prove careless of tongue. Ouen and Aden and the former Borderer, aided by several other of the more able scholars, were striving to learn and record all they could of the struggle between the forces of Light and Dark, both in the past and now. The old balances had been disturbed through all the known lands of this world, and it was becoming ever more apparent that the ancient, near dormant war could all too soon burst forth in its full fury once more. Any weapons that could be discovered to aid life's cause would be welcome, aye, and could be essential to preventing the Dark from drawing them all into its ever ravenous maw. Tarlach had told of the strange spirit woman who had been Una's friend, of the warning she had brought: that the very site of their approaching battle was a Dark gate nigh to open, and needing only a little more blood to give the thing ravening inside the strength it required to tear away the last bonds holding it back. He described the opening of that gate and of the duel waged by the spirit in their defense, which had ended in the defeat of the horror seeking entrance into their realm and the sealing of its passage, a victory she had secured at the cost of her own existence.

Of other things he had not been able to speak. He could not tell this man of the way regard had grown between Una of Seakeep and himself, of how they had drawn ever closer during their weeks together, first in peace and then in shared peril, a closeness culminating in the declaration they had made to one another on that Ravenfield beach while the gate they believed would be their doom slowly opened before them. Even were such revelation possible, he could not have brought himself to disclose the details of their later meeting in the safety of Seakeep's high round tower when they had affirmed that they were lord and lady in heart, although both accepted the stark reality of the fact that they could probably never be so joined in body or before the world. He might or might not have had the courage to fly in the face of his people's custom had he been free to act for himself, but that liberty of action was not his, and both of them were bound by the same chain of purpose.

That heavy cause itself, the reason why he had come to this continent, why he had journeyed to Lormt, was another matter. That need not be hidden, though it was Falconer business. Duratan and his associates had been good to him, receiving him kindly and giving every assistance without ever raising the questions pricking their ever active, eager minds. They deserved this much return, and courtesy had demanded that it be given.

Tarlach had told how Una of Seakeep and he had each come to recognize the specter of extinction looming over his people and of the incredible thing she had done to prevent their destruction.

The scholar had stared at him in stunned silence for several seconds.

"She . . . gave you a Dale?" he had whispered at the end of that time, stunned by the magnitude of that gifting.

His head had raised in pride as he had given his answer. "She had no will to keep Ravenfield after having gained it through blood, but chiefly she could not stand back unacting and allow a race to fade out of the universe when the means to prevent it were hers. For the same reason, she has entered into treaty with me for the joint use of Seakeep's wild country, since only thus would we have sufficient land to establish a new Eyrie and its villages."

Tarlach had stopped there, gathering his thoughts. There were stipulations in that agreement with respect to the treatment of the women he would bring to High Hallack, for Una would not perpetuate old evil, and changes in their association, male with female, would have to come. These, too, he had described as far as he was able, but much of the actual detail was still in the stage of thought only.

Duratan had remained quiet some time after he had finished speaking.

"So you came to Estcarp to seek the approval of your

officers and comrades and to gain the consent of enough
women to enable you to establish a viable community?"

"Even so."

"You realize the danger you could be facing?"

The Captain had nodded grimly. "I may have come to
meet my death if I am judged a renegade by all, and I shall
be outcast by many of the columns, perhaps all to no avail.
Even if I can gain permission to approach any of the villages,
there is no guarantee I can convince a sufficient number of
women to accompany me, even with the Lady Una's testimony to strengthen my cause."

"She will not have an entirely pleasant life if you do succeed," he had observed. "Your people will have to deal with
her long-term, and some of them are not likely to tackle well
to that necessity, whatever concessions they make with respect to your own."

"As Holdlord of Ravenfield, I am the logical choice to be
the Falconers' representative with Seakeep and its people,"
the mercenary had responded stiffly. "We two have at least
proven that we can work together." He had shrugged
slightly. "What must be endured shall be. Neither of us can
avoid the war because we fear the bite of an opponent's
steel."

He had then explained in answer to the scholar's question
that he had come to Lormt in quest of weapons, for anything
that might sway those he must approach in his favor. He had
also hoped to discover information about the lives his people
had led before their move north which could help guide him
in building a new lifeway in High Hallack, one acceptable to
all their number, male and female alike, but he had not been
able to unearth anything of significance despite all his efforts
and the untiring assistance of his hosts, not then and not
since.

Duratan saw the shadow deepen on him and guessed its
cause. "You and the Lady Una have not had any better
success?" he asked. "I had hoped you might have learned

something since you have been working with much older materials."

"Almost none. Your people could not have done more to aid us, but Lormt has very little on my kind. Apart from the heal-lore, which is indeed worth the finding, I have discovered well nigh nothing of the nature I was seeking."

He did not say that the one piece of data he had found had given him an ugly scare. The Talisman had been mentioned in some detail in one of the scrolls. Both Aden and Pyra must have read it, and they would have seen his gift to Una of Seakeep.

He had relaxed in the end. Any personal relationship between the Daleswoman and one of his race was so unlikely as to seem inconceivable, and he trusted that the healers would completely overlook the significance of the piece for that reason, as seemed to be the case in fact. At least, neither of them had betrayed any suspicion that Una might be more to him than an employer.

"What made you believe we might have custody of such records, Bird Warrior? You Falconers have been close about your affairs since you arrived on this continent."

"It is understood amongst us that we had left a large cache of documents relating to the old ways here shortly after our coming, but either there is no truth in that report, or else the material has been lost or destroyed in the great expanse of years since that time."

"It might also merely not have been rediscovered as yet."

"I know that," Tarlach replied with a sigh, "but we can give no more time to the search. The winter has been mild thus far, but we cannot trust that it will remain so. If we do not leave soon, we may be snowed in here until spring. By that time, most of the Commandants will be oath-bound again or long gone in search of a commission." He shook his head. "Besides, the Holdlady cannot stay away indefinitely from her Dale, and I am responsible to my command stationed there." If he still had a command at the end of all this.

Duratan nodded. "I knew you could not be far from that decision now that Lady Una is well. When will you be leaving?"

"In a few days, once I am certain our comrades are fit for the road."

"You will go with our good wishes, whatever their worth. We shall continue delving our records here, and if we uncover anything of significance, I will see that word of it reaches you at Seakeep."

The Falconer looked at him in surprise. "You would do that?"

"I am no different from most others in that I prefer to have a goal for my efforts. Your quest is a hard one, Bird Warrior. I fear it would be scarcely less difficult to restore these mountains to their former state than to accomplish what you would do, but all that can be done here to aid you, I shall do. I only wish your visit to Lormt had proven more profitable for you."

"It has brought me a good friend, it seems. That is not a gain to be slighted."

Bravery lay on her back, batting at Una's hand with one bandaged and three sound paws.

"You little trouble!" the woman chided. "I shall never finish dressing, much less get my hair into place if we keep this up!"

A rap caused her to glance toward the door. It was an instinctive move, but precisely the opening the cat was seeking. As Una's hair swept over her shoulder in response to the motion, Bravery grabbed for it, tangling in it with supple claws and mouth.

Tarlach's eyes were dark when he slipped into the room, but when he saw the cat, chiefly feet and wide-eyed face, peering from the flood of hair, he laughed.

The Daleswoman scowled at him as she freed herself.

"You would not be so amused if it were your hair that she was pulling," she told him tartly.

"Perhaps not," he replied with a grin, "but she was very entertaining from here. Your expression alone would have been reward enough for my visit."

She studied him curiously. The Falconer had carefully avoided entering her chamber until now, and she wondered what had brought him, and so early in the day.

He read her thought. "I just wanted to assure myself that you both were all right before your two guardians awoke and forced me to be more circumspect again."

Her jade eyes shadowed. "Did Duratan not tell you that last night?"

The warrior stiffened. "You sent him to me, then, told him there was trouble on me?"

"No, I did not. He intended to visit us both. I mentioned only that our search did not go well when he inquired about it. If he read more into my answer than that, I am sorry."

"There was more?"

"I was and am worried, Tarlach. You were like a defeated man when we parted yesterday, at least to my eyes. I do not like to see that on you, not before we have even begun to approach your columns."

"It was not our lack of success," he assured her quickly. "We both knew this was but a chance—"

"I realize that." She turned from him to conceal her face. "I am ever a weight on you!"

The man came to her. "What do you mean, Una of Seakeep?"

"I have seen the way you have been watching me, as if you fear I will shatter in a moment, and you already hold yourself responsible. It is a weight no other of your race has to endure."

"Are we the richer for that?" His hands closed on her shoulders and forced her to turn, to look at him. "It is true that we have no experience with this brand of caring, and I own I am clumsy in managing it, but I do not regret that I love you, that I cherish you even more than I desire you."

He held her against him, and his eyes closed. "The thought of losing you is a spear through the core of my being. That we must remain apart, I can endure, but I must know for my sanity's sake that you are alive and well within this universe."

She made him no answer save to rest against him. His lips tenderly brushed the rich chestnut hair so that he caught the fresh scent of the herbs with which she had washed it. Her body felt warm and soft, and he guessed she wore little beneath the blue chamber robe, which the healer Aden had probably lent her.

She seemed vulnerable and responsive, and she was beautiful, female and feminine both.

His mouth found hers, but his kiss was gentle, loving only, and he reluctantly drew away from her in the next moment lest what he already felt rising in him swept him completely. It would not take long, he knew, for he wanted this woman very badly.

In that instant, he hated all that he was and all that rested on him because he could not declare openly what burned in his heart and mind. To take Una of Seakeep in any other fashion, to make of her his trollop, though no other should ever learn of it, that was not even to be considered, not while he retained any shred of honor or any control whatsoever over himself.

He stepped back, and it was with bittersweet satisfaction that he saw she shared his regret, although she, too, separated herself a little from him. It was by no accident, he realized, that she dressed and acted as she did with him, as a comrade, deemphasizing this other part of her, which could gain them nothing and would only add to their frustration and tension.

The Holdruler smiled ruefully. If there was hunger on him, on them both, at least the gloom was gone for a while.

She tossed her head, thus easing them away from the mood gripping them and the moment that had preceded it.

"I do not usually like to issue you orders, Bird Warrior," she told him, "but I am going to do so now. We shall be leaving Lormt soon, and once we do, we—you—are not likely to be returning to these mountains again very soon. I watched you yesterday. The alteration in them lashed you, but you were intrigued by the resurgence of life. Ride them now for a few days, be alone with them, gain the assurance that one day they will again be all that you once knew, although neither of us shall see them then. I will remain here and watch over the recovery of our two comrades."

She saw what flashed into his eyes and shook her head impatiently. "Will you ever see the dark side of a question, Tarlach of the Falconers? I am not ill or injured or weary, but I do want you to have this time."

Una smiled again, reassuring and commanding both. "Go fly, Mountain Hawk. Act for yourself for once." The jade eyes sparkled. "Take care, however. I do not want to winter in Lormt, whatever welcome our hosts have for us, because you have broken your leg on a pleasure jaunt!"

6

Once away from Lormt, Tarlach felt his spirits lift, and he knew Una had been right. He had needed this time to himself, to explore and observe and be free for a while from the burden of responsibility. Only the fact that Una and Storm Challenger were not here to share it with him marred his pleasure in these few days stolen from the normal press of his life.

The first he spent finishing exploring the slopes around the old structure, and he camped there that night, but with the dawn of the following morning, he turned his attention to

the true heights, heights such as he had known and loved
since his boyhood. The Eyrie had been situated in a location
like to this as it had once been. . . .

Quickly banishing that thought and the shadow it cast
over him, he threw his head back and breathed deeply of the
cold, clear air. That, at least, had not been marred by the
Witches' spell casting.

The effects of the Turning were even more evident here
than below, where milder conditions aided the reestablish-
ment of natural life, but there was a raw magnificence about
it that both moved and held him.

This was an incredibly wild region, a realm of stone whose
grim aspect was rather emphasized than relieved by the
hardy plants finding place there. It was a fascinating world
despite or, perhaps, because of its bleakness, harsh and yet
strangely compelling to one not frightened by the stark coldness of virgin rock.

The Falconer knew where he wished to begin his hunting
and made for the place, the foot of the great cliff soaring up
behind the softer rises supporting Lormt and the farms nestled around it. He had noted its many ledges and outcrop-
pings from the vantage of the settlement below and had
yearned in his heart to explore them. Now he had the opportunity, and he was resolved not to squander a moment of it.

Tarlach went as far as he could on horseback and then
dismounted in a small natural meadow near the place where
he would begin his ascent of the cliff itself, dropping the reins
so that Lady Gay would know she was free to feed but that
she was not to wander far. There was good grass and a small,
fast stream to provide water, and he knew the mare would
suffer no want in his absence.

His eyes followed the rugged line of the rock upward. They
glowed with anticipation. The task before him was not impossible, but it would take a mountaineer's skill to master it,
and the pleasure of that testing was on him. It had been so
long since he had last met its like.

The difficulty of the way increased speedily once he did begin to climb, but its hardships were ever a challenge and not a barrier, and he steadily won altitude until at last he stood on the spot he had selected as the first stage of his day's search.

His body was hard, and his breath came normally again very shortly after he had attained his goal.

The man looked about him. Only a little of the high country was actually visible to him. He had climbed far, but the crests of the surrounding mountains remained above him.

That did not matter. He had not come here to conquer peaks but to observe a little of their slopes.

Tarlach then turned to examine the forbidding miniature world into which he had entered. The winning to this vantage had in itself been a joy, a contest just strenuous enough to be stimulating at the relaxed pace at which he had tackled it, and now he felt fresh and ready for the excitement the discovery of new things always brought him.

It was not a pretty place. In truth, he could hardly have imagined a more uninviting country or a harsher one. His mind had called this a slope, but that was merely a convenient mental label, maybe even a subconscious effort to soften what was in actuality a broad ledge jutting out from an incline so steep that the inexperienced would have judged it nigh unto perpendicular.

Because this part of the mountainside had never been forested, it had always suffered heavy weathering, a fact which combined with its severe topography to prevent colonization by the ferns and grasses and rough shrubs covering those lower, gentler slopes where the trees had not yet begun to make their return in force.

The rarity of growing things made those which did exist the more fascinating. The Captain knelt beside a stunted tree, marveling at the eerie twisting of its branches and trying to estimate the depth and course its roots had taken. He did not wish to dig around it or make any other effort to answer his questions, fearing to injure an organism whose hold on life might well be as tenuous as it was enduring.

It was a survivor, this small plant. Tarlach touched a gnarled branch gently, respectfully. This had not grown here in eight short years. It must have somehow weathered the Turning, one of the few rooted things to do so, and possibly had weathered many another near disaster in the ages that it might well have seen since it first sprouted from its seed.

Softly whistling the refrain of a song well known in his company, he left it for another patch of green which had just taken his eye.

Half an hour passed most pleasantly as the Falconer wandered from place to place, his heart alive with wonder and a delight in living which he had not known in many a long day.

Even in that short time, he confirmed that the seemingly barren cliffside was, in truth, anything but sterile. Its flora existed on a reduced scale and was thus easily overlooked, but it abounded wherever there was enough shelter to permit it to take root. Everywhere he saw growth which had been familiar to him in the heights where he had spent his youth. The plants were scarce as yet, colony patches rather than a true, ever-varying carpet, but they were back, and they were thriving. These mountains would indeed eventually become again all that they once had been.

The weathering which had created so many safe pockets for seeds and spores was less helpful to a human intruder. There was a good bit of loose stone and gravel on the ledge, and he had to place his feet carefully or risk a fall. That broken leg Una had mentioned could prove as disastrous as a tumble over the edge in a spot so wild and far from help.

Tarlach had expected to pass his time with the plant life of the slope or merely looking out over the vista beyond, but his attention was drawn to the cliff face itself when he squatted near a clump of moss of particular interest, since it was the first of its kind that he had encountered, and suddenly found himself shifting position in an unconscious effort to remove himself from a cool draught.

Surprised, he searched the rock wall behind him until he located a black fissure close to ground level. A moist finger confirmed that it was the source of the odd air current.

He gingerly inserted his hand but could not discover its end in the little distance the narrowness of the opening permitted him to explore.

The man rocked back on his heels, staring at the crack in amazement. Then he smiled. He had no cause for astonishment. Had Aden not mentioned that there were many caves of various sizes honeycombing all the highlands around Lormt? This was merely yet another part of that system.

He rose and stepped back to scan the cliff for sign of any further linking with the ghost-ridden underworld.

The movement was both careless and too quick. His foot turned as it came down on a stone, and he fell heavily.

Tarlach instinctively dug in his heels to brake himself although he was in no actual danger of rolling outward and off the ledge.

Suddenly, his legs jerked as the support of the ground under him vanished. The whole world seemed to be disappearing into a gaping chasm.

He clawed desperately with his hands, trying to push himself up against the flow of material, but the weakened crust gave further, and he dropped down amidst a rain of gravel and larger rocks.

The warrior did not lose consciousness immediately when he struck bottom. He was dimly aware that debris continued to fall from the broad patch of light above and dragged himself farther into the darkness, where he collapsed, overcome at last by the shock of the fall.

Tarlach's mind was slow in returning, but it held steady when he again woke to his surroundings.

He sat up, clutching at his head as he did so, and leaned

back against the stone wall for a few minutes, his eyes tightly closed, until the world ceased spinning and he was able to take some rudimentary stock of himself.

Physically, he could be far worse off. His body felt as though it must be a mass of bruises, and his head ached abominably, but he could discover no sign of broken bones or other serious injury. There certainly were no spurting arteries or deep puncture wounds, or he would scarcely be in any condition to search for them at this stage. There were no symptoms of shock to indicate internal injury, although only time would confirm that.

That was about the sum of his good fortune, he thought as he looked about him.

The half-conscious instinct which had driven him deeper into the cave had saved or at least prolonged his life, for a vast amount of material had fallen between the time of his passing out and his awakening. The pit had been nearly completely filled in, was totally filled for all practical purposes. Only a chink a few inches across remained open to the outer world. The single ray of light it admitted was his sole source of illumination, not much in itself but sufficient for his needs and even brilliant to eyes already adjusting to the deadly blackness all around.

The air remained good and flowed too strongly to be coming through that tiny crack above, so he could feel certain that he had fallen into part of a reasonably large cavern system.

Whether or not it connected with the outer world, he could not say. That made no real difference anyway. He could not crawl through miles of what were probably highly complex tunnels, tunnels very likely littered with countless perils, without a light or more food and water than the small amount he had taken with him from his saddlebags to sustain him until he returned to Lady Gay and hope to find his way home, not unless greater fortune than he had any right or reason to expect should be with him. Even without the ghost to contend with, he simply did not believe it could be done. The chance of coming upon another exit under such conditions was simply too slim to be considered as a viable option for his escape.

What then? He still had his weapons. They could free him very quickly of thirst and hunger and the terror of a slow and utterly lonely death.

His hand did not go near sword or knife. That was for later, when hope was exhausted and the actual pangs were upon him. Far better to crawl a while through the eternal night than to claim such release prematurely.

There was yet another possibility.

He was not so very far below the surface, no more than fifteen feet or so, and that air hole above showed that the roof was not thick. He might just be able to breach it.

Tarlach examined the debris which had followed him into the pit. It was mostly small stuff, he decided, the gravel and dirt that had accumulated in the low place to form a loose crust over the fissure and the ground around it. There seemed to be almost no big rocks with it.

Such material was likely to be treacherous, but he felt that it could be managed with the few tools he had or could fashion. Theoretically, he should be able to mount it and work his way through the roof plug to the surface.

The actual attempt would not be so simple, of course. It would be far more a dig than a climb, and he would have to fashion a succession of shelves as he went, a crude scaffolding system to provide himself with a reasonably secure workspace for each phase of the operation.

He licked already dry lips. He had one chance, two at best. If his strength did not give out by then, the roof and what remained of the crust would. Their already fragile hold would shatter under his continued worrying, and the whole mass would fall, either burying him outright or sealing him still living in what was well nigh certain to become his tomb.

Perhaps all of this was irrelevant. A horror stalked these

caves that was independent of landslide, independent of the
endless night or the agony of physical want. How long did he
have before the killer spirit of which Aden had spoke came
upon him and touched him with her blight? How much time
remained before the flesh began to rot from his still-living
body as if it were already a corpse long abandoned by its
soul?

He put the thought of that danger from him since there
was nothing he could do to avert it and set to work with all
the speed and force he dared throw against the unsettled
mound of debris.

The task the Falconer had set himself proved more physically trying and far slower even than he had anticipated. The
material comprising the landfall was difficult to dig with the
knife and flat stone he was compelled to use in place of pick
and shovel. The wet autumn and winter had imparted
enough cohesiveness to the gravel for him to be able to work
with it, but even so, hours passed during which he felt he
made no progress at all.

He was very close to panic. It was growing late, and he
would be able to keep on with this only while light continued
to pour through that very small opening.

Tarlach glanced fearfully up at it and shook his head.
Night would come quickly down here once the evening advanced and the invisible sun began its descent in earnest.

And then? He bent his aching back to lift out another
scoopful of damp gravel. Then he must sit huddled against
some stony wall until the sky far above brightened enough
for him to begin his digging anew.

Daylight would come again if another cave-in did not close
him off from it completely, but he knew in his heart and soul
that the Ghost Child would reach him first.

He tried to tell himself that this was probably a safe area,
no more than a hole in the ground, but he knew it was not
so. It was part of the caves, and he could expect no mercy,

not when darkness reigned supreme once more, perhaps not even before then.

His eyes closed, and he had to battle himself to keep on working. The healer had told her tale all too well. Death in battle, he did not court but could at least accept as part of the road he had been bred and trained to travel, but there was too much of horror in this. All his resolution could not hold him firm in the face of it.

His mounting terror worked against him, making his movements jerky and hasty, robbing his shaking hands of fine control, but it was beyond his will to master it completely. He could only set his teeth and press on, battling himself and the flying time and the damnably uncooperative stuff he must somehow mold to fit his need.

The light failed him abruptly, as he had guessed it would.

Although expected and even overdue, its loss finished him. He cast himself against the mound of debris, his body wracked by tearing sobs.

The wave of hysteria ebbed after a few moments, and Tarlach was able to grip himself again. He dropped to his knees and felt his way out of the pit area to the more secure stone-roofed tunnel beyond.

He lay down there and removed his battered helmet, resolving to rest, to sleep if he could. He was ashamed of his momentary breakdown, yet he was grateful for it, too. It had released some of the terror building inside him. The fear was still there but not the panic. If he could keep that chained during the following hours—and avoid the doom that had given it birth—he should be able to finish the work on the mound fairly early the next day, probably before noon. Then, of course, he must tackle the roof.

One thing he did know, he wanted desperately to live, and he would fight for life as long as the power to do so remained his.

7

*T*arlach groaned and opened his eyes.

A soft light filled the rocky chamber, and an elfin face was peering curiously into his own. The combination of mischief and merriment in it was so irresistible that, before he was even half awake, he had laughed and tapped the upturned nose with a playful finger as he had often seen Rufon do with his small granddaughter at Seakeep.

Then his heart froze in its beat, and he shrank back as all his horror returned to him in full force.

This was not the bright face of the Seakeepdale child with her laughing eyes and cheeks a creamy tan after a summer spent running wild on her father's farm. The little maid before him was undeniably lovely with rippling masses of brown hair and great, pale green eyes, but she was wan as no living being could be. The folk around Lormt were right to have named her a ghost, for this she indeed seemed to be.

The light appeared to be—was—emanating from her.

The spirit had started to reach for his hand but had stopped when he pulled away from her, and she was now looking at him in hurt amazement.

The man sat up quickly. "I am sorry," he said, attempting to control the shaking of his voice. He had heard that the first to speak sometimes gained an edge in such an encounter. "For a moment there, I thought you were another little girl."

"Your little girl?"

"No. Just someone I know."

"Oh."

She appeared to study him, cocking her head to one side. "Are you cold?" she asked at last.

"Not very. Why?"

"Because you are shivering so."

He stared at her, then smiled despite himself. "I suppose you frightened me," Tarlach told her with perfect honesty.

The Ghost Child laughed in delight at that.

She seated herself beside him, smoothing her dress carefully as she took her place. He noticed it for the first time and found it to be cumbersome, not like those worn by women or female children in either Estcarp or High Hallack, not now. It might be very old, given the age of the legend concerning her, but he knew nothing of women's fashion to be able to put a date on it.

The small face lifted to look directly into his. "You were asleep a long time." A new thought occurred to her. "Did I wake you?"

"No, at least I do not believe so. I was probably just slept out and woke by myself." Or his warrior's senses had reasserted themselves and roused him.

"I am so glad! I tried to be very quiet. Kathreen says that I chatter so and must not always be troubling people."

"Kathreen?"

"My sister. She is very big and very wise." Her face lighted with pride. "She is pretty, too."

"That I do not doubt if she is like to you."

The ghost vigorously nodded her agreement. "I am Adeela," she said, as if she had suddenly remembered the training in courtesy she had received.

Here the Falconer hesitated. He did not want to frighten the child and something within him did not want to hurt her, but knowledge of another's name gave a measure of power over that person in certain forms of sorcery. He was not about to reveal his to this or any other spirit even if it were not against his kind's custom to do so with those not of their own race. Only to Una . . .

Suddenly he recalled the title the Holdlady had put on him. "I am called Mountain Hawk," he told her, then inclined his head as he had seen lords in the Dales do. "I am pleased to greet you, Adeela."

The man blinked, not knowing whether to laugh or cry. He realized that he meant what he had just said.

Adeela did not notice the change in him this time. She was staring at their surroundings as if she were seeing them for the first time.

She turned back to him. "Why were you sleeping?"

"Because I could not keep my eyes open."

"No!" she exclaimed in exasperation. "I mean why were you sleeping *here*?"

"I fell in and got very tired trying to find a way out again."

"Were you looking for diamonds?"

"No," he answered with some amusement. "I stepped in a hole, and down I came."

The Ghost Child was quiet a long time. She kept looking around her and pressed close to him, as if she were growing afraid. Unaccustomed as he was to offering such comfort, he put his arm around her and was rewarded by feeling her grow less tense.

"Do you have any cousins?" she asked suddenly in a very low voice.

"Probably. Why?"

"I do not like cousins. No-el is my cousin."

Tarlach felt a chill settle in his stomach. He did not want to know why the small spirit disliked this No-el.

Memory had caught her, however, and she went on, almost oblivious to him in her agitation. "No-el told us we would find diamonds for mother in the cave. It was to be a grand surprise, and we were to tell no one until we came back with them, but the cave looked so dark and the door was so tiny that I started to cry, and Kathreen said she was sure we could find our diamonds outside if we looked hard enough."

The big eyes seemed to grow larger still as they suddenly fixed on him. "No-el picked up a stone and hit her with it until her head got all red. Then he pushed her into the cave and pushed me in, and he rolled a big, heavy rock in front of the door. He would not take it away, and I could not move it no matter how hard I tried."

Her lip was trembling, and tears coursed down her cheeks, but she was too gripped by her old fear to wipe them away. "Kathreen was asleep. She would not wake up even though I called her and called her. I called everyone, but no one would come."

Adeela rubbed at an eye with a small, balled fist. "I was so hungry and thirsty, and I wanted mother to take us out of that horrible dark. . . ."

The warrior's eyes closed. He picked up the child and held her tightly to him. Her body seemed solid enough in his arms, but it was cold, and he could not feel what should be a wildly slamming heart.

He did not really notice her strangeness now, not in the face of her fear and misery and confusion. "Your mother could not hear you, Adeela," he said softly, "and . . . and neither could Kathreen. That is why they could not help you."

She stopped crying. "Mother was down in the big hold where we were stopping, but Kathreen was right there with me. . . ."

She paused and then looked up at him. "Had Kathreen gone away? Like my grandsire?"

"Yes."

The child rested her cheek against his chest. "No-el made her go?"

"Yes, he did."

"He must be very wicked."

"Unbelievably wicked."

She pulled a little away from him. "Was he punished?"

"Probably," he replied. He stroked the soft, thick hair and sighed deeply. "That was a long time ago, Adeela. Your mother and Kathreen would not want you to be still crying over it."

He fought to keep the fury burning inside him from reaching his voice, knowing she did not need more anger and hate. She was little more than a babe, and to have suffered so much and then be condemned to this. . . .

She had not deserved any of it. She certainly had not deserved to become what she was here.

Remembering the doom she carried only caused Tarlach to hold her the tighter. If he was to die through her, so be it. The fault—the guilt—was not hers that he should hate her, and he had the means of gaining release before the horror became too much. In the meantime, he would not, could not, refuse her the comfort she had already been denied in her first great need. Even terror could not make him that savage.

The little maid grew very quiet, and he felt certain she had gone to sleep.

He gazed down at her, and the fear left him. Adeela was a child again, whatever her physical state. The horror and violence of her death, the unfulfilled need to lash out at the one who had done such wrong to her and perhaps at those who could not help her, had combined to overpower a soul too immature to deal with them, had frozen awareness and humanity and had somehow made her a force of destruction in her turn. Now that curse was broken. Of that, he was positive.

The Captain hoped he had in some way helped to bring about her release but supposed that the time for it had probably just come. Otherwise, he was at a loss to explain his own escape, unless the unlikely sight of a man sleeping peacefully in such surroundings had managed to reach Adeela's numbed mind and returned the spark of life to her paralyzed humanity.

He wondered what would happen next. She should probably begin her journey down the last, long road now that she was free and knew herself once more, but she was very obviously still here.

He smiled tenderly. Maybe she just needed to rest a bit after her countless ages of weary wandering.

* * *

Tarlach dozed again himself and had gone quite far into sleep when he felt Adeela leap from his arms.

"Kathreen! It is Kathreen! Can you not hear her?"

He shook his head but released his little companion's hand. He did not doubt that she had faculties unknown to him.

He started, his heart beating fast. The moment of her final release must be upon her! "Go find your sister. Hasten! She has been waiting a long time for you."

Adeela needed no further urging. She raced from his side. Her small body seemed to waver and then vanished completely from his sight.

The pale light disappeared along with her, plunging the cave tunnel into utter darkness.

The mercenary did not really miss it. The night was well on, and he knew morning would bring him its glow before much more time had elapsed.

His head sunk upon his breast. He was very glad for Adeela, but by the Horned Lord, he had loved having her here with him. He could too easily still meet his death in this place, and now the loneliness of it seemed magnified a thousandfold.

8

*P*yra sought out Una of Seakeep where she was working in the long reading hall shortly after the Captain had left Lormt.

She sat down beside the Daleswoman. "Duratan has told me your purpose in coming here," she said after a brief hesitation. "He learned of it from your Falconer before he rode off to meet you."

"He should have told you sooner," the other replied, concealing her surprise that the healer would broach this subject with her.

"It is a noble aim, but one that I fear is foredoomed. However he fares with his comrades and the Commandants, I doubt he will have much success in the villages, assuming he meant that part about gaining the consent of the women in the first place."

"He means it. Any force, and he loses access to Seakeep. There can be no permanent Eyrie unless he has the use of both Dales."

Pyra shook her head. "How can it work, Lady? Falconers are what they are. They will not change their ways. Their fear is too strong, and lesser things have been added to it over time."

"They have been changing, I think, slowly, since they lost their stronghold. They must accept longer commissions now, remain for greater periods of time among other peoples. They are not stupid men, and what they observe must make an impression on them. Those bound to me have never given sign of discourtesy, and Seakeepdale is managed heavily by its women since war and fever so stripped us of our males. We do try to accommodate their ways, but a certain amount of interaction has always been unavoidable."

"You believe they will just settle in like any other men?" she asked contemptuously.

"No, of course not. That will not be possible on a large scale for several generations to come, if ever." Her eyes narrowed. "Nor am I sure that would be the best solution for male or female. The women in those villages have lived their own lives for a long, long time. They may not see it as any advantage to have their daughters and granddaughters move into the lifeway followed by their counterparts in most other races.

"On the other hand, the new Eyrie may be the best, the

only, way they can keep and continue building upon what they have made of themselves."

The healer frowned. "What do you mean?"

"Think! The villages are slowly breaking apart as more and more of their citizens slip away to make other lives for themselves. Many will marry and content themselves with raising fine, strong sons and daughters, but what of those who bring other skills with them? The female healer will always be welcome, as will the weaver and seamstress, but what reception will the blacksmith and carpenter find even among the bulk of the people in Estcarp? What about the woman who would train horses or breed cows rather than merely milk them?

"I speak from knowledge, Pyra. Circumstances forced me to go well beyond the role normally carried by a Holdlady in the Dales."

"Many must have done so."

"During the time when the Hounds ravaged High Hallack, but once they were defeated and our men returned home, most resumed their more usual work and place. My sire came back to us without the use of his legs and right arm. He had to rely on both my mother and me, and later on me alone, to help him manage Seakeep. Then when the fever took both him and my wedded lord, I had to become Holdruler in fact. The neighboring lords have come to respect my abilities, but more than one of them still views me as a mare feeding outside her proper pasture."

"There may well be truth in what you say," Pyra responded after a silence of some seconds, "but consider the other part of the situation. Most villages truly do not suffer when the men come. Their visits are not pleasant, for them or for the women, but they want sons and their temporary partners want daughters, and what happens is done without force. Most villages keep their boys until their fifth or sixth year, and rarely are they subjected to violence save when a babe is born malformed.

"There are two exceptions, besides one which entirely vanished. The men come to them quite literally to rape. They take male infants at one year, and they slay at whim, women and their get alike. No one would want to be bound to their like, maybe with no option for flight at all."

"The Captain told me about that," Una said grimly. "He explained that each village is under the control of an individual column and that a few of them were traditionally rough to the point of brutality. Even before the Eyrie fell, when their members visited outside their own region, as was needful to spread the seed of the race as widely as possible, they were closely watched to prevent such violence as you mention. He himself witnessed an assault on a young girl merely because her hair was too red for the attacker's liking. His Commandant, the Falconer Warlord himself, knocked the man's weapon from his hand and dismissed him, and he then had the girl brought home untouched since she was very young and shaken."

"You would deliver others to danger like that?"

"That power over life will be ended. It is all but ended now, is it not, by the depopulation or total disappearance of the villages in question? Besides, I doubt men of that ilk will consent to the demands of the new Eyrie. According to the Captain, most of them are very fixed in the old ways."

"To the point of preferring extinction to the alterations needed to avert it?"

"Even so." Una's eyes darkened. "I only hope they do not succeed in swaying the majority of their brethren to their way of thought. If they do, the Captain will be outcast for his pains, if not actually executed, stripped of his command and denied the fellowship of his comrades."

Pyra eyed her. "He would hardly be without place, would he? Most men would consider the possession of two Dales more than a fitting exchange for rulership over a company of blank shields."

The Holdruler stiffened. "Most men are not Falconers!"

she said sharply. "They have nothing but their own, the close companionship of the men who trained them and who were trained with them and beside whom they have fought, that and the friendship of their winged ones. I do not know if land or any other relationship could replace the loss of that, not if it were riven from one of them by force and in shame."

Her fingers whitened as they pressed against the table. "That man is proud and fine. I should not like to see him grow defeated and bitter, something pitiable to those who realize what should be." Una's eyes fixed the other, sharply, as if they were spears. "As for what you have intimated, we are both women, not dream-eyed girls. That cannot be considered, not even as a question with no base in reality. He is not a boy responsible only to himself, his horse, and his falcon. If one word of such a situation were to reach his Commandant and other comrades, our hope would be irreparably shattered, and he would be less than a rabid animal in their eyes. Whether I held feeling for him or none, I could not do that to him."

"No, you could not," Pyra agreed. "Pardon craved, Lady. I spoke without right. The chains binding both of you are apparent, as is your need for care. It was not mine to raise such a question in the first place, with you or anyone else."

"We often speak as we should not otherwise do when we seek to defend our own," Una of Seakeep said quietly. "You are a Falconer yourself, are you not, Pyra?"

The healer's face became a mask. "You jest, and without humor," she warned.

"Every race has its marks, Falconers more so than most since they have bred so closely for so long a span of time. Despite those high helmets, I have come to know them well, and your features bear the same cast, very strongly so, allowing, of course, for your womanhood."

"If I were what you say?"

"You could help us if you chose, speak for and with us. Authority rests on you like a cloak whose wearing is yours by right. I think your sisters would listen to you as they would to no outsider, female or male."

Again, the Falconer woman fell silent. She remained so a long while, and when she did reply, it was obvious that she was choosing her words with care. "I like you, Una of Seakeep, and respect you, and I like your Captain, although it was my original intention not to do so. As you say, he is a fine man, and that will not be hidden despite the usual coldness of his manner and the hardness of his race. Of that I can speak, but can I ask others to go blindly to another place, another continent, to immure themselves in yet another mountain fastness, when I have no more knowledge of it, of what conditions actually are there, than any other of them?"

The Daleswoman leaned forward. "Gain that knowledge, then. Come back with us and see both Seakeep and Ravenfield for yourself. We have lost much time already because of my accident and can afford to wait another season if the delay will give us such aid. I can guarantee that no force or compulsion will be used against you," she added, seeing how the other stiffened.

"This I do believe." Her brows came together. "I must think on this before giving you my answer," she said after a moment. "I shall truly consider what you propose. Beyond that, I can make you no promise."

So saying, she came to her feet and quickly took her leave of her former patient.

The remainder of that day and the first part of the next passed uneventfully, but shortly before midday, Storm Challenger became restless and grew even more so as the afternoon progressed toward evening.

His uneasiness gradually infected Bravery and finally Una herself so that she, too, began to feel and fear that all was not right with Tarlach. Several times, she questioned the war bird closely, but his power to communicate with his comrade did not extend across the miles, and he could tell her no more than that he felt something was amiss with the Falconer Captain.

The woman tried to check her worry. Tarlach was a mountaineer by birth and training, and few if, indeed, anyone better appreciated his abilities, in a wilderness or in battle, but she knew too well how readily accident or the unforeseen could fell the most skilled of warriors. Yet he would not be pleased if she came out after him needlessly. . . .

He could have the rest of this day until noon on that to come, she decided in the end, but if he was not back by then, or if Storm Challenger, if all three of them, were not significantly easier in mind, then she would ride in search of him, come what may to their pride.

The Holdruler was glad when the time of the evening meal at last came, for she hoped that the company and talk of the Lormt leaders would distract her from the worry gnawing her mind and heart.

She was grateful that Ouen had asked her to join him in the smaller eating chamber rather than in the main hall, as was his custom when some specific or serious search was likely to be discussed at length. The number and noise of the full community would have been well-nigh unbearable to her at this point.

Una was the last to arrive. The old head scholar was there, along with Aden, Duratan, and two of the other younger men who had taken a strong interest in their research. Pyra was present as well, as was Jerro, who had not left the complex with the others who had taken part in the hunt for the killer pack. She had learned early in her stay that he was so often a visitor here that he was more or less regarded as a member of the community.

Although neither she nor the falcon, whom she had brought with her, had much interest in either food or discussion, she did her best to hold her part in the conversation, which concerned not only her companion's plans but her own and Seakeep's story as well, and she did not find her listeners' attention wandering as she told the tale of her adventures, hers and the blank shield's whose blade she had hired.

All the while, the sun dropped lower and ever lower in the sky. Suddenly, without any shadow of forewarning, such a wave of terror ripped into her that she sprang to her feet, her heart slamming in her breast. Only by an all but instinctive act of will did she clamp her jaws tight to keep herself from screaming aloud. There was no need of the falcon's simultaneous battle call to tell her the source of this panic.

"I must ride! The Captain is in peril!"

The excitement generated by her and the war bird's alarm subsided with surprising speed, and Ouen's hand closed on her arm with a steel-strong grip that restored her senses to her.

"Think, Child!" he commanded. "Before you go, where do you ride? What has happened to your comrade? Is he injured or alive at all? You have had some warning or communication from him. What has it actually told you?"

Una forced herself to grow calm, deadly calm. "He is alive, otherwise the falcon would be stricken as well, with the will to death upon him. A male bird does not long survive his Falconer's death."

She drew a deep breath. "As for the rest, I know little save that he is in some sort of trouble. It is through the winged one that I received it, and his contact does not extend a very great distance, not far enough to tell us more."

"The bird, does he know where the Captain is?" Aden asked quickly.

"No, but he can help locate him.—I must go! I have just told you how much I owe to that man, beyond the service you saw him render to me. I cannot allow him to die or suffer alone, not without making an attempt, the best in my power, to bring him aid."

"I shall ride with you," Pyra told her. "My skill with a bow may be needed again, if not my heal-craft."

"I go as well," Jerro asserted in a tone that said he would not be refused.

His sister was about to volunteer her services as well but restrained herself. "Two healers are already with you. I shall rouse the able men here in Lormt and those we can reach rapidly in the countryside and begin a second, broader hunt in the morning. Between the two parties, we should be able to find your comrade, the Amber Lady willing."

Una of Seakeep's hands twisted in Eagle's reins. Their progress was slow. After that initial surge of raw fear and the guidance it had provided, the mental signals joining Tarlach with Storm Challenger, which had permitted the short-lived, violent link with her, weakened or lessened to the point that they were well-nigh undetectable. They had to feel their way along the ever steeper trail he had taken, hoping against hope that the tenuous contact would not break entirely.

The bird did eventually lose the eldritch trail, and only the joint linking of falcon, woman, and cat enabled him to pick it up again, but their pace decreased even further lest it be severed a second time, maybe beyond the reclaiming.

The small party rode cautiously, tensely, through the night, in silence lest any noise or speech should distract those following the mind signals of the missing man.

An hour after midnight, Una abruptly came erect in her saddle, as did her nonhuman comrades. Fear! Once more terror drove into her, this time with the immediacy of real need heavy in it.

It passed as had the Falconer's first sending, and she made herself release her own dread which had risen in answer to it. Tarlach was still alive, then, and still fully aware of himself and his surroundings, but he was hard pressed.

She told the others about this second contact, once more concealing the nature of it, then the woman fixed all her mind and will on the task before her. Her face was set and white. She greatly feared, she was nigh unto certain, that her lord's plight was a dire one, but she swore in her heart that she would find the mercenary Captain and find him in time, however far or high he had gone.

9

*T*arlach did not sleep again. He waited quietly in the seemingly eternal blackness while dawn began to grip the eastern rim of the riven highlands.

It was some time longer before the light gained enough strength and altitude to make itself perceptible to him, but at last, a grayish beam broke the dark.

He was on his feet as soon as the first glimmer streamed down through the minute window in his prison. The task still ahead of him was dismally real, as was his hunger and his limited supply of water.

The last represented his greatest danger now, for once that was gone, he would not live long. His ability to work would hold only a few hours after real thirst began, and then all that remained was to choose between the merciful speed of his blade or lingering agony. Death itself was certain.

He drank heavily of that waning supply of water as he ate, however. The labor he faced was not only hard, but it would demand a great deal of concentration and a high degree of precision. Dehydration could drastically and insidiously impair his performance in both areas.

About a quarter of the mound remained to be scaled. The man started on it at once, knowing it would take time and that the hard, delicate excavation of the roof must then begin.

The debris was more difficult to handle, if anything, than on the previous day. The mound had settled somewhat and had lost some of its moisture to evaporation, and he was forced to trust his weight entirely to the treacherous stuff.

Despite that, his progress was decidedly better. With the terrible, draining fear gone, he was able to handle himself far more efficiently both physically and in mind.

He worked more knowledgeably as well. His troubles of yesterday had taught him much about the nature of this material; he would not repeat the mistakes he had made then.

Fortune was with him that morning. The errors he made, the inevitable accidents and mishaps, were few, and none caused serious delay. The work was hateful and heavy, but he pressed on with it, and by what he judged to be midday, he had reached the roof.

The Falconer rested at that point, taking his first major break since he had begun his assault on the mound.

He leaned against the wall, closing his burning eyes. He wished he had the trick of relaxing his muscles at will, that he could disassociate himself entirely from his body for a while. He would not have believed it could ache so.

Thirst was now an incessant scream within him. He sighed and reached for his uncomfortably light supply of water. Brooding over his problems would not lessen them.

He shook the flask and then with deliberate recklessness drained half of what remained. If he did break free, the surface ran with potable water; if he failed . . . In either event, the further sparing of so minute an amount of liquid was quite pointless.

Tarlach stood looking at the plug of material which he had been calling the roof for several minutes without making any move toward it.

He was afraid of it, afraid because the slightest error, the mildest unkindness of fate, would most probably bring, not delay, but either instant death or utter ruin.

To remain here was the same ruin, and so he forced himself

to climb the mound until he had reached the place from which he was to work.

Before raising any tool, however, he studied the roof very carefully, trying to plan his assault. Only a miracle would save him if he merely attacked it without any regard to logic or order.

The greater part, that behind him, was but a continuation of the mound. The material directly above and before him was crust, like to that which had given beneath his weight yesterday. Beyond this lay the solid rock roofing of the cave itself.

It was the last that he must reach, but that would not be possible from here, not directly. In no place did it approach his makeshift scaffold closely enough.

It would be equally impractical to dig out through the crust and then try to crawl across it. The weakened gravel would no more support him now than it had on the previous day.

He shook his head as if to deny what he knew must be his course. To make good his escape, he must come up on the fairly solid mound and then leap from there to firm rock.

It was a long jump, frightening because his life was at hazard, but far from an impossible one. He knew he had matched and bettered it on a number of occasions before and had scarcely given the feat much thought.

The work went very slowly for the relatively small amount of material to be moved. He could probably have safely hurried himself a little since the stuff seemed to be holding together reasonably well, but he had come so far now at the cost of so much labor that he did not want to risk everything for the sake of a few additional minutes.

Carefully, infinitely carefully, he scraped away the imprisoning soil until at last, the final layer crumbled under his cautious blows and the vast blue sky shone above him.

Tarlach cried out in the same moment and threw his hands

over his eyes. He crouched down, shielding his face in his arms until the tearing stopped. Very gradually, he allowed more and more of the light to reach his eyes, giving them the time they needed to adjust to what was now a dazzling glare.

He tried to imagine what would have happened if he had been closed in complete darkness all these hours and could only shake his head. He would probably have been blinded, at least temporarily.

When he could at last bear the daylight once more, the Captain wriggled up out of the pit onto the solid mass of the debris that had choked it.

He lay there a moment, glorying in the feel of moving air on his skin. He laughed aloud when the chill of it began to bite through his sweat-soaked clothing. All that hard work had kept him warm if nothing else!

The man sobered abruptly. He felt the touch of hysteria in himself and forced his mood to quieten. He was not free yet, not by a long ride.

He looked about him and became very grave all at once. The border between brittle crust and true roof which had been so clearly marked underground was invisible up here. Everything looked the same, and even the chaos wrought by the landslide did not show clearly where safety began and danger ended. He must depend upon memory and, to a certain extent, on his sense of direction since the edge between stone and gravel was most uneven.

His hand reached for the waterskin, more a nervous gesture than the prompting of thirst, but when he felt the first touch of the liquid upon his lips, he recorked the flask and returned it to its place on his belt. If he fell again and lived, he just might want to try repairing any damage done to his mound-ladder and make another attempt at freeing himself. The sight of the open sky made suicide seem a far less attractive prospect than it had been in the dark of the tunnel below.

His eyes swept the ground in the direction he knew he must

leap, trying to discover some clue by which he could gauge his distance.

He could find nothing, nothing at all.

Tarlach grinned suddenly and stepped back several paces. Better go too far than spare himself and wind up in the pit again, he thought as he started running as fast as he could on the loose soil. He launched himself from the relative safety of the mound.

Once airborne, it seemed that he could never reach his goal, that so weak a spring could carry him no farther than the flimsy center of the crust.

He was down again before he could begin to panic, scrabbling desperately for a hold on the blessedly solid ground.

Partly solid. That beneath his right leg gave way, taking much of what was around it down as well. He felt himself begin to slide, but his fingers had clawed into firmer ground and held while he fought his way up, crawling until he had reached a place unmarred by any sign of collapse.

The man just lay there while his heart resumed something of its normal beat. He was filled with the rapture of being alive and free, and he was content to remain still and wonder at the miracle of it all.

As the intensity of the emotion ebbed enough for rational thought to regain its customary control, his mind approved of that course lest his very relief betray him into further danger.

At last, when he felt rested and reasonably calm once more, he arose and cautiously began his descent from that high and perilous place.

Storm Challenger's cry of joy drove all awareness of her weariness from the Lady Una. Her hand clamped down on the falcon lest he be tempted to try his as yet unhealed wing, but she touched her heels to Eagle's sides. The winged one had his trail now, and she, in turn, had hers.

Then she needed no guide. Tarlach was there, riding toward them. He was incredibly dirty and one wing of his helmet was bent nearly double, but he sat straight in Lady Gay's saddle and seemed to have no difficulty in doing so.

She did not need the bird's eager, impatient demands to spur her forward, nor did either of the others, and they all reached the Falconer nearly in the same moment.

His astonishment at seeing them was complete, but the Holdruler only shrugged at his question. "Your winged brother was concerned, and we took his worry seriously, apparently with good cause. What happened?"

"I met with the Ghost Child. . . ."

Pyra gave a small moan, and her hand flew to her mouth, while Jerro turned his head aside.

Una of Seakeep made no sound, but her face changed to the color of death, not so much white as gray, and her lord knew the heart had gone out of her.

The Falconer quickly reached over to her. His hands closed on hers as she gripped her reins with convulsive, unfeeling force.

"Curse me for the fool that I am! I have taken no hurt, nor shall I now, I think."

He glanced at the other two. "The decay strikes quickly, does it not, within the hour Aden told us, yet it was the middle of last night or very early this morning when I encountered the spirit. Also, I heard nothing of the crying which is supposed to accompany her attack."

"You are right, Bird Warrior," Jerro replied, "but how did you escape, once having met her?"

The battered helmet lowered. "Pardon craved," he said, "both for my unthinking callousness just now and for asking your indulgence a while longer, until we are with Ouen. He and some of the others should hear this as well, and I am weary enough not to want to go through it more than the once."

* * *

None of the four said much on their return. All of them were tired, and all were engrossed in their own thoughts.

Tarlach's free hand stayed with his falcon, gently caressing and reassuring him, but his head was bowed and his mind obviously far distant.

Una paced him, keeping her mount close to his. Guilt and grief for what might yet come to pass filled her heart, and she could not keep from studying him, seeking for sign of the dissolution the deadly haunt had always before brought with her.

At last, he felt her eyes on him and turned to her, smiling faintly. The fear on her was not difficult to guess.

"I think I am truly sound, Lady, apart from being bruised on every inch." His eyes shadowed then, and his voice both tightened and lowered still further. "If . . . if it turns out that I am not, that . . ."

"You will be allowed to go," she replied. "As a man. This do I swear." Her head raised, and she made herself smile. "I believe that you are right, though, that however you did it, you have escaped the spirit's blight."

By pressing their horses hard, the four reached Lormt again before the setting of the sun. Weariness ate into their very bones, but they went at once to Ouen's chamber where Duratan and Aden waited with the aged scholar. There, the Falconer Captain at last told his story.

He omitted mention of his fear, of how he had shamed himself when night had closed over him, but of his meeting with the Ghost Child, he withheld no detail that remained in his memory, although he spoke with a low voice and a flush marring what could be seen of his face. His role had not been that which would have been expected of one of his race.

He concluded with his theory concerning Adeela's condition and what might have caused her release, and after answering the few questions his account had left unanswered, he took his leave of his audience, wanting nothing more than to wash the grime of the underworld from himself and seek the peace of his bed.

Dead silence filled the small room for several minutes after he had gone, then the others went as well, leaving Ouen to take his own rest.

Una slowly made her way to her chamber, her heart sick and heavy with consciousness of the doom her lord had so narrowly escaped. She was completely absorbed in her grim thoughts, with Tarlach's danger and her total failure to meet it despite the warning she had received, and she started like a young maid when Pyra came suddenly up beside her.

The Falconer woman apologized but only walked quietly with her until they reached Una's door. There she straightened, throwing off the weariness bowing her shoulders. "I have made my decision, Una of Seakeep. I will go to High Hallack with you and your Mountain Hawk."

10

"Rise up, Captain, or do you intend to sleep your life away?"

Tarlach turned onto his back in response to the familiar voice and groaned as his battered muscles protested the sudden movement.

"Brennan! When did you arrive?"

"Not long ago." The Lieutenant sat on the edge of his bed. "You have been busy by the sound of it. Battling Dark-bred killer hounds, laying a ghost. You appear to be making a habit out of this business of becoming a local hero."

"Where did you hear about all that?"

"Everyone around here seems to be so excited by your adventures that even our appearance has lost its chilling effect. One old fellow by the name of Morfew accosted us as we dismounted with a rather disjointed account of both affairs. We were finally rescued by another local who looked more like a tradesman than a scholar but was as well-spoken as any of the others. He gave us a fuller and more comprehensive report."

"That would be Jerro." The Captain felt a moment's unease, but he was not usually a bad judge of a man, and he did not believe Aden's brother would have revealed details he would realize were a source of discomfort to his subject.

He threw his blanket aside and sat up, braving the chill of the room air.

Brennan's eyes fixed on the bruises purpling his chest and arms. "What in the Horned Lord's name happened to you?"

"I fell into a pit, remember?—It is not a matter for laughter, Lieutenant."

"No," his comrade conceded with a broad grin, "but I cannot help recalling your pride in the fact that you are supposed to be the best rock weasel in the company."

"Perhaps that is why I am still here to endure your abuse," he retorted calmly.

The Captain suddenly became aware of Storm Challenger's soft crooning and shot a quick glance at him. He expected to see him fussing over his mate but instead found him introducing himself to a fine young male falcon, who, upon feeling the direction of the man's gaze, was quick to give him the salute of his kind.

He looked to Brennan in puzzlement. "Where is Sunbeam?"

The other lowered his eyes to conceal the hurt in them. "Winged Warrior followed me almost as soon as I entered the camp, and she just left me, as if I were nothing to her at all.—No, that is not true, but she did freely give me up to him."

"I am sorry, my friend," he said softly. "It has always been different with the females."

That was so. Until the Eyrie fell, they would not even

follow a man and had only consented to do so now in some of the columns in order to remain near their mates and assure a nesting each year—adapting to altered conditions as their slower human comrades were just beginning to consider doing. Their linking with their chosen warriors was not as powerful as that which developed between male and male. The fall of one was deeply mourned by the other, but neither man nor female bird died following the loss of the other partner, and there were usually several widows in the company. These normally eventually chose to pair with another Falconer, although no pressure to do so was put on them, often saving the man's life or restoring his sanity as a result, or else helping by their experience to ease a young warrior's assimilation into the veteran fighting unit.

Their comparative aloofness was not difficult to understand. Once, female falcons had paired with the women of his race, but they had severed that contact with Jonkara's coming in order to preserve their kind from her control. It was to have been a temporary break, and the female birds had fought with their male counterparts to aid the men and the unchained women in their efforts to win free of her hold, but their desertion, however needful, had gone far in breaking their former partners' spirit, thereby in a sense temporarily aiding the Dark One's cause. It had also been the example upon which the surviving men had drawn when they had sought the means by which they might defend themselves against future domination.

"She remained in the camp?" Tarlach asked after a moment.

"No. Sunbeam accompanied us back to Lormt, where she promptly bonded with our employer."

"What?"

"There is no blame on the Lady. We can all swear to that, stunned as we were. We witnessed the whole thing. It had taken place before she so much as realized what was happening."

"This we did not need," he muttered. He had known Una could speak with the war birds but had not even thought to consider this possibility, that one of them would choose to fly and fight with her, especially since she already had Bravery.

He reached for his clothes, which had been neatly laid out for him on the table. All had been cleaned and repaired, he noted, as had his helmet, and his other battle gear had been restored to good order. He must have been well out not to have roused when they had been removed and returned again. Storm Challenger, of course, recognized the intruder and his purpose and had raised no alarm.

"I shall have to see the Holdruler, and with no delay."

The other eyed him in some amusement. "You might as well use her name," he remarked. "The rest of us do amongst ourselves. It is too cumbersome to keep playing with titles." The lightness left his mood, and he became deadly serious. "You should know this, Tarlach. The company met and voted before our departure from Seakeep, all of us, with unanimous result. We want another Eyrie as well, and we want it in the place you have chosen. Whatever the Warlord and the other Commandants decide, we stand with you."

Tarlach started to shake his head, but Brennan went on quickly. "Five hundred men. It is not what you want, but neither is it the handful or part companies that have already split off in the hope of fashioning some permanent place for themselves or for all of us again. They cannot succeed in bringing us back to what we were, but with luck, we might just be able to accomplish our ends and preserve our kind as more than a remnant."

"Not without women," he reminded him.

"That, too, we discussed. Seakeep is man-poor, and its people have no more desire than we do to wither into oblivion. Perhaps some arrangement could be worked out with them, Dalesfolk though they be. We are not mates so strange, after all, as were the Were Riders.

"The resulting offspring would be different from either of

our peoples, but they might be the stronger for that, and we should be able to hold what is most basic to us. Then, too, the mixing of our blood might just bring us out of range of Jonkara's power entirely so that we need never dread her awakening again."

"Truly," his commander said with a sigh, "but if we are forced to ride that road, I fear we shall face even heavier compromises than we would with our own." Tarlach shrugged. This might all be a moot question. "I may not live long enough to begin negotiations if the judgment goes badly against me."

"Then I will assume command and our work with it, and Rorick is prepared to take up our cause should I be felled along with you.—Do not look so surprised, my friend. You are not the only one concerned about the fate of the Falconer race or the only one willing to risk himself in our cause."

The Captain's head lowered. "I stand corrected. I have undervalued you, all of you. For that, I crave pardon."

"Ah, you just fell victim to your usual habit of trying to assume the whole burden yourself. I only spoke of it now so that you would know you did not stand utterly alone."

Tarlach was more powerfully moved than he would have wanted even this close comrade to guess, but he was chilled as well. "You believe I will have a need to know it?" he asked quietly. "Was Varnel's reception so cold?"

It was impossible to imagine that the Falconer Warlord had not learned of his acquisition of Ravenfield and the circumstances surrounding its conquest. Elfthorn and the other Sulcar he had saved would have carried the tale to Estcarp even without the report of their own warriors, some of whom would have returned here since those events had occurred. Every Falconer in High Hallack had probably learned of it all within a couple of months after the attack he had led. His own identity would be readily guessed by the size of his company.

"Cold, no, but neither was he minded to be very communicative, at least not with a lowly Lieutenant."

"The treaty with Seakeep?" Tarlach asked sharply. That he wanted to describe himself, before rumor had any play with it.

Brennan shook his head. "He said nothing about that, and I doubt he knows of it. We have kept that pretty close, and you can be assured that I volunteered no information not required of me. I was happy just to escape out of his sight again as soon as I could."

His commander smiled despite his concern. "Varnel is not so bad. His snarl is usually far more impressive than his snap with one of our own."

"Perhaps, but you were the only fledgling he ever chose to name his son. The rest of us prefer to keep a sound distance between us and the good Commandant." The blue-eyed warrior grew grave again in the next moment. "He asked if you planned to remain a Falconer or settle into the Dale as its lord and seemed even more pleased by my surprise that he should raise such a question than he was by my assurance that you had no thought of abandoning your people or company."

"The Warlord is blessed with a very keen imagination," Tarlach said grimly. "If that possibility has occurred to him, I had best ride now. . . ."

"He is no longer there, Tarlach. That is why we have returned here.

"Varnel issued a Council Call. To our full force, the first since we received word that the Eyrie was to die. Every Falconer free and able to respond has been commanded to join him or to take ship after him."

"Take ship!"

"He is bound for Linna. The same summons was sent ahead to those operating in High Hallack before he ever set sail, which was some six weeks ago now. We are to join him as soon as the Holdlady is fit to make the journey and we can secure a vessel to carry us.

"Even the villages have been uprooted to accompany him. He is apparently not blind to the fact that they may be empty by the time he returns if he leaves them completely unattended."

"Varnel is blind to very little," he replied. "Why in the name of the old Eyrie did you not bring or send me word of this?"

"Because Varnel expressly forbade it and ordered us to remain in his abandoned camp until now to be certain we should not be tempted to forget his order. He said we would probably not be free to move much earlier anyway, and he did not want to set you worrying before you were ready to come to him."

The Captain's expression grew even darker as his comrade continued speaking. Just how much did the Falconer Warlord know or guess?

"The Lady Una is ready to travel," he said. "We can take our leave almost immediately." His mouth tightened. "What must be endured shall be, but I hope by the Horned Lord that we are not the subject of this council. If we are, I have very little hope for our plans." Or for himself.

Tarlach started purposefully down the now familiar corridor and rapped sharply on Una's door. Her response came almost instantly, not only confirming her expected presence there but the fact that she had been waiting for him.

He went inside and was greeted by the sight of Sunbeam perched on the desk in an attitude of patient endurance while Bravery gave her such a washing as no falcon before her had likely ever received.

"I was wondering how those two would take to one another," he said to the Holdlady, who was watching the pair affectionately but in open dismay. "It seems I need not have worried."

"No. They have always liked one another. I am sorry, Tarlach. I did not even imagine anything the like of this could happen, much less court it."

He smiled. "I know, my Lady. Brennan was quite certain on that point."

"Will . . . it cause trouble?"

"That I do not know," the mercenary answered frankly. "We shall just have to see how events develop."

"It is permitted, though, that I am bonded with Bravery and Sunbeam both?"

"There has been no precedent as far as I know. As with many other matters, my Lady of Seakeep, we appear to be breaking an utterly virgin trail in this matter."

The warrior's eyes darkened momentarily. "The danger to all three of you is greater. The loss of one will affect two rather than a single partner, though the survivors might also be able to support and strengthen one another in a manner impossible for the rest of us." He sighed. "It is a question I hope we do not have to see answered."

"A hope I most heartily share, Comrade."

Tarlach gave a greeting to his war bird's mate and rubbed Bravery behind the ears. He faced the Holdruler after that and related the intelligence Brennan had brought.

"I can be ready to go within the hour, within the half hour if need be," Una assured him, "although I would prefer the longer time to bid farewell to our hosts here."

She hesitated but decided to speak openly since she had permission to do so. "Pyra will accompany us. She has promised to report back to her sisters in your villages on her reaction to Seakeep and Ravenfield."

The man stiffened. "A Falconer?"

"Yes. She was naturally reluctant to reveal herself before now."

Tarlach nodded, but his expression was dark. His anger was against himself for his blindness, and a sense of the enormity of the task before them settled heavily on him. He knew full well the importance of his mission to all his people. He was about to champion the right of choice for their women in the matter and the necessity for changing and softening some of their centuries-old stand with respect to them, yet so little heed had he paid to this one who had helped care for Una in her need that he had completely overlooked the characteristics which should have told him what she was within moments of seeing her. It seemed he had as far to go in schooling himself as he did with the most stubborn man in Commandant Xorock's notoriously harsh column.

"Inform her of these new conditions," he told his companion gruffly. "She may not want to risk exposing herself with so great a number of us at such close proximity. I will not of my own choice allow her to be taken, but what can five hundred do against that many?"

She frowned. "It will not come to that."

The mercenary's head lowered. "It should not, but . . . I know I play the coward, but I felt easier about my plans with the breadth of an ocean lying between us and the better part of the Falconer host. A three-weeks' march is no defense at all."

His shoulders squared. "Come what will, we shall not permit Seakeep or Ravenfield to be ravaged in our warring."

"There will be no warring!" Una of Seakeep snapped. "Listen to me, Tarlach, and give your people and your War-lord more credit. You have seen a very real peril overshadowing all your race, and right or wrong, everything you have done or hope to do is to try to avert that danger. Perhaps despite that, the alliance you have made with me may cause you to be condemned, but would this Varnel wreak unmerited vengeance on two innocent Dales as well, directly or through your own private struggles? Would he be so stupid as to do so, given the fact that your Falconers must have the trust of other peoples if there is to be a market for your swords? A Holdlord would have to be desperate indeed to introduce a known firebrand into his domain."

"No. No to both your questions. Varnel is a fair and thoughtful man. He could not otherwise have attained his position or have held us together as well as he has these last eight years."

He smiled then. "You are right, Una of Seakeepdale, as you usually are. I was but adding needless weight to my concrete worries.—I will leave you now to ready yourself. I want to depart for the coast as soon as we can and courtesy permits."

11

Three-quarters of an hour did not pass before the Falconer party along with the Lady Una and Pyra assembled in the windswept courtyard. The whole community, scholars and laborers alike, gathered there as well to bid them good speed and good fortune.

Tarlach took his final farewell of Ouen and those others who had given him so much help and lay his hand on Lady Gay's neck in preparation to mount.

He stopped and turned at the soft, quizzical calling of the name Una had put on him.

Two children were standing by the gate. The closest, she who had spoken, he knew at once.

"Adeela!"

His voice was all she needed to single him out from the other high-helmeted warriors, and she literally plummeted toward him.

Glancing in dismay, first at Una and then at Brennan, he went to his knee to intercept the racing child.

Adeela cast herself into his arms, hugging him joyfully. "Oh, Mountain Hawk, I am so glad to see you! We were afraid we might not find you here, and we had to warn you about the Sultanites."

He looked over her shoulder at her companion, another little maid, this one about ten or perhaps eleven years old.

If Adeela did not know with whom she dealt, this one obviously did. She had made a desperate attempt to grab the younger girl and now stood watching him in horror.

"Kathreen?" he asked. It was hardly a remarkable guess under the circumstances and considering the resemblance between the two. She was not as exquisite as her sister, but there was a delicate prettiness about her that was most appealing. Had she been permitted to grow into adulthood, she would have been a rare beauty.

"Yes. Pardon craved, Bird Warrior. My sister does not know . . ."

"No offense taken," he assured her quickly. "Do not frighten her. She has known enough of that."

Every eye was fixed on the newcomers. Una was openly enchanted by the lovely child in his arms. Ouen's customary kindness and warm welcome was open for the reading, and so, too, was something else, a curiosity and hunger for knowledge so intense as to be well-nigh physically painful. It was a measure of him that he held his peace despite his longing to question the pair.

Tarlach's own comrades gave no open sign of their feelings whatsoever. Were they merely frozen by surprise like so many around them, or did they but rein their fury until they could draw apart from the others?

The Captain's head raised. The spirits'—for such both patently were—coming was not by his instigation, nor had he sought the little one's overly enthusiastic greeting, but he would show them both courtesy and whatever measure of warmth of which he was capable.

"These are not living children," he informed his command, then gave his attention to the older girl. "Adeela mentioned a warning," he prompted.

She nodded with unchildlike gravity. "We, or I, carry news of great importance, but it will only frighten many of these folks around us like my dear Morfew. Could your comrades and Lormt's leaders not talk with us alone somewhere?"

"Of course, Child," Ouen answered at once. "Come inside where you can give us your message in comfort."

Brennan matched his pace with Tarlach's. "I thought there was only one ghost and that you had sent her down the long road," he hissed.

"So did I, Comrade," his commander muttered in response, "and I am weak enough to wish that I had. Whatever their motive for this return, I fear we are not going to find much comfort in the news they carry."

They would soon find out. Ouen led the mercenaries and his own close associates to one of the small study halls he himself favored and, after having his younger colleagues scrounge the additional chairs they needed, bade them all be seated.

Adeela started to protest when the Captain set her down, but Una came swiftly over to them, Bravery in her arms.

"Will you help us, Adeela? We must all talk with Kathreen now and be very serious, and my Bravery can be a fierce little pest when everyone ignores her. Do you think you could play with her and keep her happy for a while?"

The child's eyes brightened, and she stroked the cat. "Oh, yes, Lady! I shall be very gentle with her!"

In short order, she was settled in a corner with Bravery and a bow string donated by Pyra to serve as a toy.

When the Holdruler returned to the table, she found the others already in place. She, like all the rest, fixed her attention on the elder ghost child, who was sitting, eyes downcast, as if she were not sure how to begin.

Tarlach broke the silence at last. "Adeela told us what

happened to you, but perhaps you would give us a bit more detail if you have the time."

Kathreen nodded. "We have all the time we need. What would you like to know?"

"Did you live in Lormt or on one of the farms outside it?" Aden asked her.

"No. The mountains had just turned then, too, and many people were moving from place to place. Lormt had not been built long, but it was strong and safe, and travelers would stay here a while to rest and get themselves ready again before finishing their journeys.

"Father had to move our household—some Dark Ones poisoned our old land in revenge because he would not join them and nothing could grow on it any more—and we were stopping here a while."

She shuddered. "No-el was with us. He was the son of our sire's younger brother and was much older than we. He had been father's heir before my birth and remained heir after Adeela."

Tears filled her eyes. "I never knew he hated us. No one did. He had played with us and kept us happy during the journey, especially Adeela. . . .

"When we went to that cave, I thought it was another game, that he had some bright stones hidden away for her to find. He had done that before, to her delight."

She looked up. Her misery was so open that Una very nearly begged her to forget that past entirely, to go down the last road with a fresh mind and never again think of what had happened before.

"You chose to remain in this realm after he struck you down?" Una asked gently. All, Lormt folk and Falconers alike, listened intently for her answer. That was a journey each one must someday face, one they had until now been forced to accept as an utter unknown. Now they had before them an informant who had known at least the first stage of

it, and they were eager for anything she could tell them about
it.

With an effort, the spirit mastered herself. It was hers to
perform as an adult, and this she was determined to do.
"After No-el . . . after I died, I knew I should go, but I could
not bear to leave my sister. She was so little and so frightened
shut up there in the dark."

She fixed her eyes on her hands, which were resting tightly
clasped on her lap. "She did not know what was happening
or what to do but only ran around and around the cave, not
even realizing when she fell or struck herself. When she became too exhausted for that, she lay near the entrance, crying
and calling me and our parents and even No-el to help her.

"I tried to stop her, to hold her, but I . . . I could not make
her see me." She bit into her lip. "I thought it might be
because Adeela was too young and too upset, but when I
went home, it was the same. I could not make them realize
I was there. I could not even touch anyone. My hands went
right through them."

Tarlach glanced at Una, then his eyes closed. The quick
death of a warrior in battle was one thing, but this. . . . and
what had followed was as bad, worse. He could scarcely
imagine what such an experience must be like for a man,
much less for this sensitive, loving child.

The girl was not aware of his reaction. She had begun an
unpleasant task and was prepared to see it through to the
best of her ability.

"Since there was nothing I could do to help her, I went
back to wait with Adeela until she should join me. I suppose
I was hoping to reach her somehow, to tell her there was
nothing to fear.

"She grew so quiet near the end that I was certain some
part of her must feel me close, but when she did break free,
it was as if she had been possessed by some maddened wild
thing. She was as bonny as she had been before being locked
in that cave, but her face was . . ." Kathreen frowned, reach-

ing for words. "It did not dance or play any more, as if she were not inside there at all.

"I tried to go to her, but she did not seem to notice me. She whirled here and there through the caves without seeing or being aware of anything."

The girl shuddered again and stopped speaking. This next, she hated, but it was part of their history and had to be told.

"Days passed, and people searched for us. No-el became afraid that our bodies would be found, or, even worse for him, that Adeela would somehow be discovered still living, and he came back to better hide what he had done.

"Adeela . . . Adeela was there. She felt him in the underground and came to him. He could see her plainly and see her body lying there, too. No one knew what she could do then, but he screamed and ran.

"It did no good. She flew after him. She was fast, faster than any horse you would ever want to see run. Adeela did not look at him, not really, just through him, but she threw her arms around him. Then she seemed to lose all interest in him." Her eyes fixed on the table before her. "He . . . he had started dying before he reached Lormt.

"I thought at first that this terrible deed was the end, that she had avenged us and could now put death away, but, of course, she could not. She was not my small sister any more, just some kind of anger or hate who looked like her. Adeela is the sweetest, gentlest little maid in all the world. She would never hurt anyone, no matter what he did to her."

"How is it that she could be seen?" Duratan asked, interrupting for the first time. "You remained invisible."

"Adeela never became a real spirit until the Mountain Hawk released her."

"It was you who cried after each attack?"

She nodded. "I could not bear it. Most of those poor people did not even deserve to die. . . ."

"Why did she spare me?" the Falconer commander inquired quickly.

"I think it was finding you asleep there in the dark. At least, she was staring at you with her old curiosity when I caught up with her. All the other people had been afraid, and some of them had tried to kill her."

"I figured that might have had something to do with it.— You did not try to contact her immediately?"

"I did, but she still could not hear me, so I just waited, hoping."

Aden's throat felt tight. "You spent all those years, those centuries, imprisoned in the dark?" she asked in a low voice.

"Oh no! I have been on the surface many times, in Lormt and in the cottages around. I loved to hear you all talking and discussing things, even when I could not understand everything you were saying."

The woman looked at her, stricken. "You were here, in our very halls, and we let you go again without help or comfort?"

"How were you to know?" Kathreen reasoned practically. "I was so happy when I was in Lormt. Poor Adeela was always safely asleep then, when it was not winter." Her lip trembled momentarily. "She . . . she did not know to be sad when she was awake."

"Why could you not stay with us altogether, then, Child?" Ouen inquired. "You were unable to stop your sister—"

"Oh, but I could! I kept her from ever coming out of the caves. She could not pass through me, you see, and I was always able to reach her before she went outside. It was only in the dark itself that I could not control her."

"You should be free now, both of you," Tarlach observed, "yet you are still in this world, visible to us."

"We would not be able to talk with you properly if you could not see us, so the Amber Lady let us have that gift. She can do a great many things, you know."

"Gunnora?" Una whispered. "You have seen her?"

"Yes, and she is truly wonderful!" The girl smiled at the memory of that meeting. "She held us close and gave us such welcome that we felt we were already home, though I knew we had a long, long way to travel before we reached that."

The softness left her, replaced by purpose. "She knew what you did for Adeela, Mountain Hawk, how you were kind despite your fear, how you saw she was innocent despite the awful harm she caused, how you were gentle with her instead of hating, even though you knew she might make you die very horribly. The Lady said there was no fitting reward for that, but a dreadful danger was coming to this whole world, and she might at least bring you warning of it. I . . . I said that since you had helped my sister, I wanted to do it, and she agreed.

"Gunnora told it all to me very carefully. I did not quite understand everything, but she said that did not matter as long as I told it to you correctly."

"Go ahead, Kathreen. Just take your time and do not be frightened of us."

"Many gates open into this world. In fact, the ancestors of all of us humans originally came here through one. Well, we are good for this place and for each other, more or less, but some gates lead to places where the people are very bad."

"The Dark!" Brennan hissed.

"No, just bad people in this case, or bad for everyone else except themselves. These ones are all warriors, the men are, and they work for a lord—they call him a Sultan—that they think is a kind of human form of their god. They do not believe any other people have worth or rights, and they conquered their whole world.

"That happened a long while ago in their time, more than four hundred years ago, and they believed all the other poor people, whom they used for slaves, had no fight left in them. They were wrong, though, and the people met and worked and trained together. They were able to keep it all secret since no one was afraid enough to watch them, although they were always careful, of course.

"When they were ready, everyone attacked at once, all over the whole world. The Sultanites were taken completely by surprise, and many of their armies were wiped out and the rest had to run, taking all their people who had moved into the conquered places with them.

"Now they are all back in their original country and are fighting to hold that. They are brave and very skillful, and there are a lot of them, and they have only one short border to defend. The whole rest of their holding faces on the ocean, and their enemies as yet have no ships or the skills to manage them. Still, they know they cannot win. Their land is very dry and does not grow a lot of crops, not enough to feed them all. It is flat, too, so it would be hard to defend once their enemies got inside."

"Their position is a bad one right enough, and amply earned by the sound of it, but how does their plight concern us?" Tarlach asked.

"Long ago, there used to be men there who could call on a kind of Power. The Sultan at the time was afraid of them and killed most of them and their families, but some of the more powerful ones had been able to make gates of a sort and escape into various realms. They were not proper gates and could be used only twice, once from each end, and then with great difficulty, but I suppose that was for the best. Their enemies had no way of following them once they were gone.

"Two, two brothers, were killed before they could leave, and all this while, their passages have remained unused."

"They lead into our world?"

"Yes. They wanted to live together.—No one there can make gates any more, but a scholar learned about these and discovered how to work them only a year ago. They would have been tried eventually anyway, but now everything is so desperate that spies were sent through one of them. They traveled around here, by boat mostly since their gate opened from and into the ocean, and looked about when they could land without being noticed, which was always at night, then they went home again. That was the hardest part, but they proved it was safe, and they reported that the country nearby was suitable for them. That meant they thought they could conquer it quickly."

"Through their remaining gate," the Falconer leader said. "What are their plans?"

"They are going to send a big fleet with all the soldiers they do not need right away. When they have enough land safe enough to try it, they will summon the rest of their people, letting their enemies have their old world."

"Where in Estcarp will they put to shore?"

"Not Estcarp. High Hallack. They have chosen Seakeep-dale's harbor, Mountain Hawk. It is nearest to where they will come through, and they think there are so few people there that they can kill them all and settle in before anyone even knows they have come."

"Seakeep!" Brennan exclaimed.

"It is not unreasonable," his commander told him. "The harbor is small, but it is good, and it is the only one along that stretch of coast. Those farther south, if they were explored at all, are busy, and most have large companies of blank shields wintering in and around them.—I am right, Kathreen, in assuming they are looking more for an easy landing than a fight at this stage?"

"Yes. They have only about three months to reopen the gate, and they will need nearly four weeks of that, with no disturbance at all, to do it. They have to be on solid, very high land, too, otherwise they could not bring up sufficient Power to hold it open long enough to be able to get all their people and animals and goods through.—I do not really understand how it works. . . ."

"Nor do we," Ouen reassured her. "It is not necessary that we do, is it, Captain?"

"No. What is important is that these Sultanites must be kept from reaching any of Seakeep's mountains.—They are armed with normal weapons?" The Kolder had possessed

strange and terrible arms and had supplied some of them to
Alizon. It could well prove the same here.

She nodded vigorously. "Lady Gunnora said that especially. They use swords, spears, the usual things. No sorcery."

"How many soldiers are aboard that fleet, Kathreen? The
Amber Lady must have told you that, too."

"She did," the child replied promptly. "Sixty thousand."

It was just a big number to her, more or less meaningless,
but those listening to her sat back, stunned. Many of the
peoples, entire races, occupying the lands they knew were not
so numerous and had not been even before war had been
loosed to ravage them.

"Whatever their strength, they will have to be stopped,"
Tarlach stated flatly. "If once that host wins past Seakeep
into the lands beyond; it will take many years and the loss of
almost countless lives to drive them forth again, if they can
be ejected at all, which I doubt, not after they have brought
their people through to support them."

"We are hardly unaware of that," Brennan snapped. "We
lack the power to alter reality, not the desire to do so."

"Perhaps," the Captain told him.

Both his voice and his expression had become thoughtful.
He rose to his feet abruptly and started pacing rapidly, a trait
his comrades recognized from of old when some matter of
serious import was before him.

All watched him for several minutes, none speaking or
moving lest they disrupt his train of thought.

At last, he stopped and faced his companions once more.
"Victory is impossible as matters now stand, but we should
be able to hold these invaders back for a time, for a long time
if fortune grants us a sufficient number of days in which to
prepare for their coming. Kathreen, can you tell us when that
will be?"

"The Amber Lady said in about two weeks, Mountain
Hawk."

The Falconer turned on his heel, away from them. His shoulders fell. They were finished, then, before they had begun. They could not reach High Hallack in less than two months even if they found a ship waiting to carry them when they reached the coast.

Una of Seakeep watched him a moment. She could read the defeat on him and shared it, but then fire flashed in her eyes, and her head snapped toward the child. "Gates have brought us to this pass, and a gate can save us out of it! Kathreen, return now to Gunnora and carry this message to her, that her warning is worthless, no, a work of cruelty only, unless she also provides us with the means of acting upon it. Let her open a gate to Seakeepdale for us now, to the round tower, so that we can lay whatever plans we may and implement them with no further waste of time."

Tarlach whirled around. "Be sure to add my name to that request and also ask that a second gate be opened if possible leading to Linna."

He smiled at the Holdruler's frown. "Do not scowl, Lady. If you are willing to risk angering the Great Ones in our cause, do not imagine I am so small as to hold back. Falconers will perish as well as Dalesfolk if these Sultanites sweep High Hallack."

His eyes fixed on the ghost child. "Go with our thanks, Kathreen, and may you and Adeela journey well to a good ending."

Adeela regretfully left Bravery and came to her sister in response to her call. She raised a small hand in farewell to Tarlach. There was no other motion on the part of either child, but in the following instant, both were gone, vanished from sight and from the realm of living men.

12

No one moved within the hall as seconds crawled by as slowly as if they were hours.

Nothing happened, and it seemed that nothing would happen, but then the air in the room's center shimmered and what appeared to be a long tunnel walled with back-lighted clouds stood open before them.

The Captain waited another moment before finally releasing his breath. Only one gate, but he had not really expected the other. The Amber Lady had done so much. The rest lay with human hands and human-wielded swords.

"Go quickly," he said softly to his comrades. "Bring our horses and gear. We shall have time for that, I think, but the Lady Una and the Lieutenant shall remain here with me in case it does begin to close. We, at least, must go through it." Fortunately, the hall was on the first level and the corridor and doors were wide enough to permit passage for the animals, as was the gate itself.

Pyra quietly took her place beside the three.

He shook his head. "Stay here. We go to fight and probably to die, not to build a new life as I had hoped."

"All the more reason to have another healer in your company. Lady Una will be of little service in that capacity, I think, since she will probably claim her place beside you, as is a Holdruler's duty. As for the rest," she shrugged, "what must be endured shall be."

She saw the way his head raised and smiled in amusement. "I have heard you use that phrase, Mountain Hawk, but it is uttered in the villages as well and in the same context. We are of one race, after all."

"And of one stubbornness," he muttered, but he made no further attempt to dissuade her.

* * *

Their comrades were not long in returning, but once all was ready, they stood frozen, looking into the mist-shrouded passage, none wanting to be the first to enter it.

There had been no taint of the Dark on the two children—the falcons would have detected that—and it was patent that Kathreen had believed fully every word she had spoken, obviously half by rote, but what if it had not been Gunnora who had schooled her? Could a spirit be so duped?

What if that powerful being were not of the Light at all and this gate led to some inescapable prison or Shadow-ruled demon's hall? It, too, was free of open corruption and was fair enough to look upon, but the senses were not always to be trusted where illusion might too easily be at work. This was witchery of the highest order. . . .

Bravery stretched and walked to the passage, her tail held high. She meowed once, impatiently, and leaped inside, vanishing as she did so. Sunbeam gave a single sharp cry and plunged in after her.

Una's shoulders squared. She grasped Eagle's reins more firmly. "The rest of you can come with us or go by sea, but I follow my cat and falcon."

The Captain pushed ahead of her. If they were to meet disaster, it was his to shield her, if only for a brief moment. . . .

He was caught up in a breathless rushing motion that left him completely disoriented. He could not have told in what direction he moved or if he still stood upright at all.

Something, someone, was beside him. A hand pressed against his. He could feel the scars circling it, and his fingers closed around it, comforting but also taking comfort as they whirled together through the seemingly endless mist.

The eldritch motion stopped as suddenly as it had begun. The Falconer stumbled and swayed, then found his balance.

He looked about him and discovered that he and Una were standing in Seakeep's one inhabited valley, at the foot of the road leading up to the round tower that had been their goal.

He quickly released the Daleswoman's hand and hastened to assist and steady their companions and mounts, who were coming through behind them.

He did so with raised head and eyes flaming with pride and something more. That these men would have followed him straight against any military foe, he had known, but in traveling that strange tunnel, they had chosen to put themselves into contact with much that they most greatly feared—powerful sorcery, sorcery of a strength similar to that which had once enslaved and very nearly broken all their kind. Never had he honored them more in his heart than he did in this moment and never had he been more deeply aware of either their devotion to their duty or their love for him.

He shivered, then, deep within his own heart. His orders, the war to which he would commit them, would soon send all too many of them to their deaths.

He had no time to brood upon that. Their arrival was nothing if not dramatic, and both horsemen and warriors running on foot were already racing toward them, having delayed this long only to confirm the identity of the newcomers.

The first to reach them drew rein beside him.

"Captain, what . . ."

"Explanations must wait. Summon both Rorick and Rufon to the tower if they are not already within. We have a council before us. A council of war."

Soon the three Falconer leaders and both Una herself and Rufon, her liege man and long-time aide, were assembled in the rather small chamber where the Holdrulers of Seakeep had ever met with their advisors when matters of grave import lay before them.

Tarlach recounted all that had transpired at Lormt, concluding in great detail with the spirit child's warning.

When he had finished speaking, he spread his hands. "I

could have wished for more specific military information, but we must be grateful for even this much and act as best we can upon it."

"Act!" Rorick exploded. "Did the trip through that gate rive you from your senses? No army could reach us in two weeks, even if one were already mustered and waiting for our call."

"We must use what we have on hand to hold them off."

"Five hundred of us, six hundred if you count Seakeep's garrison, most of whom are women, trained, yes, but whose only battle experience has been in chastening a few bandits?"

"They have had some pretty intensive Falconer schooling in these last months," Una reminded him. That had been part of their treaty, a minor part, but Tarlach had insisted upon its beginning at once as a gesture of good faith.

"Lady, they might be Falconers with no better effect! There are sixty thousand warriors coming against us! With those odds, they need not even be passable fighters to sweep us all away and not even notice that we had ever been here."

"Maybe." Rufon had battled Alizon's Hounds beside the Lord Harvard. He knew fighting men and those who led them, and now his attention was fixed on the Captain. "You do see some hope for us, then, Mountain Hawk?" he asked, picking up the name as instinctively as those others who had heard it.

He nodded. "This valley is narrow in every part and shrinks still further just above the final fields skirting the place where land and beach meet. If we can throw up a wall there, no more than the number mounting it would be able to come against us at any one time, and we could hold a full third of our force in reserve to act as reinforcements for particularly hard-pressed sections and replacements for our inevitable casualties. In the meantime, some help will be reaching us from Seakeep's neighbors."

"Not much, I fear," Una interjected. "I know these Hold-lords around me. They are good men, brave men, but the fever left them with little more in the way of able-bodied troops than it did me, and some they needs must keep with them, however fully they believe our declaration that High Hallack's stand has to be made here, that individual Dales will be quickly swallowed up if the invaders get past us, even as was the case with Alizon. They cannot send us what they do not possess. Do not forget, none of them trained their women as we did.

"Ravenfield is the only one with a sizable male population, and Ogin made sure there was no fight in any of them. We can expect nothing of people so cowed. They would flee at the first sign of a determined foe, giving us more trouble than help."

"The lords around will be more generous with supplies?"

"Yes. That help will not be denied."

"That should be sufficient. It is not in any Dale that I am thinking of placing our hope."

Seakeep's Lady frowned. "In whom, then?"

"Falconers. Remember the Warlord's summons? His ships should be making Linna about the time our courier arrives there, and most of us serving in High Hallack should already have assembled in obedience to his summons. Even with all the columns united, we would not equal a third of the invaders' strength, but given a strong defensive position here and the losses any attacker must sustain in assailing the like, we would have good hope for victory, and even as we fought, the Dales would be mustering to take over for us should we fail."

"Will your people respond?" the Holdlady asked him. "They have not come to Linna to fight, nor could even the greatest of the Dales hope to pay so many—"

"Forget payment!" He gripped himself. His was a race of mercenaries, after all. "This is a Blood Call, Lady. The attack to come is as much directed against us as against you since we are also present in High Hallack, and the war to be fought is for all the world, even as was that against Kolder."

"There will still be a fierce long time before we can hope

for help to reach us.—The journey is not so far by sea. . . ."

"Fate has foiled us there," Rufon told her. "The *Tern* was holed only this morning. We have her ashore, but the damage is severe, and for the smaller boats to attempt to voyage so far in this season . . ."

"We must forget the sea," Tarlach told them. "By the time the Warlord arrives, the invaders will be here, and nothing is likely to be able to get through their fleet, not without a battle too costly for us to consider. They outnumber us too heavily for us to meet them thus. In fact, I want all Seakeep's vessels brought ashore and so placed that they can be destroyed instantly should our defenses go down. No use in giving our foes the use of them."

The Falconer flushed slightly. "Do you concur, Lady?"

Una only laughed. "You are our battle leader, Captain, not I. The right of command is yours."

"What else would you have us do, Captain?" Rufon asked him smoothly.

"Start work on the barrier at once, dividing our people into two shifts, no, three, so that the labor need never stop. We have no hours for the wasting.

"Besides this, bring everything movable including all the livestock not essential to our immediate efforts into the mountains. Nothing of value must fall to the invaders in the event of our defeat."

"Except ourselves."

"We shall not go down lightly, and the dying will be the easier for knowing those dependent upon us will not be slaughtered or enslaved immediately upon our fall.

"For that reason and for the support of the survivors in the event of disaster, all noncombatants must withdraw into the highlands as soon as the wall is up and establish themselves there in very small groups so that the taking of one will not mean the end of all.

"We shall have to continue the fight as hidden folk, as partisans, if these Sultanites succeed in gaining their foothold here. Let the people remember that as they settle themselves. We, all this continent, could have very great and very direct need of them in the time ahead." His lips pursed. "That is in the event of our defense's failure. For now, those not able to fight will be supplying us, aiding us as if they were actually in the valley with us, and attending to our severely wounded. They will be the better for being removed out of immediate danger, and we shall be relieved of the worry of caring for their needs."

"Daria will not like that," the Holdruler remarked dryly. "She is no coward."

He smiled. "Tell her and her assistants that their gifts and oaths bind them to service, and that can best be rendered well back in the highlands, all save the few who must be here to give immediate aid."

"Suppose the barrier is not complete when the Sultan's fleet comes?" Brennan asked.

"We retreat and try to stop them at the pass into the valley. There can be no thought of trying to hold them off from the tower. The same applies if our defenses are breached and cannot be resealed. Warriors will always be assigned to form a rear guard. It will be theirs to give the rest time to escape. Should we lose the pass as well, as is likely, we take up a guerrilla war until the invaders can be ousted once more."

"It all sounds reasonable," Una agreed.

She glanced at Tarlach. "I can see no point in trying to conceal any of this from our people."

"None. That would be as fatal as the Sultanites' swords."

"How many couriers must we send?" Brennan questioned. "Essential as their mission is, I hate to lose the use of their swords."

"Only one, or a couple at the most. We cannot spare more."

"If I may make a suggestion, Captain," Rufon interjected quickly, "We cannot risk sending a woman or girl to your Warlord with so much depending upon his response, and neither can you afford to deprive yourself of any sound warrior." His one hand slapped his empty right sleeve. "I should be of little use swinging a sword, but otherwise I am hale of body and as good a rider as most of your own comrades. Let me serve as your messenger. It will be a hard race, and I am better able for it than an old man or a boy too young for battle would be."

The mercenary was silent a while, as if he were reluctant to accept the other's logic, but at last he nodded. "Very well, Rufon. I shall prepare a report explaining the situation and will also order one of the widows to fly with you to add credence to your position."

He paused at the mention of the falcon and seemed to slip into his own thoughts. When he roused from them some moments later, his expression was very grave. "I must ask something more of my command. The bond uniting us with our winged brothers is powerful, and one does not usually long survive the fall of the other. For now, however, for the duration of this confrontation, I ask that this release be waived, at least temporarily, if that can be done. We simply will not be able to afford the loss of a second fighter for every one brought down, and we can anticipate all too many casualties. For the men, it will be a matter of enduring the agony of their loss. For the falcons, it is a more difficult sacrifice, the refusal to yield to the workings of death already active within them, yet I must beg them to remain as well.

"The widows, of course, must join at once, for the length of the battle, with bereaved warriors."

He sighed as the weight of his responsibility settled on him in all its crushing force, then his head raised. "We must begin at once. Lady Una, Comrades, go to our peoples and tell them all that has transpired here. See what can be done about starting the barrier and also," he added suddenly, "about tearing down the dock. Let our unwelcome guests ferry themselves in by dory since we cannot prevent their landing altogether.

"I shall join you as soon as I have completed my request to the Warlord."

Una came to the chamber she had given over to Tarlach for his use from the time the Falconer company had first come to Seakeepdale, the chamber once used by the old Holdlord himself.

The Captain was just folding the report that he had composed. He sealed it, then gave her a sympathetic smile. "You told them?"

"Yes," she replied. "They accepted the news quietly."

"I would have expected no less. Rufon is ready?"

"Just about. He is loading his saddlebags now." The woman eyed him somberly. "I am glad you agreed to let him go, dearly as I shall miss his support. I was afraid that you might try to send me in his stead."

"He was right. I could not have given the commission to a woman."

"I could not have gone in any event," she told him. "You know that, Tarlach. A Holdlord would have to remain, and I can do no less."

"Stay to die."

"If that is to be."

He turned away from her. "I wish I had the courage to order you from here, Holdruler or not."

He gripped himself and forced himself to look at her again. "I am not entirely a brave man, Una. Too many I love will fall in this, and I should be glad to have you out of it, but I only know that I do not want to face it without having you beside me. I do not want to see you ride from here and know I shall probably never see you again. I do not want to die without the comfort of your presence." He stopped himself, and his eyes closed. "I do not even have the strength to keep silent and not burden you further. You have enough to bear without having my weaknesses put on you, when I should be showing you strength only."

"I am aware of your humanity, my Lord," she said softly, "and I am weak enough myself that I very much needed to hear that from you just now."

Una made herself smile and drove the tightness from her voice, although it did not leave her heart. "Come, my Lord. We have tarried long enough. Guests are coming, and we have a deal of work before us to prepare a fitting greeting for them."

13

*D*alesfolk and Falconers alike threw themselves into the task of preparing the mountain-girth hold to meet the invasion whose success or failure would determine the fate not only of this one Dale but of all those around it and probably the very history of their world besides.

The labor before them was massive, enormous, seemingly hopeless at its outset, yet the wall that was to be their screen rose with marvelous speed.

Material, they had in plenty, and nature had set it near to hand. Every stone, every rock, every boulder was cleared away from the beach and the shallow tidal waters so that neither shelter nor missiles remained to aid the Sultan's dark cause. More came from the surrounding slopes, great boulders, some more like to miniature cliffs than single rocks, requiring the combined strength of all the hold's dray horses and oxen to move them onto the logs that would roll them to their final place. The huge blocks were prized and more than worth the effort expended in placing them, for they were proof against any ram, and they quickly filled space along the line that could never have been closed in time had its builders depended entirely upon more conventionally sized materials.

The long, squat wall which took form out of the mountain of debris the defenders brought to it was no thing of beauty, but it was strong, and they believed it would serve them as they intended.

It was relatively low, only high enough that a man might not leap over it even using his spear to aid his spring. More height should not be needed. The Sultanites were expecting no opposition and would not be likely to have carried formal siege equipment with them.

The seaward side of the barrier was straight and smoothly finished so that neither those trying to scale it nor hooks meant to tear it down would find ready purchase upon it; that facing the keep had more the appearance of a rubble pile and sloped sharply down from the platform where the defenders would stand. This last was situated in such a way that archers could crouch behind it to fire through the slits provided for the purpose without exposing themselves, or warriors might stand to wield swords or other weapons, screening themselves by means of their shields.

An officer's rank did not exempt a Falconer from labor when his unit faced heavy need, and both the Captain and his two Lieutenants strained and sweated beside their subordinates whenever the nearly ever-present press of their other duties lifted enough to permit it.

Both Tarlach and Brennan had been so occupied all that morning and were well spent with their efforts. They cast themselves against the huge boulder they had just manhandled into place, breathing heavily, their eyes closed. It was good just to rest for a few minutes, to draw the cold, sweet air into their gasping lungs.

At last, the Mountain Hawk opened his eyes to look into the gray sky. "If the Sultanites do not come to batter us, the elements soon will. Those clouds bespeak a storm."

"That is all we need."

Tarlach levered himself up so that his elbows supported him. His eyes ran the length of the wall. "Actually, we have been fortunate. The work is done now, and we can rest as easily in rain as on a clear day. I wonder when it will strike?"

"That is hard to say. Perhaps tonight. Perhaps tomorrow. There should be some heavy squalls before it hits in full force at any rate."

"We cannot grudge its coming, I suppose. This is the season for gales, and the weather has been considerate to have held off troubling us for so long."

"So have our supposed enemies. Perhaps that will continue and they will choose to make their landing somewhere far from this coast. I confess I should feel more secure meeting them elsewhere with a number of warriors beside me more nearly equal to theirs, even though countless other clashes were certain to follow."

His commander smiled sympathetically. "Our thoughts run alike, my friend. I should not even complain about the wasting of all the effort to which we have gone in preparing a proper reception for them."

The men straightened as a slender figure approached them.

Pyra moved quickly and lightly through the mass of workers. She was carrying a stone water jug, which she handed first to Tarlach, then to Brennan.

The latter drained a good part of its contents before returning it to her. "Thanks given," he said as he did so. "No wine is as sweet."

"It is but another of Seakeep's riches, Bird Warrior.—You have chosen a fine site for your Eyrie," she said to the Captain. "I will give you that."

"It is a pity you cannot see it under normal conditions," Tarlach told her with real regret. "These people are brave and able, but they would rather be working with their animals and land and with that wild sea out there than preparing for war."

"Like it or nay, they have risen to the emergency well. They have both my liking and my respect." She smiled, a trifle gravely, perhaps, but the effect was pleasant on her sharp features. "At least all this has put one false belief of ours to rest. We thought you Falconers never did anything but fight, beyond training with the feathered ones and your horses, of course. I see instead that you are well able to work and do so in a manner that proves you are no strangers to it."

"Who did you imagine maintained our camps, or the Eyrie before its fall?" Brennan demanded. "We have no servants or keep no slaves."

"How were we to know that?" she countered archly. "You worked well to hold your lives a mystery to us." She settled the heavy jug so that it rested more comfortably on her hip. "The Lady Una looks as if she could use a break. I had best go to her."

"Tell her to pace herself more carefully," Tarlach ordered with no good humor. "I would not see her kill herself trying to match my warriors."

The woman only laughed. "The Holdlady is no such fool, I can assure you. The work she assumes, she is fully capable of performing."

Pyra joined the Daleswoman a few moments later, and Una accepted the water she offered as gratefully as had the two men.

"You should be resting," she chided after returning the jar. "You were at this yourself most of the night."

"Some of us have to draw support duty each day."

The jade eyes studied her. "You are getting a strange view of us."

"Your Mountain Hawk just made almost the same comment."

"I am glad," the Holdruler said softly. "That means he is still holding some hope for the future."

"It also means that he has a real care for your people. For you as well. He believes you are working too hard."

Una of Seakeep sniffed. "I have not noticed him sparing himself any!" Her eyes shadowed again. "I would have us talk of Seakeep, Pyra. How do you see us?" As long as Tarlach of the Falconers could hope there might still be life after this and the chance to build and grow, she could do no less.

"I like your people a great deal," the other woman replied. "Your women are much like ourselves, and your men and boys are natural and content with them as they are. It is a fairly unique situation from what I have observed and an enviable one, and I would be very careful indeed about introducing males from the Dales around in here, whatever your need for mates. Few of your people would be content at being forced back into the old rules of life now.

"Your blank shields are harder to know, harder to read. They are never less than courteous, and they do work well with your folk, but they are not your comrades, not yet."

"No, but that would be a great deal to expect in so short a span of time, would it not?"

"I am not faulting them, Lady. I would not have expected so much from them or believed they could do so much had I not witnessed it day by day."

"The rest may come as well, assuming any of us survive this." Una shook her head ruefully. "It has been an interesting time, right enough, but I knew what was involved when I hired their swords."

"Did you?"

"Not all of it, perhaps," she replied, smiling. "I certainly did not anticipate their remaining with me so long or that I should have them as permanent and close neighbors." She straightened. Tarlach was looking at them, inquisitively, as if he would speak with her, and she took her leave of Pyra to go to him.

Brennan gave salute to the Holdruler, then left them. Tarlach's smile came easily once they were alone, and she could see that he was pleased with the progress they had made.

"We have beaten your schedule, Mountain Hawk," she told him with equal satisfaction.

"That we have, Lady."

Her eyes ran the length of the wall. "It is finished?"

"It is. A little smoothing of the platform still remains to be done, but nothing even vaguely essential."

"I can begin moving my people out, then, those who are not to fight, and have them take the rest of the stock?"

He nodded. "As soon as possible.—There is no thanking you for your role in all this. None of the work would be even nearly half completed if my comrades had to carry the whole of it, and it is with you that the credit for managing your folk belongs. That alone would have been a sufficient contribution, and you have organized their retreat to the Highlands as well."

She eyed him gravely. "Does it surprise you that I have proven able?" she asked him quietly.

"No, Lady," the mercenary answered thoughtfully after a brief pause, "not any longer. You were Holdheir, and duty and responsibility were both bred and trained into you." A smile just touched his lips. "Recognizing your competence does not lessen my gratitude for it."

"I am glad to hear you say it," the woman replied with a little sigh. "I do not feel particularly competent when I think of what lies ahead."

"You will carry your part, Una of Seakeep. Perhaps a lone warrior can afford to feel strong and at ease before a battle if there exists such a fool, but no one bearing the weight of command may do so. Fear is my companion as well and has been since we first learned of this threat."

Her eyes searched his and found that he had offered her no idly phrased comfort.

"Thanks given for those words," she said softly. "I think I shall lean upon them often in the days ahead when my courage would otherwise fail me utterly."

"All of us use memory so, my Lady."

Una lowered her eyes to veil the suddenly born pity in them. She would never be able to comprehend how these mercenaries bore with the life they led, the constant danger of it, the constant loss and threat of loss.

She had once believed them to be a callous lot, being almost totally isolated from any but blatantly superficial contact with their fellows. She had recognized her error in that even before Tarlach had come to them and knew now that Falconers were bonded very deeply one with the other, and she shuddered in her heart at the realization of what the coming confrontation would mean to the man beside her. Scant wonder he had been able to use her so gently and wisely just now. He understood all too well the need for reassurance, the need to have reserves, whatever their nature, upon which to draw and lean when all else became horror only.

She lay her hand on his arm, keeping her touch very light. "Do not try to be too strong, Mountain Hawk. It is needful for my people that we be allowed to give as well as to receive. Let us, let me, bear what we can for you in whatever lies ahead."

14

The threatening storm continued to hold off all through that night, and the new day opened dark and cold but dry and with the wind falling well short of gale force. Only the sea gave indication of the anger that might yet tear down upon them, for the waves were uncommonly high, covering many of the offshore rocks normally visible, and they were rough and cruel in their striking.

Tarlach was standing at the window of the high chamber in which he and Seakeep's other leaders were gathered, staring out over that turbulent ocean. He had been there most of the morning, silent and so seemingly moody that his companions, even Storm Challenger, had left him to himself.

He straightened suddenly as decision firmed in his mind. "Pull the sentries back from the wall," he said without turning. "Let the watch be kept from the round tower only. When the alarm is given and the ships are actually visible from ground level, let only a few, Dalesfolk all of them, go to the wall, and let them move with apparent confusion and astonishment. The barrier is low, and what goes on behind it will be visible from the fleet's masts. I would have our enemies begin at least their first assault without being aware of our true strength and resolve."

Rorick grinned in appreciation as he moved to relay the command to one of the sentries waiting in the hall outside. This one well merited the rank he held.

"Hasten!"

All whirled at the note in the Mountain Hawk's voice. He was standing very stiffly, his hands pressed against the deep ledge of the window.

The Lieutenant snapped out his orders, then raced back to join the others, who were now crowded around their war commander.

A forest of as-yet-tiny spikes fringed all the horizon.

They grew rapidly in size, becoming, first sail-shrouded masts and then entire ships, warships and troop carriers by the look of them, all painted the deep purple that was apparently their Sultan god's color, and above each of them floated high and proud the crescent standard which had so long been the terror and the chain of the world that had given birth to those sailing them.

Tears swam in Una's eyes despite the effort of her will to block them. "So many, so incredibly many of them!"

She was not ashamed of her weakness. All of her companions had paled, for the force coming against them was more fearsome in its stark reality than ever their inner dread and imagination had made it.

The Holdruler felt a sharp, uncheckable tremor pass through the Captain's body, which was pressed closely against hers in the narrow space, but whatever his feelings in that moment, the gray-eyed man was perfectly calm in his bearing, seemingly sure of his course in this task a hostile fate had set him to do.

"There they are, Comrades," he said softly. "Free men drove them from the realm they had believed securely chained. Now let us see what sort of welcome the free people of this one can give to them."

The arrogance of the Sultanites filled the defenders, Dalesfolk and Falconers alike, with cold fury. There was no concealing the defensive nature of the low wall stretching between the beach and the greater part of the valley, nor could it be concealed that some few warriors stood behind it, yet the newcomers conducted themselves as though they were oblivious to it, coolly arranging themselves and their goods just out of arrow range.

Perhaps they were so assured—and contemptuous—because no opposition had been offered them, not so much as a single word of question or protest, but it was Tarlach's will that no move be made until the alien host began its assault, and the apparently few defenders held firm and quiet in accordance with his command.

More than any potential human foe, the weather held the invaders' attention. It was steadily worsening, not yet a full tempest but lashing out with frequent squalls of both wind and rain that roiled even the well-sheltered bay and made the use of the small boats, necessary for disembarking, treacherous in the extreme.

That could not be helped. They wanted to have the bulk of their army ashore before darkness closed down. Once the fast-approaching night was upon them, the work would have to stop entirely and the ships drop anchor where they were until daylight once more filled the sky—if the obviously building gale would permit it to be resumed at that time.

The defending officers watched their progress from the

tower window all that day until their numbers swarmed upon the beach like the seemingly frenzied but ordered mass of ants working within their hill.

The darkness of spirit which had been on him in the morning had remained with the Mountain Hawk, a sullen weight his comrades were powerless to break or lift.

In watching that proud, seemingly infinite army, he could at least feel with Estcarp's Witches. Had he their Power, he would drop the mountains upon these invaders, would sink the very land beyond the wall into the sea to save the Dale and the people he had come to love.

It was only toward evening that he at last opened his thoughts to those waiting with him. "Those soldiers out there are not under the command to conquer for their Sultan's honor but to claim a new base for all their race, and time is of some import to them. It is possible that they might sail from here again if they find Seakeep too difficult to take and fall upon some other now unsuspecting target."

"There is nothing we can do to prevent that," Brennan told him, sighing within his own heart; if there was ever a grim possibility, this man would find it, and he feared Tarlach had come all too close to true prediction this time.

"They would be forced to remain here if we could destroy their ships."

The Lieutenant stared at him for one moment as if he believed madness had stricken him. "How do you propose we manage that?"

"The Horned Lord has sent us this storm. It may be possible to utilize it."

"How?"

"Their sailors are not used to working in our seas or with our weather systems, and they most assuredly are not familiar with the tangle of rocks and the fierce currents gracing Seakeep's coast. If they believed themselves secure only to have their anchors suddenly released during the height of a tempest such as will soon break here, might their surprise and uncertainty not leave their vessels at the storm's mercy just long enough that a great many of them would come to serious grief, particularly if all were simultaneously so afflicted?"

"Cut the anchor ropes?" Rorick whispered, his voice low with horror.

"Partially cut them. The tempest must be at full power for it to work, and I doubt swimmers could function in the midst of that."

The Captain's face was hard, without any touch of lightness or even of hope in it. "Our people would have to act in complete secrecy and return again in complete secrecy. Any hint of what we had done would probably negate all."

"How could that possibly be accomplished?" Una gasped, no less stunned by his suggestion than were his own comrades.

"By lowering ourselves with ropes down that cliff from which we rescued the survivors of the *Mermaid Fair* once night has fallen and being raised again by the same means when we have completed our work upon our respective targets."

His eyes met hers. "What think you, Lady? Both your people and mine have trained long and hard in these waters, but are we good enough to reach our targets under the conditions that will be prevailing out there, do what we must, and then return again? We can afford no floating bodies to be discovered before our plan fulfills itself. The storm may not develop sufficient force until well after dawn."

"Yes," the Holdruler answered after only the briefest hesitation. "It will not be an easy task, but I think we are the equal of it."

"So be it. We shall set out once there is sufficient darkness to conceal us."

Only a single candle illumed Tarlach's quarters, although the tightly secured siege shutters would have blocked a conflagration from the sight of the invaders on the beach and out on the water so far below. The Falconer lay fully clothed upon his bed, his right arm covering his eyes to shut out even that dim light. He wanted no part of seeing, no part of awareness.

He could not put the thought of what he was to face away from him so easily, however, and yet another shudder shook his body.

The man willed the tremor to cease. This he would have to conquer, he thought grimly, and do it damn quickly. There would be no going down that cliff if he could not so much as bring himself to its edge.

His terror was excessive. The mercenary realized that. He knew those waters and the dangers they contained. By the Horned Lord, he had compelled himself to enter them often enough to train alongside his comrades and the Dalesfolk, and they had frequently been rough and angry.

This was different, though. His mission was real and the storm was real, real as it had been that night he had carried the rope to the prow of the *Mermaid Fair,* real and terrible as his time aboard the dory from the *Dion Star,* and far, far more was riding upon his success.

He was relieved when a soft knock announced Rorick's presence, and he sat up to give the Lieutenant greeting.

The newcomer settled himself into a chair until his Captain should finish smearing his face with black grease and drawing on a pair of dark gloves.

"Did you sleep at all?" he asked Tarlach.

"No." He might as well be truthful, he thought. None of the others were likely to have fared any better in that respect.

Rorick nodded. "I am rather glad to hear it. If you could be that much easier about this than the rest, I would be decidedly worried." He watched his chief pensively. "Are you sure you want to risk the Holdruler on this jaunt?"

His commander turned to look at him. "She swims like a seal. None of her people and few of ours can match her in the water."

"If she is lost, we could be accused—"

"We are all likely to be lost," he snapped, "if not tonight, then later." He reined his temper. "I have no choice but to use our best swimmers, and unfortunately Una of Seakeep is numbered high amongst them. It is bad enough that I cannot risk all our officers by taking you and Brennan. We shall return. This is no suicide mission."

"Do not taunt fortune! If the Grim Commandant does not entirely command that storm-tossed ocean, he at least bears very high authority there."

Tarlach smiled. "Chiefly over the careless for this night, my friend. I trust that none of us shall prove guilty of that fault."

The Captain was ready by then. He checked the two knives sheathed at his waist for keenness and took up his cloak.

He felt better. His dread was no less, but the activity of these final preparations and the need to speak coherently with his comrade had given his mind something concrete upon which to fix, and he found he was able to master himself once again. If he could bring himself to enter the ocean at all, he should be able to perform as need and fate demanded of him.

15

The party standing upon the broad ledge was a large one, consisting as it did of both those soon to enter the ocean and those who would handle the ropes and attend to the swimmers upon their return.

No noise issued from any of them, no needless movement which might, through some quirk of fortune, betray their presence to the ships trying to ride out the storm on the sea below; because of the sharp turn of the cliff, the ledge and those upon it were completely invisible to the warriors on the beach itself.

Una huddled deeply into her heavy cloak. The gale was already high and seemed to gain strength with every passing minute. She hoped they had not delayed too long, that it would not grow too powerful too soon. Tarlach was right. They all had to reach their targets, and they all had to return to their place again.

She glanced at the dark figure of the Captain. He was standing only a few feet from her, unmasked, of course, in preparation for the effort to come, but had she not known it was he, she would not have recognized him, so deep was the storm-enhanced darkness.

He was holding himself stiffly, and his face had been set when they had left the round tower. It was too much, she thought. The fate of a continent, a world, was too heavy a responsibility for one man to have to carry, and doubtless he was as nervous as any of the rest of them as well over what he himself must soon face. No sane man challenged an ocean without qualm.

Her eyes closed, and she battled down her own fear. They were not here to die, but a hard and dangerous task was before them, and the time to set out was almost upon them.

Tarlach waited tensely while the ropes were prepared and tested. He was to descend with the first group.

Now!

His body felt oddly uncoordinated, and he thought his legs must surely buckle as he moved forward to grasp the rope.

It was not yet too late. He could still spare himself. . . .

His fingers closed around the rough fibers of what was to be both his road into terror and his salvation out of it.

The Falconer went to his knees and crawled forward until he reached the edge of the natural platform. He moistened his lips with a tongue gone nearly as dry. This would be the most difficult part, this turning and letting himself down into that black emptiness and the fearful, churning force that was his goal.

Closing his eyes, he reversed his position so that he faced the sturdy wall of the cliff. He clutched the rope almost convulsively as he slowly lowered his body over the edge.

There was an instant of panic as he seemed to be suspended in nothingness, but he gripped that, raised his legs and moved them inward until they made contact with the solid rock.

The improvement in his position, both physically and psychologically, was instantaneous and significant. The wind was not yet so strong that his muscles were unable to stand against it. With a firm brace against the cliff face, he no longer spun and twisted helplessly with each new gust.

It was an eerie feeling, this walking down the almost perpendicular wall like some great spider descending along a strand of its web, and he might almost have enjoyed the strangeness of the sensation were it not for his knowledge of what lay at this journey's end.

The sea was very near now. The Captain could hear the roar of her as she strove to batter down the sturdy heartstone of the land. Already, he shivered under the lash of occasional high-flying spumes of spray. The rain, heavy and chill as it was, did not have the bite of this.

The warrior gasped as a sheet of frigid water poured over him. It was still chiefly wind-borne foam, but the backlash of angry water striking resolute stone had a part in it as well.

Somehow, he retained his grasp on the rope despite the shock of it. A fall from here would not be perilous to man or mission, but it was best to accustom oneself to the touch of cold water before attempting to function in it, and there could be no thought of clinging to the line for even the few seconds necessary to allow his body to acclimatize itself once he actually submerged himself, not in the maelstrom now existing where land and ocean met.

He remained in place until another and yet another wave

had slapped over him, then loosened his hold and plunged straight down into the storm-swept darkness.

He knew fear, stark, blind, primal fear, during the fraction seconds of his fall, whatever assurance his reason tried to draw from the knowledge that the water directly beneath was deep and utterly free of obstacles, however thickly they were scattered only a few feet farther out.

Tarlach struck and sank quickly. He plunged deeper and still deeper until he felt sure he was below the turmoil rending the upper layers. Once at that point, he struggled into a horizontal position.

The mercenary Captain was a strong swimmer and a fast one, and he put forth his full effort now. It was imperative that he be as free as possible from the white water and sharp, conflicting currents fringing the cliff before he was forced to rise to the surface for air.

At last, his lungs warned him he must begin his ascent. Up, he went, carefully testing the way lest he be caught in some eddy or struck down by a breaking wind wave on the surface. It was essential that he retain full control over his movements. The waters around him were no longer clear of debris, and he had no wish to be slammed against any of the rocks or islets littering the region. What would be a relatively light, even an insignificant, accident on land could well prove fatal out here.

The Falconer broke surface. A grin of triumph momentarily lighted his face. He had indeed come far and had managed to place himself in an almost perfect approach to the first of his targets.

He remained above water but a few moments, only long enough to take his bearings and to draw a fresh supply of air into his lungs. Movement was far easier and safer below.

A sense of elation filled him as he deftly swerved to avoid a sharp spire lifting up out of the ocean floor. The long, hard hours of training to which he had subjected himself and his comrades were proving their worth this night. Even with visibility so poor and with the surface so roiled by the ever-rising tempest that he was compelled to remain much deeper than was his wont, he was functioning as if such movement were as natural to him as was the handling of a spirited horse. Barring some viciously ill cast of fortune, he knew now that their mission would be a success and that they would all return from it.

Tarlach was not so foolishly optimistic or so ignorant of the medium through which he moved as to imagine he could hope to avoid all injury. The water was too dark and the material littering it of too high a density for that even were the surface dead calm.

He proved more successful at avoiding obstacles than he might have hoped. On four occasions, he did hit against rocks he was either not a quick enough, or a strong enough, swimmer to escape entirely, but those were mere grazes, bruising his flesh but drawing no blood or so much as tearing the sturdy material covering him. For a time, during the second of these incidents, he had cause for fear, when he surfaced into a cresting wind wave. It had caught him up in its mindless anger, but he was able to regain enough control to dive again and was soon below the reach of its fury, before it could break him against the nearest of the three islands in whose midst he had floundered.

At last, the dark shadow shape of a warship loomed very near to the Falconer. It looked huge and ominous, a patch of infinitely deep blackness against an almost equally lightless sky.

His heart beat rapidly. It was not fear spurring him now, or at least not the deadening dread he had known since he had first conceived this mission. The familiar tension that ever preceded battle was upon him.

The man dove, and when he rose again, he was beneath the curved side of the first of the three targets assigned to him.

He remained well back in its shadow so that his eyes might accustom themselves to the additional darkness and, thus, be sensitive to whatever light there was in the sky beyond. The contrast must be sufficient for him to detect the anchor rope with some kind of reasonable speed . . .

There! He darted toward it as swiftly and silently as a shark and grasped it. Tarlach took yet another deep breath and followed the line down to the point where he would make his cut.

Hooking his left arm and leg around it to give himself support, he drew the foremost of his daggers and brought it to bear upon the rope.

The fibers were thickly packed and tough, and even his keen-edged weapon did not slice through them quickly or with any ease. The task was complicated, too, by the fact that it had to be accomplished well below the surface so that no chance movement of either the vessel or the water around her could expose the sabotaged moorings before the time for their breaking was come.

His relatively slow progress did not cause him to fear discovery. No one could have seen him even were the deck above crowded with sharp-eyed men looking directly at this place, nor would the slight motion his sawing imparted to the line give him away, not with the movement of the warship under the lash of wind and wave. As for sound, he made none, and he would have felt little concern were the very opposite true; he doubted he should be detected this night if he hammered directly upon the hull.

At last, he replaced his knife in its scabbard. A little of the rope still remained intact, enough to hold against the punishment the vessel was now taking. When the tempest worsened another few degrees, only a very few, it would give.

There would be another to assume its work. The Sultanite sailors were not such fools as to trust to one anchor in a gale the like of this.

The Captain was not long in discovering it and in subjecting it to the same treatment as he had given to the first, save that he left barely enough of it that it should not part prematurely to give the invaders warning of their danger; one glance at the severed end of it would be sufficient to reveal that no natural force had caused it to separate.

That done, he moved on to his second target. It was very close, and he was fortunate in locating one of the lines within minutes after reaching its shadow.

He was more accustomed to handling the Sultanites' ropes by then, as well, and cut it perceptibly more quickly than he had that first one.

Tarlach sought for its mate, but it eluded his eyes.

He raised himself out of the water in an effort to gain a better perspective. The cut rope to which he clung was more than a little slippery, and he would not have cared to climb far on it, but it gave his arms and legs purchase enough for this, particularly with the sea still supporting the better part of his weight.

His eyes slitted with the effort of focusing in this grossly inefficient light as he resumed his search.

A mighty blast of wind, the strongest thus far released by the storm, struck the vessel above him.

The hull rolled under the impact of it. The man's attention was fully fixed on the darkness beyond, and he did not become aware of his danger until it came crashing down upon him.

His skull seemed to explode. His limbs lost their power to grasp, and he sank as if weighted. He tried to fight the water, but his body would not respond. The neck must be broken. . . .

Tarlach's mind returned to find his lungs screaming for air. He could not have been senseless for more than a moment, he thought numbly, or they would have begun sucking in water.

Even before he could begin to curse whatever power had restored him to consciousness only so that he must experience both his helplessness and his dying, his arms and legs began thrashing wildly in a purely instinctive effort to save himself.

Feeling almost drunk with relief, he forced himself under control and sped upward, not caring where or how he broke surface only so long as this horrible burning anguish in his chest should be ended.

The mercenary found himself very near to the partially severed rope from which he had dropped. He grasped that and clung to it, drawing in great draughts of cold, impossibly sweet air.

Gradually, his breathing returned to a rate more nearly approximating its norm, and he stirred himself to complete his work.

He discovered the second rope at last, located considerably farther from the first than had been the case on the other warship. That notwithstanding, he was but moments in reaching it, not much longer in sabotaging it.

His final target lay a goodly distance from the first two, from all the rest of the fleet. The Sultanites apparently preserved preeminence of person even under battle conditions, and this was their flagship. There was no crowding of her.

The Falconer submerged. His recent accident had not affected his ability to swim, he thought wryly, although his head throbbed violently after it. No one following his grim profession could afford to study himself too closely if he hoped to live very long, much less to prosper at all.

Flagship or nay, his last victim was no better secured than her sisters had been. He found the ropes, and soon she, too, rode with unsuspected death hovering over her.

Tarlach rested for a few minutes. His heart felt strangely heavy. His work was done, successfully done, yet it was not in him to rejoice. His own trial was far from ended. The ordeal of the return remained, the long swim back to the cliff. There would be no stages to break the constant labor, the constant need for vigilance and almost superhuman concentration upon his surroundings the increased strength of the storm now demanded. He would have to complete it in one unbroken dash across this unfriendly ocean, knowing all the while that her most potent hate would be reserved for the very end when he would be most wearied by his long efforts.

The Captain filled his lungs and dove. He had proven himself the equal of this challenge already tonight and would meet it as well a second time. The quick decisions he would be compelled to make and sheer physical effort would soon force his imagination back into more acceptable bounds.

So did it prove. He came into even less trouble, in fact, than he had encountered upon the approach. The pounding inner urge for speed, the nervousness for his mission no longer drove him, and he reduced his pace a little, giving himself a few precious extra moments in which to spot potentially deadly obstacles around him and plan his best course for the avoiding of each.

Although he longed for the peace, the comfort, he would find at its crest, the cliff seemed all too soon to loom up over him, casting the sea below into the deepest shadow.

He was in greater danger now than at any other time during this night save for that moment when his carelessness had given the rolling warship power over him. Other swimmers would be converging on the cliff face below the ledge. He had to avoid colliding with any of them and had somehow to escape being smashed against the unyielding stone while searching for one of the ropes.

That hunt proved monstrously hard. A great number had been lowered. He knew that, but he knew, too, that each was no more than a slender thread tossing in the vast, dark fury of the storm. It was not possible to seek for them on the surface where what little light there was might have aided his search. That was maelstrom only. No creature could survive long there.

He remained under water as much as possible, but his body needed air, and each time he was forced to go up for it, he was cruelly buffeted in that madness of breaking waves and the backwash they created until he wondered if he would meet his death here after all.

It was a bitter long time before the man succeeded in finding and grasping one of the precious lines. Once he did, he followed it down with nearly frantic haste lest the next of the eternally charging breakers wrest it from his hold again.

His lungs were nigh to bursting by the time he reached the weighted loop that formed its end. Ignoring his pain, he worked his legs through the noose and cut away the stones holding it down. Three times in quick succession, he raised himself up and then dropped upon the rope with the full force and weight at his command. That done, he sat back in the loop to wait.

Would it be enough? Would the prearranged signal be read by those above, or would they lay the vibrations to the workings of wind and wave?

They must act soon! Already, his chest heaved, struggling against the will that kept his lungs from drawing in the water that would end their agony and his life.

Tarlach knew he could hold on only seconds longer before that reflex conquered. He began to make his way to the surface, drawing the line up with him. By doing this, he realized full well that he could cause the rope to foul, but to remain longer was death.

The line tightened. It began to rise swiftly.

He ceased his own efforts and permitted it to catch up to him, turning all his strength and will to battle desperately against the nigh unto overwhelming urge to breathe, only to breathe . . .

His head broke water. He drew in air with such speed and force that it set him coughing. That did not matter. Nothing did beyond the fact that his body was once more free to take what it needed of the precious gas.

The Falconer remained in that state of numbed euphoria barely long enough for him to be drawn free of the water.

There was yet work for him to do if he was to escape injury on this final stage of his attack.

As he had done when he had been lowered into the sea, he used his legs to keep himself away from the wall. It was a harder task this time. The wind was higher and stronger. It tore at him viciously, threatening to rip him from his place even now, when safety was so close.

The rain was enough in itself to throw him down. It fell in a seemingly solid sheet that struck with the force of a blow, its power redoubling the strength of the gale driving it.

Tarlach rested his forehead against the rope during a rare momentary lull. He was infinitely glad he was not forced to actually climb.

He could not have done so. He had been too long in the water. His muscles missed the buoyancy of it, and his usually supple body felt as heavy and unwieldy as if it had been fashioned out of some dense tropical wood. It would not have obeyed him well enough had he tried to put such a demand upon it. He had been all too right in ordering that the rescue of the swimmers be handled in this manner.

The journey up the cliff was of too short duration for cold to be a danger at the present temperature, but still, it was a bitter lash, as if nature herself would score him for the lives his deeds of this night would cause to be lost. It knifed through his saturated clothes like the talons of those unnameable things native to the caverns of which the Great Hall of the Demons itself was but a part.

His hands were growing numb, but the man only clamped them the more tightly. If they loosened now, he would crash back, down, probably to be broken upon the cliff as the sea seized him once more.

Would this weary ascent never end?

Tarlach compelled his impatience to quieten. He ceased to battle his discomfort, accepting that there could be no escaping it. His part was to endure, and this he was determined to do in a manner befitting a Falconer officer. Whatever his present misery, he knew it would not last much longer.

It did not. He saw the lip that marked the edge of the ledge scant inches above him. Hands reached over to steady and lift him. Then he was standing upon firm ground, leaning heavily on Brennan for support. A cloak was wrapped about him and a flask held to his lips. The brandy burned pleasantly in his mouth and sent a thin stream of warmth flowing down through his frozen body.

Rorick was there as well. He took part of the swimmer's weight from Brennan.

The two Lieutenants urged him to begin moving back toward the rear of the ledge and the steep path leading down into the valley.

This, the Captain resisted. He could not go yet. . . .

Brennan understood what held him.

"Una is already down," he shouted, almost screamed, to make himself heard above the combined roar of the gale and the tempest-lashed waves; there was no fear that his voice would carry to alert their foemen now. "You are one of the last."

Tarlach nodded his thanks. He went with his comrades, allowing them to more than half carry him to the place where his mare was waiting and to lift him onto her saddle.

Brennan mounted as well, and the two mercenaries rode for the shelter of the round tower, leaving Rorick to return to the work above.

16

A dull, grayish light filled his chamber when the Falconer Captain awoke. The air was cold outside the heavy blankets covering him, and he could hear the muted howling of wind and rain and sharp, terrifyingly loud explosions of thunder.

Those last accompanied searing flashes of white brilliance so intense that he was forced for a time to screen his eyes beneath the covers until they could become somewhat adapted to the enormous alterations in illumination within the room.

He shuddered in his heart to think of the fate of anyone unfortunate enough to be in the water when even one of those awesome bolts streaked down to meet it.

A sickness filled him. If he and his comrades had done their work well, there should be many men now helpless before that fearsome force.

Ignoring the chill against his bare shoulders, he sat up.

Brennan was standing by the window. He had been gazing at the world outside, whatever little of it was visible through the turmoil of the rampaging elements, but turned when his chief stirred.

"You might as well lie back again. The Lady Una has confined most of you swimmers to bed for several hours yet. She wants you all well rested and somewhat recovered from your bruises before the attack begins."

"She has put herself under similar bonds, I suppose?" Tarlach asked sarcastically.

"She is not hurt, and we need one of you to remain in command."

"She cannot fight a war!"

"Rorick and I are there to keep an eye on things. Everything is well in hand. Nothing is going to happen with the storm lashing like this, but just in case, we have the wall manned and reinforcements at ready." He scowled. "Stay where you are, will you! I never thought I would support a female's stand above my commander's, but she is the one showing sense. There will not be much time for sleep later, so make the most of the luxury now."

Brennan came over to him. He sat on the edge of the bed. "Are you all right? That was a nasty crack you took on the back of your head. We were afraid for a long while that you had suffered real injury from it."

Tarlach grinned. "My skull is too thick for that."

He recounted all that had happened.

The Lieutenant's lips tightened during the telling. "Your being in the water saved you," he said after his commander had finished. "You were pushed down through it instead of being crushed. Still, you were incredibly fortunate."

"What about the others?"

"All safe. A few bad lacerations but nothing to hold anyone back from the fighting. Most are probably still asleep."

"Where is Storm Challenger?" he asked, suddenly becoming aware of the empty perch beside his bed.

"Off sulking with Sunbeam and Bravery. They did not appreciate being confined to the round tower last night."

"Falcons do not sulk!"

"The cat has apparently been giving them some lessons." Brennan's expression grew troubled. "The Lady Una is fully bonded with her as well, is she not?"

"Yes," Tarlach answered evenly.

"You have known this for some time?"

He nodded. "I was afraid of the reaction if it became known. First Seakeep needed us as a united force, and now our own people do."

"I have said before that you must start trusting us, Tarlach." Brennan arose and went to the window, turning his back on the other.

The Mountain Hawk's head lowered. He was shamed. The rebuke was merited, the more so in the face of the unwavering support this man, the whole company, had given him. "Pardon craved, my friend. I have had to feel my way along strange paths of late, and I fear many of my judgments may have been ill-considered."

"I know that," the Lieutenant responded wearily. "We all do, but if you must fight a different sort of war, we want to have our part in it, even as we will carry our part on the wall outside."

Tarlach sighed. "I wish . . ."

He pressed his fingers to his eyes. He had more to concern him now than this. "What time is it?"

"Three hours past noon."

The Captain's eyes darkened. The day was almost gone. "How fares the fleet?"

"As we would have, apparently, from the few glimpses we have been able to get of it." Brennan glanced toward the window. "Perhaps that is just as well. I count myself no traitor for saying that it would not be an easy watching."

"That it would not," Tarlach agreed bleakly. "Whatever they be, it is no matter of pride to see men broken by a force nothing human can hope to face and withstand."

The fury of the great tempest did not waver at all during what remained of that day or during most of the following night. It began to lessen just before dawn and then eased off so rapidly that it was no more than a heavy rain by morning. Visibility was good by then, and the Seakeep leaders crowded together at the window in their high council chamber.

Although physically close to his companions, Tarlach felt utterly isolated from them, isolated from everything in the world around him. His body was stiffly held, tense, his expression intentionally emotionless as he gazed out over the beach and the sea beyond it.

The ocean was almost completely clear of ships, and those few remaining were but shards, hopeless wrecks that would never again dance over any wave. The Sultan's mighty fleet had been annihilated. Not so much as a dory remained of all that had been.

The strand was littered with debris, that and other things. The sea was beginning to give up her victims.

Not all the bodies washing up there had come from the ships. Most of them had not. The storm-driven tide had claimed far more of the beach than was its wont, and a considerable part of the invading army had been unable to avoid its mighty, hungry waves.

His head lowered. The toll might be fully as high as half the Sultanites' original number—they had certainly lost a third of their force—yet what did that massive slaughter mean to Seakeep? His was still so much the lesser force as to scarcely seem an obstacle to the intended invasion at all.

The Holdlady's thoughts were little brighter as she watched the stunned aliens gather what they had thus far recovered of their dead for burning, an essential precaution if they were to avert the pestilence otherwise almost certain to fix upon their damp, incredibly crowded camp. At least, the remnants of their broken warships provided them with fuel enough for their grim work if they could no longer support the cause of the living.

"They will not sail from here now," she said, speaking aloud to herself rather than to the others. "We accomplished that much for our neighbors."

"Let us not claim too much credit," Tarlach told her, rousing himself out of the dark thoughts which had been holding him. "The storm might have done as much without our intervention."

She shook her head. "I think not. Less than half of those ships would have been left, maybe less than a quarter of them, but that would still have been more than enough to work grief upon some other unsuspecting port."

"We have made our own case the more desperate," the Mountain Hawk said without taking his eyes from the activity going on below. "They have no choice but to take us now."

"We realized that would be so," Brennan told him quietly. "Rabble may break under heavy adversity, but we never believed those ones down there would do so."

"When do you think they will make their move?" Una asked the Captain. The fury of the storm and sheer shock had thus far shielded them, but they all knew that respite would not be long-lived.

"Sometime before noon, I would say. They will settle their

camp first and secure their supplies. They were fortunate in being spared the most of them and are not likely to risk exposing them to any more heavy weather if they can avoid it."

He turned away from the window for the first time. "We will have little warning. Tell those on the wall to be prepared for a sudden assault and put the reserves on alert. Reinforcements must reach the line almost immediately if it is to hold. After this first blow, we will keep it at full strength, and this will no longer be a concern unless our line is breached."

"Perhaps they should move up now," Rorick suggested doubtfully.

He shook his head. "Our enemies will have found a few cut ropes by this time and know we are organized and daring. I would keep our true strength from them a while longer. They will discover that soon enough, and then we shall have no further weapon to throw against them save our skill and our courage under arms."

17

Rufon sped from the valley without a backward glance at either the round tower or the ocean that would all too soon cradle the warships of their enemies.

He was heavy with a sense of frustration and with the dead feeling that his mission was a hopeless one, at least as far as saving those he loved was concerned. The Mountain Hawk and Seakeepdale's Lady would cast themselves day after day into the thickest and most furious part of the fighting. Even with all their skill, it was not likely they would be able to avoid their enemies' blades until help could reach them.

No aid would be coming to the Dale for many long weeks yet. They all must accept that fact and everything it portended. Linna lay far from the sea-girth hold, and the land separating them was wild and rough. He would be fortunate indeed if he could cross it and return again without meeting with some accident or other ill happening that would cause him serious delay.

The man forced patience upon his heart. There was no purpose in railing against circumstances he was powerless to alter, and it but wasted energy he could better spend elsewhere.

Time went by, better than two weeks, without change in the routine the man had set for himself and his nonhuman companions. Fortune rode with them, and they experienced no unexpected delay.

The stops he was forced to schedule were more than bad enough. However much he might resign himself to the limits terrain put upon their speed and to the breaks he had to permit each day to refresh both himself and the animals, Rufon bitterly resented the coming of darkness when he must stop entirely. All those hours lost, and in the end, Seakeep's fate and this world's might be lost with them.

He was quite without choice. The distance to be covered was simply too great to permit another such race as the Mountain Hawk had ridden to Lormt for the Lady Una's sake. Without sufficient rest and food, man and beast alike would falter and fall before a fraction of the journey was ended.

That was, at the least, a predictable delay. Other forces were at work which could sweep infinitely more time from those who would save the embattled Dale.

The weather had turned sour. As yet, it was merely raining heavily, making riding unpleasant but causing no delay. That would not remain true for many more hours. The storm was gaining steadily in force and would be a full tempest before morning unless some miracle scattered it. Once it reached its full potential, there would be no going on until the better part of its force was spent again.

* * *

Several hours passed. The Dalesman began to feel decidedly nervous about his route and altered it abruptly so that he left the rift he had been following well below.

The steeper, rougher ground of the mountainside might slow him somewhat, but narrow highland valleys could too easily become riverbeds during a downpour like this. He had no wish to find himself in the path of any such flood.

He would have had to come up to this level anyway. There was a large cave that travelers from Seakeep had used before, during their infrequent journeys to Linna. It was the only really acceptable resting place on this part of his route if the weather should be significantly foul.

He had better find it, and soon, the veteran thought grimly. More than his and his companions' comfort was at stake. There were dangers in a gale such as this, too many and too heavy to permit travel, at least during its height.

He should have passed the cave already according to his recollections, but the storm and the more recent change in the path he followed had so much slowed his progress that he had not yet reached it.

Rufon of Seakeep fervently hoped he had not. If he had somehow gone by the only place in this area able to shelter both himself and his horse, if he had failed to see its dark entrance during one of those increasingly more frequent times when the rain drove so heavily that visibility ranged scarcely a foot beyond his eyes, then they all faced a hard night and maybe a perilous one. The cold was increasing and so, too, was the falling of branches and even of whole trees.

His already tight lips grew still harder. His mission could be ended before dawn once more touched the eastern sky.

There! The yawning blackness that marked the mouth of the cave he sought was before him.

The Dalesman longed to race for it and fling himself and his weary mount into its shelter, but warrior's discipline was too much a part of him to permit any such unguarded action. He drew rein well away from it.

He watched his gelding carefully, the horse and the falcon, who had been sheltering beneath his cloak. His own senses were in a great part negated by the sheer fury of the elements, but animals were possessed of other gifts scarcely comprehensible to humans, and those of well-trained war comrades were highly developed.

When neither of the pair showed sign of unease, Rufon started forward, still moving cautiously.

He slid from his saddle and advanced toward the entrance on foot. Under his cloak, he held the torch and the flint kit he had readied during his last break in anticipation of this moment.

The falcon darted inside ahead of him. She remained within for several seconds, then returned briefly to circle him and dash back, into the cave, out of the driving elements.

Despite that reassurance, the man tensed as he slipped inside and moved quickly to set his back against the wall to his right.

Nothing sprang at him, and he hastened to fire his torch and penetrate beyond the half light of the entrance.

Rufon found himself in a great chamber about thirty feet square. Walls and floor were equally rough, with fissures and cracks marring both in several places. At least two of the former appeared to lead farther within the mountain. The roof was probably very high in proportion to the cave's other dimensions; it loomed beyond the feeble power of his single torch to reveal.

One feature of the place pleased him greatly, a small cave-let situated just behind the left-hand lip of the entrance that seemed to have been created to fill a traveler's needs. No light from his fire would leak outside to betray his presence to the world beyond, and at least a little heat would be held within its relatively confined space.

He hastened outside again. The storm was likely to hold

him a long while in the cave, and since a couple of hours of reasonable light remained, he would do well to utilize it by drawing in as much fuel as possible and also as much fodder as he could collect. It would be wise to spare what he could of his remaining supplies for later need. He had not made Linna yet.

There was little twilight that evening, and darkness came rapidly once it began to fall.

The veteran settled back to wait out the storm. His small fire would never banish more than the edge of the chill and damp, but that did not trouble him overmuch. He had often been less comfortable than he was now. The cold in here was not sharp enough to give pain, and the fire did serve to dry his clothes once more.

Hunger would be no problem. His food might be the familiar journey rations, dry and nigh unto tasteless, but it filled the stomach and met the body's needs, and he was not inclined to complain because daintier fare was lacking.

In truth, he was too tired, too physically and emotionally battered, to concern himself with much beyond his most basic requirements. The hard stone floor would be no deterrent to sleep that night.

The little he had, he shared. These falcons were war birds, hardy and able to care for themselves, but he had observed the attention their human comrades paid to them, and he was resolved to give no less to the one accompanying him. She doubtless had no greater love for damp, cold air than he did himself, and if his cloak and the warmth of his body could provide her with a measure of comfort, he was more than pleased to offer her both.

The tempest roared on in all its awesome strength through the rest of that night and the day following while the courier bowed down his impatience and endeavored to make himself content in his waiting.

Beyond the necessary care of his mount, which brought him several times into the larger chamber, he rarely left the cavelet. It was cold in the outer cavern, very damp throughout, and wet near the entrance from the rain carried in by the fierce wind whenever it so swung about as to blast in through the wide mouth. Nothing was to be seen through the downpour that he should expose himself there, nor did caution demand that he do so. He knew himself to be safe from attack; nothing, animal or human, would be moving through this.

Only once did Rufon remain at the uncomfortable post for more than a few minutes. He had finished his evening meal and was just replenishing the fire when an awesome roaring began, a grinding, seemingly continual explosion deeper and more terrible than the sharp crash of the thunder.

The Dalesman sprang to his feet and raced for the entrance. He could see nothing and praised the Flame that he could not. That eldritch rumbling was the voice of a suddenly released flood tearing through the valley below. Had it so moved that some wild surge swept upslope to the point that it became visible to him, it would very probably have filled the cave as well. Whether he and his companions would have been able to withstand the battering until the water had receded again, well, he was only glad not to have seen that question put to the testing.

His head lowered. This proved the wisdom, the necessity of stopping and remaining here until the gale blew itself out, but he quailed in his heart to think of the price that might yet be exacted for this long delay.

He wondered how his people were faring. Had they been able to complete the wall before the tempest had broken? Had the Sultanites arrived? This was about the time the spirit had set for their coming.

If so, it was a harsh welcome they had received from the realm they had thought to despoil. He knew storms, and this one ruled for a greater expanse of sky than that directly above his sheltering place. There would be no fighting while the weather held thus, save against the wind and the waves lashing the beach.

Rufon returned to his camping place, shaking his cloak vigorously before entering it to remove the rainwater clinging to it. He had no wish to bring any more damp than necessary inside with him.

He leaned back against the wall and resolutely willed himself to relax. There had been little time for rest since he had left Seakeepdale, and there would be less still once he was again free to set out. It behooved him to use it well while he could.

The anger of the great storm finally spent itself during the early hours of the following morning just before dawn began to grip the sky.

The rain still fell, but travel was once more possible, and the Dalesman set forth as soon as he was certain the alteration in the weather was a true one and not merely a lull that would quickly give way to madness again.

The pace he set and maintained was a killing one, allowing rider and mount just enough rest that they were able to continue with their race, for with every fast-flying moment, Rufon realized that more blood was being spilled at Seakeep's newly constructed barrier—if that barrier still held at all.

For nearly three days longer, Rufon continued to ride until at last he crested the final rise separating him from Linna town.

He paused there, to rest and to look down upon the cluster of buildings that was his goal, and his head raised in triumph and hope. Filling all the land surrounding the seaport was a great camp. Those he sought were here.

Setting his heels to the sides of his tired horse, he began the final stretch of his long journey.

A question came suddenly into his mind. Falconers

masked not only their faces before those of other races but also every sign of rank or personal identity. How was he to find the man he needed to see? Would he, a Dalesman of no apparent authority, be taken to the Warlord of this strange people merely because he claimed he bore a Blood Call and needs must speak with him immediately?

He smiled then, and his fingers rather shyly touched the proudly held head of the falcon riding the perch before him. "Well, Winged Lady," he told her, "this must be your part, I think. Find this Warlord of your comrades and let him know the need that is on us."

He had no more power to speak with the war bird than he had with his horse, but she uttered a soft cry, as if in understanding, and took wing, streaking toward the encampment below with obvious purpose.

Only a short time passed before two Falconers rode out to meet him, and escorted him back to their camp. They drew rein before a large tent set approximately at its center and then left him after first giving salute to the man standing in its entrance.

The Falconer chief was tall and slender of build with a wiry, lithe look about him that reminded Rufon of Tarlach. There was no questioning that he was a veteran fighting man and that he was long familiar with the burden of great responsibility. Both his carriage and what could be seen of his features allowed no doubt of that.

Even as the Mountain Hawk would have done, he stepped forward quickly and caught the horse's bridle.

"The Horned Lord's welcome, Dalesman," he said. "Alight now so that my aides may care for your mount and come inside yourself. I have ordered that food and drink be prepared for you."

The interior of the tent was divided into two parts, the larger to serve the Warlord for living and work space and a small screened-off area in which he probably slept. It was furnished comfortably enough, rather surprisingly so, and as

Rufon looked about him, he received the impression of a man of both taste and discipline.

For only a moment could he permit his attention to so wander before his host's eyes fixed on him. They were so pale a gray as to be almost silver, and they held and pierced him as if they would delve his very soul.

"The winged one reports that you have come to me bearing a Blood Call," Varnel said.

He nodded. "I do, Lord." Falconers normally did not claim title, but this man was ruler of his race and must be so honored. "From the Company Captain bound to Seakeepdale. He has sent you this report, which contains a full account of our situation. Ours and yours."

The Warlord took the thick letter but continued to study the messenger. "You are acquainted with its contents?"

"I am, my Lord. A written message might be lost or destroyed, and it was needful that this information reach you. The falcon, too, can doubtless give you a good part of it if you question her."

"What is your name, Dalesman?"

"Rufon. I am aide to the Lady Una, Holdruler of Seakeepdale, and so served the Lord Harvard, her sire, before his death."

"I thank you, Rufon," he said. He glanced at the entrance as an aide pushed the flap aside. "Your meal is ready. Eat now and rest a while until I have read this. I shall send for you again then, perhaps to question you or to hear your own assessment of the situation. Sometimes the opinions of those native to a place can be most helpful in the planning of our moves."

"I am at your service, my Lord."

The sun was better than two hours set before Rufon was once more admitted to the Warlord's quarters.

Varnel greeted him courteously, but there was a gravity, a heaviness, about him which told that he had read his Captain's report and accepted the reality of the threat it described.

"The invaders had not yet arrived when you set out?"

"No, Lord. They will have come by now, though, if the ghost's information is accurate."

"You believe this spirit as well?" he asked.

"The Mountain Hawk does. I know fighting men, Lord, and I trust his judgment."

"Mountain Hawk?"

The Dalesman flushed. "The Captain. The phrase was somehow put on him while he was in Lormt, and we of Seakeep have picked it up. No discourtesy is meant, but it is difficult to work without a name when dealing closely with a person over an extended stretch of time."

To his surprise, the Falconer smiled. "I know. We frequently encounter that problem."

His mood darkened again in the next moment. "Sixty thousand men. I do not command a third that number. Your Mountain Hawk is correct. If they cannot be met and held at some strong defensive position where they can bring only a small part of their force against us at any given time, we do not have a hope of stopping them. Whether his proposed wall will suffice, or whether it was completed at all . . ."

"We cannot know that until we reach Seakeep, my Lord."

The silver eyes pierced him suddenly. "There have been some strange tales about this Seakeep," Varnel said, "and about Ravenfielddale as well. A Falconer has never held such a position before, and I am wondering what my Captain's plans may be. His comrades were reticent to the point of mystery about the whole subject when some of them returned to my camp last fall."

"That would be Falconer business, Lord," the Dalesman replied carefully.

"Would you lie to protect him?"

Rufon's head raised. "What are you asking? The Mountain Hawk has done nothing that would bring disgrace upon him or upon his race. Throughout the whole time that I have known him, he has conducted himself with courage, nobility, and integrity. As for defending him," he added almost fiercely, "I would give my body's life, and my soul's with it, for his sake, as would every other man and woman and every child old enough to so choose in Seakeepdale, even as we would for our own Holdlady."

Once again, the Warlord smiled. "Peace, Dalesman!—So my son's ability to draw the loyalty of those with whom he serves extends beyond our own race?" He saw the other's look of astonishment, which he had, indeed, intended to elicit. "It has always been our custom to so name some of the fledglings we train."

"He wins loyalty because he merits it," Rufon told him flatly. "Did you not hear among those tales you mentioned how he saved those Sulcar mariners?"

"That I did, both from some of my own warriors and from Captain Elfthorn himself. He has not been slow in spreading the story of his rescue and of the events that followed it."

"Then you know your Captain—your son—is a credit to all your kind." Rufon shifted uneasily. "Time flies, my Lord. Your people have been warned now, but the Dales have not. Will you send couriers—"

"No."

The Dalesman's head snapped up. "I am sorry to have troubled you, Commandant. I have several miles to travel yet this night. . . ."

Varnel raised his arms in a gesture of surrender, all the while laughing silently. "Your temper is sharper even than the Mountain Hawk's! Be easy, Rufon of Seakeep. I will not send messengers because I have already done so."

He reddened. "I crave pardon."

The Falconer laughed again, this time aloud. "No need. I baited you. Sit. It takes time even for a race of blank shields to break a camp the size of this one."

A great weight seemed to lift from the other's heart. "You will ride with me, then?"

The Warlord nodded. "All but one company of convalescing men that I have set as a guard over our villages and the couriers I already mentioned. I have heard enough about Seakeep and Ravenfield that I feel the need to see them for myself, and I prefer to do it with their lands unviolated and their people unslain."

18

Jarlach allowed his weary body to slide down along the wall until he sat upon the fighting platform. He closed his eyes and tried to will his mind to shut out completely all awareness of the horror that had been his life for better than a full month now.

They opened once more. It was no use. The reality of this barrier and all beyond it was not to be banished merely by desire and the willing.

All was strangely quiet. The defenders were too spent for more than a word of thanks to those bringing them food and water, and the Sultanites made little noise while removing their dead. They had no need for speech, he thought dully; that work was well familiar to them by this time.

It was all too familiar to him.

The Captain roused himself to look along the platform to right and to left. There were too many missing who had stood there when these accursed invaders had begun their first charge nearly five weeks before. The wall they had raised with such haste had proven to be an excellent defense, but it could not shield everyone forever, could not deflect every dart and blow. All those felled were not dead, of course. The most of them were not, but warriors had gone from here to claim their places in the Halls of the Valiant.

A surge of grief twisted in his heart as memories of those he would not see again in this realm of the living crowded for place in his mind.

Was Rorick among them? The Lieutenant had been carried down during the last of the fighting, a spear transfixing his body. Such chest wounds were not invariably fatal, but the very great majority of them proved to be so, even in those surviving long enough to reach Daria's care.

Tarlach would miss him if he did perish. They all would, and they would sorely miss his skill and his courage in this battle. Whatever the outcome of his wounding, he would not be returning to the barrier. Either it would have fallen or relief would have come and the Sultanites be crushed long before he was healed.

Injury should have dismissed a lot more of them. There was not a single warrior in all the defending line who did not bear some wound upon his body, and few of the falcons were not similarly afflicted. Most carried several, and some of them were significant enough that they would have forced retirement from the fray under any other circumstances.

They did not have that privilege here. As long as a soldier could still stand and both attack and defend with reasonable effectiveness or a war bird take to the air and fight, he needs must remain in his place.

He himself had been fortunate thus far. He had received a half dozen or so cuts during the course of the siege, but they were no more than that and did not interfere with his combat ability or even cause him much in the way of discomfort. They gave him nothing at all of what could be termed pain. He could give the Horned Lord thanks that Storm Challenger was as yet unscathed.

The Mountain Hawk straightened a little. He examined his spear critically, both point and shaft. Their enemies would not be long in clearing enough of their fallen away from the base of the wall that they could function effectively there once more, work the defenders permitted to go on unhindered because it afforded them respite as well. When that moment came, their attack would be renewed.

His mouth hardened. Tarlach took no joy in slaughter, particularly when he could not but admire the tenacity and the raw courage of his opponents.

They had to be given that, these Sultanite warriors. They fell like flies into a fire, they shivered and at times swam in their sandy encampment, they endured inhuman crowding and watched wounded comrades perish who should easily have lived save for the obscene conditions under which the army was forced to exist, and still they came on with an ardor and a singleness of purpose the Falconer knew neither he nor any other of his people could have equaled.

They had the hope, no, the certainty of conquest to spur them, of course. The invading soldiers could see how few actually opposed them. They knew they need only wear them down to the point that the wall could not be adequately manned. Only one post need go, only one. If they could but get across the barrier in number in any place, swarm behind and around the pitifully tiny band of defenders, the whole would be theirs in a matter of minutes.

Officers and warriors alike were pressing harder and ever harder for that moment. Pride and honor were both pricked that their many should be held at bay by so very few. Beyond this, beyond even their race's dire peril and the command laid upon them by their Sultan god, the need for victory was on them. Every man of them realized that they must break through before their supplies gave out, before the even more dreaded shadow of sickness seized upon them, as it inevitably must if they remained confined much longer on this minute beach, ever under the stench of bodies burning in the fuel of their own fat.

Brassy trumpets sounded from beyond the wall, and the high-pitched, wailing shout that had for so long been the terror of their distant world rent the air.

Una of Seakeep leaped to her feet. They were coming again, a purple-turbaned, seemingly undammable sea of hate and death.

Seakeep's archers felled the first row of them, but those following after leaped their bodies before they had quite hit the ground, racing madly until they reached the stubborn barrier.

There, they began to climb, one bracing the other, forming living ladders to bring their comrades into combat range of those holding High Hallack against them.

A turban rose above the wall. The Holdruler waited a moment, then struck hard as the face became visible. Another replaced it and yet another.

She tried not to look into those faces, tried not to become conscious of them as such. It was not butcher work she did, for that implied personal safety and ease in the killing, and neither applied here. The Sultanites were coming up too fast, and each winning the ability to use his arms was a deadly opponent.

One gained the wall. Una failed to throw him down with her first blow, and before she could bring her weapon to bear again, a second foeman was before her.

The woman plunged her spear into the heart of the first and withdrew it again with a quick, wrenching motion, whirling to face the second warrior in the same moment, catching her spear in both hands as she did so.

The invader brought the razor sharp edge of his scimitar down squarely upon it, putting the full force of his arm behind the blow. The strong shaft shivered and shattered as if it had been fashioned of brittle glass.

The Holdlady had anticipated that and did not freeze in momentary confusion at the destruction of her weapon as the other had believed she would do. The Sultanite's charge was quick but careless, fatally careless, for Una lunged with the point-bearing segment of the spear, impaling her enemy upon it.

It had taken but moments to fell the two, but even in that brief span of time, a third had topped the wall.

The woman dove at him as if maddened, ducking low to just barely avoid the wide sweep of his scimitar. She struck the invader a sharp blow across the forehead with the remaining portion of her spear. It was no club, but all her force had been behind that blow. The Sultanite's hands flew to his face, and he dropped back, down over the heads of his fellows, unbalancing the one coming up behind him and taking him down as well.

Una sprang to her feet and drew sword to meet the challenge of the next climber only to see Sunbeam tear into his face until he fell, blind and screaming, into the seething mass of humanity below.

How much longer would the attack continue? It was growing late, and twilight was fading into something darker, but hers had not been the only position severely threatened, and the Sultanites kept up the pressure of their assault.

The battle raged on and on through the deepening shadows, but the early advances generated by the unexampled ferocity of the original attack could not be sustained. The defenders threw their enemies from the wall and kept them from it, and at last, the thrice-welcome notes of the retreat were sounded.

Tarlach waited until he felt sure that the call had been one of genuine release and not merely a summons for regrouping and then gave a similar call upon his own horn.

He came down from the wall as soon as its new guardians were in place. So weary was he in body and spirit that he had to will himself to wipe off his blade with the hideously stained rag he kept on his belt for that purpose and resheathe it.

Like all the officers, whose minds must be fresh enough to quickly and accurately respond to the challenges of each new day, he would pass the night in sleep and away from the barrier.

The Sergeants and rankless warriors were divided into a series of shifts so that about a third of them were granted the same privilege as their leaders each night and claimed the comparative ease of reserve service the following day. The other two-thirds had to keep the wall, half on watch at all times lest their enemies attack suddenly in the hope of surprising and overpowering them.

They were fortunate to have even this much respite. It had not been so during the first four days of the invasion. Then, the Sultanites had sent wave upon wave against them, hour after hour without break longer than that needed to clear the fallen from the fighting space around the savagely contested barrier, until they had at last come to know that there would be no quick conquest here and to realize that they themselves were weakening under the constant lack of rest, a lacking their enemies' vastly superior position allowed them to counter somewhat despite their poverty in numbers. Since they must be able to fight for an unknown number of days longer—they had not guessed then that the battle would stretch out into weeks—they had been forced to give over their efforts during the hours of darkness almost entirely.

The Falconer Captain went first to the cottage where the most gravely wounded were taken to receive treatment and await transport into the highlands.

Brennan was standing by the door, his head lowered.

His own heart fell, although he felt no surprise.

"Dead?" he asked when he reached the other's side.

"Rorick? No. Actually, he was not so direly hurt and will almost certainly recover. They have taken him already."

Tarlach nodded. The supply units came down as soon as the night was enough advanced to cover their activities from the invaders' eyes. The injured went back with them.

"Any recruits?"

"A dozen from Cliffdale."

Not enough, his commander thought wearily. They would

help a little—every sword helped—but his needs were far greater.

The neighboring Dales had responded to Seakeep's call as Una had predicted they would, generously with goods but, despite her every effort, with very few fighting men.

His shoulders sagged. How much longer did they have before their casualties, phenomenally light as they were, eliminated their reserves, before they were forced to lengthen the distance separating each defender on the wall, before their surviving soldiers were too few to hold their enemies back? Had he been insane to imagine Seakeep could stand until help could cross all the distance from Linna to reach them? Had it been madness to think help would be coming at all?

The Mountain Hawk forced himself to straighten again. Such thoughts were for himself alone, were not to be encouraged at all. The very fact that they tormented him must be concealed. It was not his to reveal such weakness before those dependent upon him, not even before this one who was his friend.

The two officers soon parted, the Lieutenant seeking out the meal wagon just come down from the keep, Tarlach going directly to the cottage the Falconer officers had claimed for their headquarters so that they might remain as close as possible to the embattled wall.

He knew he should eat but could not bring himself to do so. He wished only to study the inevitable reports Una and Brennan, who had commanded the reserves that day, had prepared, take whatever action was necessary based upon them, and then sink into oblivion for a few precious hours, their enemies willing.

"Captain!"

He paused at the call and turned to watch the Holdruler's approach. He quickened his pace to meet her. The Lady Una amazed him. Of all the officers, she had held up best. She was wan and haggard, but her energy was all but undiminished.

Rather, he corrected himself, she willed that it appear so, knowing how it would distress him to see her otherwise and how much the commander of Seakeep's war needed to be able to depend upon his comrades. These Dalesfolk had strength, right enough, and this one more than most.

"What news, Lady?" he asked when she had come up beside him.

"Reinforcements, much good they will do us. We must give them greeting all the same."

He looked at her sharply. Her lack of enthusiasm for these much needed newcomers was patent and quite incomprehensible.

"Reinforcements? How many?"

"One hundred and twenty. From Ravenfield." Her expression clouded. "What do they want here? We are hard pressed enough to care for ourselves, much less for them."

"Be silent!" the Captain snapped suddenly in a tone that startled and stilled her. "They have come to us in force, which is more than can be said for any of your other valiant neighbors."

He gripped his temper. Weariness and strain were gnawing at all of them; it was his to remain conscious of that and allow it no sway over him. "At least, we compelled them to undergo the same training as we gave Seakeep's people since we annexed their Dale. They need not be as good to give us excellent service better than any of those less rigorously schooled."

"You know their history," Una said.

"They have not fought, but, Lady, neither had a great many of these other Dalesfolk we are being forced to use, not against an enemy such as this. We have both seen what they have managed to accomplish these past weeks.

"As for the Ravenfielders' lack of spirit, their coming here reveals some spark of that. They alone of all this region's Dales were not summoned to our aid. They have marched into peril of their own wills and by their own initiative."

He glanced back in the direction from which the Holdruler had come. "Shall we make our recruits welcome, my Lady?"

The Mountain Hawk studied the newcomers closely. They were a fine enough looking unit, physically strong and well armed, but it was obvious they read his companion's lack of belief in them and that they shared it in full, hardly an encouraging attitude in men soon to face an enemy of the Sultanites' caliber. He would have to do what he could to alter that, and alter it quickly.

He bade them welcome and offered them his thanks, frankly stating the defenders' need of their support. This done, he dismissed the most of them, telling them to refresh themselves as best they might.

Their leader, a big, able-looking Sergeant who called himself Torkis, he kept beside him. "I would have you see where you will be stationed tomorrow."

The man gave him salute. "As you will, Captain."

Tarlach moved briskly through the Seakeep camp until he came to the place where the wall joined with the great cliff flanking the beach on its right side. "Half your number will stand here. The rest will remain back at first, although I will not number them amongst the reserves. I may want to draw some or all of them into the line almost immediately if the invaders strike as hard as they did during their last assault today."

The other nodded but then looked closely upon him. "It is right that you should know that there is some doubt as to how firmly we will stand against any foe."

The Falconer's eyes flickered toward him. "Did you come here intending to fly?"

"No, Captain."

"Then let me hear no more of such talk." His attention fixed once more on the fiercely contested barrier. "You can expect to fear. There is none of us free of that. Own it frankly and then rein it.

"You began Falconer war training almost at the same time Seakeep's warriors did. We have proven that makes you more than the equal of those soldiers out there on an individual basis, and this wall ensures that you shall usually meet them thus. They come up fast, right enough, and occasionally two or three must be faced at one time, but this, too, lies within our ability to handle. If someone is too heavily pressed, he is not alone. I have purposely crowded the line so that comrades may aid one another without leaving any portion of it uncovered.

"If one of you or many of you cannot hold, that we can manage as well. It happens time and time again each day. It is the work of the reserves to move in quickly to counter such weakenings."

He turned so suddenly that Torkis started to find his eyes fixed upon him. They had an incredibly piercing quality when wielded so. "They have to be given time in which to act. Whatever the pressure, you must hold until help can reach you. If you break before that, you are slain and the most of the rest of us with you."

The other man lowered his head, then raised it again. "I can promise little. I do not know what we are capable of doing, but at the least, we should be able to provide some sort of delaying action for the rest of you."

"That is all any of us are doing, Sergeant."

He sighed then and looked hastily away lest the despair welling up in him be read.

One rider and one falcon had gone forth from here, and the way was long and rough between Seakeep and Linna. Right now, it seemed impossible that they should get through in any reasonable time, much less win the aid of the army they sought and return again with it before the beleaguered garrison was utterly swept away.

Una came to Tarlach's cottage as soon as she had seen the newcomers settled.

She frowned at finding him still alone, but she supposed she should not grudge Brennan a few additional minutes of rest apart from his duties, and she made no comment as she bent to help him with the stack of reports still awaiting his attention as she did each night.

Both of them were tired and little inclined for speech, but there was an additional heaviness in the woman's silence that bespoke some burden of mind.

The Falconer watched her for a few minutes, but when she gave no indication of revealing the cause of her trouble or of admitting that she was troubled at all, he roused himself and reached over to her so that his fingers brushed the back of her hand.

"You have cause to be angry with me," he said gently. "I was beyond my right before."

"For snarling at me? Hardly. I would that you would flare out for a fact. The fate of a continent is too much weight for any man to have to bear, and you will allow yourself no release at all, not even with those of us closest to you." Her eyes fell, and she turned away. "Knowing that makes me even more ashamed. . . ."

"Of what?" he demanded. Of all the remarks she might have made, this was about the last he would have expected.

"I failed you utterly in Lormt. I knew you were in difficulty. Both Storm Challenger and my own senses told me that, yet I waited until your peril was actually upon you before coming in search of you. I was afraid I would anger or embarrass you if I acted prematurely."

She could not keep the sob out of her voice, although no tears followed it. Una knew that this was her exhaustion talking, even as weariness had made Tarlach snap at her earlier, but she could not seem to stop herself. "I live in terror of betraying you again, here."

"You have never betrayed or failed me, nor shall you! I am more likely to serve you so with my grand plan of standing off these invaders in this place and my promise of aid that might never come."

He smiled to see the quick anger flash in her eyes. "You frown to hear such nonsense from me, though it is more firmly based than your own fears. Let us both put aside pointless guilt and concentrate on what must be done here. That gives us problems enough without our inventing more."

He raised her hand and kissed it, then lifted his head to look at her again. "I was right about wanting and needing you beside me. I do not know if I could even stand without your strength to support mine."

"You would stand!" Her voice lowered. "We both must. Fate has given us no other choice."

19

Dawn had not yet begun to brighten the sky when the Falconer serving as his aid roused Seakeep's war commander.

Tarlach was enough disciplined to swing instantly from his bed, although mind and body cried out to remain at rest.

He ate quickly and with better appetite than usual, the result of his fast of the previous evening, and hastened to wash and clean his face of beard.

That last ritual was no hollow vanity but a form of warfare in itself, a sign to comrade and foe alike that pride and spirit lived yet, despite hardship and the rage of the hostile army ever ravening for his life and his cause's utter destruction.

He managed a grin at his reflection in the dim glass. No, vanity had no part at all in it. This gaunt, grim image would not fuel that.

He had scarcely finished before Brennan came into the room. Exploded into it.

The Captain sighed inwardly, guessing what had so roused

his friend. "A fair day to you, Lieutenant," he said casually. "You have seen the line?"

"Are you insane? Manning so large a portion of the wall with those Ravenfielders is little less than suicide!"

"Our reserves are there to support them. At the least, they will give our tried warriors a few hours' extra rest."

"As likely as not, it will be a few minutes!"

"Even that is a help—Brennan, our people need their aid. I believe we are safe enough in trusting to it as long as there is good support near to hand. Besides, I want to bring them into action as quickly as possible. The doing is easier than the anticipating."

"Why not use the full of their number, then?" the other asked sourly.

Tarlach replied with a slow smile. "I am not quite that trusting, my friend. We might not be able to manage the emergency so easily if a hundred and twenty should break all of a sudden. The success of half their company will serve the others nearly as well as active involvement of their own even if I do not draw upon them during the day."

"You will not utilize them as reserves?"

The Mountain Hawk shook his head. "No, not for a day or so until they see our needs for themselves."

Brennan nodded. Reason supported that. The warriors backing those on the wall had to be able to respond instantaneously, almost instinctively, to the demands of the battle. Danger developed too quickly at times for them to depend upon previous instructions or to wait upon the commands of officers.

The blue eyes fixed on him. They mirrored deep concern. "To all this, I yield, but not that you must place yourself so near to them. Even were they noted for being a valiant people, they are still untried."

"All the more reason that they should have an officer's support," he responded quietly.

"Tarlach, listen to me. We need you too desperately to risk

you so. Change places with me or even with the Lady Una. At least then, you will have proven warriors beside you if you should come into trouble. We are both more expendable."

"I cannot, Comrade. They know your opinion of them and do not need that to reinforce their own."

He smiled. "I shall not be in their midst, you know, just beside their position, and I will have their Sergeant at my right. He looks to be an able man, whether those with him be so or nay. Whatever little safety there is for any of us shall be mine in full measure."

The two men hastened to take their places, although there was still no trace of light in the sky; neither of them believed their enemies would delay their attack very long once dawn began to unfold in earnest.

That assumption proved no false one, and the first gray streaks of light revealed the invading host already massed to begin their assault.

Tarlach's eyes closed. There seemed no lessening whatsoever in their number. By the Horned Lord, was their Sultan god restoring their slain and wounded to them each night?

The blast of their trumpet and the chilling cry following it drove that bit of folly from his mind.

He looked to the Ravenfielders. The invaders' war cry did not trouble them. They had been told to expect it, and it was no more to them than the battle shout of any other people.

The size of the enemy army was another matter. No one could see that vast horde arrayed against him without quailing, and these perceptibly wavered. Would they shatter completely?

The Sultanites were at the barrier, scaling it. The newcomers shuddered under their impact but then steadied.

To their own infinite amazement, they kept their enemies off the wall. Some weakened, some went down, but their comrades on either side were ready with aid, and never once was their position seriously breached. When the invaders were at last driven off, they watched them retreat with a new feeling of pride, and their Sergeant's head was high when he raised his bloodstained blade in salute to the Falconer Captain. This was a moment they would cherish and would build upon, any of them who survived what was yet to come.

The Mountain Hawk acknowledged Torkis's salute before turning his attention back to the fleeing Sultanites. He had seen them recede thus so many times, sometimes in what amounted to a route, and as on every one of those previous occasions, he raged in his heart because he could not capitalize on their momentary weakness and confusion. If his army had not been so hopelessly tiny, victory should have been his.

His head bowed in his despair. As always before during these last dreadful weeks, the invaders came to an enforced halt at the waves' edge, regrouped, and charged again.

Time after time, the incredibly vicious assaults were repeated throughout all that day. The Sultanites were angry, and they were growing worried both for themselves and for their comrades in their falling homeland. They needed no exhortation from officer or from priest to tell them the inevitable result of any further delay in their program, not with the fairly heavy rationing already in effect in their camp. No respite was given their enemies now, not so much as an hour's quarter. The fallen were drawn away from the feet of those still battling, each one instantly replaced by soldiers coming up from behind, as the great army strove to crush the incomprehensibly stubborn defenders by this one fierce, unbroken onslaught.

The massive attack and the new rage and increased purpose firing it proved to be an awesome challenge to those trying to hold the gate to their homeland. Here at last, they faced all the power of the Sultan's host, not for minutes, but for long and weary hours.

They withstood its fury as they had withstood its every effort for over a month, but as the day grew old and the sky started to darken to announce the approach of another night, weariness lay upon them like a blanket fashioned of flexible iron.

Tarlach's face was white and lined with exhaustion, and he had to fight himself just to continue wielding his spear. His movements were no longer as smooth, his responses no longer as swift, and he bled from shoulder and thigh because of the openings his waning powers had given his enemies. Both injuries were nicks, unworthy of notice at all, but they were grim heralds of what must come, and come soon, if he did not have some rest.

It happened at last. The Falconer brought his spear up too slowly, then so poorly timed his strike that his target easily avoided it, gained the wall, and brought his own weapon into play before the defender could move against him again.

The Sultanite bore a spear as well, short and heavy of shaft. Tarlach leaped aside to escape its barbed point, did escape it, but in so doing abandoned his guard.

He was aware of his danger even as it developed and quickly brought his weapon up to cover himself again, too quickly for his opponent to check the swing of spear and thrust with it a second time. The man was wily, however, and very fast. Rather than attempting to counter the motion of his weapon, he utilized it, striking with its shaft to catch the Falconer squarely in the breast.

The full of his considerable strength was behind that blow, and the Mountain Hawk was thrown back under the force of it, off the platform to crash on the rubble-strewn ground beneath.

He remained conscious, but the breath had been driven from him. He lay still, looking up at the missile whose release would seal his doom. Storm Challenger was deep in a battle of his own and could not break off to help him this time. . . .

The spear flew.

Another warrior hurtled from the wall, interposing himself between the Falconer and the fast-flying dart.

The weapon struck true, and Torkis of Ravenfield jerked violently, his back pierced by the spear he had thereby deflected from its intended target.

He had saved the Captain his deathblow, but he had also wrought his undoing. The unconscious man could not turn aside in his fall, and his body struck Tarlach's with the force of a catapulted missile. Dazed as he already was by his own fall and by the blow which had precipitated it, the Mountain Hawk was rendered utterly helpless. He was still aware of his surroundings, just barely aware of them, but he was powerless to aid his comrade, to even determine whether aid would serve any purpose, powerless to rise, although he knew the breach in the wall's defenses must be sealed. . . .

Warriors were around him, most black clad, some wearing the Ravenfield uniform. Torkis was lifted off him, then he himself was raised and borne toward the cottage where the wounded were being tended.

The motion and the pain it elicited overmastered his strained senses. The world whirled madly for an instant, and blackness closed over him.

20

$\mathcal{T}$ arlach drew up a chair so that he might sit beside Torkis.

The big man had been incredibly fortunate, enough so that one might almost have believed the Horned Lord had intervened directly to save him. Because of the angle at which he had jumped and the manner in which he had twisted his body, the spear had pierced the heavy muscle of his right shoulder, traveled through the flesh across his back, and emerged through the left shoulder. It was a painful wound, one which had cost him heavily of blood, but it was not dangerous provided significant fever did not seize him, and there was little likelihood of that. Pyra had taken the steps necessary to prevent it before releasing him into the commander's care.

The Sergeant little liked that this much attention should be given him, and he was not slow to protest once the Mountain Hawk had seated himself.

"I am not nigh to death that I should take your bed, Captain."

"It is yours for the next few nights all the same. I shall not be gainsaid in that. Besides, neither of us will have enough time to spend in it to make this worth the arguing."

Tarlach himself had suffered no injury apart from the myriad of deep bruises blackening his body. That would not have been the case had the Dalesman not acted as he had, and his eyes darkened. It was precious poor return he could make for such sacrifice, and that was what Torkis's move had, in fact, been. "I would I could send you to the highlands altogether."

"For this?" he snorted. "Such a pinch is not sufficient to keep a man off the wall!"

"That will be necessary for tomorrow at least," the other told him calmly. "You are to remain with the rearmost reserves, assuming Pyra will permit you to rise at all."

"If you imagine I will allow my comrades to go up there alone—" he began hotly.

"My mind is set, Sergeant. That wound will interfere with your movements until it settles a bit. If you were stricken again because of it or if it reopened, I should lose you for the duration or, perhaps, permanently. I need you too badly to permit that."

The Ravenfielder's face was starting to look pinched, and he gently touched his bandaged shoulder. "I keep you talking too long. Sleep now, or I shall violate my own command and force an opiate on you. Then I should have to order yet another warrior out of combat to guard you until you woke out of its hold and were capable of your own defense once more."

The other glared at him. He grinned in the end and settled back. "I must yield. You would do it."

"Believe that I would, Comrade."

The mercenary leader rose and moved toward the door. He remained there until he saw the Sergeant's breathing become relaxed and steady, then slipped from the room and quietly pulled the door shut beside him.

All the energy seemed to go out of the Mountain Hawk once he found himself alone and, for the moment, free of the need to maintain the appearance of undiminished strength.

There were papers on his makeshift desk that needed his attention, but he did not so much as look at them when he took his seat more out of habit than through any conscious willing.

It was the army he commanded that filled his mind until the thinking tore the heart out of him. They were valiant and skilled those warriors out there, uncomplaining under the harsh task fate had set them. It was his to do as well by them.

He could not but fail them in that. There was no way he could give them victory, and he would not be able to give the most of them life, not even that of a heavily hunted partisan. He now believed that it would be only a very small minority who would be able to make their escape in accordance with his plan when the barrier was at last breached.

He shook his head. He was tired, too tired, or he would not be wallowing in himself like this. Despair had to be fought, not nurtured . . .

He straightened at the sound of a knock, but the blankness betraying his almost totally spent spirit could not be forced so quickly from his eyes, although he made no delay in rising and returning Pyra's greeting when she came into the cottage. He did not bother to set his helmet over his head and face.

The healer read that which gripped him aright but chose not to remark directly upon it. "I could have expected to find you looking worse, I suppose," she declared gruffly after a few seconds of close scrutiny.

The Captain could not but smile for all his weariness and depression. "And also a great deal better, I warrant."

"That, too—The Sergeant is asleep?"

"He is now."

"The privileges of low rank!" she muttered somewhat enviously.

Tarlach glanced at his desk and the work waiting upon it and sighed. "Torkis would not be lying there if that hole were not in his back, I think, but, yes, authority does carry some measure of disadvantage to balance its privileges."

He eyed her curiously. He was not surprised to find the Falconer woman here. Given his own fall and the fact that he had assumed responsibility for the significantly injured Ravenfielder, he had actually expected to see her before now.

Another had not yet come, and a chill gripped his heart. "The Holdruler was not wounded?" he asked in a voice held steady by force of will.

"The Lady Una was fortunate today and took no injury. There is just more to be done with your second Lieutenant out of the line."

"Truly, and I am neglecting my share of it by talking here." Tarlach slowly came to his feet and moved toward the door. "I had best see how the others are faring now. The paperwork will wait so long."

He should have attended to that immediately upon the close of the day's hostilities, but Torkis's need plus the healer's insistence that he rest a while himself before attempting to rise had delayed him.

Pyra lifted a hand to stay him. "The Holdlady is quite capable of handling that tonight, and I imagine I am not so ignorant of a commander's duties after heading a women's village that I cannot give you a bit of help here. I may not know much about arranging the manning of a defensive wall, but rest assured that I am well familiar with a supply roster.

It seems to me that I have been shirking this part of it all until now."

"No one can accuse you of that, healer, but I confess I welcome the aid. I am uncommonly weary tonight."

"Little wonder! By all rights, you should be ordered to bed yourself."

"We could all use about a week of that," Tarlach responded ruefully.

Pyra went to the desk. "Show me what is to be done, Bird Warrior."

The Falconer woman proved as efficient at detail work as she was in the healing arts, and they were able to quit the desk again in a surprisingly short time.

"You have my thanks," the Captain told her. "I had not thought to see the end of this for some while yet."

"If nothing else remains, we can consider ourselves free to get a bite to eat before the meal wagon goes back up."

She saw him shrug and shook her head. "You fasted last night. There must be no more of that, Mountain Hawk."

"Did the Lady Una tell you that?" he demanded irritably. He knew that the two women were friends, and females talked even as men did.

"No, though by rights she should have done so since I bear the responsibility for keeping us all on our feet. Your head Lieutenant mentioned it."

Brennan?

The healer saw his surprise and smiled. "Your comrades are concerned about you. More than one of them fears that you will drive yourself down."

She stood up. "It may be a task to take food, but you will weaken all too quickly without it. I shall bring you something if you do not feel up to going for it yourself."

Tarlach stiffened. "There is no place for such service here, nor could I accept the like from you."

"Come with me, then. It shall be one way or the other."

* * *

The night was a pleasant one, cold but without real bitterness and quieter than either had known in many long weeks. The peace of it tore their war-wracked spirits, pierced them, waked such intense longing that neither healer nor warrior could bear to close himself within walls away from it, whatever the desire for sleep. They ate slowly and then returned to the cottage that had become both the Captain's office and his quarters.

There was a low wooden bench by the door, and Tarlach seated himself upon it, resting his back against the whitewashed wall. His eyes closed. The slightly damp coolness of the stone felt good to him, as if he were fevered.

Pyra hesitated, then seated herself beside him. Like the Mountain Hawk she said nothing but only sat back, drinking in the quiet of the night.

Storm Challenger settled on the man's arm, crooning for attention until he began to stroke the soft feathers.

Tarlach glanced at his companion. "That you are a competent healer and work as such is a given, but there is no gratitude strong enough for the care you have shown for our winged ones."

"None is required," she said softly, "no more than for that which I give to yourselves." Her voice tightened. "By the Amber Lady, how I hate to see their fragile bodies torn! War is human work, not theirs. They involve themselves in it for love of us."

Their human comrades loved them deeply in return. That much, at least, she had learned in these last terrible weeks. Only today, she had seen a Falconer draw apart and, thinking himself unobserved, weep like a child for the war bird whose life all her skill had not been able to save. Her heart had ached for him and ached because she could do nothing more for him than quietly withdraw and leave him to his grief.

With the falcons, it was different. She found that she could comfort them, the females particularly, but also the males, at least temporarily. Much of whatever time she had, she devoted to them, and even when she slept, it was usually cradling one or more of the birds who had been wounded in body or heart.

So much sacrifice, she thought, yet neither she nor the officer beside her could deny that it was needful. Seakeep, all High Hallack and all the world beyond, depended upon their strength now.

Her eyes closed momentarily. Seakeepdale was made for peace, for joy and life and the labor needed to secure both. . . .

"This is a good land," she ventured at last after several minutes' silence. "It is beautiful in itself, and its people are as fine as I could imagine or wish."

Ice filled her soul. Soon death could sweep the most of them and slavery crush the rest.

"We must win this war, Mountain Hawk," she said steadily, with deadly purpose.

The same thought, the same fear, had touched the man's mind as well. "We shall win it. Here or elsewhere, we shall conquer. What Alizon could not take, these accursed outsiders shall not have, either."

Partly to conceal the emotion on him, partly to dissipate it, the mercenary straightened out of his relaxed position and started to rise.

He slumped back again with a gasp of pain as his battered muscles violently protested the sudden movement.

Pyra started in alarm, then recognized the cause of his trouble. "Have you stiffened so much already?" she asked with no small concern.

Tarlach found his voice. "I shall have to work this out before I mount the wall tomorrow," he said through set lips.

"If you do not, you will not be in the line. You cannot fight when you are unable even to get to your feet."

She did not attempt to assist him. Such help, he might accept from one of his comrades or perhaps from the Lady

Una if they were alone like this, but she knew he would not take it willingly from her.

The Captain steeled himself. His face remained strained, and he had to lean upon the wall to rise, but he knew his body would not betray him like this again. He would not permit it to do so.

"I shall be ready. Do not fear for that."

21

*T*he Mountain Hawk was about to leave his chamber the following morning when Brennan entered it.

He read the manner in which the Lieutenant watched his movements and frowned. "Did Pyra not believe me?"

"She knows better than to trust any Falconer in such a matter, my friend. We have a tendency to carry endurance too far. How do you feel?"

"Well enough to avenge my aches upon our enemies."

Tarlach noticed a faint red line on the otherwise fair skin of his comrade's neck. It ran from a point just beneath the ear to his high collar, as if a sword tip or spear point—he believed it was the former—had just broken the skin there. "You did not escape entirely unscathed yourself, I see. That was a little close."

"I should have found it most inconvenient had it come any nearer," he admitted.

A flash of white caught Tarlach's attention. The other's left hand was completely encased in a thick bandage. This was not the way in which their healers were binding minor injuries, and the lightness at once vanished from his tone and expression.

"What happened **to** you?"

"Grabbed a **sword**," Brennan replied laconically. "It is

nothing permanent. My left arm shall just be confined to shield work for a while, that is all."

"This is why Una took the work for me last night instead of you?"

He shrugged. "There were graver wounds than mine. It was late by the time the healer's aides could look to me, and I believe they did not finish any too quickly once they did start work."

"You believe? They sent you to sleep?" Only in the case of delicate, immediately essential surgery or with wounds of such gravity as to demand evacuation were opiates administered. That spoke ill for the nature of the damage the hand had sustained.

"Pyra assured me there will be no loss of function." He grinned. "Come, friend, or you shall begin to embarrass me! Let us prepare to give our guests their morning greeting."

Dawn was an exceptionally lovely one and gave promise of an extraordinarily beautiful day to follow.

A fair setting to contrast with harsh deeds, Tarlach thought bitterly, for the scene unfolding before him in the ever-strengthening light was that which had met his eyes for what now seemed like the better part of eternity to his weary mind.

No, there was a difference in the great host massed upon the beach, a new incredulity.

The Sultanites had struck with everything they had possessed the previous day. They had accepted that the wall still stood when they had retired at last with the coming of night, but they had not expected to find it defended like this when morning again broke, its garrison calm, staunch, quietly, perilously defiant, as it had been from the beginning of its ordeal. Reason still declared that victory must be theirs, but now, looking upon those steady, awesomely deadly warriors, they doubted. For the first time, they doubted.

That was of no consequence. They, too, steeled themselves, and their general brought his trumpet to his lips.

He did not wind it.

Another call broke upon the brisk morning air, high and strong and clear, as could only have sounded from a Falconer battle horn.

Black-uniformed riders appeared suddenly upon the high trail leading into the valley, their number beyond ready counting although they were but the vanguard of the great Falconer host.

They paused for what seemed an eternal moment and then, as a second command was given, this time the order to charge, they tore down the steep way toward the barrier and their goal beyond it.

Wave after wave of warriors followed, an army that seemed in this moment vast almost beyond possibility to both the frozen invaders and their equally stunned opponents.

Above them flew the falcons, thousands of them, in a great, solid wing that blackened all that part of the sky.

Tarlach's eyes narrowed momentarily. The human force was not nearly so great. . . .

His head raised in a fierce pride. The females! All of them, even those from the columns where none would follow a warrior, had joined with the army in their world's defense.

He watched them come, riders and war birds. This was his race as none had seen them since they had come north in the distant past, full in strength and pride and with a cause worthy of their skill and courage before them.

They were not the lesser party. For the first time, the true ravages of storm and sword came home to him, and he realized with both shock and an instinctive horror that human would match equally with human. With the intervention of the falcons, Seakeep's army was the greater by a vast margin.

The Sultanites, too, were aware of the blow fate had struck

them. Their position was suddenly a very different and terrible one. They were soldiers to the core and hastily reformed themselves into the square that would best permit them to meet the foes so rapidly pouring down upon them, but they knew their efforts to be hopeless. Each looked upon the Falconer host and realized that the time of his doom was come.

Tarlach ordered every third of his warriors to stand aside to give the newcomers, who abandoned their horses before reaching the foot of the barrier, free access to the beach below but refused to permit them to follow after. Even now, with their salvation come, he would not allow the wall's defense to be weakened, not while any force at all remained to their enemies to threaten it.

His face and stance were impassive. He moved closer to Una, who held the place beside him, but he neither touched nor spoke to her.

The Mountain Hawk did not really watch what followed after the two armies joined in earnest and wished he might leave the wall altogether. This was slaughter on a scale he had not witnessed before, not even in the charge that had completed the breaking of Alizon's power, and he hoped he would never have to see a repetition of it again. With all his heart, he prayed he would never be party to the like.

The Sultanite warriors were both courageous and skilled. They sold their lives dearly, but this was a fight without hope. Their heavy losses at the wall and their losses to the ocean before their assault had even begun, the hardships under which they had lived and fought since that time, insured that they could not conquer. Spent as they were and lacking as they did any defense save that provided by their own bodies and shields, it could not be otherwise.

Despite that and the fact that the Falconers were fresh, their long ride not withstanding, the invaders might have held them long before going down had it not been for the war birds. Diving and fighting as an independent body, they were a force of irresistible power and terror, the more effective still against these aliens, who had from the beginning responded to them with the well-nigh superstitious horror of those who had never paired thus in war or friendship with beings of any other species.

There was no question of quarter, none of surrender. This, the Sultanites would not accept, would not consider accepting. The magnitude of their failure and its consequences for all their race made the continuation of life inconceivable in their minds, even had they not borne the disgrace of having been kept from what should have been a quick and sure victory by so pitifully few opponents. If the Falconers' swords spared any of them, they would fall upon their own.

The mercenaries soon came to recognize that fact and to accept it as inevitable although butchery was not their way, and they had both the respect for their enemies and the compassion to grant them the faster and more honorable release they sought.

Una of Seakeep lowered her head and averted her face from the slaughter below, but despite her hatred of that and the deep weariness of her body and spirit, she was filled with a sense of wonder. It was over, and they had conquered. They had conquered the impossible, and they lived, the most of them.

The weeks just past seemed unreal to her now, as if they had been a strange, Witch-inspired nightmare.

It had been no illusion, her mind countered, and she recognized that she had been altered by it all. She was now what she had never thought or wanted to be, a veteran warrior with so much blood upon her sword that she could not number the lives she had taken.

The Daleswoman remembered the first time she had ever slain, that day a seeming eternity ago when she had first encountered Tarlach of the Falconers. The mercenary had told her shortly afterward that killing became easier but to beware the man for whom it was a pleasure. She shuddered now in her heart, wondering what sort of depravity could find delight in such infinite horror.

Tarlach did not. She could all but feel his disgust at what he needs must watch, his desire to be gone from this place, although his rank would allow him no escape until the inevitable conclusion of the battle had been reached and the last Sultanite had fallen.

Neither could she go, nor would she have left him. He needed her now, the little comfort of her presence which was all she was permitted to give him.

Una looked upon this man who had become her life more closely and more critically. The ordeal had ravaged him. How deeply, she feared even to think, and she trembled at what might yet lie before him, this time at the hands of his own people, these very ones who had ridden to the salvation of them all.

The Captain looked once more at the great pyre being lighted on the beach below and shuddered, though to his race, flame was clean and a fitting couch for a warrior's shell.

He had long since dismissed his command, and most of the warriors had left the wall. Only he and Una of Seakeep remained on this section of it.

"Will you take charge here, Lady?" he asked. "There are matters to which I must attend before speaking with Varnel."

She smiled and nodded. "Do not work too hard, Mountain Hawk. I shall come to you as soon as I can, and together we should be able to put it all to flight in short order."

22

Tarlach had been in his quarters in the round tower for some time and was deeply absorbed at his desk when a sharp rap and the almost simultaneous opening of the door brought Column Commandant Varnel into his presence.

He rose quickly and touched hand to his sword in salute to his commander, then the two men clasped arms in the friendship greeting of their kind which they used when they were free from the observation of strangers.

The Warlord drew back and studied the younger man intently for several seconds.

"I have never seen you look so tired, Tarlach," he said at the end of that time.

"The reaction is beginning to set in, I suppose. I am lucky to be alive at all. We all are. If you had not come . . ."

"You knew that I would."

"Yes, but I could not be sure that it would be in time."

His head bowed, and his eyes fell on the neatly lettered paper on his desk. It had been too late for some. "My casualty lists," he said, seeing the other had followed the direction of his gaze. "Most would call my losses miraculously light, yet to me . . ."

"That is part of command," the Warlord said gently, "a spear in the hearts of us all save for those officers so callous of life that their comrades' deaths have no effect upon them. To my mind, they are scarcely half human and are an eventual danger to any hold or any company with which they are associated."

Varnel deliberately turned the paper over. He then went to the fireplace and after gazing into it a moment, drew up two chairs before it and lowered himself into one of them.

"Someone went to the trouble of laying this fire. Let us not be so discourteous as to waste its warmth."

The other did not move to join him, and he sighed. "Sit down, Mountain Hawk. I do not enjoy craning my neck when I talk to a man."

Tarlach obeyed. "Where did you hear that name?"

"From your courier and from just about everyone else since we arrived.—Your situation here and in Ravenfield is unique, my friend. I want to have the details, everything, from the time of your first involvement with them."

The Captain's heart gave an ugly jolt, and he could feel the muscles of his stomach tighten. Here it was, then, the moment that would confirm hope for their kind or, perhaps, work his utter doom.

"The decisions and the actions I have taken are mine only. No other of my company or our allies must be faulted for them."

"If nothing else, I trained you to be direct," Varnel observed.

"You trained me to care for my own as well!"

His hands balled but released again. He had known from the moment he had made his choice that this meeting must eventually come.

Tarlach described all that had occurred since his fateful meeting with Una of Seakeep, described his growing fears for the Falconer race and the solution the Holdruler had offered to provide and the conditions under which she would do so.

Both were silent for several minutes after he had finished. "Ravenfield by itself will not serve us?" the Warlord asked at the end of that time.

Tarlach shook his head. "Not alone. There are fine, fertile valleys there for the villages and a good site for an Eyrie, but there would not be room to house the columns and maintain our mounts." Even when the old Eyrie was at its height, the bulk of the warriors camped and trained beyond its walls.

"Only with Seakeepdale's lands at our disposal as well would we have sufficient space."

"And to win the use of those, we must accept this treaty?"

The Mountain Hawk frowned, fighting both despair and his anger at the Commandant's tone. "It is just and very little to give in return for what we shall be gaining. The Lady Una is placing great trust in our honor by allowing us and our descendents access to her lands. She is sincere in her desire to aid us, but she can hardly be expected to condone, much less reseed, what she sees as a deep wrong, an evil, to accommodate us utterly."

His eyes suddenly fixed the other like burning spears as anger welled up in him at the memory of the Daleswomen's role in the fight just ended and the service the healer Pyra had given these last weeks. "So it is an evil, one we should fight long and hard to break were we used as we do those who were once our own."

The Mountain Hawk gripped himself. This would not advance whatever miniscule chance he had. "Is such a great deal being asked of us?" he demanded. "Those joining us here, at the risk of placing themselves and their offspring in a tight and deadly prison, must do so by their own freely given consent and then remain by their consent. We must treat with them and with the Dalesfolk, high and lowly born alike, with respect and forego the power of life and death over the villages."

He studied his commander somberly, trying to gauge his reaction, but Varnel's face was a mask. He would hear everything before he would make his decision.

"We are not being asked to live as do the men of other peoples," Tarlach continued. "Some changes will probably take place over time, perhaps sooner than we could now imagine given the closer contact we shall perforce have to maintain, but at the outset at least, neither columns nor villages should suffer that much actual disruption of their lifeways."

Tarlach smiled suddenly, briefly. "That may be as welcome to our females as to ourselves. They are not likely to be any more eager to have us in close association with them than we are for their company. They have by all signs done very well without us for a very long time."

Varnel started. "That, I had not considered."

"Until this crisis hit us, I had thought of little else in these last months except the ramifications of this proposal," Tarlach told him wearily. "If it be true, it will make the transition easier for all of us. The worst we will have to face at the start is their training and that of the Dalespeople, which we must give them as we do our own. Courtesy has ever been demanded of us when dealing with outsiders, and extending that to members of our own race, even with the slightly increased contact we can expect, should not be an unendurable hardship."

The Warlord came to his feet. He stared for a while into the fire, then turned to his companion once more. "You know what this means?"

The Captain's mouth hardened. "If rejected outright, it may cost me my life or see me outcast. If accepted at all, it will never be by more than half our race. We will be split, sundered, riven column from column, comrade from comrade." His eyes fixed Varnel's. "I know full well that mine will be the responsibility for dividing our people in a schism such as we have not seen since Jonkara won her victory even in her seeming defeat when terror of her return rent us male from female," he concluded as the bitterness within him surged forth with a force that for a moment threatened to sweep him utterly.

Varnel studied him. "You bear a weight of anger," he said quietly.

"It is chiefly fear," the Mountain Hawk replied, his head lowering in shame and in the defeat he could already taste. "I knew what I faced when I first agreed to the Holdruler's proposal, and I accept the consequences of that decision, but

I do not hunger for death or disgrace. If I did not believe to the depths of my soul that this was our one hope of surviving as a viable people, I would not so much as consider it, but I fear, I know, that if we, or a sufficient number of us, do not choose to walk the path I describe, extinction only lies before us."

The Commandant came over to him and lay his hand on his shoulder. "There will be no condemnation of you, whatever my decision regarding your alliance with Seakeep."

Tarlach had to fight himself not to laugh. "No? I think Xorock will have something to say about that, and both Gurrin and Langhold with him."

"Those three have no right to any say with respect to the continuation of our kind!" Varnel shot back. "It is in a good part because of them that we are in our present difficulty, or at least that we have reached this stage of it already.

"Commandant Xorock thought so little about our future that he simply left his village behind when we had to abandon the Eyrie, never bothered with it at all. Of course, no one was left when we went back, whether they were all dead or had left or were in hiding, but we lost the whole lot, including any get fathered on them in his warriors' final visit. The other two have followed his ways and each of them has succeeded in losing so many of their females that they now have less than half the number they brought with them out of the highlands despite a good seeding of offspring since then."

The Warlord shrugged at his surprise. "Did you imagine I was oblivious to this drain?"

"Pardon craved, my Lord. I was arrogant and a fool besides to imagine that I alone . . ."

His companion smiled. "A fool, perhaps, but no one can fault you with arrogance."

"How do Breen's and Arnel's villages fare, and yours?"

"The others have lost about a tenth of their population, mine no more than five percent, and that flight occurred primarily in the first couple or three years of our exile."

"It is better than I had believed," Tarlach said with relief.

"For now. Even so, you are right. Without a place of our own, our eventual doom is inevitable. That is the reason I sent out the Council Call and then set High Hallack as the site. I wanted to shake some of our more hidebound brethren enough out of their complacency that they would at least listen to me." The silver eyes pierced him. "I chose Linna because it was the port town nearest to Ravenfield. I had heard of your gaining the Dale and hoped that we might use it even as you suggest. Now you tell me this is not possible without involvement with Seakeep and its Holdruler as well."

"It is not," he declared positively. "You shall see maps, and we can ride through something of both Dales once matters here have settled a bit."

"I will need to examine both before making my final judgment."

"Together, they are suitable," the Captain assured him.

This was as much as he could expect, more, yet an infinite grief filled him. "Even by entertaining the plan, you will lose—"

"We will lose somewhat less than half our force," the Warlord stated flatly. "Each man must make his own choice, but Xorock, Gurrin, and Langhold will violently oppose any such agreement, any easing of our treatment of our females, any altering of our lifeway whatsoever. Their columns are loyal to them, and the bulk of our warriors are likely to follow their example. Arnel and Breen will probably go with me if I can present my case well, and our troops with us."

"You will stand with me, then?" the Mountain Hawk asked. It seemed impossible in this moment that he had not been summarily dismissed, a broken outcast without rank or place. That Varnel should actually agree with and support him . . .

"Assuming that I find your proposal workable," his commander replied grimly. "As you say, what other choice do we have?"

The Falconer chief shook his head. "We face difficulties on every side, and gaining the support of our warriors may be the least among them. My column alone should suffice, without any of the others. It is the response of the villages that most concerns me."

Varnel's eyes darkened. "Those belonging to Xorock's faction will not abandon their road to escape. They have no reason to anticipate better treatment from us than they have known from their own columns, and we cannot expect that more than a handful will give us enough of their trust to accept our assurances.

"As for the other villages." He shrugged. "Who knows how mares think to gauge their response, even if this healer you mentioned does testify for us?"

"If we could get the equivalent of one village to start . . ."

"It would not be enough, not for long. Another peril threatens us that you have not seen, my friend, or not seen clearly enough." Varnel was quiet a moment, then went on slowly. "When I was a boy and even when I was first commanded to visit the villages, the destruction of a deformed babe was a rare and terrible event, a sickness on the soul of all involved, and in truth, I shall be glad to lose the right to so remove defective get. It is no less terrible a deed today, but it is far less rare. In some villages, it must be done seemingly every other season." Tarlach's breath caught, and the Warlord nodded. "If we are showing the sign of too close inbreeding now, what will happen to us if we limit our choice of mates still further?"

"It might be possible to introduce some now blood," the Captain said thoughtfully, recalling his discussion with Brennan, "not enough to alter us, but—"

"What other blood?" the other demanded with a harsh incredulity. "We are not regarded by the world at large as ideal mates."

"Some of these Daleswomen, perhaps. I imagine Seakeep's people have no desire to fade, either, to let what they have striven and fought to preserve fall to strangers with their going, yet they are extremely man-poor, and I have noticed no eagerness to bring in mates from other places. It may be that the females here are reluctant to put themselves in the position of being forced back into and again limited to the kind of work their people hold to be appropriate for their sex. Our lifeway offers an alternative, and a few might find it attractive enough to adopt or partly adopt it."

The Captain pressed his fingers to his eyes. "We talk of the future's problems when we do not as yet even have a present."

Varnel smiled. "You have never lost the tendency to see the single cloud in a blue sky, Mountain Hawk. Let me worry about that present for the moment. The deciding lies with me, and rest assured that I shall make no delay about it." He sighed. "I suppose I had best begin by seeing the Holdruler."

Tarlach shot him a look of surprise, and the Commandant's brows raised. "You did not imagine I would ratify your treaty without interviewing the second party to it, did you?"

"No, I suppose not. The idea just seems strange."

"Such dealings will be necessary from time to time if we go through with this," he said without enthusiasm. "I might as well get started now since there can be no avoiding of it."

Varnel glanced at the door. "I will go to the chamber she has put at my disposal. Would you have one of your sentries or the Dalesfolk bring her to me there?"

"Of course, Commandant."

"I know you have much to do with your company, but stay here a short while. I shall be wanting to see you again fairly soon."

"I will await your call, my Lord."

23

*V*arnel turned with an inner sigh at the sound of a knock but was surprised to find Rufon standing before him instead of Seakeep's ruler.

"The Holdlady will be pleased to receive you at once, Lord," the Dalesman said blandly.

The Falconer stiffened but then nodded, accepting the correction. A Holdruler gave audience. He—or she—did not appear at the command of others in her own keep.

He picked up the cloak he had draped across the back of the chair nearest him and swung it about his shoulders, then followed Rufon to a small council chamber, the very room in which the Dale's danger and defense had been discussed weeks before. A woman awaited him there, and because it was needful, he made himself study her.

She was not clad in the trappings of a nobly born Daleswoman but rather in the breeches and tunic of a warrior, though she was without arms and armor, and he was an acute enough judge of motive to recognize that she had probably done so out of consideration for her guests, to reduce as much as possible their awareness of her sex.

Although she was, like Tarlach, bone weary and drawn with strain, she was beautiful by the standard of any people he had yet encountered. More than beautiful. There was strength and intelligence in her finely wrought face and that pride which comes of worth and hard-earned right.

There was tension on her as well. She knew the importance of this meeting to the plan she had proposed, and its outcome was apparently of personal as well as official importance to her.

With her were a very small tortoiseshell cat and a falcon,

a female, who gave him and his own Sky Glory salute as soon as they entered the room.

Una of Seakeep studied the Falconer Warlord intently in her turn. He was, as Rufon had described him in his quickly given report, tall and slim of body. His hair was probably dark to judge by his lashes, and his eyes were close enough to silver to merit the name. From what she could see of them, his features were good but stern of cast in the manner of his kind. He bore himself as a man well used to both the privileges and the heavy burdens of high authority carried in greatly troubled times.

She knew that he had just come from conference with Tarlach, and a quick rush of relief swept through her. There was no open rage burning in him at the least.

Her newborn sense of assurance faded in the next moment. Lack of apparent violent emotion meant nothing. Such a man could be expected to be tightly controlled.

She had to fight herself to hold her own nervousness, her fear, in check. This one could be the pillar of her lord's hope or the blade that would cut down dream and perhaps the dreamer as well. She could only pray that she would be able to advance their cause or, at the worst, do nothing to harm it.

The Holdlady gave the traditional greeting of her kind to both Varnel and to his war bird. That last courtesy surprised him, for those outside his own race rarely gave full respect to the winged ones, but he quickly responded as custom demanded.

Una made no attempt to touch him, but she moved a little nearer to him. "No words of gratitude can express what we all feel, Warlord. You have restored life to Seakeepdale and all sheltering here."

Her voice was soft, he noted, and a marvelous quiet rested on her like an invisible cloak. "We rode and fought for our own kin, Lady, and for all this world. It was a cause to which we were glad to give our service."

He decided to broach at once the subject that was paramount in both their minds. "It appears that my people in turn have reason to thank you, for your good willing if nothing else."

"You have spoken with the Mountain Hawk, then?" she asked evenly, although she knew the answer full well. He had also come to at least a partial decision. He would not have asked to see her otherwise.

"Yes." He took the chair to which she indicated with her small, scarred hand. "I have heard his version of the tale. Now I would hear yours. From its beginning."

The Daleswoman braced herself, then began her story. She took her time with it, knowing that he did want full detail, and held nothing back save only her love for the man she had called Mountain Hawk and his for her.

The Warlord's head bowed when she had finished, partly to conceal his smile.

"In detail, you agree precisely with my Captain, but your emphasis is very different."

She started to frown but realized his meaning and smiled herself. "The Mountain Hawk tends to reduce his own role, but I assure you that no other here will allow that."

Una eyed him cautiously, trying to determine his response, but between the screening helmet and the control under which he kept himself, she could read nothing for certain.

She did know that he was putting her to the test. "We mean him no insult by our enthusiasm, but we consider that his service to Seakeepdale has been such that neither our custom nor human feeling itself can permit us to treat him as a mere hireling or to consider him as such, him or any of those with him."

She drew a deep breath, then went on, trusting to her instinct that she would do better speaking plainly to this man rather than holding herself too meekly before him.

"I crave pardon on my own behalf and on that of my people if we seem to challenge your ways at any time. We do not pretend to understand them all, but your Captain has conducted himself with extraordinary courage and sense of responsibility toward us, and he has shown the same with respect to his own. It is incomprehensible to us that he might be penalized for that."

"He will not be," the Falconer said quietly. "You have my word on that."

Relief and joy surged through her but quickly faded again. "Not officially, perhaps."

He nodded, acknowledging her point. "To some, he will be a renegade, whatever my ruling, and he does now have friendships he values amongst them. What must be endured shall be, Lady. There is no avoiding that loss. Our need is too great for him to withdraw his suggestion even if he willed to do so. I should have to pursue it despite him, and his would still be the blame for having instigated it all."

"You will pursue it?"

"I am doing so now, Lady."

His eyes fixed her suddenly, pierced her. She had seen Tarlach do this, but still, she had to steel herself not to cringe visibly under his gaze.

"Warlord?" she made herself ask coolly. It was best to establish from the outset that Seakeep was an equal partner in this and that its Holdlady was a true ruler, to be dealt with as such, not a nonentity to be cowed and forgotten.

"My Captain has told me what you expect to gain. A market for your horses and produce, defense, and warrior training for your folk seems small payment for the benefits accruing to us."

"Payment? Walk to that window, Bird Warrior. The wall is visible from it, and before this danger came upon us, there was the Mountain Hawk's effort on my behalf in Estcarp and the matter of his preserving Seakeepdale from Ogin of Ravenfield."

"There are few Holdrulers who would give over a Dale in the name of gratitude."

"I am Una of Seakeep, not any other. I know that the Mountain Hawk explained my reasons to you already, but I will state them again.

"Whatever the circumstances forcing me to mount that attack, it would be repugnant to me to retain and use for my own profit a Dale I had taken from its rightful lord by blood, the more particularly since I was next in line to inherit, he being without lady or get. It would be even more unthinkable to allow a brave people to perish when the means to preserve them was mine." Her eyes went to the two falcons sharing Sunbeam's generous perch. "It would be worth fighting for your kind only to guard what you have established with these winged ones. That must not be lost, Falconer, whatever else you gain or relinquish."

"What we have established?" he countered. "You appear to have a share in that relationship. This bird is not here by chance."

Una knew she had taken a risk by drawing Varnel's attention to her war bird, in having her here at all, but her bonding with the falcon was too well known to Tarlach's company and among her own people and would soon have come to his notice in any event. Concealment now would of a certainty flare back in her face then. "Sunbeam followed me after her warrior joined with another falcon while in your camp last fall. I do not know why she chose me and did not even believe such a thing was possible before it happened, but I welcome her and would not be parted from her. She gave me my life several times during the course of the siege," the woman added, her voice softening.

"And you hers?"

"I was privileged to come to her aid, yes."

"It is not ours to question a falcon's choosing," he admitted gruffly after a moment.

The Commandant nodded, as if to himself. "The winged ones like these highlands and have already declared themselves pleased to settle here, and this country is as a lodestone to my warriors, fairer even than that which we lost. If I decide for it, more than a sufficient number will want to make it theirs. I am more worried about whether we can attract the other settlers we require.

"I realize you have little personal knowledge of Falconer women, but you do have one of them here with you."

The Holdruler stiffened. "She is my friend and has given us such service. . . ."

Varnel scowled. "So I have been given to understand. You and your blank shield seem one in your doubt of my honor."

"Merely because our own is bound up in this matter," she answered evenly.

"No harm will come to her, but I do need to question her. There is no point in going any further with this, or in destroying the Mountain Hawk's standing with a large number of us, if we can expect no support from the villages."

She inclined her head in acquiescence. "She will be brought to you when you require her."

"The Captain mentioned that he believed some of your own women might have an interest in joining or partly joining with us. Do you think that likely?"

Una did not conceal her surprise. "I had not considered the possibility," she admitted.

She pondered the idea. The desire for children, to continue their line in Seakeep, would not be enough in itself to overcome custom and the expectation of a warm, sharing relationship, although she believed that was what Tarlach had been thinking. Falconers, men and women alike, were accustomed to resorting to temporary matings to continue their kind, but her people would find that insufferably demeaning, especially now. They knew their worth after all they had accomplished since Alizon's Hounds had swept down upon High Hallack. On the other hand, Seakeep's predominantly female garrison and support staff had been thrown into very close association with the mercenary company during the course of the siege and, to a degree, even before it. It was not impossible that some interest, some attraction, might have developed between individuals.

"It could come to pass," she said slowly, "though I would make no promise or so much as hold it out as a hope to you."

At that moment, the Commandant's falcon, who had been watching the woman intently throughout the interview, uttered a short, sharp cry and flew to Una's shoulder. Grasping tightly, as if in warning, with his feet, he began pulling impatiently at the woman's collar with his beak.

The Holdruler remained perfectly still, although she was fully aware of the razor-keen talons and bill just inches from her face and recalled with terrible clarity the damage those weapons could inflict. There was no anger on the war bird, and her own two comrades were not concerned, though both openly showed their annoyance at his behavior.

It took but a few moments for Sky Glory to find the chains lying beneath the garment and draw Gunnora's blessed symbol and the silver falcon free of the screening material.

Varnel's eyes fixed on the last, then raised to her face. They burned like angry stars. "Do you know what that is, woman?"

"Of course." She compelled herself to answer calmly, although she knew her death might be only seconds from her, and Tarlach's with it. She realized full well that the Warlord had recognized the piece and knew who had fashioned it. "A Falconer's Talisman. It cannot be wrenched from me by force or guile or threat, and possession of it entitles me to the aid of any Falconer or Falconer unit free to serve me, provided only that my cause lies within the scope of their honor. That is an authority upon which I have never been compelled to draw," she added. "The Mountain Hawk's company bound themselves and remained without compulsion."

"If you know so much, it must have come to you as a freely given gift and not as something accidentally found."

"Naturally. I should have recognized such a thing as the work of your people and returned it.—Your bird has shown himself to be sorely lacking in basic courtesy. I ask that you order him back to the perch."

The Warlord complied. "All falcons can sense the presence of a Talisman, and my comrade believed I would be interested in this one since the fact that you bear it surprised him. Nevertheless, I crave pardon, Lady. Yours is patently the right to carry it since it consents to remain with you, and you should not have to suffer interference by either bird or man for doing so."

All the same, he continued to study her intently for several fraction-seconds. In the end, he went to the door. Rufon was standing on call outside to serve either his Holdlady or her illustrious guest.

"Bring the Captain to us. We needs must speak with him now."

Tarlach felt his heart grow cold at the sight of the Talisman gleaming on the woman's breast. However, he merely gave salute and waited for his commander to speak.

"This was yours?" Varnel demanded without preamble.

"Yes." A man's Talisman was his own, and he owed no one, not even the Warlord of his race, any accounting with respect to his use of it. "I have already replaced it." Although only one could be held at any given time, a warrior was free to fashion another should he lose or make a gift of his original piece, though both were rare occurrences indeed.

The Commandant looked from one to the other of the pair.

"It is a small recompense for the giving of a Dale," he said in the end, addressing the Mountain Hawk, "although she does seem to appreciate its significance to us." He faced Una. "You are wise to wear it concealed, Lady. There are too many who would wonder at such a gifting, particularly under the circumstances in which we find ourselves."

"That is why I do hide it and why I am so angry with your falcon for exposing it," she said as she slipped both the

Talisman and Gunnora's amulet back into their customary place.

Whether Varnel actually believed the escape he had given them or not, he dismissed the subject as a matter of discussion to the infinite relief of both his human companions.

"Assuming that the remainder of my inquiries turn out as I now believe they shall, I will stand behind the agreement you two have reached."

His upraised hand stilled the words of thanksgiving both began to speak. "Perhaps you should be a little slower in bestowing your gratitude. There is a difficult time ahead for all of us, even for you, Una of Seakeep, but the brunt of it will fall on the Mountain Hawk."

"What must be endured shall be," Tarlach said grimly but with real resignation.

"Truly, but I am determined to see you as well armed as possible for the fray." His eyes sparkled at his officer's puzzlement. "There is little profit in a Captain's arguing with Commandants even in a people like ours where discussion is encouraged. Let us see how this looks on you."

As he spoke, he removed his cloak and set it about the Mountain Hawk's shoulders. It was black like those worn by all their race, but it was lined with silver.

Una saw Tarlach's look of exultation and turned to the Warlord for the explanation she had already guessed.

"It is a Commandant's cloak, Lady," Varnel told her. "Normally, it would not be worn save in our own camp or, once, in the Eyrie, but you are our ally in this and should rightly know what power we have."

"That is most well done, Warlord," she answered him. The Holdruler allowed some of the wild pride surging through her to have access to her voice and face. She had made known the honor in which she and all her Dale held this man whose sword she had hired. She could be expected to evince strong pleasure in his advancement now. "No man in all our people's history has ever deserved it more," Varnel affirmed.

Tarlach's eyes fell as the first rush of excitement passed. "I command but a company, Lord, five hundred men, less now. That is a far cry from a column."

His commander chuckled. "You are imagining midnight when it is high noon, Commandant. Have no fear. You will have your column, and in very short order, I think. There will be many warriors eager to ride behind the Mountain Hawk after this, and I shall let you have those you want of any coming to us from the schismatics' columns as well. You should be able to double, aye, and treble your command and without ever being compelled to accept any but the ablest of our kind."

He sighed then, and the lightness left him. Thrice deserved as this promotion was, fate had decreed that it must serve as much as a weapon to allow Tarlach to stand firm in his war of need and change which had been thrust on him as it was an honor and a source of growth and heightened responsibility.

"There is one more with whom I must speak before word of our intention goes beyond this room and your own company. Have this healer brought here now."

Pyra studied the Falconer Warlord warily, but she stood straight before him, her head high, and her eyes did not fall when his met and searched them.

"You know why we have summoned you?" Varnel asked in more statement than question.

"I believe so, but I might also be mistaken."

The silver eyes narrowed. "You actually say that you will not be trapped into betraying your friends?"

"Would you deal so, blank shield?" the healer countered calmly.

He glared at her but then smiled. "If needful in a cause this important, but I do not play that game now. I must know, to the best of your ability to answer, what sort of response we may expect if I announce the Commandant's alliance with

Seakeepdale and ask the villages to settle Ravenfield." He nodded to himself, pleased both at her fast comprehension and equally quick delight at Tarlach's advancement, but he went on without comment. "I do not want to place this burden on him if it will be without purpose."

Pyra was quiet a while. "My testimony will help," she answered at last, "but my own village is the only one for which I can speak with even probable certainty.

"Even though I can freely stand beside the Mountain Hawk and the Lady Una and the others I have come to know here, I shall have to report, too, that these Dales are isolated and rugged and that escape from them will not be easy should that prove desirable or necessary.

"You will receive recruits, I believe, not all by any means, but many. Our experiences with our males have not been unduly harsh, and as a whole, we like the lives we lead, the independence and fullness of them, enough to take considerable risk to preserve and perpetuate our ways.

"That will probably also hold in other villages that have kept the old history as we did and that have been visited chiefly by well-controlled warriors. From the others, you will get little support. They will not be able to give you sufficient trust to put themselves so utterly in your power, nor can they be blamed for its lack. They have been hard used, Warlord."

"Will there be enough, Pyra?" Una asked urgently. "The future of your race will rest with them."

"Yes," she replied slowly. "You should win over just about enough if the Amber Lady is with you."

The healer's eyes narrowed almost imperceptibly as she looked at her friend. Her two friends. The Mountain Hawk was that as well, she realized, despite his reserve, his usual formality of manner with her. Both of them were giving so much to this cause, and neither would gain at all from it, not in any personal sense.

Not unless someone took an active hand in their affairs. She smiled deep and hard within herself. One worry, one black concern, had been eating at her the more she considered her people's position if they came to High Hallack. It would have to be raised, and she would do so now, but with a solution to present instead of merely as a question and a demand for a concrete resolution, although by speaking she would be putting herself into peril.

"There is one grave fear on me," the Falconer woman said, "and in order to lay it to rest, I must ask the Lady Una and the Mountain Hawk to do a most difficult thing." She looked from one to the other of them. "This is all the harder because you have done so much already . . ."

"Speak plainly!" Tarlach commanded sharply. What dart would the woman throw into their plans now, when he had believed them just about settled?

"I have heard the Holdruler state on several occasions that she could never have made such an offer to any other race, whatever their need, that only Falconers could be depended upon not to eventually become a plague on her own Dalesfolk or their descendents.

"It seems to me that we Falconers must think on that ourselves. Ravenfield is ours freely, but our warriors' use of Seakeep's lands is dependent upon this alliance, and that Dale's future is not so certain."

She paused, marshaling her thoughts. "It is not common in High Hallack for a Dale to be ruled long-term by a woman. This one may not be wealthy in comparison to others, but it would still be a prize to a landless man from outside or to local lords with more sons than estates to bestow upon them. Besides this, the lady herself is uncommonly fair to look upon, which would sweeten any bedding. She will be under ever-increasing pressure to wed again, and perhaps her own heart may even eventually incline her to some suitor.

"What if she does so choose, either by desire or for reason of state? Suppose Seakeepdale's new lord does not honor our agreement, it having been instituted by a mere female? What if their heir does not, or his heirs?

"I cannot bring my sisters here only to find ourselves or our daughters or granddaughters—or our sons, since we shall no longer lose complete contact with them—trapped in a space too small for our needs, perhaps at perpetual war for land, which I understand we have never yet been forced to undertake, however much we have aided others in such frays. We should be in a worse position than we are now."

"You have some solution?" Una asked, stunned. She had not thought of this, and she realized the other woman's fears were very well-founded.

Pyra nodded curtly. "I do, Lady, little though you might like it. You and the Mountain Hawk must marry, by High Hallack's custom and by our own ancient ceremony, the memory of which is still preserved in my village, thus binding the two Dales by the normal, unquestionable laws of inheritance."

For a breath's space, only dead silence greeted her proposal, then a flush of anger darkened what could be seen of Tarlach's face and flashed from his helmet-shadowed eyes.

The Holdlady colored as well, first in outrage and then again in the shame of a proud and beautiful woman who had grown accustomed to the management of her own affairs.

Pyra smiled in her heart. Whatever happened to her in the next few seconds, these two, by the very naturalness of their response to her interference, had preserved themselves before the Falconer Warlord.

Varnel's hand clasped the hilt of his sword. "Though we both be guests under this roof, I should drive this blade through the dearest part of you," he snarled.

"Think, man!" she snapped, trying to control the hammering of her heart enough to hold her voice and expression steady. "The villages can live well in a small space. It is your columns and your herds that cannot."

With great difficulty, the Warlord controlled his fury. The

Horned Lord might curse her, but there was no denying the mare's logic. She had found the barb that might pierce their newly born hope to its death—and the means of blunting its point did they choose to avail themselves of it.

He looked at the other two. "She may have farseen what the rest of us did not," he said slowly, with great bitterness. "Despite that, despite what this alliance means to my race, I will not put such a sword to this warrior's throat. Or to this lady's," he added, compelling himself to accord Una the same consideration.

Tarlach had recovered from his initial shock and now realized what Pyra had done. He was still furious at having been thus manipulated, but his eyes, when they met the Hold-lady's, were both laughing and exultant.

"Seakeepdale's Holdruler has proven herself a valiant and worthy ally," he said slowly, for he knew he must choose his words carefully. "If this be necessary to secure our aim, and if it is not totally repugnant to her, then I will yield to it." Real bitterness poisoned his voice for a moment. "I will be no more deeply cursed by those who condemn me whether I wed with her or nay."

His manner softened again. If he could gain this, then the future might indeed hold more for him than purpose and pain. . . .

"Your answer, Lady, or do you require more time?"

"No," she replied, her head raising. The healer did not know of her vow to take no other lord but Tarlach of the Falconers, for that lay between themselves alone, but the argument she had raised was a strong one, and she seized upon it. "As Pyra says, heavy pressure may be put on me to join with a man I honor and trust less for far weaker cause than this. You have my consent, Bird Warrior."

Una of Seakeep sighed in her heart. She detested resorting to subterfuge when she longed rather, to declare to all the world her love and desire for this man.

She smiled then, in mind, since she durst not do so before

Varnel. That was but a minor shadow on the glory blazing within her. It might be necessary to conceal their true feelings for a time, perhaps a long time, but the impossible had happened against every dictate of reason and, seemingly, of hope. They themselves were not bound to screen their hearts from one another. The way before them would never be an easy one. Both knew that, but they would now be able to walk it together, sharing fully in whatever it offered, be it hardship or joy. That would be blessing and gift enough, for her and, she saw when she again looked into his face, for the man who was her lord.

Afterward

THUS they went forth from Lormt, this handful of those who would stand against as dire a flood of the Dark as any monster this world could raise. While the thought of the Kolders and all the ruin those had wrought in their time, clung, to feed our foreboding.

We thought of what we might do, for, let these invaders get a foothold, a port, a settlement in the Dales, how else might the rest of our world be able to thrust them forth again?

Nolar and I once more visited Elgaret in her guardianship of the great Stone. In its sanctuary we sought that which would enhance what talents we possessed. Elgaret spoke mind to mind with those who remained of the Witches, Nolar channeled and fed that sending with all she could control.

I searched for Kemoc with the farthest mind reach I had ever tried. And I was successful, but it was also true that no army might be mustered in time to reach overseas to the Dales. However, there might be, he thought, other forces which could possibly set astir for us. He spoke of Hilarion, the adept who dwelt by a western sea of which we knew but little, but who, because of his very dwelling place, had knowledge of wind and wave greater than that of ordinary mankind.

Even as it had done for the Turning of the mountains, Power

gathered, yet time was against us and also distance. For those of the greatest talent were now very few—and what they could do half a world away was little.

We paid three visits to the Stone and at the last I threw the crystals which I had not had the heart to do earlier. I read therein what seemed to crush all hope.

They fell but did not scatter—so I thought I looked upon a constricted battlefield. A ring of yellow, which I believed marked the Falcon breed and, within it, a vast upsurge of blood red—the enemy.

Yet the yellow did not give way and, while the line thinned, there was no faltering. My hand moved without my willing and I shook the bag until it was almost empty.

The crystals which foretold ill separated themselves into an ugly pile and lay to one side, dull and cold. However, those of green, and blue, of white, all the colors of the powers which meant life to us, and those akin in blood or deed, flickered to the battle.

And the red—went down—buried!

Nolar caught my arm and cried aloud as might one on a field where right had triumphed. I, too, voiced a shout, that which came from a Borderer's throat when he charged.

Our cries echoed about the chamber of the Stone and there settled within me such a feeling of joy as I had never before known. My hand clasped Nolar's and I looked into her great eyes, which were of such deep beauty, which now gladly sought mine.

Thus long before the coming of the Sulcar messenger that Mountain Hawk sent to us with the full story of that valiant stand, we knew that the balance between Light and Dark still held steady for us.